Adrian McKinty was born and grew up in Carrickfergus, Northern Ireland. He studied law at Warwick and politics and philosophy at Oxford before emigrating to New York in 1993. He lived in Harlem for seven years working at various jobs, with various degrees of legality, until he moved to Denver, Colorado to become a high school English teacher. In 2008, he emigrated again, this time to Melbourne, Australia with his wife and kids. Adrian's first crime novel, *Dead I Well May Be*, was shortlisted for the Ian Fleming Steel Dagger Award and was picked as the best debut crime novel by the American Library Association. The first book in the Sean Duffy series, *The Cold Cold Ground*, won the 2013 Spinetingler Award and was longlisted for the Last Laugh Award. The second Sean Duffy book, *I Hear the Sirens in the Street*, was shortlisted for the Ned Kelly Award.

PRAISE FOR *IN THE MORNING I'LL BE GONE*

'Powerful . . . [these are] exceptionally smart police procedurals' Christine Tran, *Booklist*

'Smart and irreverent . . . a clever and gripping set-up that helps make Duffy's third outing easily his best so far' John Dugdale, *Sunday Times*

'Hugely enjoyable' John O'Connell, *Guardian*

'This is an older, more s⌐   ⌐ and willing to take chances   ⌐lock Holmes and Edgar Alle   . . . there is plenty of exciten   ⌐arn' Maurice Hayes, *Irish In⌐*

'Terrific Troubles-set thriller' *Sun*

'McKinty is particularly convincing in painting the political and social backdrops to his plots. He deservers to be treated as one of Britain's top crime writers' Marcel Berlins, *The Times*

'Not content with constructing a complex plot, McKinty further wraps his story around a deliciously old-fashioned "locked room" mystery, the solution to which holds the key to Duffy's entire investigation. Driven by McKinty's brand of lyrical, hard-boiled prose, leavened by a fatalistic strain of the blackest humour, *In the Morning I'll Be Gone* is a hugely satisfying historical thriller' Declan Burke, *Irish Times*

'McKinty has rightly developed an international reputation with his stories . . . Written in spare, razor-sharp prose, and leading up to a denouement that creeps up on you and then explodes like a terrorist bomb, it places McKinty firmly in the front rank of modern crime writers' Geoffrey Wansell, *Daily Mail*

'McKinty's series is settling in as one of crime fiction's most reliable attractions . . . builds to a genuinely thrilling climax' *Mail on Sunday*

'Structurally, *In The Morning I'll Be Gone* is gemlike, embedding a locked-room mystery within a terrorist thriller' *The Age*, Australia

'Already claimed as the finest of the new wave of Irish crime writers, McKinty is as good as any novelist around. His lovely flair for language is matched by his feel for place, his appetite for redemptive violence leavened by some seriously mordant wit and his seriously cool appreciation of characters who reject conformity. His Duffy novels echo, among many, Dennis Lehane and Robert Crais' *Weekend Australian*

PRAISE FOR *THE COLD COLD GROUND*, THE FIRST OF ADRIAN MCKINTY'S SEAN DUFFY THRILLERS

'*The Cold Cold Ground* is a razor sharp thriller set against the backdrop of a country in chaos, told with style, courage and dark-as-night wit. Adrian McKinty channels Dennis Lehane,

David Peace and Joseph Wambaugh to create a brilliant novel with its own unique voice' Stuart Neville

'It's undoubtedly McKinty's finest . . . Written with intelligence, insight and wit, McKinty exposes the cancer of corruption at all levels of society at that time. Sean Duffy is a compelling detective, the evocation of 1980s Northern Ireland is breathtaking and the atmosphere authentically menacing. A brilliant piece of work which does for NI what Peace's *Red Riding Quartet* did for Yorkshire' Brian McGilloway

'The setting represents an extraordinarily tense scenario in itself, but the fact that Duffy is a Catholic in a predominantly Protestant RUC adds yet another fascinating twist to McKinty's neatly crafted plot . . . a masterpiece of Troubles crime fiction: had David Peace, Eoin McNamee and Brian Moore sat down to brew up the great Troubles novel, they would have been very pleased indeed to have written *The Cold Cold Ground*' Declan Burke, *Irish Times*

'*The Cold Cold Ground* is a fearless trip into Northern Ireland in the 1980s: riots, hunger strikes, murders – yet Adrian McKinty tells a very personal story of an ordinary cop trying to hunt down a serial killer' John McFetridge

'McKinty's *The Cold Cold Ground* has got onto my five best books of the year list as it is riveting, brilliant and just about the best book yet on Northern Ireland' Ken Bruen

'*The Cold Cold Ground* confirms McKinty as a writer of substance . . . The names of David Peace and Ellroy are evoked too often in relation to young crime writers, but McKinty shares their method of using the past as a template for the present. The stories and textures may belong to a different period, but the power of technique and intent makes of them the here and now . . . There's food for thought in McKinty's writing . . . *The Cold Cold Ground* is a crime novel, fast-paced, intricate and genre to the core' Eoin McNamee, *Guardian*

'Adrian McKinty is the voice of the new Northern Irish generation but he's not afraid to examine the past. This writer is a legend in the making and *The Cold Cold Ground* is the latest proof of this' Gerard Brennan

'Detective Sergeant Sean Duffy could well become a cult figure . . . McKinty has not lost his touch or his eye for the bizarre and the macabre, or his ear for the Belfast accent and argot . . . McKinty creates a marvellous sense of time and place . . . he manages to catch the brooding atmosphere of the 1980s and to tell a ripping yarn at the same time . . . There will be many readers waiting for the next adventure of the dashing and intrepid Sergeant Duffy' Maurice Hayes, *Irish Independent*

'McKinty [has] a razor-sharp ear for the local dialogue and a feeling for the bleak time and place that was Ulster in the early 80s, and pairs them with a wry wicked wit . . . If Raymond Chandler had grown up in Northern Ireland, *The Cold Cold Ground* is what he would have written' Peter Millar, *The Times*

'Adrian McKinty is fast gaining a reputation as the finest of the new generation of Irish crime writers, and it's easy to see why on the evidence of this novel, the first in a projected trilogy of police procedurals. At times *The Cold Cold Ground* has the feel of James Ellroy, the prose is that focused and intense, but then there are moments of darkest humour, with just a hint of the retro feel of *Life On Mars* thrown in' Doug Johnstone, *Herald*

PRAISE FOR *I HEAR THE SIRENS IN THE STREET*, THE SECOND SEAN DUFFY THRILLER

'It blew my doors off' Ian Rankin

'A strain of rough and visual, sly and lyric narrative prose in service of one hell of a story. Sean Duffy is a great creation, and the place comes alive – a uniquely beautiful and nasty part of the world' Daniel Woodrell

In the Morning
I'll Be Gone

Adrian McKinty

A complete catalogue record for this book can
be obtained from the British Library on request

First published in this edition in 2014 by Serpent's Tail
First published in 2014 by Serpent's Tail,
an imprint of Profile Books Ltd
3A Exmouth House
Pine Street
London EC1R 0JH
website: www.serpentstail.com

ISBN 978 1 84668 821 8
eISBN 978 1 84765 931 6

Designed and typeset by Crow Books
Printed and bound by CPI Group (UK) Ltd, Croydon, CR0 4YY

10 9 8 7 6 5 4 3 2 1

Take every dream that's breathing,
Find every boat that's leaving,
Shoot all the lights in the café,
And in the morning I'll be gone.

Tom Waits, 'I'll Be Gone' (1987)

My friend you must understand that time forks
perpetually into countless futures. And in at least one
of them I have become your enemy.

Jorge Luis Borges, *The Garden of Forking Paths* (1941)

1: THE GREAT ESCAPE

The beeper began to whine at 4.27 p.m. on Wednesday, 25 September 1983. It was repeating a shrill C sharp at four-second intervals which meant – for those of us who had bothered to read the manual – that it was a Class 1 emergency. This was a general alert being sent to every off-duty policeman, police reservist and soldier in Northern Ireland. There were only five Class 1 emergencies and three of them were a Soviet nuclear strike, a Soviet invasion and what the civil servants who'd written the manual had nonchalantly called 'an extra-ter-restrial trespass'.

So you'd think that I would have dashed across the room, grabbed the beeper and run with a mounting sense of panic to the nearest telephone. You'd have thought wrong. For a start I was as high as Skylab, baked on Turkish black cannabis resin that I'd cooked myself and rolled into sweet Virginia tobacco. And then there was the fact that I was playing Galaxian on my Atari 5200 with the sound on the TV maxed and the curtains pulled for a full dramatic and immersive experience. I didn't notice the beeper because its insistent whine sounded a lot like the red ships peeling off from the main Galaxian fleet as they swooped in for their oh-so-predictable attack.

They didn't present any difficulty at all despite the sick genius of their teenage programmers back in Osaka because I had the moves and the skill and all they had were ones and zeros. I slid the joystick to the left, hugged the corners and easily dodged their layered cluster-bomb assault. That survived, I eased into the middle of the screen and killed the entire squadron as they attempted to get back into formation. It was only when the screen was blank and I saw that I was nudging close to my previous high score that I noticed the grey plastic rectangle sitting on the coffee table, beeping and vibrating with what in retrospect seemed to be more than its usual vehemence. I threw a pillow over the device, sat back down on the rug and continued with the level. The phone began to ring and it went on and on and finally, more out of boredom than curiosity, I paused the game and answered it. It was Sergeant Pollock, the duty man at Bellaughray Station.

'Duffy, you didn't answer your beeper!' he said.

'Maybe the Soviet army blocked the signal.'

'What?'

'What's going on, Pollock?' I asked him.

'You're in Carrickfergus, right?'

'Aye.'

'Report to your local police station. This is a Class 1 emergency.'

'What's the story?'

'It's big. There's been a mass break-out of IRA prisoners from the Maze prison.'

'Jesus! What a cock-up.'

'It's panic stations, mate. We need every man.'

'OK. But remember this is my off day so I'll be on double time.'

'How can you think of money at a time like this, Duffy?'

'Surprisingly easily, Pollock. Remember double time. Put it in the log.'

'All right.'

'Another fine job from Her Majesty's Prison Service, eh?'

'You can say that again. Let's just hope we can clean up their mess . . . Listen are you OK with going to Carrick? I know you haven't been back there since you were, uh, demoted. I could always send ya to Newtownabbey RUC.'

'Never fret, Pollock. I shall thrive on my native heath.'

'I hope so.'

I hung up and addressed the Galaxian fleet hovering silently on the TV screen: 'Return to your alien masters and tell them that we Earthmen are not so easily crushed!' And with that I pulled the Atari out of the back of the TV and flipped on the news. HM Prison Maze (previously known as Long Kesh) was a maximum-security prison considered to be one of the most escape-proof penitentiaries in Europe. Of course, whenever you heard words like 'escape-proof' you immediately thought of that other great Belfast innovation, the 'unsinkable' *Titanic*. The facts came drifting in as I put on my uniform and body armour. Thirty-eight IRA prisoners had escaped from H Block 7 of the facility. They had used smuggled-in guns to take hostages, then they'd grabbed a laundry van and stormed the gates. One prison officer was dead and twenty others had been injured. 'Among the escapees are convicted murderers and some of the IRA's leading bomb-makers,' said an attractive, breathless young newsreader in the BBC studio.

'Well, that's fantastic,' I muttered, and wondered whether it was anybody I'd personally put away. I made a cup of instant coffee and had a bowl of Frosties to get the Turkish black out of my system and then I went outside to my waiting BMW.

'Oh, Mr Duffy, you won't have heard the news!' Mrs Campbell said to me over the fence. I was wearing a flak jacket, a riot helmet and carrying a Heckler and Koch MP5 submachine gun so it wasn't a particularly brilliant deduction from Mrs C, but I gave her a grim little smile and said, 'About the escape, you mean?'

She tucked a vivid line of burgundy hair behind an ear. 'Yes, it's shocking, they'll murder us all in our beds! What will I do with my Stephen upstairs on disability?' Stephen's 'disability' was a steady diet of cheap gin and vodka which meant that by lunchtime he was as pickled as Oliver Reed during the making of *The Three Musketeers*. She was a handsome woman, was Mrs Campbell, even with her troubles and her 1950's nightdress and a fag-end hanging out of her mouth.

'Don't concern yourself, Mrs C, I'll be back soon,' I said, trying to sound like Christopher Reeve in *Superman II* when he reassures Lois that General Zod will be no match for him. I'm not sure she quite got the element of self-parody in my Reeve impersonation but she did lean over the fence, give me an ashy kiss on the cheek and whisper 'thank you'.

I responded with a little nod of the head, walked down the path and got into my BMW. Before I put the key in the ignition I got out again and looked underneath the vehicle for mercury tilt bombs. There were none and I re-entered and stuck in a cassette of Robert Plant's *Principle of Moments*. This was my fourth listen to Plant's solo album and I still couldn't bring myself to like it. It was all synthesisers, drum machines and high-pitched vocals. It was a sign of the times, and with the autumn upon us it was safe to say that 1983 was turning out to be the worst year in popular music for about two decades.

I drove along the Scotch Quarter and turned right into Carrickfergus RUC station for the first time in a long time. It was a very strange experience, and the young guard at the gate didn't know me. He checked my warrant card, nodded, looked at me, frowned, raised the barrier and finally let me through. I parked in the crappy visitor's car park far from the station and walked to the duty sergeant's desk. There had been a few changes. They'd painted the walls mental-hospital pink and there were potted plants everywhere. I knew that Chief Inspector Brennan had retired and in his place they had brought in an officer from Derry called Superintendent Carter. I didn't know much about him except that he was young and energetic and full of ideas – which, admittedly, sounded just ghastly. But this wasn't my manor any more so what did I care what they did to the old place?

Running Carrickfergus CID branch on a temporary basis was my former adjutant, the freshly promoted Detective Sergeant John McCrabban, and that was a good thing. I went upstairs, slipped into the back of the briefing room and tried not to draw attention to myself.

'... might be of some use. We're instituting Operation Cauldron. Blocking every road to and from the Maze. Our patch is the access roads to the north and east, the A2 and of course the roads to Antrim. We are coordinating with Ballyclare RUC...'

Carter was tall with a prominent Adam's apple and brown curly hair. He was rangy and he leaned over the podium in a menacing way as if he was going to clip you round the ear. I listened to his talk, which spoke of dangers and challenges and finished with an echo of Winston Churchill's 'Fight Them on the Beaches' speech. As rhetoric it was wildly over the top but some of the younger reserve constables clapped when it was done. As we were filing out of the briefing room I said hello to a few old friends. Inspector Douggie McCallister shook my hand. 'It's great to see you, Sean. Jeez, if you'd been here five minutes earlier you would have caught up with McCrabban and Matty but they're away with the riot police. How ya been?'

'I've been fair to middling, Douglas. How's your new boss?'

Douggie rolled his eyes and lowered his voice: 'If he wasn't a six-footer I'd have said that he was a short man in need of a balcony.'

'Oh dear. You could always do the old Thorazine-in-the-whiskey trick.'

'Total abstainer, Sean. Tea drinker. Wants to ban booze from the station, from the whole island, too, if his pamphlets are to be believed.'

'I think they tried that approach in America with decidedly mixed results.'

'Aye well, one crisis at a time. Let me sort you out with a duty roster. Can you still drive a Land Rover?'

'Does the Pope shit in the woods?'

I got my armoured police Land Rover and headed out with a group of nervous constables to a place called Derryclone on the shores of Lough Neagh. It took us over two and a half hours to get through all the police roadblocks so that we could reach our destination and set up our own roadblock. This was the much-vaunted Operation Cauldron in action.

Radio 3 was playing Ligeti's *Requiem* and the sombre mood wasn't helped by the black clouds and the light rain and solitary crows cawing at us from sagging telegraph wires. When I opened the back doors of the Rover two of the men were reading their Gideon *New Testaments*, one appeared to have been crying and the sole Catholic reservist was, embarrassingly, fingering a rosary.

'Bloody hell, lads! It's like a Juarez minibus on the *Dia de Los Muertos* in here. Come on! This is routine. We are not going to encounter any terrorist desperadoes, I promise you.'

We set up our block along the sleepy B road by Lough Neagh and after an hour or two of nothingness it was evident to even the gloomiest young peeler that none of the Maze escapees were coming our way.

We saw helicopters with spotlights flying back and forth from RAF Aldergrove and on the radio we heard that, first, the Secretary of State for Northern Ireland had tended his resignation, and later that Mrs Thatcher herself had resigned.

No such luck. No one had resigned and I prophesied to the boys that when the inquiry into the break-out was published no one above the rank of inspector would even get a reprimand. (You can read the 1984 Hennessy Report for yourself if you want proof of my uncanny fortune-telling abilities.)

Another Land Rover arrived at our roadblock from Ballymena RUC and the coppers spoke in a dialect so thick we had trouble understanding them. Much of their conversation seemed to involve Jesus and tractors, an unlikely combination for anyone who doesn't know Ballymena. Yet another Land Rover came in the late evening: this one carrying lads from as far away as Coleraine. No one had thought to bring hot chocolate or hot cocoa or food or cigarettes, but the inspector from Coleraine RUC had brought along a travel chess set just to have the satisfaction of beating all of us. I told him my Boris Spassky story (Reporter: 'Which do you prefer, Mr Spassky, chess or sex?' Spassky: 'It very much depends on the position'). But he was not impressed and mated me in eleven moves.

It began to rain harder around midnight and the night was long and cold. In the wee hours we finally stopped a car: an Austin Maxi with an elderly female driver who'd been trying to get home from church since lunchtime. In the boot, alas, there were no escaped prisoners. She did have a tin of shortbread and after some discussion, in the interests of good community relations, we let her keep it.

Bored senseless, we listened in on the confused and contradictory police radio traffic. There had been some rioting in West Belfast but this was an obvious ploy to distract the cops so central command hadn't diverted many troops or peelers to deal with it.

Just before dawn there *was* a bit of excitement on the southern part of the lough when an army helicopter pilot thought he had seen someone hiding in the reeds. The radio barked into life and we and several other mobile patrols were scrambled and sent down to check it out. When we got there a small unit of Welsh Guardsmen were shooting into the water with machine guns. As the sun came up we saw that they had done a good job of massacring an exhausted flock of Greenland geese who had foolishly touched down here on their journey to the south of France.

The Ballymena boys grabbed a goose each and we drove back to our outpost. I sat up in the Land Rover cab and tuned in BBC Radio 4. The latest news was that eighteen of the escapees had been recaptured but the others had got clean away. At noon we got the list of their names. They were all unknown to me except for one . . . but that one was Dermot McCann. Dermot and I had gone to school together in Derry at St Malachy's. A really smart guy, he had been Head Boy when I had been Deputy Head Boy. Handsome, good at games and charming, Dermot had planned to go into the newspaper business and possibly into TV journalism. But the Troubles had changed all that and Dermot had volunteered for the IRA just as I had once thought of doing at around the time of Bloody Sunday.

Through various machinations I had joined the police and Dermot had served several years in the Provos before getting himself arrested. He was a highly gifted IRA explosives expert and bomb-maker who'd only been betrayed in the end by an informer. The grass fingered Dermot as an important player but there was no forensic evidence so some clever peeler had fitted him up by putting a fingerprint on a block of gelignite. He'd been found guilty and until his escape he'd been doing ten years for conspiracy to cause explosions.

I hadn't thought of Dermot in a long time but in the weeks that followed the break-out we learned that he had been one of the masterminds behind the escape plan. Dermot had figured out a way of smuggling guns into the prison and it was his idea to take prison officers hostage and dress in their uniforms so the guard towers wouldn't be alerted.

Dermot got to South Tyrone and over the border into the Irish Republic. I heard later from MI5 that he and an elite IRA team had been spotted at a terrorist training camp in Libya. But even on that miserable Monday morning on the eastern shores of Lough Neagh with the mist rising off the water and the rain drizzling from the grey September sky I knew with the chilly logic of a fairy story that our paths would cross again.

2: THE LITTLE ESCAPE

It was late on a cold December day and Prisoner 239 was doing now what he did best: waiting. He had not always been good at this. As a boy he had been aggressive and forward. At school he had been brilliant but often impatient and rash. It was in the Maze prison where he had learned about waiting. As an IRA leader he'd often been put in solitary, where waiting had been his only companion. He had waited in the Maze for five years: learning, scheming, plotting. And here, in this concrete coffin on the edge of the desert, although it was harder to keep track of time, he was waiting again. In the first few days after his arrest he had raged and fumed and banged his fists against the iron door. 'This is all a huge mistake!' he had yelled. 'We were invited here!' But it hadn't done any good. All that it had done was make them rush in with rubber hoses to shut him up.

He knew that he was not alone in the facility but here there were no prisoners in the cells on either side of him, which increased his sense of isolation, as did the high window, the enclosed exercise yard and the guards, who had been instructed never to talk to him or respond to his questions. But it only took him a few days to remember his old skills. He learned again to use the time and not to let the time use him. He read the French novels they gave him and what was left of the English newspapers after the prison censor had had his way with them. Censor is a lowly position in every culture and no doubt what the man cut from the pages revealed more than they could possibly imagine.

He began writing his thoughts down in the journals they left for him. On every other page he made drawings from memory of his mother, siblings and scenes from Derry. He must have known that when they took him to the exercise yard or the shower block they read and photographed what he had written, but he didn't care. He wrote poems and notes for political manifestos and stories about his childhood. Perhaps he even wrote about me, although I doubt that, and certainly my name was not mentioned in the materials British Intelligence subsequently gave me. In truth I was never one of his best friends; more of a hanger-on, a runner, a groupie . . . For a while in the sixth form I was even a comic foil, a court jester . . . until he tired of me and promoted some other loser into that position.

As the weeks dragged on, Prisoner 239's journal entries grew more elaborate. He described his experiences growing up in the Bogside in the 1950s and 1960s. He talked about that awful day in Derry when the paratroopers had shot dead a dozen civilians who had only been marching for equal rights . . . He mentioned how Bloody Sunday had galvanised him and every other young man in the city.

Including me, of course. In fact the last time I had seen Dermot McCann in the flesh was when I had meekly sought him out and asked whether I, too, could join the Provos. He had turned me down flat. 'You're at Queen's University, Duffy. Stay there. The movement needs men with brains as well as brawn.'

Of course, after I had joined the peelers he had no doubt expunged all thoughts of me from his life . . .

On that last December day, Prisoner 239 had taken the thin white mattress off the bed and placed it on the cell floor. He wrote in his journal that if he lay in the corner of the cell near the door he could occasionally see a thin cirrus cloud through the high slit windows. He could smell the desert on the southern

Khamseen and although he wasn't supposed to know where he was being held, he knew that he was south-east of Tobruk, probably less than a dozen miles from the Egyptian border. Freedom . . . if he could get out and make a break for it. And if anybody could get out of a Gaddafi dungeon it was Dermot McCann.

He lay on the floor and wrote about the sky as it changed colours throughout the late afternoon. He described the *ful* and flat bread they brought him at six o'clock. He wrote about the night-time prison symphony: keys turning in locks, the squeak of sneakers along a polished floor, men talking on the floor below, a distant radio, vermin outside in the hallway, a lorry clanking along one of the border roads and, when the wind was right, the howling of jackals at one of the desert wadis.

Prisoner 239 wrote and waited. He explored the vistas of his own mind and memory. 'Society improveth the understanding,' he scribbled on the very first page of the book, 'but solitude is the school of genius!'

On that final December evening, he lit a red candle stub (red wax was on the notebook), made a drawing of a fox, fixed his blanket about him and went to sleep. No doubt he woke with the sun, and when the guards came into his cell to bring him breakfast perhaps he sensed the change in their mood and attitude. Maybe he noticed that they were smiling at him and that one of them was carrying a brand-new suit of clothes.

3: THE INCIDENT

December. It had been a year now since I'd been thrown out of CID and reduced from detective inspector to the rank of sergeant – an ordinary sergeant, that is, not a *detective sergeant*. As you can imagine, after you've been a detective it's very difficult to go back to regular uniformed police work in a border police station. The official reason why the RUC had busted me was because I'd broken a lot of chicken-shit rules, but really it was because I had offended some high-ranking FBI agents over the DeLorean case and they'd wanted to see me brought down a peg or two.

Police stations on the South Armagh border were future finishing schools for alcoholics and suicides, with the added frisson of being shot or blown up on foot patrol, but what did me in was the night we had to take Sergeant Billy McGivvin home after he'd caused a drunken scene in a pub. Billy lived in my neck of the woods and I'd actually been to his house once for dinner, so I was put in charge of delivering him safely back . . .

It was after nine o'clock at night and we were driving up the Lower Island Road into Ballycarry village. There were three of us. Sergeant McGivvin and myself in the back, Jimmy McFaul driving up front. In theory it was a double-lane road but in fact it was merely a widened cattle track and Jimmy had us almost over into the sheugh because a car was coming the other way.

To avoid dazzling the other driver, Jimmy switched off the

full-beam headlights as the car went past. I looked through the Land Rover's bullet-proof windows but there was nothing to see: thick hedgerows on either side of the road and boggy pasture beyond that.

The Land Rover made a clunking sound.

'What was that?' I asked.

'I don't know,' Jimmy said.

'It was something.'

'You think someone shot at us?'

I had heard bullets thudding off the armour plate of a police Land Rover dozens of times and none of them had made a sound like that.

'I don't think so.'

'Well, we got to get McGivvin home,' Jimmy said.

The week before, Billy McGivvin's wife had taken their three kids and flown the coop. A lawyer told McGivvin that she was in England and that she was divorcing him because of repeated drunkenness and domestic violence. McGivvin had decided to refute her claims by going to the Joymount Arms in Carrickfergus and getting blotto. He had begun swearing at the other patrons, calling the women 'bitches' and 'hoors', and when they'd tried to make him leave Billy had pulled out his service revolver.

McGivvin was a terrible police officer before his wife had left him and no doubt now he was going to be a lot worse. That didn't concern me. What concerned me was the possibility that he was going to throw up over my uniform, which was only two days back from the dry cleaners.

'It's all right, mate, it's all right,' I kept assuring him. 'Soon be home.'

'Blurgghhhh,' he replied, and drooled on the plate-steel Land Rover floor.

We reached Ballycarry village without any trouble and found his farmhouse on Manse Street. Jimmy parked the Rover and dragged McGivvin out into the drizzle. We couldn't find a key, even under a plant pot or the mat, so we had to break in through the back door.

We stuck McGivvin in the recovery position on the downstairs sofa. We put a bucket next to him and loosened his shirt buttons. There was an enormous velvet painting of Jesus marching in an Orange parade that Jimmy felt might be in vomit spatter range so we took it off the wall and put it in the dining room.

There was a step ladder perched ominously under the light fitting in the kitchen. An ideal place for a noose. I collapsed the ladder and shoved it under the stairs. 'How many Freudians does it take to screw in a lightbulb?' I asked Jimmy to change the mood.

'Dunno,' he said.

'Two. One to change the lightbulb, the other to hold the penis – I mean ladder.' Jimmy didn't get it. 'I think that'll do,' I said.

We walked back to the Land Rover and got inside. We were just in time to hear the *Chart Show* announcing the Christmas Number 1 for 1983. It was 'Only You' by Vince Clarke – re-recorded by some tedious a cappella group.

'The musical taste of this country baffles me these days,' I said.

Jimmy smiled his twenty-four-year-old smile and said nothing.

I persuaded him to switch the channel to Radio 3 and Bach took us back to South Armagh.

When we parked at the police station I noticed that the driver's-side wing mirror was cracked. 'Look at that,' I said. 'Could we have hit something on the road?'

'Nah, it was cracked before we left. I'm pretty sure.'

There was no sign of blood or other forensic material.

It's probably nothing, I thought, and we went inside the heavily fortified barracks to complete the remainder of our shift.

4: SUSPENSION WITHOUT PAY

We were nearing the end of the foot patrol, which as any peeler or squaddie will tell you is the most sickening part of the whole business. We were close to the police station on the top of the hill and to be shot within sight of home would be very irritating.

The village was empty. It was a quiet Saturday morning, well before the market. We walked down the middle of the road along the white lines.

The houses on the left-hand side were in the Irish Republic, those on the right were in the United Kingdom of Great Britain and Northern Ireland. Our job was to patrol this border and prevent smuggling and the free movement of IRA arms, personnel and money. The geography made it an absurd situation. When Northern Ireland had been created in 1921 everyone had assumed that it was only going to be a temporary solution to the problem of Ireland's self-rule. No one seriously thought that the complicated twisty county lines of Fermanagh, Tyrone and Armagh could possibly become the permanent and policeable border between two separate countries. Yet they had and this border now ran through fields, villages, sometimes through farms and individual houses. All along it there were exclaves, enclaves, salients and other utterly unpatrollable cartographical features.

And here in the village of Bellaughray the border ran through the centre of town. Technically we were supposed to keep to the right-hand side of the road, because anything over that white dotted line would be an incursion into the sovereign territory of the Irish Republic and, in theory, a diplomatic incident; but if you did keep right you were exposed to snipers all along the County Monaghan hillside, so when I was leading the patrols, I kept us on the Eire side of the street, where the houses would protect us.

Walking slowly and in single file, we reached the central Bellaughray roundabout, and now it was only three hundred yards to the station.

I had taken eight men out in full body armour and we were heavily laden with flares, radios and Sterling machine guns. As usual it had been an exhausting patrol. We had walked across boggy fields, over sheughs and stone walls, through swamp and slurry and cow shit. We had found no trace of IRA men or petrol smugglers or sheep stealers, or sheep shaggers come to that, but nevertheless we had all put our lives on the line for the last hour and a half.

The IRA snipers were good and thanks to Yankee dollars they had acquired sophisticated high-velocity rifles. They knew our routines and routes and could easily have been waiting for us from a concealed den or lair up to three thousand feet away.

But they weren't. Not this morning anyway. We went through the roundabout in single file and reached the tiny Catholic chapel.

The hedge around the wee red-brick structure bothered me. It was thick and you couldn't see through it and anything could have been lurking behind: a man with a gun, a concealed explosive device . . .

I sent Constable Williams to recon it while I signalled the rest of the patrol to drop to one knee. Williams went ahead, looked behind the hedge and found nothing.

He gave me the thumbs-up.

'OK,' I said. 'Let's move out. Nearly home, lads.'

As was typical of these late December days the sun was more or less gone now, swallowed up in the mouths of huge chalk-coloured clouds that were tumbling down from the Mourne Mountains. But even on the coldest days fear and the heavy equipment kept us drenched with perspiration. It was starkly beautiful out here under the austere slopes of Slieve Gullion. This was a hallowed landscape: Cuchulainn's kingdom in the era of the *Táin Bó Cúailnge* and in St Patrick's time the *Terra Repromissionis Sanctorum* – the promised land of the Saints. No Saints about today, or sinners come to that.

I walked on point for a couple of minutes and then nodded at Constable Brown, whose face assumed the startled look of the stag in Landseer's *Monarch of the Glen*.

'Go on, son, I'll be right behind you,' I assured him.

He walked about twenty yards and froze. 'Vehicles!' he yelled.

I looked up the street. Two cars had parked themselves laterally at the ends of the road; one was a blue Ford Cortina, belonging to Mr McCoghlan, the local butcher, I thought, and the other was an orange Toyota that I didn't recognise. I wondered why they had blocked the road off. An ambush? A double car bomb? Or something completely innocent?

Smoke was coming from both exhausts. I raised my fist so everyone could see it and then I pulled it down. Everyone dropped to one knee again.

'There goes my arthritis,' Constable Pike complained.

'Just get down,' I said. 'And keep your wits about you.'

Eventually everyone assumed a crouching or half-kneeling stance – all the better to hit the deck if it was a car bomb and white-hot shrapnel came tearing towards us.

We waited. A raven landed in the road ahead of us and began pecking at something. The cars just sat up there, blue smoke curling from their exhausts, the engines turning over quietly. Constable Daniels started whistling 'What's New Pussycat?'

more or less off-key. I took out my binoculars and looked at the scene. There were two men in the two cars and they appeared to be talking.

'Hopkins, go up there and investigate!'

'Why me?' Constable Hopkins asked.

'Because it's your turn on point,' I said.

'When Inspector Calhoun leads the patrol he always investigates anything suspicious,' Hopkins protested.

'That's why they pay him the big bucks, isn't it? Now get up there and investigate before I take my boot to your arse!'

'All right,' Hopkins said moodily.

'McBeth, you go with him, staggered formation, at least twenty feet behind. And both of you stay on your toes!'

Hopkins and McBeth went up to the two parked cars while the rest of us held our breath.

I knew what the pair of them were thinking.

This is how it ends.

Bang.

An explosion of cordite into the layered chevrons of ignition powder. Logarithmic expansion. The explosive thrown out of its plastic casing. Vermilion fire. An entire life lived and ended in an instant . . .

McBeth and Hopkins reached the cars and talked to the men inside and came back to us.

'Two old geezers having a chinwag. It's all clear,' Hopkins said.

I nodded and just as I got to my feet I heard a loud crack from somewhere up in the hills. I didn't need to give the order to hit the deck. Before I could even open my gob everyone was already on the ground.

'Anybody hurt?' I yelled, and called the roll.

'Pike?'

'I'm OK!'

'Brown?'

'I'm all right.'

'Daniels?'

'OK.'

'McCourt?'

'OK.'

'Hopkins?'

'Despite your best efforts, Sergeant, I'm OK, too!' he said bitterly.

'McBeth?'

'Aye, I'm all right.'

'Did anybody see where that came from?'

No one had. No one had seen anything and no one knew what the sound had been. Up ahead the two old geezers were still talking.

The question was how long we should remain lying here. We couldn't hug the tarmac all day. 'OK, Pike, McBeth, McCourt, get over to the left-hand side of the road and scan those bloody hills. If you see a scope glint or a puff of smoke shoot it. The rest of you, let's retire by half-squad at three-quarter pace up the road. When we're a hundred metres past them, we'll stop and cover them. Everybody clear?'

'Yes, Sergeant Duffy!' several – but not all – of them said.

Pike, McBeth and McCourt ran to the ditch on the Irish Republic side and pointed their machine guns at the hills. Of course, if it *was* a sniper he'd be concealed and thousands of feet away and the effective range of the Sterling was a hundred feet max, but if the three of them blazed away together they might hit something.

The rest of us got to our feet and ran up the road. We stopped and let Pike and his mates reach us.

We did this twice more until we reached the station.

No one shot at us. If it was a sniper, he was a very cautious one. One shot and then done. We patrolled this road every day. His opportunity would come again.

I let every man in the squad go into the barracks ahead of me and then I went in last. I didn't completely relax until the thick iron gates closed behind me. As usual I was utterly exhausted when I walked through the double doors of the locker room, but the bastards didn't even give me a chance to get my body armour off . . .

The bastards were two tall, humourless, plain-clothed goons from Internal Affairs. They were wearing old-fashioned black woollen sports jackets over white shirts and matching red ties. One had a ginger peeler tache, the other a black one.

'Sergeant Duffy?' Ginger Tache asked in a vague Scottish accent.

'Yes?'

'Come us with us to Interview Room 2,' he said.

'Can you hold on a minute?' I said, and made them wait while I took off my kit.

I followed them along the concrete corridor to the interrogation room, normally reserved for suspects. They were in there with Constable Jimmy McFaul. Jimmy had evidently spilled his guts about something because there were tears in his eyes and he couldn't look at me.

I had no idea what this could be about. The cannabis I had lifted from the evidence room in Carrickfergus? But that was a long time ago and what had Jimmy to do with that?

'Have a seat, Duffy,' Ginger Tache said.

'Can I get a drink? I've been on foot patrol along the border. Thirsty work, but you proud boys in Internal Affairs wouldn't know about that, would you?' I said, and went back outside, got a can of Coke from the machine and put it against my forehead. I popped the can, took a big drink and joined them again.

I sat next to McFaul. 'What's going on, Jimmy?' I asked him.

His eyes were fixed on his boots.

'Were you driving a police Land Rover on the Lower Island Road, Ballycarry, at approximately 9.45 p.m. on the night of 20 December?' Black Tache asked.

'What?'

'You were the only Land Rover on the road that night. There's no point in denying it,' Ginger Tache added.

'Your mate has told us everything. You were on the road and you were driving and you hit someone and you didn't stop,' the other goon said.

'Jimmy, you said *I* was driving?' I asked him.

Jimmy said nothing and kept looking at the space where his lying eyes intersected with the floor.

'You hit someone, Duffy. From what Constable McFaul says you didn't even realise it, but you hit a man,' Black Tache said.

'Is he OK?' I asked.

'You knocked him into the sheugh with the wing mirror. He was shook up and he broke a finger, but he'll live. Twenty-year-old lad on his way back home from football practice. He had his rucksack on his back. You hit that. That's maybe what saved him from a more serious injury.'

'Thank God for that,' I said.

'He's still going to sue us, though, isn't he?' Ginger Tache said.

'I don't know what the Ghost of Fuck-ups Past here has told you but I wasn't driving that night. I was in the back of the Rover trying to stop Sergeant McGivvin from choking on his own vomit or puking on my green union suit. Sergeant McGivvin will verify that.'

'We've already asked him. Sergeant McGivvin doesn't remember anything of the incident,' Black Tache insisted with a sleekit smile. 'So, it's just your word against Constable McFaul.'

I nodded. *So that was how it was going to be.*

'Both of you are hereby suspended without pay until the conclusion of this inquiry,' the big Scottish bastard said.

'You can keep your gun for personal protection, but you are not permitted to leave Northern Ireland and you are *not* to report for duty,' Goon No. 2 added.

Jimmy accepted the verdict and slunk out of the interview room. He had got his story in first. He was the grass and I was going to be the fall guy. In other words I was completely screwed. Ginger Tache sat down in Jimmy's seat. 'I'm Chief Inspector Slater,' he said, offering me his hand.

I didn't shake it. I knew this game of old. First the stick, then the carrot up the arse. 'What's all this about?' I asked. 'Just tell me the bottom line.'

'The bottom line? It's over for you, Duffy. You are not being graded on a friendly curve. You should see your file, mate. Christ on a bike. It's got red flags all over it. You were lucky not to have been kicked out in '82. You've been on probation ever since,' Slater said.

'I wasn't driving the Land Rover,' I said.

'What do we care? You're our boy for this month. A nice juicy sergeant. All we need is our quota and you're it,' Slater said.

'I wasn't driving!' I insisted.

'Your mate Jimmy says you were. He's clean and we've got your dirty, dirty file clogging up the works.'

I lit a ciggie. At least Jimmy hadn't told them about my Freudian dick joke. But it didn't matter. Nothing mattered. The wheels had already been set in motion. 'So it's all been settled, then, has it? I'm the scapegoat?'

'You've been in the RUC, what, eight years?' Slater asked.

'Closer to nine,' I told him.

Slater leaned in towards me and smiled an ugly yellow-fanged grin. 'It doesn't have to end in scandal, does it?' he said.

'OK, give it to me. What's the deal?' I asked.

'You're not eligible for a pension or benefits but we'll give them to you if you accept full responsibility and quietly resign without this becoming a big deal.'

'And if I don't resign?' I asked.

Slater made the throat-slitting gesture. 'Full disciplinary proceedings. Make no mistake: you will be found guilty and you will be dismissed the force without severance or a pension. And don't think being a Fenian will save you. In your short, not so brilliant career you've managed to piss off a lot of people.'

I nodded, stubbed out my cigarette on the desk and got to my feet.

'I'll think about it,' I said.

5: THE LETTER

The New Year. 1984. But there was no Big Brother watching us. No one gave a pig's arse. Ireland was an island floating somewhere in the Atlantic that all sensible people wanted to drift even farther away, beyond their shores, beyond their imaginations . . .

The year limped in. The days merged. One morning it was sleet, the next rain.

I walked the town and when I got home I checked the post to see whether my dismissal papers had come through for me to sign. Carrickfergus was a mess: large areas had been zoned for demolition and reconstruction. It was EEC money and the locals saw it as a good thing, and it wasn't because it only meant that we were high on the EEC list of Towns That Are in the Shitter.

I walked the streets and drank in the pub and watched TV late into the night, when it was all public information films warning kids about the dangers of drowning in quarries or lifting up strange packages which were really trip-wired explosives.

One night the elderly woman across the terrace had some kind of seizure and started screaming, 'He's coming! He's coming!' Who was coming was never explained, but she had proclaimed it in such a convincing way that a minor panic had ensued and the whole of Coronation Road had come out.

Another night we heard a two-thousand-pound bomb in

Belfast so clearly that it might have been at the end of the street.

Signs, portents, single magpies, black cats, bombs, bomb scares, helicopter traffic . . .

Finally one morning a white envelope sitting on the hall mat.

I took it to the living room and stirred the embers in the fireplace. I lit a fag, took a deep breath and ripped it open. A boilerplate full 'confession' to be signed, notarised and returned to RUC Headquarters in Belfast.

The terms were comparatively generous. In recompense for an admission of wrongdoing I would take early retirement and receive a pension, although I hadn't put in enough time.

I read through the document twice, poured myself an emergency Glenfiddich and signed everything that needed to be signed.

At nine I went into Carrickfergus and found Sammy McGuinn, my barber, who was also a notary public. Sammy was the town's only communist and it was he who had turned me on to the strange delights of Radio Albania. He read the document and shook his head. 'I know you don't see it now, Sean, but this is a very good thing. As a member of the police you were nothing more than a lackey in a tyrannical government oppressing the will of the people. A Catholic, too! Smart lad like you.'

'It was a job, Sammy. A job I was good at.'

'Power is bad for the soul!' he said, and went on to talk about Lord Acton, Jurgen Habermas and the Stanford Prison Experiment.

'Yeah, could you just notarise the form for me, Sammy?'

'Of course,' he said and added his seal and signature while muttering something about Thatcher and Pinochet.

'I can see you're down, I'll throw in a haircut,' he said, and put on the happiest music he could think of, which was Mozart's Symphony Number 40.

Mrs Campbell saw me coming out of the barber's: 'In getting your hair done, Mr Duffy?'

'I don't get me hair "done". I get it cut,' I replied dourly.

I crossed the street to the post office, bought a first-class stamp, fixed it to the return envelope, mailed the letter, and just like that I was off the force.

6: THE VISITORS

Time moved on. Days to weeks. Weeks to months. Cold February. Damp March. As Ezra Pound says, life goes by like a field mouse, not even shaking the grass. Usually I went to the library and read the papers: parochial news, fossilised editorials, a narrow frame of reference. I sometimes checked out classical LPs and did nothing until six o'clock when it was seemly to get quietly hammered on Polish vodka or County Antrim poteen, listening to Wagner or Steve Reich or Arvo Pärt. Strange millennial music for strange millennial times.

I went to the dole office and they told me that there was no point signing on. With my retirement money coming in I would be means tested and would not be eligible for any other kind of income support. The unemployment officer told me I should move to Spain or Greece or Thailand or someplace where my monthly cheque from the RUC would go a long way.

I felt that this was good advice and I got a few books on Spain out of the library.

I walked the streets. Observed. Observed like a detective. Kids playing football. Kids painting death's-head murals on gable walls. Fiddle players and cellists outside the bank busking for coppers. Men in the High Street offering to recite you any poem you could think of for the price of a cup of tea.

One evening in the pub I got into a fight. Standard fare. Old geezer bumped me. I said 'Excuse me, pal.' Out came the fisticuffs. I got him with a left and before I knew what was happening the bastard had jabbed me five times with his right. Chin, stomach, kidneys, stomach again . . . He must have been sixty if he was a day. He helped me to my feet and bought me a drink and spun me a yarn about winning a middleweight belt and training John Wayne for his performance as an ex-boxer in *The Quiet Man*. It was a likely story but I was so addled I couldn't tell whether it was legit or bollocks . . . I went home in a taxi, drank a vodka gimlet, took 10 mg of Valium, half a dozen aspirin and went to bed.

In the wee hours I woke and looked at the aspirin bottle next to me and wondered whether this had been a cowardly, half-hearted suicide attempt. *Cowardly* because I still had my service revolver, which as an ex-policeman I was allowed to keep for up to a year after I'd left the force. That was the way to do it. Point blank with a hollow-point .38 slug straight across the hemispheres.

My guts ached and I walked to Carrick hospital and a surprisingly full waiting room. Lynchian post-midnight bus-station characters. The Open University on a black and white TV. A beardy physicist: 'Life is a thermodynamic disequilibrium but entropy will take us all in the end . . .'

Yeah.

My guts were killing me so they put me on a drip. The doctor on call said that I would live but that I wasn't to mix my medicines. He gave me a leaflet on depression. I went home, wrapped the bedsheets around me and went on to the landing. My newly installed central heating had sprung a leak and the repairman had said that he needed to get a part from Germany to overhaul the whole organ-like apparatus. It would take weeks, he explained, maybe over a month, so I'd rented another paraffin heater and in truth I liked it better. The paraffin heater was my shrine and I bathed in its warmth, its sandalwood aroma and the light of its magenta moon.

I lay before it and let the hot air wash over me like a blanket.
A long time ago I had killed a man with a heater like this.

No. Was that me? Did such a thing really occur?

Or was it a fragment, a dream . . .

Oarless boats . . . Dream ships . . . The half-light of the wolf's tail.

Dawn.

I went downstairs.

Rain. Sky the colour of a litter box. An army helicopter skimming the dogged brown hills.

I caught a glimpse of myself in the hall mirror. I was skinny, scabby, pale. My nails were long and dirty. My hair was unkempt, thick, black, with grey above both ears and on the sideburns. I looked like the poster boy for an anti-heroin ad. Not that I'd go that route. Not yet. And speaking of the exotic gifts of the Orient . . . Wasn't there a . . .

I rummaged in the rubbish bin under the kitchen sink and found a roach with an inch of cannabis still left in it. I made a coffee and topped it with a measure of Black Bush. I went back into the living room, searched among the albums until I got the *Velvet Underground & Nico*. I put on 'Venus in Furs', drank the coffee, lit the roach off the paraffin-heater flame and inhaled. Paraffin. Hashish. John Cale's viola. Lou Reed's voice.

Revived somewhat, I went outside and picked up the milk bottles. There was a strange car four doors down on the Coronation Road bend. A white Land Rover Defender with two shadowy figures inside. A man and a woman, she in the driver's seat. I made a mental note of the car, popped the top off the gold-topped milk and poured it into my coffee mug. I stared at the car and drank. It began to drizzle from a dishwater sky.

'Jesus is Lord!' another one of my enthused neighbours yelled as a morning greeting. I took a final look at the car, closed the door and went back into the living room.

'I am tired, I am weary. I could sleep for a thousand years,'

Lou Reed sang as I lay down. The music ended, the stylus lifted, moved an inch to the left and the song began again.

There was a faint creaking sound from outside. Someone at the gate. The post or the paper or—

I grabbed the revolver from my dressing-gown pocket and checked that it was loaded. But somehow I knew that the people in the Land Rover were not going to be terrorist assassins . . .

I heard voices and then a confident rap on the door knocker.

I went into the hall, looked through the fisheye peephole every cop had installed as a necessary precaution.

The man was a tall, balding, slightly harassed-looking guy who would make an ideal 'innocent bystander injured in shooting' story for the news. He was wearing a blue suit and his shoes were shined to autistic levels of perfection. He was about twenty-five. The woman was brown-haired, pale, thin, grey-eyed. Somewhere around thirty. No lipstick, make-up, jewellery. She was wearing a black sweater, a short black skirt and black low-heeled shoes. She wasn't pretty, not classically so, but I could see how some men would lose their heads for her (some women, too). There was an intensity, a self-possession to her that was uncommon.

I put the .38 back in my dressing-gown pocket and opened the door.

'Mr Duffy?' the man asked with an English accent.

'Yes.'

'May we come in for a moment?'

For just a sec I wondered whether they were, in fact, a really good hit team. It would be the sort of thing a really good team would do. Ask whether they could come in and when the door was safely closed and your back turned, plug you . . . but they were almost certainly those English Jehovah's Witnesses that I'd heard everyone complaining about down the fish and chip shop.

'Aye, go into the living room, just to the right there. Do you want tea?'

Both of them shook their heads. Perhaps, like Mormons, they didn't drink tea or coffee.

'Are you sure you don't want any? The kettle's on,' I shouted.

'No thank you,' the woman said.

I made myself a mug, poured a packet of chocolate digestives on to a plate and carried it back into the living room.

She had taken the leather chair and he had been relegated to the sofa.

They took a biscuit each. Missionaries didn't deserve the Velvet Underground so I put on Lou Reed's fuck-you masterpiece, *Metal Machine Music*, an album of feedback loops and screeching guitars.

'Do we have to have the music?' the man asked.

I nodded. 'Of course! In case *they're* listening,' I said.

'In case who's listening?' the man wondered.

I pointed vaguely at the sky and put my finger to my lips. I sat down, dipped a chocky biscuit in the tea and ate.

'So . . . Jehovah,' I said.

'Who?' the man asked, and blinked so slowly you wondered whether Lou Reed had given him a mini-stroke.

I brought the teacup to my lips and nodded at the lass. I looked into her strange pale eyes and suddenly remembered that we had met before.

I froze in mid-drink. You know poker, don't you? So you know what's it like when you're playing Texas hold 'em and you're sitting there with a three and a five off suit and it's the big blinds and you're short stacked and the dealer spreads the flop and it's a two, a four and a six . . . and just like that you've gone from the shit-box seat to the bird-dog seat in the blink of an eye. The blink of a bloody eye . . .

And now I was feeling slightly foolish sitting here in my dressing gown and fluffy slippers.

'We've met, haven't we?' I said to her.

'I don't think so,' she said in a refined English accent with an ever so slight foreign echo to it.

I got up and turned off Mr Reed. 'Oh yeah, we've met before. Not a hundred yards from here in Victoria Cemetery, in 1982. You left me a note about a case I was working on. You're MI5, aren't you?' I said.

Neither of them had any idiosyncrasies that would render them vivid but that was the point, wasn't it? I had only seen her for a fleeting moment and her hair was a different colour, but it was her. The fact that I was right was communicated only by a momentary eye twitch and a slight pursing of the lips.

'Any chance of getting some names?' I asked.

'I'm Tom,' the man claimed.

'And I'm Kate,' the woman claimed.

I took a big gulp of the sweet tea and set it down on the coffee table.

'So, Tom, Kate,' I began. 'Exactly how badly are you fucked and why do you think I can help you get unfucked? There are plenty of coppers. Plenty of good coppers. What is it that I bring to the table? Eh?'

I gave the man a wink and his lip curled in distaste. He didn't like my new-found pantomime joviality. She, however, smiled. 'You bring several things, Sean. First, you're very good at what you do. Second, we don't want the man we're looking for to know that we're making a special effort to find him; of course, he knows that the police are after him, but if two people like Tom and myself were to go around asking questions . . . Well, that just might set the alarm bells ringing a bit louder than we'd like. And third and most important of all, the *personal*. You actually know the individual that we're seeking.'

'You went to school with him,' Tom added.

I digested this information. Part two was a half-truth. She and Tom wouldn't be going around asking questions – they'd have proxies in the RUC or Special Branch to do that. But MI5 were like those English officials in the Raj who could never completely trust their sepoy soldiers. The RUC was leaky and unreliable, whereas I was safely outside the system. I would be grateful to have a job. Grateful and pliant.

I sipped some more tea, had another biscuit and lit a cigarette. Of course, it was obvious who they were talking about: I had only been to school with one man that MI5 could possibly be interested in and that man was Dermot McCann.

'Mr Duffy, if I could just suggest a—' Kate began, but I cut her off.

'You see, the thing is, love, I've retired. I'd like to help you but you've arrived too late. I'm putting the house on the market, I'm selling up and I'm moving to Spain. I've picked out a nice wee spot with a view of the Med and with my RUC pension coming in every month I'll be sitting pretty.'

'What will you do with your time?' Tom asked.

'Nothing. Relax. Listen to music. Did you know that Haydn wrote one hundred and four symphonies? Who's heard more than half a dozen of them?'

Kate bit her lip and looked at me benevolently. 'Look, Sean, we deeply regret the way you have been treated in the last year.'

'Who's we?'

'We work for the Security Service, as you intuited,' Kate said.

I was excited now but I let my anger bubble through: 'It's easy to say that you *deeply regret it* but you didn't actually lift a finger to help me, did you?'

'It wasn't our purview,' Kate said.

'Or maybe you caused the whole thing, eh? Maybe you've done it to get me on the way down and then you chaps swoop in as my saviours from across the sea? If that's the case, I'm afraid it's backfired pretty fucking spectacularly. I've moved on. I've moved on mentally and spiritually and very soon I'll have moved on geographically too. I'm done with Northern Ireland and the Troubles and Thatcher and MI5 and this whole disagreeable decade. I'm very happy to take my wee bit of hard-earned scratch and go to Spain,' I said.

Tom looked concerned but after a moment's thought Kate shook her head.

'I don't think so,' she said.

I set my teacup on the mantel, stubbed out the cigarette in the dolphin ashtray and rubbed my chin.

'No, believe me, I'm leaving. I'm like Macavity the fucking Mystery Cat. I'm not here. I'm already gone.'

Kate sighed, waiting for the histrionics to be done with.

I slipped in the dagger. 'And if you want me to locate Dermot McCann for you before I go it's going to come at a very high price.'

Tom was shocked to hear the name *Dermot McCann* so early in the conversation but Kate merely arched an eyebrow.

'What price?' she asked.

And now we had the 64,000-dollar question. What the hell *did* I want?

'Full reinstatement to the rank of *detective* inspector. Full remission of pay and seniority. My record to be expunged of *any* wrongdoing. A posting to a police station of my choosing. And something else . . .'

'What?' Kate asked.

'An apology for the way I've been treated. An apology from the top.'

'The Chief Constable?'

'From Thatcher.'

'From Mrs Thatcher?' Tom asked, amazed at my chutzpah.

'Well, not from fucking Denis.'

'You must be out of your mind, chum!' Tom exclaimed, his eyes bulging in his head.

'That's what I want. Take it or fucking leave it.'

'You know we could make things very unpleasant for you,' Tom said.

I got to my feet and got close to him. Practically nose to nose. 'No, mate, you don't want to be starting in with the threats, that's the wrong tack completely,' I said.

Kate cleared her throat, stood and brushed imaginary crumbs from her blouse.

'I assume a letter of regret signed by the Prime Minister would be sufficient?' she asked in a businesslike voice.

'Maybe,' I said.

'Well, we'll have to see what we can do, then, won't we?' she said.

She waved Tom to his feet.

I saw them to the front door. 'We'll be in touch,' Kate said.

'You better make it soon, love, I hear Valencia is lovely this time of year.'

'Actually, it's surprisingly inclement,' she said, and walked briskly down the garden path.

7: CHIAROSCURO

Ireland in shades of black and green under the gibbous moon. Ireland under the canopy of grey cloud, under the crow's wing, under the crow's wing and the helicopter blade. A night ride over the Lagan valley and the bandit country of South Armagh. The music in my head was Mahler's Ninth Symphony, which opens with a hesitant, syncopated, motif evocative of Mahler's irregular heartbeat . . .

I'd never liked helicopters: hills looming out of the fog/engine failures/surface-to-air missiles – especially the latter. RAF choppers in Ulster flew with magnesium-flare countermeasures streaming constantly from the back of the aircraft, but for bureaucratic reasons the army had not yet adopted this sensible precaution. Fortunately the flight from Belfast was short and I could soon see our destination.

Bessbrook army barracks had grown up around a converted mill built by Quakers in the nineteenth century. It was now the regional headquarters of the British army in Armagh and the busiest heliport in Europe. Hundreds of soldiers were ferried from here all over the border region and it was here that many of the intelligence agencies and the military police had their command centres.

Within the coils of razor wire and blast-proof perimeter walls there were squaddies of every stripe: infantrymen, chopper pilots, SAS, engineers, signals, Royal Marines, you name it.

Bessbrook was a bundling of all the British army's best assets in one basket. It was surrounded on all sides by unfriendlies, and if the IRA ever got its shit together for a big push Bessbrook would make a nice little Dien Bien Phu.

We dropped to five hundred feet. Everywhere arc lights, spotlights, red flares. The town of Newry just two klicks to the left; the border to the Irish Republic only a stone's throw to the right in a patch of forbidding darkness.

'Brace yourself! We do a hard landing. You get out, we take off,' the gunner explained.

'What do you mean by hard landing?' I asked, but by this stage we were in a rapid descent. The Wessex touched down on a huge white H.

'This is you! Get out!' the gunner yelled.

I nodded, undid my harness and took off my headphones. I ran out of the chopper and as soon as I was safely out of the way the Wessex took off again.

A young military policeman with a clipboard walked towards me.

'Inspector Duffy?'

Inspector?

'I'm Duffy.'

'This way.'

We went through a metal blast door and I followed him deep into the concrete labyrinth. We had gone two levels down and through several different security zones when we reached the lowest level of all: a dank, grim sub-basement.

'It's like Hitler's last days down here.'

The MP had clearly heard that one before but he smiled anyway.

I was taken to an interview room and left with a jug of water, a chair, an ashtray and the *Daily Mirror*. I read the *Mirror* and smoked a tab.

The headline was about magician/comedian Tommy Cooper, who'd had a heart attack the previous night and died live on TV.

Everyone thought it was part of his act and continued laughing while he struggled for breath on the stage floor. 'It was the way he would have wanted to go,' many of Cooper's friends were quoted as saying, but you couldn't really believe that.

Tom and Kate entered ten minutes later. Tom was wearing a black polo-neck sweater over a pair of brown slacks and brown tasselled loafers. He was trying hard to be casual but there were bags under his eyes and his face was ashy. Kate was wearing a white shirt and faded blue jeans. Tom was carrying a tape recorder, she a briefcase. He set up the tape recorder, hooked it to a microphone and pressed record.

'8.01 p.m., 16 April 1984, Bessbrook, County Armagh, Northern Ireland. Interview with Sean Duffy, formerly of the Royal Ulster Constabulary,' he said.

'Still formerly, eh?'

Kate opened her briefcase and passed me a sheet of paper. It was a legal document temporarily reinstating me into the RUC until 31 December 1984 with the rank of detective inspector.

I looked at it and then at her. She could tell that I wasn't pleased.

'What's this 31 December bullshit?'

'I'm afraid it was the best we could squeeze out of the Chief Constable,' Kate replied.

'He really doesn't like you,' Tom added.

'Where's my letter from Thatcher?'

'The Prime Minister was apprised of your request and declined to sign a letter of apology or regret at your allegedly unfair treatment by Her Majesty's government,' Kate said with an attempt at a sympathetic smile.

'Did you even ask?'

'Yes, we did ask.'

'That sour old bitch!'

I looked at her and at Tom and at the black tape spinning round on the recorder.

'Sean,' Kate said softly. There was something odd about her face, something difficult to explain. Under that severe brown bob she was attractive and intelligent, you couldn't tell what she was thinking or where she was from or even how old she really was – I wouldn't have been surprised to learn that she was twenty-two and fresh out of Oxford or fifty and a long-standing veteran of the Cold War.

'This is the best we can do, for now,' she continued.

'It's not good enough. I want full reinstatement and an apology. Those goons called me a "Fenian bastard", practically to my face. Do you have any idea what it's been like putting up with bollocks like that over the years?'

Of course they didn't. Not really. Their religious wars were done. The English had got over all this hundreds of years ago.

Tom drummed his fingers on the table.

I looked up to the ceiling. What *was* I going to do? Go to bloody Spain? Eat tapas and listen to frigging flamenco?

'I'm willing to drop my demand for a letter of apology but I'm not going to compromise on anything else,' I said.

Tom shook his head at Kate, as if saying, *I told you so, he's a fucking prima donna.*

'Sean, look, this is the best deal we were able to get. A temporary reinstatement, a return to the CID. Your old rank back! It took a lot of haggling to get just this through the RUC hierarchy.'

'It's worthless. All this means is that come 31 December I'll be chucked out again on my ear,' I said, waving the paper like a sadder and wiser Neville Chamberlain.

'No, that's not the case,' Kate insisted.

'So what *does* it mean?'

'It means that you'll be temporarily reinstated with a proviso that at the end of the year the reinstatement will be made permanent . . . if certain conditions are met.'

'And what are those conditions?'

'That you do no harm to the reputation of the RUC, that you don't violate any direct orders from senior RUC officers and, finally, that MI5 gives the Chief Constable a favourable report on your activities with this service.'

I wrinkled my nose in disgust. 'So I'm back on probation and effectively I'll be serving two masters. Trying to keep the cops happy and MI5 happy at the same time?'

'I suppose so,' Kate said.

But, restoration to the police? To my former rank? To be a detective again? The old thrill was coming back . . .

'I'd like to see all this in writing.'

'Don't push it, Duffy,' Tom muttered.

I leaned back in the plastic chair, looking at poor Tommy Cooper's grinning face under his red fez.

'What are you thinking, Sean?' Kate asked.

'*Albion perfide* is what I'm thinking.'

'Yes. You're right to be cautious of the service but wrong to distrust me. I make it a point of giving my word only when I know I can keep it.'

'Oh, you're good,' I told her, but in truth her words were strangely reassuring.

'And if you really want me to, I can write you a note explaining the conditions and provisos of your full reinstatement,' Kate added with a smile.

I nodded.

'Well then,' she said, opened her briefcase and passed me several forms to read and sign. There was no drama. We all knew what I was going to do.

I put my signature to two different versions of the Official Secrets Act and a form indemnifying the Home Office from death or injury that might happen in the line of duty. When I was done Kate carefully took the forms and put them back in her briefcase.

'Jolly good. Now, you must understand that what we're about to tell you is highly confidential . . .' Kate began.

'OK.'

She cleared her throat. 'All right, then . . . We've known for a few years that the IRA has been receiving weapons training in Libya. Following the mass break-out from the Maze prison last September we were able to track nine or possibly ten IRA escapees to Tripoli. Through the work of our sister agency we have been able to identify most of those individuals. One of whom, as you correctly guessed, is Dermot McCann.'

'He's quite the lad, isn't he? You really should have kept a better eye on him.'

'Indeed. Now, relations between Colonel Gaddafi and the IRA have been somewhat complicated, fraught, one could even say, and in the late autumn of last year our sister service managed to plant a story with the Gaddafi regime that the IRA men were in fact agents of the Mossad. Gaddafi had all of them arrested and thrown in one of his dungeons.'

'Nice work.'

She shook her head. 'As is typical of the somewhat baroque schemes of the SIS this disinformation created only a short-term gain and may actually have hurt our cause. Gaddafi has since released all of the IRA personnel and has redoubled his efforts to equip and school them.'

Tom took up the story: 'SIS did do us one favour, though. They were able to get a copy of McCann's prison journal. Unfortunately it's not terribly helpful, but we'd still like you to read it.'

He passed me two dozen photocopied pages in a black binder. I flipped it open and saw it contained doodles, political commentary, drawings, poems and a potted attempt at autobiography.

'You've read this already?' I asked.

'Yes, and I'm afraid that McCann was not foolish enough to write anything incriminating.'

'Do you have the original?'

'We do.'

'I'd rather read that, if you don't mind.'

Kate nodded and Tom passed me a little notebook covered with candle wax and which smelled of sand and sweat and *ful medames*.

'What else have you got on Dermot?'

'We've been able to gather precious little information about the IRA's activities in Libya but evidently the men were given bomb-making and weapons training. And we think they were split into two or three separate cells.'

'These cells have the money and operational capability to subsist completely independently of the IRA Army Council when they return to the British Isles,' Kate continued.

'That must have made you nervous. You've got a mole in the IRA Army Council, haven't you?'

The blood drained from Tom's face. Kate reached across the table and stopped the tape recorder. 'Inspector Duffy, you really shouldn't speculate about things like that,' she said tersely with an unattractive but oddly fascinating furrow between her eyebrows.

She rewound the tape to the point where she had said 'British Isles' and hit the 'Record' switch again.

'Last week we received the somewhat alarming information from SIS that the IRA teams were given false passports and some of them may have already departed Libya.'

'Brilliant. So they're long gone.'

'Yes.'

She folded her hands together on the tabletop and looked at Tom. He had nothing to add.

'Go on,' I said.

'Go on with what?' Kate asked.

'That's it? You've no more intel?'

'I'm afraid that's it,' Tom said with a sheepish grin.

I lit myself a cigarette and let the nicotine dissolve into my bloodstream for a minute or so before beginning my spiel.

'Let me see if I understand you correctly. Up to ten IRA men have received sophisticated bomb-making and weapons training in Libya. Some of them were escapees from the Maze prison and those boys were already highly skilled explosive engineers. Gaddafi's secret service has given them false passports, money and materiel and many of them are probably already in the UK plotting a major IRA bombing campaign. Is that about the size of it?'

'That's about the size of it,' Kate said.

'I think,' Tom began, but before he could tell us these thoughts the lights went off and we heard muffled thumping sounds all around the base. Some sort of attack? If so it was a half-hearted affair and after two minutes the lights came back on again. I noticed that Tom had puffed my cigarette to a stub.

'So what exactly is my role to be in all this?' I asked Kate.

'We'd like you to help locate Dermot McCann for us. He'll almost certainly be the leader of one of the cells, perhaps of the whole unit.'

'Dermot's been on the run for a while now. Presumably you've already tried the conventional approach?'

'Special Branch, the prison service, MI5 and even the SAS have been looking for him,' Kate replied.

'Phone taps? Mail diversion . . .'

'All that and a couple of ground teams.'

'Who exactly are you tapping? I know that Annie divorced him a few years ago.'

'Annie's living at home with her mother and father, but we've tapped that phone anyway, just to be on the safe side.'

'Who else?'

'Don't be cross, Sean, but I'm afraid I don't have the clearance to tell you all the names. I can assure you that we tap the phones and intercept the post of every known family member and associate.'

'And you've heard nothing?' I said.

Tom shook his head.

It was my turn to shrug. 'I'm not surprised. Dermot's extremely disciplined. He'll never contact his family or friends, not while his cell is operational. Dermot's no mug. It'll be a tough gig.'

'We caught him once before,' Tom offered.

'No, you didn't catch him. The police fitted him up. Dermot would never have left a fingerprint anywhere, certainly not on one of his own bombs. Special Branch planted that print,' I said.

Kate smiled at me. 'Perhaps we'll have to take more extreme measures this time.'

I didn't like her tone.

'Well, I certainly won't be your assassin,' I told her coldly.

'We don't need you to be. We just need you to do what you do best,' she replied.

I lit another fag, threw the match at the ashtray and it landed on Tommy Cooper's big chin. 'I'll need a list of Dermot's friends, relatives, old prison buddies and acquaintances. Basically every person that you're wire-tapping and the circle beyond that.'

'We can do some of that.'

'And I'll need an office. I was thinking Carrick police station. It's handy and I know the score. They've got some tight-arsed new boss there, a Chief Super from Derry. You'll have to square it with him.'

'We can do some of that, too,' she said.

'I'll need a warrant card that says I'm an inspector in CID. You better stick me in Special Branch. It won't scare the punters but it sometimes puts the wind up uncooperative peelers.'

I couldn't think of any more demands off the top of my head.

'That all sounds reasonable,' Kate said.

'Good.'

'Good.'

Kate offered me her hand and I shook it.

Tom walked me to the helicopter landing pad.

On the chopper ride back I read Dermot's journal: the autobiography, the political theory, the knock-off poetry, a utopian plan for a thirty-two-county, democratic socialist Ireland. If this was the authentic Dermot McCann and not just nonsense he had composed to give his guards something to read, he had become a little embarrassing.

Society is intrinsically dead and Stasis is the defining characteristic of the postcapitalist regime. All consensus in the post textual narrative is used to oppress the sectarian inverse. If one examines the preconceptualist paradigm of Ireland before the Norman Invasion one is faced with a choice: either accept this rural hierarchy or embrace an anarchy of tribal kingdoms. We must build a footbridge to the past and between classes and constructed sectarian identities. And if pretextual rationalism survives the Revolution I do not believe that we will not have to choose between capitalist post dialectic theory and a form of capitalistic Marxism . . .

Pages and pages like that. I looked for acrostics or hidden meanings but didn't find any. Perhaps it was satire on a high level.

We landed at Carrickfergus UDR base, where a Mercedes was waiting to take me back to Coronation Road. I kept reading in the car. The only really interesting part of the journal was the biographical material: early life in Derry, schooldays, anger at his beatings under the rough hands of the Christian Brothers, 1950s music, radicalisation after 1968, protests, prison. Nothing about yours truly. Nothing about our meeting after Bloody Sunday. And nothing of that curious moment in the sixth-form study when he'd slapped me across the face for some slight that I'd inadvertently made.

The car dropped me at 113 Coronation Road.

I went inside and grabbed a can of Bass and sat next to the telephone.

I called my mum and dad and told them I was back on the force with my old rank. My mum started to cry. I started to cry.

I called McCrabban.

'Crabbie, it's me.'

'Gosh, Sean, I haven't heard from you in forever. What's going on? I heard you quit the force?'

'No! Me, quit? Just a rumour. I'm back. Back in CID,' I said, hardly able to contain my pleasure.

'Really? That's great news!'

'I'm running a case for Special Branch. I was wondering if you'd mind me taking a wee office in Carrick. I know it's your patch and I don't want to impose but—'

'Don't think twice about it! It'll be great to see you, Sean.'

'Thanks, Crabbie.'

We chewed the fat and I hung up and settled in with the case files on Dermot. Kate had also given me the full MI5 intelligence report on McCann, complete with photographs and a family tree. To my surprise I found that I knew most of it already. Dermot had three brothers and two sisters. One of his brothers was inside doing twenty years for murder, the other two had emigrated to Australia to open a restaurant. His father was deceased and his mother lived with his sisters Orla and Fiona in Derry.

All his surviving relatives were solid Republicans who would never talk.

I finished the Bass, poured myself a whiskey, put on the Velvet Underground and reread everything again.

On the third go through the journal I noticed something that I'd missed the first two times: a tiny doodle of a curly-haired woman that had been scratched out. If you looked carefully through the scribble you could see that the woman was wearing a necklace that had tiny letters on it: 'A' scratch, scratch, 'I', 'E'.

'Annie,' I said aloud. They were divorced, yes, but perhaps he still carried a torch. My first order of business would be to drive up to Derry and ask his ma and sisters what they knew and then plough the more fertile territory that might be a disgruntled ex-wife . . .

Nico began singing 'All Tomorrow's Parties'. Somehow it seemed totemic. 'This case is going to be all about the women,' I prophesied out loud.

Completely correctly, as it turned out.

8: FIRST DAY OF SCHOOL

The man in the mirror: a facsimile of me but scrubbed, shaved and wearing an ill-fitting white shirt, red tie and leather jacket. Ill-fitting because I'd lost a lot of weight in the last six months. Easily a stone and a half, through a diet of marijuana, ciggies, vodka, lime cordial and little else. I scuttled down the stairs and stepped quickly out on to the porch. Spring was here in the form of daffodils, bluebells and a slick street after a shower of rain. The McDowell kids kicked a football in my direction. I hesitantly kicked it back. 'Off for a job interview?' Mrs Campbell asked solicitously from Mrs McDowell's porch, where she was enjoying a cigarette.

Thanks to gossipy Sammy McGuinn everyone on Coronation Road knew that I had resigned from the peelers.

'No, no, no! Sure, he's back in the polis now! The scunners saw the error of their ways and put him back, so they did!' Mrs McDowell said.

'Is that so?' Mrs Campbell asked, looking at me for confirmation.

'It is!' Mrs McDowell insisted between puffs, while nursing a baby at her breast. That was, what, kid number ten for her?

'Are you back in right enough, Mr Duffy?' Mrs Campbell asked.

'Well, I—'

'He's in the Special Branch now! A detective inspector no

less,' Mrs McDowell yelled for all and sundry to hear. That certainly was what it said on my new warrant card, which had been posted to me last week: *Detective Inspector Sean Duffy, RUC Special Branch, Assigned to Carrickfergus RUC.* How Karen McDowell knew this I have no idea but her old man did work as a letter carrier for the Royal Mail . . .

Mrs Campbell's face glowed with excitement. 'Oh, congratulations, Mr Duffy! I am so happy. I had a feeling that that, uhm, misunderstanding you had with the higher-ups would soon get sorted,' she said.

'Thank you,' I replied and cleared my throat. 'Well, I don't want to be late. First day back and all that.'

'Wait there!' Mrs Campbell commanded, and ran into her house.

She came back with a comb.

'Bend over the fence there, love.'

'That's not necessary, I—'

'Bend over the fence!'

I leant over the fence and she combed my hair to get the cowlicks out.

'Ta,' I said sheepishly, and walked to my somewhat battered 1982 BMW E30. I checked underneath it.

'Any bombs today, mister?' one of the McDowell sprogs asked me.

'Not today.'

'Ach,' he said, with mild disgust.

I got inside, tuned the radio to Downtown and drove to Carrickfergus police station. The guard inspected my warrant card and with a suspicious shake of the head he let me through.

I parked the car in the small CID section, walked by the potholes filled with rainwater and diesel and went inside.

At the incident desk there was a fat copper with a silver moustache and skin the colour of lard. The old desk sergeant used to do the *People's Friend* crossword and have a hard time with it. This guy was halfway through *Middlemarch*.

'Detective Inspector Duffy reporting for duty,' I announced.

'Aye, you're expected,' he muttered without looking up.

When I got up to the first floor I saw that there'd been even bigger changes since my last visit. Most of the office walls had been torn down and the space filled with cubicles. CID had been moved from their prime location at the windows overlooking the lough to the drafty cinder-block extension at the back of the building. Apple computers had replaced the typewriters on most desks and the dull yellow light bulbs which I'm sure had been churning away since the 1930s had been ripped out and replaced with fluorescent strip lights.

All the old comfortable wooden furniture was gone, replaced by plastic tables and chairs. Many of the coppers were new, young, fresh-faced goons pretending to work at the computers. Some might have been actually working but at what I couldn't imagine. A couple looked up when I appeared at the top of the stairs but then cast their gaze down again when they saw that I was not a person of import.

Jazzed-up muzak versions of the great American songbook were piping through a quadrophonic sound system. I suppose the purpose of this was to provide a calming atmosphere, but you could easily imagine a day when someone would crack at the fiftieth iteration of 'Mack the Knife' and shoot the speakers off the wall.

I was desperate to see my old CID sparring partners but I knew that the first order of business was to report to Superintendent Carter. He had taken the offices by the window, turning the old evidence room into his new domain.

I knocked on a door which was frosted glass in a black mahogany frame.

'Duffy, is that you?' he said in an impressive psychic display.

'Yes, sir.'

'Don't stand out there like a bloody eejit, come in!'

He was sitting behind a huge desk also fashioned from a mahogany-like material. He was wearing his superintendent's uniform and he'd grown long sideburns which gave him a Gilbert and Sullivan air.

'Inspector Duffy reporting for duty, sir,' I said, saluting.

'You don't salute if you're in civvies, Duffy. Sit down.'

I sat opposite him. The desk was empty but for a single folder with my name on the top of it. Behind Carter there was a Union Flag and a photograph of the Queen on a horse. There was also a somewhat smaller family portrait of Superintendent Carter, Mrs Carter and two grisly youths.

'Let me read you something interesting, Duffy,' Carter said.

'It's not my horoscope, is it, sir? I don't believe in that stuff,' I said.

He put down the file and pointed a finger at me. 'That's the kind of attitude that got you sacked in the first place, Duffy. Now, shut up and listen.'

He cleared his throat and he began reading. It was the lowlights of my personnel file and I tuned out for most of it.

' . . . I thought we'd seen the last of you, Duffy. A bad apple everyone around here said. Good riddance, I thought. And I'm home last Sunday, at home, mind you, when I get a phone call me telling me that I am to make space for one Detective Inspector Sean Duffy of the Special Branch. This can't be the same Duffy I've been hearing about, says I to myself, but then I find to my amazement that it is. How is it that you were kicked out of the police for a whole host of crimes and misdemeanours, the latest of which was running some poor sod over, and yet here you are? Like magic! Special Branch! An inspector!'

'Well—'

'How did you do it, Duffy? Did you write to *Jim'll Fix It*? Is the Chief Constable your da? You're not related by blood to any of the crowned heads of Europe?'

'Not to my knowledge, sir.'

'What are you doing, Duffy? And why is it that you've come back *here*? To my parish?'

I looked him coldly between the eyes and was proud that I was now sufficiently mature to avoid the incivility of a smirk. 'I'm not at liberty to say, sir,' I said without any inflection.

His face turned red. He put down the piece of paper. A blood vessel pulsed on the left-hand side of his neck.

'It's like that, is it?'

'Yes, sir, it's like that.'

'I don't like it, Duffy. I don't like it at all.'

'I'm sorry about that, sir, but that's the way it is . . . I've been told that I've got an office around here somewhere?'

'Aye, back in CID next to the toilets,' he said with satisfaction.

'All right. Well, I will wish you a good day, sir . . .'

He jumped to his feet, came round the desk and grabbed me by the arm.

'Who are you working for, Duffy?' he asked.

'I can't say, sir.'

'What's this all about? Is it about me? Is it something I've done, or am alleged to have done?'

I sighed. 'Will that be all, sir?'

There was a nice beetroot quality to his cheeks now, and to really set a stroke in motion I gave him another uniformed salute, turned on my heel and marched out.

A jazz trio version of 'The Last Train to Clarksville' took me across the office to the squalid CID section at the back of the building.

Matty and McCrabban were shoved into a little room with bare breeze-block walls overlooking the car park and the railway lines. The attitude regular cops had towards CID always surprised me. Why the contempt? It was the detectives who actually went around solving the crimes. I mean, who knew what regular cops actually did? I'd been a regular policeman for the last year and I still didn't know.

I opened the door and went into the CID den.

'Room for one more, lads?' I asked.

The boys were genuinely pleased.

Handshakes, slaps on the back. To put McCrabban at ease I said: 'Listen, mate, I'm Special Branch now, a DI on special assignment, I haven't come to poach, this is still your manor.'

McCrabban was relieved, but he tried not to show it. Tall, almost stooped, he had filled out a bit since I'd seen him last but his pale skin was just as pale and there was no trace of grey in his hair.

'Temporarily in charge, Sean. They're supposed to be bringing in a detective inspector in the summer.'

'They always say things like that. If you hang tight you'll probably get the job.'

Matty had cropped his hedge hair and there was a bit more colour in his cheeks. His beak-like nose and prominent teeth were less to the fore in his still-youthful face. He still didn't look like a peeler but that was OK because he never really wanted to look like one.

'It's magic to have you back, Sean, in any capacity,' Matty said.

'I heard they stuck you down in some trench in South Armagh,' Crabbie added.

'Aye, they did. They were doing their best to kill me, I think. But I lived to spite the bastards.'

'You have nine lives, Sean,' Matty said.

'Who wants to sneak out to the pub? My shout.'

'Carter keeps us all on a pretty tight leash,' Matty said.

'Come on. What's the worst that can happen?'

'You would know,' Crabbie said.

We retired to the Royal Oak next door and the boys filled me in on a year's worth of office gossip and I told them straight out that I was looking for Dermot McCann and I might need their help at some point.

'You've to keep it under your hats, lads. It's a Special Branch op and those nutters are as paranoid as anything,' I said.

Neither of them, I knew, would breathe a word of it.

We had a quick round of drinks and we ran into my old boss, Chief Inspector Brennan (Retd), who'd heard I was back and had come by to say hello. He'd always had a tragic Polonian air about him, but now he was old and shabby and his nose was a metro map of capillaries. And worse than all that, he was drunk. Drunk at 1.30 in the p.m. He insisted on standing us all a double Johnnie Walker and he told a few inappropriate stories about me and my insolence in the 'bad old days'. Eventually he looked at his watch and muttered something about a golf game.

'There goes the ghost of Christmas future,' Matty said.

Murder, suicide or cirrhosis – those were three of the most popular ways out of the RUC. The lads were depressed now and I walked them back to the station, requisitioned myself a desk, a chair, a lamp, a phone and a brand spanking new Apple Macintosh computer.

Satisfied with my day's work I drove home again.

'How was your first day back, Mr Duffy? I hear Superintendent Carter is a bit of a hard horse,' Mrs Campbell asked.

'Well, he's certainly a—'

She lowered her voice to a whisper. 'Mrs Rattigan says his wife left him for a fancy man over the water. Left the bairns, too. Boys, I think.'

'Yes, it looks like he has had a couple of trials and—'

'That's his second wife, of course, his first wife died, car crash, *he* was driving. Three sheets to the wind, they say, although that's just what I heard.'

'What? Carter killed his wife in a vehicular—'

'Well, I won't keep you, Mr Duffy, your phone's been ringing off and on for the last hour, someone's looking for you.'

I went inside, made a cup of tea, put on some nerve-calming Delibes.

I got the phone on the fourth ring.

'How was your first day back?'

'It was fine, Kate,' I told her.

'Have you made any progress locating our friend?'

'Not . . . as such. This was more of a settling-in day.'

'I see.'

'Anything from your end?'

'Nothing. He's not calling home or sending letters home and there's no trace of him anywhere. Frankly I'll admit that it's got some of us a little rattled.'

'He's biding his time. When he shows his hand it's going to be something big. Dermot knows his history. I remember him telling me once that it was the King David Hotel bomb that got the Brits out of Palestine.'

'True. But it was Gandhi who got us out of India a year earlier.'

'Dermot's no Gandhi,' I said.

'No, he isn't. So what's your plan of attack?'

'Nothing special. I'll just start interviewing people.'

'When?' she pressed me.

'You're hassling me a wee bit, aren't you?'

'Because they're hassling me. We all have our bosses.'

'How about tomorrow? I'll go up to Derry to see his mum and his sisters and his uncle's not a million miles away. They won't tell me anything, but all I can do is ask.'

'Derry?' she asked.

'Aye.'

'You want me to join you? I'm in Rathlin. It's not a million miles away either.'

'You live on Rathlin Island?'

'I have a house here. It's been in the family for a long time and it's better than sleeping on the base, I can tell you.'

'Don't you have better things to do than attend a wild-goose chase?'

'Not really, no.'

'Dermot's mother lives in a bad area. The Ardbo Estate. This will sound dramatic, but I couldn't guarantee your safety, Kate.'

'I can look after myself.'

I thought about it for a moment. It was always useful to have a partner who could pick things up that you couldn't. A female partner was even more useful.

'All right. I'll meet you at the Ballycastle ferry car park at nine. Will that give you time to get over?'

'Yes.'

'See you then.'

I made beans on toast for dinner and watched the TV news.

Things were quiet. A couple of attacks on police stations. A few fire bombs left at shops in Ballymena. It looked like the Libyan boys were still waiting to make their presence felt and I knew they wouldn't wait for ever.

9: THE TWO SISTERS

I set the alarm for six, checked under the BMW for bombs and ran it up the coast to Ballycastle. Driving rain made the road slick and dangerous on the clifftop sections but I kept the Beemer at a quare old clip anyway.

Kate was waiting for me at the Ballycastle ferry car park.

She was wearing a long black wool duffel coat and a black beret tilted to one side. It was fetching. It made her look young. Twenty-something. Fashionable. On her way up.

'You live on Rathlin Island, then, right enough?' I said, pointing across the Irish Sea to the L-shaped island five miles from the mainland.

'Yes.'

'I never met anybody who lived on Rathlin.'

'Well, several hundred people do.'

'Is it not inconvenient for an MI5 agent?'

'Not in the least. There's a regular ferry service. Phone line. Electricity. Views to die for, of course.'

'And safe, too, I imagine,' I said.

'Oh yes. Safe. There hasn't been a murder on Rathlin in a couple of hundred years. Of course, that was a multiple murder. The massacre of the entire population . . .' she said, and smiled.

'Well, get in. It's probably best if you don't say anything. I'll introduce you as . . . Not sure that I caught your second name?'

'Use my mother's maiden name. Randall.'

'OK. I'll say that you're Detective Constable Randall but if you speak with an English accent the jig will be up.'

'I can do an Irish accent. My father's old Anglo-Irish gentry.'

I rolled my eyes. 'I'm sure you're great but it's probably best if you keep your gob closed.'

She got in the car.

'*Your* parents live around here, don't they?' she asked.

'Yes.'

'We can drop in on them if you want.'

'I don't want.'

'Gosh, you're all business, aren't you?'

'Aye, I'm all business. When I'm on a case I'm on a case.'

I fumbled in my cassette box and put on the B side of *Kind of Blue*.

Miles Davis is usually a way in to someone's musical background, but Kate didn't object, hum along, or make any other comment. Instead it was the same intense, stony 'I'm just stepping outside for a moment' stiff upper lip.

I wasn't impressed. She was trying too hard.

We drove along the busy A2 to Portstewart. The rain was elemental and you couldn't see a thing – a shame, because on a fair day this was the most attractive part of the coast. I kept us on the road through Coleraine and Limavady, where I finally stopped at a little café I knew.

'Are you hungry?' I asked Kate.

'I might be,' she said, looking sceptically at the place, which was just a bog-standard roadside joint.

'They do a mean Ulster fry when Suzanne's working and you can always tell when Suzanne's working because her Vincent Black Shadow is parked outside.'

'Is that thing over there a Vincent Black Shadow?'

'Yes.'

'Is the fry the speciality of the house?' Kate asked.

'Aye.'

'I'll try it, then.'

'My treat,' I insisted.

We went inside. I ordered two Ulster fries and two teas. I grabbed an *Irish News* and a *Newsletter* and we sat in a booth by the window. I read the sports news and Kate the proper news.

Our fries came: potato bread, soda bread, pancakes, eggs, thick pork sausages, fatty bacon, black pudding – all of it pan-cooked in beef dripping.

'I don't think I can eat this,' Kate said.

'And a round of toast!' I yelled to Suzanne.

Kate nibbled at the toast but I needed to get some weight on so I got most of the fry down my neck.

The rain hadn't let up so we ran out to the car, almost going over into the mud. We drove on and were in Derry just after ten.

For the thousand years before the Normans had come to Ulster late in the twelfth century this had been the territory of the O'Neills, a particularly fierce and independent people. The English settlers had renamed the city Londonderry and survived a famous siege in 1690 by King James' Catholic armies. After 1690 east of the Foyle had remained a Protestant, English city and west of the river had become Catholic Derry. The city, tragically, had remained divided between Catholic and Protestant ever since. We drove into the Catholic Bogside, which can be an intimidating place for outsiders, what with the IRA murals and the maze of estates. Not for me, though, even though I was a peeler and they would have kidnapped and killed me at the drop of a hat. I had gone to school here and I knew the town and its ways inside and out. It was good to be back, in fact. Belfast would never feel like home, but Derry . . . yeah, I could handle Derry.

We drove through the Shantallow Estate with its rows of grey houses, street urchins, bonfires, burnt-out cars and welcoming AK-47 motifs on every gable. Then it was across the A515 to the Lenamore Road and the Ardbo Estate.

Just a mile from the border with Donegal in the Irish Republic, this place was basically unpoliceable. The RUC and the British army claimed that there weren't any no-go areas in Northern Ireland but I'd be surprised if the writ of Queen's law ran true here.

Unemployment was well over fifty per cent and the houses were hastily built low-rise and terraced jobs owned by the biggest landlord in Europe, the Northern Ireland Housing Executive. Not that that was any kind of a boast. A third of the homes were boarded up or otherwise derelict and the rest were in various states of disrepair. Gangs of children and packs of stray dogs roamed the neighbourhoods. Garbage and old clothes lay strewn or stacked in little Charles LeDray-style pyramids. All the trees that had been optimistically planted on the estate were gone to bonfires, and the menagerie you saw through the windscreen included horses and goats which had been let loose to graze on the landscaping between the brown low-rise tower blocks.

Some kind of empty factory was an eerie red shell to the west, and to the north there was the strange, looming presence of the Donegal Mountains.

'If you want to bottle out of this, I can turn us round easily,' I said, seeing the look on Kate's face.

'I'm not remotely worried,' she lied.

Once upon a time this had been a sought-after place to live. A bold, gleaming 1960s slum-clearance project, and it had stayed that way for a few years at least. Derry had largely escaped the worst of the Troubles until that fateful day: Sunday, 30 January 1972, when British army paratroopers had overreacted to reports of an 'IRA sniper' and shot dead thirteen unarmed people during a civil rights march.

IRA recruitment had soared overnight, and within months vast tracts of Derry had been effectively ceded to the paramilitaries.

'Look in the glove compartment. There's an address on a piece of paper. What's it say?' I asked Kate.

'22 Cowper Street.'

'OK, Cowper Street, I think I know where that is.'

I drove deeper into the Ardbo Estate, through crumbling tower blocks and terraces, until I found Cowper Street. I wasn't enjoying the look the kids were giving me as I drove my BMW past them. Thirteen-year-old boys with mullets, spiderweb tattoos and denim jackets who would just love to steal and joyride a car like this.

None of the houses had numbers and I had to drive round the loop twice, which was plenty of time to attract attention. I finally realised that No. 22 was a four-storey tower block constructed from cinder blocks and a dirty, slate-coloured concrete. Windows had been put in on all the lower floors and graffiti told me that this was the territory of the Irish National Liberation Army – yet another of the many Nationalist paramilitary sects.

I parked the BMW outside No. 22, got out and waited for the pack of kids to approach.

'Say nothing,' I mouthed to Kate. 'And try not to make eye contact.'

'I *live* here, Sean. You're treating me like I'm a green lieutenant on his first tour of duty in Vietnam.'

'This isn't Rathlin Island, love. Just do as I say, OK?'

The roving gang of boys approached.

I gave two pound coins to the tallest and meanest of them, who was going with the skinhead/denim jacket/hobnail boot look and who happened to be carrying a piece of wood with a nail sticking out the end of it.

'There's ten quid more in it for you when I get back, if, and only if, there's not a scratch on this vehicle,' I told him.

He sized me up and nodded. 'Aye, I'll fucking see to it,' he said.

I thought it was about a fifty-fifty shot whether he'd steal it or guard it.

'All right, let's go,' I said to Kate.

There was a slight twitch to her lip, which might have been the first sign of nervousness she had exercised that day.

'The Francis Hughes Hunger Striker and Resistance Fighter Memorial Block,' No. 22 Cowper grandly called itself.

Over the entrance there was a massive graffiti mural of a paramilitary gunman holding a Kalashnikov in one hand and an Irish tricolour in the other as he led an assorted group of refugees through an apocalyptic landscape. It was actually rather good, rising above the naive primitivism of most gable murals to become something that was convincingly terrifying.

I went inside, holding my nose against the stench of urine.

I found a heavily graffitied floor plan and saw that 4H was a corner flat on the fourth floor.

I walked jauntily towards the lift. My years of police training were not required to ascertain whether it worked or not. The elevator shaft was a gaping hole with smashed machinery, garbage and a pram lying at the bottom of it. If there'd been a live or dead baby in the pram I wouldn't have been surprised.

We found the stairs and walked to the fourth floor. The architect had assumed that the stairs would be seldom used for they were narrow and dimly lit through broken windows. They stank of vomit, beer, rotting leaves and garbage. The occasional black, shoe-sized stain was not the mould I first suspected but, in fact, dead, decaying Norwegian rats.

Kate had the sense not to say 'charming' or anything like that. This transcended her acute English sense of irony.

We got to level four and took a breather.

'Are you quite sure MI5 is intercepting the mail for this place? Services seem pretty basic around here to me,' I said to her.

'If this is Dermot's mother's place, I can assure you that we're reading her post and tapping her phones.'

'If you say so,' I muttered, and wondered what MI5 agent would have the balls to come out here to INLA central, break into Mrs McCann's flat and install a phone bug – if indeed that was how you installed a phone bug.

We walked along a dank, dark corridor and knocked on the door of flat 4H.

'Who is it?' a woman asked.

'Police,' I said.

'Fuck off!' the woman said.

'It's about Dermot,' I said.

There was a pause and some discussion and finally the door opened. Dermot's ma, Maureen, was slight, about five one or two, a fragile wisp of a thing with her hair in a greying black bob. Her eyes were hazel, her lips red, her skin like grease paper. I'd seen screen vampires with more colour in their cheeks. She was in her fifties now and clearly she didn't remember me, although I'd been to Dermot's old house in Creggy Terrace half a dozen times when I'd been a kid.

'What about him?' Maureen asked.

'Could I come in, Mrs McCann?'

'What about Dermot? Is he dead? Have youse topped him?'

'No. We haven't. Can I come in?'

'Are you the police right enough?'

I showed her my warrant card.

'I'll give you five minutes of my time and not a minute more.'

We went inside.

The flat was large, tidy and well maintained, but stank of cigarette smoke, booze and quiet desperation. There was a spectacular prospect to the north-east of Donegal, Derry City and Lough Foyle.

'Who is it, Ma?' Fiona McCann said from behind an ironing board in the kitchen.

Fiona was two years older than me and I remembered her from my visits to Dermot's old house. Back then she'd been extremely beautiful in a way that other Derry girls weren't. In a way Irish lasses weren't. Her complexion was dark and her eyes were dark and her voice had been deliberately modelled on Janis Joplin's. There had always been something exotic about her (and the whole clan, come to that). The exoticism of fallen aristocrats, or exiled royals adrift in a far-off land. Fiona had gone to America for five years, worked as a nurse, had a kid, left her husband and come back to Derry just as Dermot was going inside, her father was dying of congestive heart failure and her other brothers and sisters were leaving for anywhere else. Not exactly the brilliant move of the decade that one.

'It's the polis, they've come to talk about Dermot,' Mrs McCann said.

Fiona looked up from the ironing board. Her red hair was streaked with white and there were deep crevasses in her cheeks. She looked fifty or even sixty and I wondered whether she was using the big H. There was a fag-end hanging out of her mouth and she was already lighting another in anticipation of the first one dying.

'They haven't lifted him, have they? Is he all right?' she asked.

'We haven't lifted him. He's still on the run,' I said.

Fiona's eyes narrowed.

'Is that you? Sean Duffy?'

'It's me. And this is Detective Constable Randall.'

'Fucksake. Sean fucking Duffy! Coming round here asking about Dermot,' Fiona said, practically spitting the words from her mouth.

'Is that wee Sean Duffy?' Mrs McCann asked in a more welcoming tone, before adding, 'Would you like a dish of tea?'

'I wouldn't say no, if it's no trouble, Mrs McCann,' I told her.

'Ach, it's nay bother. Have a seat. Have a seat. What about you, love, tea?'

Kate shook her head. 'No thank you,' she replied.

We moved aside a stack of slim poetry books and took a seat on a cushionless sofa.

Fiona turned off the iron, stubbed the first cigarette out in a full Rothmans ashtray, walked across the room with the fresh one and sat opposite us on an upturned plastic delivery box that served as a living-room table.

'I heard you joined the police. Couldn't believe it. How do you sleep at night?' she asked.

I'd been asked this question so many times I had a prepared set of responses with ascending levels of sarcasm (depending on my contempt for the interrogator), but this was not the time or place for those. I ignored the query and asked: 'How come you're living here? What happened to your house on Creggy Terrace? That was a lovely place.'

It was, too. Light-filled, airy, five bedrooms . . .

'Ach! They burned us out!' Fiona explained.

'Who?'

'Who knows? UVF, INLA, UDA . . . what does it matter? The house is long gone.'

'Was this after Dermot went inside?'

'Of course it was! Do youse think they'd have had the nerve to touch us with Dermot still out?' Mrs McCann said, coming back with the tea and coconut buns she had clearly made herself. They looked on the ancient side but it would be impolite not to take one.

'How did you end up in the peelers?' Fiona asked.

'I suppose there just wasn't enough excitement in my life.'

'I'm surprised you're still alive. They've got a bounty on Catholic peelers, don't they?'

'They do indeed.'

I took a bite of the coconut nasty. All I could taste was baking soda and treacle. I swallowed some tea to get it down. That, too, was vile. Maybe the pair of them were trying to earn that bounty right now.

'So does Orla live here too?' I enquired.

'Is that what it said in your wee intelligence reports?' Fiona asked with a cackle.

I nodded. 'That's exactly what it said. It said that the three of you were sharing this place.'

'She's moved out,' Mrs McCann said, sighing.

'Don't tell him where, Ma, it would be collaboration!' Fiona hissed.

'I'll tell him! I'll tell anybody that wants to know. Orla's mitched off with Poppy Devlin, so she has. One of his wee Shanty hoors now! High as a kite, so she is. We are scundered! Can't put our heads out the door for the shame of it!'

I was shocked and there was a leaden silence while I digested this information. Dermot McCann's sister was whoring for some drug-dealing pimp called Poppy Devlin? Did Dermot have no currency left at all in this town?

Christ Almighty.

Maybe Dermot didn't care what his family was up to, or maybe the old IRA operators were all being driven out by a new generation of drug dealers flush with cash who weren't interested in politics or 'the struggle'.

'Who is this Poppy Devlin?' I asked.

'What are you doing here anyway?' Fiona asked.

I showed her my warrant card. 'I'm RUC Special Branch. I'm looking for Dermot. I'd like him to turn himself in.'

Fiona laughed without any sign of mirth. 'You're a good one, you are, Sean Duffy.'

'I'd like him to turn himself in before the Brits find him and top him.'

'The Brits will never find him, so they won't!' Mrs McCann said.

'We'll not tell you where he is, even if we did know, which we don't. Do you think he'd call us? Do you think he's that much of an eejit? Have you forgotten who you're dealing with?'

I shook my head. 'I haven't forgotten, Fiona. But if he does get in touch will you do me a favour and mention what I said? It would be better if he turned himself in. If the SAS find him they'll kill him. He's got the Brits terrified.'

Fiona walked across the room and jabbed a finger in my chest. 'We'll be telling him nothing! And we'll be telling you nothing! He never liked you. He never trusted you. I thought you were all right. But I see that I was mistaken. Now get out of here before I show you the back of my hand!'

I got to my feet.

Kate rose a moment later.

'Thanks for the tea and cake. Delicious as usual, Mrs McCann,' I said.

The old lady smiled. 'You were always a good boy, Sean. Ach, it's just a shame things went the way they did, isn't it?' she said dreamily.

'Aye, it is.'

I turned to look Fiona in the face. Her cheeks were red and again there was that weird light in their eyes, indicative of some rogue royal bloodline which had ended up in this ghastly sink estate in the arse-end of nowhere. 'I'm fond of Dermot. I wouldn't want anything to happen to him. That's not a threat. I just don't want him to give the Brits an excuse to kill him in cold blood. They're pulling out all the stops looking for him – hence my involvement – and it would be better if he turned himself in. Please pass on the message if he gets in touch.'

This made her furious. 'Will you fuck off, copper, or do I have to throw you out meself!' she hissed.

I opened the door, and when Kate came through Fiona spat on the ground at our feet and slammed it shut.

We walked back down the stairs in silence.

'Was that normal? Are you happy with the way that went?' Kate asked as we reached the bottom.

'It went exactly the way I expected it to go. It's the way it's going to go with all of Dermot's family. No one is going to tell us anything.'

'So how are you going to get a lead on him?'

I lit myself a cigarette and offered her one.

She shook her head.

'To be honest, love, I haven't the foggiest,' I said.

Kate bit her lower lip. 'So what *is* next?'

I drew in the tobacco smoke and let its warmth coat my lungs and clear my head. I rubbed my chin. 'Well, there's his uncle who's still in the Derry area. We'll try him next. And then, Annie, his ex-wife down in Antrim living with her ma and da. We'll try her.'

'And then?'

I shook my head. 'The rest of his family is across the water. Didn't you say they're all in America and Australia and places like that?'

'Yes.'

'That's a bit beyond our jurisdiction, isn't it? And his old comrades are either in prison or on the run from prison . . .'

'So, again, my question, what *will* you do?'

'If no one will talk?'

'If no one will talk.'

'Hope that somebody changes their mind or that Dermot slips up.'

Although she attempted to hide it I could see that she was disappointed in me. She'd put her neck out for me and promised her bosses miracles but I was no miracle worker. I was an average, maybe a below-average, detective in a rather mediocre police force. Nothing more, nothing less. She'd given me another chance and I appreciated it but one man could do very little.

We walked out of the building and found the hoodlum king guarding my car against all comers. I gave him the tenner.

'Where would I find a fella called Poppy Devlin?' I asked.

'The offy on Carlisle Gardens. Don't go to him. He's pricey. I can sort you out if you're after some brown, or,' he looked uneasily at Kate, 'a wee milly or something?'

'Nah, you're all right, son.'

We got in the Beemer. It was raining so I put on the wipers. This part of Derry was better behind rain and wipers.

'Where to now?' Kate asked.

'We'll go see the uncle.'

I made sure that first I drove past the offy on Carlisle Gardens. It was the usual concrete bunker covered in metal grilles and graffiti. Under the overhang there were a couple of goons in Peter Storm coats chatting and chain-smoking.

I clocked them and the location and the vibe.

I'd be back.

'Where's the uncle live?' Kate asked. 'You said he lived around here?'

'He's in Muff. Just over the border in Donegal.'

'Oh God, I suppose we'll have to go through the Foreign Office to get permission to interview him.'

'Nah. We won't even have to go through a police checkpoint.'

'What? How's that possible?'

I drove along the Lenamore Road and took a left down a semi-concealed slip road that I knew. It was a seldom-used country lane that went through a now-derelict farm. The lane was rutted and flooded but the Beemer handled it with only minimum complaint.

'What is this? Is this a smuggler's trail or something?' Kate asked, a little bit excited by the prospect.

'Nah, smugglers use better roads than this,' I said.

'What are we going to do if we run into an army checkpoint? I didn't bring my proper ID and you've got a gun. How are we going to explain ourselves?'

'We'll be fine,' I assured her.

The lane ended abruptly near Derryvane and we were nearly all the way to Muff before Kate realised that we had already crossed the border and were now in the Irish Republic.

10: ORLA OF THE GOLDEN HAIR

Jonty McCann lived just beyond Muff on the R238 in a newly renovated granite Victorian manse overlooking Lough Foyle. Sheep and cows were all around and the smell of fertiliser was in the air.

I parked outside the white, cast-iron gate and got out. I ditched the leather jacket and got my raincoat from the boot.

'You wanna come in for this one? It'll be the same story.'

'I'll come in,' Kate said, still a little nonplussed by the ease of our border crossing. If *I* knew of a secret unpatrolled road from Northern Ireland to the Irish Republic the terrorists must know hundreds . . .

Jonty's garden was planted with sweet pea and red and pink roses.

The house looked neat and well maintained.

It said on the bio that Jonty was a builder, but he was also a retired INLA divisional quartermaster who had organised operations that had killed scores of people over the years: police, army, civilians and the leaders of rival factions, including a couple of top IRA men. In theory there was a truce between the IRA and INLA, but Jonty had to know that some day someone might come looking for revenge.

We knocked on his blue front door.

It was opened by a young woman with brown hair and green eyes who was wearing a Snoopy sweatshirt and green wellington boots. I knew I should have been scoping her but it was the sweatshirt I was obsessing about. Snoopy was wearing the shades of his Joe Cool persona that had been fashionable briefly about ten years ago. How had the sweatshirt survived through so many spin cycles?

'Looking for Jonty McCann,' I said after Kate nudged me.

'Yes,' Kate said.

The young woman looked at Kate and was somewhat reassured. She certainly didn't look like an IRA assassin.

'What for?' the young woman asked.

'Private business,' I said.

'What sort of private business?'

'It's private, that's all I can say.'

'He doesn't like to be interrupted when he's fishing.'

'I don't think this will take too long.'

She examined my face, trying to figure out what I was, exactly. I showed her my warrant card.

'I'm an RUC detective and I have no authority here in Donegal whatsoever. If Jonty doesn't want to speak to me he can tell me piss off and there's not a thing I can do about it. But I don't think he will. This will only take five minutes.'

She nodded. 'He would never talk to a policeman.'

'I suppose I could ask him and see?'

'I suppose you could ask. All right . . . He's fishing down the lane.'

'Where's that?'

'Go round the side of the house and head down towards the water. I'll let him know you're coming.'

'Aye, do that.'

I smiled at her and she closed the front door.

She was probably going to call him on a walkie-talkie, or more likely he'd already heard this entire conversation on an open mike. Sending us down here on foot would give him ample time to get his gun out and prep for us.

Sure enough, at the bottom of the brambly lane Jonty was

standing there in front of a fishing stool and two rods. He was facing us with his right hand in the pocket of his Barbour jacket.

He looked younger than his fifty years. Thick black hair and bushy beard, no worry lines at all. Clearly he wasn't being tormented by bad dreams of men who had begged him for their lives. We'd met once before when Dermot had been captain of the school team in the Irish Inter Schools Debating Cup. Of course, we had won the tournament and Dermot had been rightly feted by the school. I'd been on that team, too, but Dermot was always the star of the hour and I imagine Jonty wouldn't have remembered me at the victory party at the Londonderry Arms in Carnlough.

I put my hands up and motioned to Kate so that she did the same.

'What do you want, peeler?' Jonty asked with his hand still in his pocket.

'I'm looking for your nephew, Jonty. I'm looking for Dermot,' I said.

'Dermot? Why would I have any idea where he is?' Jonty said.

'And even if you did you wouldn't tell me.'

'No.'

We stared at one another. My hands up, his right still on the trigger of his gun.

'Has he contacted you at all since he escaped?' I asked.

'I'm not going to tell you anything. You're just wasting your time here, cop,' Jonty said.

'Did he contact you from Libya at all?' I asked.

'Libya? Where's that?'

Jonty was a veteran of dozens of interrogations in his time: the RUC, the Irish cops, the British army, British Intelligence . . .

He could go on like this for hours.

I looked at Kate. This was mostly for her benefit, so that she could report back and tell them that I had at least tried. But I was also curious about Orla.

'If he does get in touch, tell him that Sean Duffy was asking for him,' I said.

Jonty's eyes narrowed.

'I know you. Working for the Brits because we wouldn't have you. You'll take anyone's shilling, will you? Or is thirty pieces of silver more the asking price?'

I yawned. You'd think they would have come up with more original lines after all this time.

'Do you know a pimp called Poppy Devlin?' I asked.

He shook his head.

'Maureen tells me that your niece, Orla, has taken up with this character.'

'I wouldn't be surprised. Orla will listen to no one. She goes her own way and what she does is her own business.'

'I remember Orla. Beautiful wee girl and smart with it. Could you not do something about it, Jonty? Everyone's very upset.'

'Don't you speak about it! Don't you speak about anyone in my family! It's not your concern, copper! We've done all we can for Orla! All we can do and more! And I can't go back to Derry now. It's impossible! Do you understand? All I can do is use my influence from here.'

'But Jonty, if—'

He pulled out the 9mm and pointed it at us.

'Enough! You've made me raise my voice, peeler. You've made me scare the fish. I think it's time you went back over the border to the Six Counties, don't you?' His voice was shaking with cold menace.

'OK, take it easy, mate. We'll go,' I said.

I backed up a few paces.

'Go on, then!' he snarled.

Kate and I turned and walked quickly back to the car.

When we got in the Beemer Kate lit one of my fags with a trembling hand.

'Are you OK?' I asked her.

'I thought for a moment he was going to shoot us. No one knew we were there. He could have done it and got away with it easily,' she said.

'He could have. But it would have ruined his fishing.'

I got the car going and in ten minutes we were back over the border into Northern Ireland.

'I suppose I'll take you home, then,' I said.

'I suppose you should,' she agreed.

I drove through Derry and then along the coast.

Kate had no conversation so I put on Radio 3.

She seemed to be digesting the day's events.

Radio 3 was playing *Einstein on the Beach* by Philip Glass, a piece I had actually seen in New York in the presence of the composer.

I tried to tell Kate about it but she wasn't interested in the least.

When we got to Coleraine, she told me to pull over. 'You'll want to go home along the A26 and the M2. There's no point driving out of your way to go to Ballycastle. I'll get the bus. They're every twenty minutes.'

'Are you sure? It's really no trouble.'

'No. Leave me at the bus station and then you go on home, Sean. It's been a long day.'

'All right, then,' I said.

I drove to the bus station. It was four o'clock now.

'Will you make the last ferry to Rathlin OK?'

'Oh yes. And if I ever miss it there's a man in a little boat who'll take you over for a couple of pounds.'

I nodded. 'Not the most productive day ever, was it?'

'No, it wasn't.'

'But that's police work. I expect it's the same in your profession.'

'Why did you keep bringing up that Dermot's sister, Orla?' she asked astutely.

'Well, clearly there's been some sort of factional fighting in the city. The McCanns have been more or less driven out. Jonty's living in exile over the border, the rest of the family has emigrated, the mother and Fiona are in some shithole flat and no one apparently can do anything to help Orla . . .'

'What does all that mean?'

'Dermot used to be a big man in Derry, but the years in prison have allowed other people to rise up in the vacuum. Dermot's never been fond of the limelight. He likes to move the pieces from behind the scenes, but that's not the way to intimidate anyone, certainly not people on the ground. He'll need to prove himself if he wants to become a major player again.'

'How?'

'You know how. Maybe he can turn the family fortunes around with some kind of IRA spectacular. It'll have to be something big, something very big . . .'

'Like?'

'I don't know.'

She opened the car door and the rain came pouring in.

'Do you think any of them will help us find out where Dermot is?'

'Not a chance, not in a million years . . . Of course, they might slip up.'

She bit her lip and nodded. 'The wire taps, you mean?'

'Aye, the wire taps.'

'There's always that. And the ex-wife, you're going to interview her too?'

'Annie. Yeah.'

'One might have more hope with an ex-wife than a mother or a sister?' she asked optimistically.

'Annie will be a tough nut to crack.'

'Did you know her too, back in the day?'

'Oh yes.'

She gazed at me for a couple of seconds and looked at her watch.

'I must say I'm feeling a little let down,' she said.

'What were you expecting?'

'I don't know.'

'I hope you haven't oversold me to your bosses.'

She dodged the question. 'You know none of them seem that well off . . . Perhaps if we offered them money?'

I laughed. 'This isn't Bongo Bongo land.'

'You'd be surprised, Sean.'

'I'm sure I would be, but not with them. Believe me, you can't buy people like the McCanns.'

She looked at her watch again. 'Well, I have a ferry to catch and a report to write.'

She gave me a half-wave, got out of the car and ran for the bus.

When she was safely on board the Ballycastle express, I headed for the roundabout and drove back along the A37 and then the A2 again back into Derry.

I was cutting against the rush-hour traffic and it was no problem getting over the bridge on to the Bogside.

I found the off-licence on Carlisle Street and parked the Beemer outside. The rain was much heavier now and the two men from earlier had gone.

I unbuttoned my raincoat so that I could get easy access to my shoulder holster. I took a breath, got out of the Beemer, locked it and went inside the offy.

Crates of Harp and Bass were stacked along one wall, there were a few bottles of cheap plonk and the spirits were safely tucked away behind the broad wooden counter. The kid behind the counter was a skinny, freckly, sandy-haired wee mucker, completely out of his depth. He was wearing an Undertones T-shirt, which meant that he couldn't be all bad.

'Help ya?' he asked, looking up from *Coronation Street*, which was playing on a small black and white TV.

'I'm looking for Poppy Devlin,' I said.

His eyes returned to the TV. 'Back room,' he muttered, and then added, 'He's *Mister* Devlin to you, mate.'

I walked through the stacks of beer until I came to a dingy black door with a sign on it that said 'Strictly No Admittance'.

I pushed on it and went inside.

Three skinny girls were squeezed on to a fake leather sofa, chain-smoking and also watching *Coronation Street* on a TV resting on a glass coffee table. All three girls were pale, heavily made-up and wearing miniskirts. Two of them had bleached blonde hair, one was a natural blonde.

All three were strung out on heroin. None of them looked at me as I came in.

Orla was the natural blonde, but it took a moment or two before I recognised her. She was thin, ghostly, fragile like a porcelain doll. She had track marks on her left arm and cold sores on her mouth. I'd known her only as an annoying little kid on those rare precious occasions when Dermot had allowed me to come over to his house after school. She was the runt of the family. Eight or nine then, twenty-four or twenty-five now. She'd pestered Dermot and me to watch her perform a song she'd written with two of her friends: they were going to be the female, Derry version of the Monkees. The song lasted about twelve bars before it descended into giggles and Dermot, irritated, had summoned me up to his room to show me some novel by Sartre or Camus.

'Hello, ladies,' I said to the girls, and again none of them so much as registered me.

A curtain moved on the left-hand side of the room and a moment later two guys pushed it aside and came into the room. Classic double act. One big, one small. The big guy clearly the heavy: he was wearing a leather jacket over a lumberjack shirt, with the butt of a shooter sticking out from the jacket pocket. Not the most useful place for a firearm, but perhaps that wasn't his weapon of choice. Resting on his shoulder was a large aluminium baseball bat.

'I'm looking for Poppy Devlin,' I told them.

'That would be me,' the little one said. He was a cadaverous, jaundiced wee shite with thin lips and beady black eyes. His greasy hair was combed to the right, in a style that Hitler had made fashionable, and on his left shoulder there was a tame white rat. There was a certain jumpy magnetism about him and I could tell that he was no dummy. He'd be the sort of boy who would know exactly who he could fuck with and who he couldn't, and I'd bet he never missed a payment to the local IRA and INLA chieftains who provided him with area protection.

A small-time hood. Hoors and H. They could tolerate that.

'I'll need some of the brown stuff,' I said.

'I'll need to see some cash,' he replied.

I reached under my raincoat for my shoulder holster. I whipped out the revolver and before anyone could react I smacked the big dude in the face. I didn't give him a chance to squeak, I cracked him in the forehead with the butt and kicked him in the kneecap. When he still didn't fall I hit him again in the temple and this time his legs trembled and he went down like a hundred-year-old maple in the Ontario woods.

He smashed through the glass coffee table and the TV upended and landed on the floor in a dull explosion. The girls started to scream.

I pointed the revolver at Poppy Devlin.

He wasn't fazed. 'You'll answer to McGuinness for this,' he said.

'I need some brown,' I said.

'This way,' he muttered.

I followed him into a side room with a dartboard and a TV showing the same episode of *Coronation Street*. There was another room beyond it with a couple of mattresses lying on the floor. This was where you fucked the girls or where the girls slept or both.

The heroin was in a metal filing cabinet that Poppy unlocked with a key.

He had about half a pound of the stuff in there, refined and probably cut with any old shite, packaged into scores of convenient dime bags. I grabbed a handful of them and a roll of banknotes.

'You can keep the rest,' I said.

'You really don't know who you're fucking with, pal,' he said.

I smiled at him.

'Let's get back to the ladies.'

Hysteria, screaming, crying and the appearance of the guy from the cash register with a sawn-off shotgun. I ducked behind Poppy and used him as a human shield.

'What are you going to do with that?' I asked the kid.

I had my left hand on the scruff of Poppy's jacket and I was pointing my revolver squarely at the kid.

'I'm going to bloody shoot you,' he said.

'Nah. A sawn-off machine like that will hit everybody in here except me. Your boss will take the brunt of it and even if I do catch some, I'll make sure he's dead before your ears stop ringing.'

He thought about that and nodded.

'It's a bit of an impasse, then, isn't it?' the kid said.

'No, no impasse. Drop the gun or your boss gets it in the head,' I said, shoving the barrel of the revolver into Poppy's neck.

'Drop the gun, Skinny,' Poppy said.

The kid shrugged, set it on the floor and put his hands up.

'What's your name, son?' I asked him.

'Everybody calls me Skinny Mickey.'

'What do you call yourself?'

'Michael Forsythe.'

'OK, Michael, you and Poppy are going to drag your mate outside. You carry him under the arms. You, Poppy, you lift his feet.'

Michael was wiry tough and without too much difficulty they dragged their prone associate through the offy and out into the street, where it was still pouring.

'Now what?' Poppy asked.

'Now this.'

I clobbered him in the noggin and knocked him out cold. I pointed the gun at Michael. 'Run along home, Mikey boy, this isn't any of your business,' I said.

He shook his head.

'I can't do that,' he said.

'If you stay here I'll have to kneecap you and you wouldn't want that, would you?'

He shook his head. 'No, I wouldn't want that, but I don't want anything to happen to the girls,' he said rather gallantly.

I looked him in the eye. 'Listen, son, I'm not going to harm the girls. Quite the opposite. I'm getting the girls out of here. Away from here. I give you my word on that.'

We held the look for ten seconds.

'All right,' he said. 'I believe you.'

'Good, now fuck off, before I have to impart a further lesson.'

He set off at walking pace and I saw him stop at a bus shelter on the far side of the street just to keep an eye on me, which was fair enough.

I went back inside, jumped over the counter and got half a dozen bottles of the strongest hooch I could find – 110-proof vodka from Poland. I ran into the back room.

'OK, ladies, everyone outside now!'

'What are you going to do?' one of them asked.

'If you have things to get, get them and go outside!' I yelled. I broke open a bottle of the vodka and began pouring it over the room. I broke open another. The soberest of the three girls got the picture, grabbed the other two, scurried them into the back room and came out with a handful of bags and clothes.

'Outside, ladies, wait for me under the overhang!' I told them.

I poured the contents of the vodka bottles over the back room, making sure to coat the locker containing the heroin. I went to the toilet, grabbed two bog rolls and lit one of them with my Zippo. When it was good and burny I threw it at the sofa. There was a whoosh of red flame that nearly took my eyebrows off. The plastic in the sofa began to peel off in strips and the foam combusted immediately.

'Bloody thing's a death trap,' I muttered to myself.

I picked up the dropped baseball bat, walked into the off-licence, beat open the till, took out the bills and put them in my pocket. Then I smashed as many spirit bottles as I could, lit another toilet roll and threw it into the mess.

The flames leapt from bottle to bottle like some kind of demonic entity and soon the white ceiling tiles were on fire. The white rat sprinted between my legs into the dark. I went back outside, where it was drizzling. The limpid sun had long set behind Donegal and it was full dark now. The girls were sharing a cigarette and seemed OK. I counted the money. About a grand all told, which represented quite an impressive little score.

I gave the two bleached blondes two hundred quid each and told them to fuck away off from here and never come back. They were dazed and initially uncomprehending and I had to give them a shove to get them moving.

'What about me?' Orla asked without much concern.

'We'll get to you in a wee minute,' I said.

Poppy was coming round now.

I bent down towards him and shook him awake. When he had fully come to I pointed the revolver at his greasy face.

'Do you know who this is?' I asked him.

'Who are you?'

'No. This girl. Do you know who she is?'

'It's Orla.'

'Her name is Orla McCann.'

'So?'

'She's Dermot McCann's sister.'

'So? Dermot McCann? He's yesterday's news, chum. He has no sway here.'

The off-licence was really starting to burn now and we'd have to move away in a minute . . .

'Yesterday's news, you say? You couldn't be more wrong. He's tomorrow's news, Poppy. You've only gone and hoored out the sister of one of the IRA's top commanders. Hoored her out and got her hooked on H.'

I cocked the revolver and put the barrel against his forehead.

'No, please, I didn't know, I didn't—'

I put my finger to my lips.

'Ssssh, Poppy. Sssshhh and listen. Are you listening?'

'Yes.'

'You've got one hour to leave Derry. You've got twenty-four hours to leave Ireland. If you ever come back you're dead. If you ever talk about what happened here today you're dead. This is a message from the very top. Is that understood?'

'I won't, I—'

'Is that understood?'

'Yes.'

'Good. Now start running.'

'Where?'

'I don't care. Just start fucking running!' I screamed at him.

He ran across the parking lot and kept going until he was out of sight.

The fire was buckling the glass front of the offy now so I slapped the big goon on the cheek until he started to come round.

I took Orla by the arm. 'You're coming with me.'

I put her in the front seat of the Beemer and drove across the car park to where the kid called Michael was still waiting.

I wound the window down and beckoned him over. 'You seem like a good kid, take this and get yourself sorted out,'

I told him, and offered him two hundred quid.

He shook his head.

'It's your money, mate, you earned it working for that greasy fuck,' I said.

He grinned at that, nodded and took the cash. I wound the window back up and drove across Derry to Mrs McCann's building on Cowper Street in the Ardbo Estate.

'I'm not fucking going here,' Orla said.

I grabbed her by the back of the neck and squeezed hard. 'It's here or the fucking river. Your choice.'

I kept the squeeze on until she was close to blacking out.

'Here,' she gasped.

'If you run away, I'll know and I'll find you, do you understand?'

'Who are you?'

'Get out of the car.'

We walked up the stairs to the fourth floor. I knocked on the McCanns' door.

Fiona opened it. She saw me and she saw her sister. Fiona was about to begin a harangue but she caught the look in my eyes and buttoned it, hugged Orla and both of them burst into tears.

I let them hold each other for a minute and then I walked them inside the flat.

Mrs McCann observed the scene. 'Oh, the wee hoor's come running back, has she. Well, she can—'

I silenced her with a look.

'You will say nothing. Not one fucking word,' I told her.

I reached into my raincoat pocket and produced the bags of heroin. I gave them to Fiona.

'You were a nurse, weren't you?' I asked.

She nodded.

'This will stop her from getting sick. You'll have to figure out the dose. And once she's weaned off, then it'll have to be cold turkey. You think you can manage that?'

'We can manage,' Fiona said.

'This is her money,' I said, handing over four hundred quid. 'It's hers, this will help you see her through.'

'Thank you.'

'Remember, no lectures. No nonsense. She's back and that's all that matters,' I said to Mrs McCann.

'All right,' she said, crying now too.

'What about Devlin?' Fiona muttered. 'He'll come for her.'

'No he won't. You'll never hear from Poppy Devlin again.'

We stood there for a few seconds and I turned to go.

'We're still not going to tell you where Dermot is,' Fiona said.

'I know. That's not what this was about.'

'What was it about?'

'It was for old time's sake.'

I went downstairs, got in the Beemer and turned the lights on. The rain was harder than ever so I maxed the wipers and the defogger. I drove through the Shantallow. Fire engines were arriving from the Waterside to put out the fire in Poppy Devlin's off-licence, but as was traditional a mob had turned out to gawp at the blaze and throw milk bottles and stones at the firemen to keep them away. I rummaged in the cassette box and sought out my Blind Willie Johnson tape. I fast-forwarded until I got to track four: 'Tear This Building Down'. The box guitar strummed and Blind Willie Johnson growled the words: 'Well, if I had my way Lord, in this wicked world Lord. If I had my way Lord I would tear this building down . . .'

The rain finally came to an end and I made good time on the ride south. When I got back to Carrickfergus it was only ten o'clock but I was so tired I went to bed immediately and, for once, I slept the sleep of the just.

11: THE MOTHER-IN-LAW

I made a cup of Nescafé, added some condensed milk, one sugar, stirred it all up and carried it into the hall. I put on the radio. It was The Smiths and Morrissey's Manky whingeing carried me through breakfast and a lightning shower.

I dressed in black jeans, a black polo neck and my black sports coat jacket. I put on my shoulder holster and noticed there was dried blood on the butt of my Smith and Wesson .38 Police Special.

I washed it under the tap in the kitchen. A pimp's blood from a crazy last night and I wondered why I hadn't kept just one block of the smack. I was still wondering that when McCrabban found me spacing out in the CID incident room at Carrick station.

'What are you doing, Sean?' McCrabban asked cheerfully.

'I came in to get some maps of Antrim town, but now I'm just sort of daydreaming,' I told him.

'May I ask why you are going to Antrim?'

'You may, Detective Sergeant McCrabban. I'm going to Antrim to interview Annie McCann, Dermot McCann's ex wife, to ask her if she happens to know his whereabouts these days.'

'If she does, she won't tell you,' McCrabban said.

'Of course she won't tell me.'

'But you have to do it anyway.'

'That I do, laddie. The Brits have me jumping through hoops.' McCrabban nodded thoughtfully.

'What are *you* working on?' I asked him.

'Nothing much,' he admitted. 'Death, murder and chaos everywhere but nowt in our parish.'

Next door the phone in my tiny windowless office was ringing. I didn't even know it had been connected.

'Later, mate,' I said.

I went into the bare room and picked up the receiver.

'Duffy,' I said.

'Sean, it's me, Kate. I was looking for you at home.'

'Well, you found me at work.'

'Sean, can I ask you something?'

'Sure.'

'You didn't drive into Derry last night, torch Poppy Devlin's off-licence, burn it to the ground, take Orla McCann out of there, return her to her mother and threaten Poppy Devlin with death if he didn't leave Ireland within twenty-four hours, did you?'

'Nope.'

'Good. I knew that couldn't have been you. You wouldn't want to jeopardise everything we've done for you with a hot-headed and silly act like that, would you?'

'Certainly not.'

'That's what I said.'

There was an awkward silence.

'Sean, I know I said I would come with you today but I find that I'm swamped here. Would you be cross if I stood this one out?'

'Not in the least. I'll give you a full report. I promise.'

'Thank you, Sean. Please do. You can't imagine the bureaucracy.'

'Oh, I think I can. But I promise I'll fill you in.'

'Please be discreet.'

'Always am.'

'Yes. Ciao.'

I hung up and went out to find the Crabman. He was in a cubicle, cleaning his pipe.

'Busy?' I asked him.

'Not especially.'

'Fancy a run up to Antrim?'

'And let Matty steer the ship?' he asked sceptically.

'And let Matty steer the ship.'

'OK, then.'

When we reached the outskirts of Antrim town I handed him the Ordnance Survey map. 'Where does Annie McCann live?' McCrabban asked.

'After the divorce she moved back in with her parents. It's a wee village called Ballykeel just outside of town. Take the map and direct me. It's complicated around here. If we take the wrong turn, we could end up on the motorway or the airport road. Those airport-road coppers can delay you for hours with all their questions.'

Crabbie unfolded the map. 'I'm not seeing the village.'

'It's off the A6 towards Lough Neagh. You can't miss it. Come on! We're coming up to the first roundabout.'

'Ballykeel? Oh, I see it. Actually, you could miss it, it's tiny. Go straight through the roundabout and take a right.'

'And then what?'

'What's the actual address?'

'Number 3, Lough Neagh Road, Ballykeel, County Antrim.'

'I see it. Go through the next roundabout and head for the lough. Don't go into the town, just follow the signs for the lough.'

I followed his directions, avoiding Antrim completely.

Lough Neagh was the largest freshwater lake in the British Isles but it was surprisingly underdeveloped, and visiting the villages dotting its shores was often like stepping back into an Ireland of a hundred or several hundred years before. Ballykeel lay a mile from Shane's Castle, the residence of Lord O'Neill, one of the ancient Anglo-Irish families of the area. The village houses were whitewashed stone cottages, many with original thatched roofs. There was a spirit grocer and a newsagent and not much else. Lough Neagh itself lay to the south, a vast, still, pale-blue presence with no boats and few birds. We were surrounded by woodland: oak, ash, elm and wild apple trees.

We found number 3 Lough Neagh Road, which was an old two-storey coaching inn or post house. It was a handsome structure, built from local stone with a small stable block to the right.

'They must have money,' I said.

'Maybe, but I think you can get these old barns cheap. The money comes into it when you try to do them up, then you'll need deep pockets.'

'I think they do have money, though. In the briefing notes I was given it said they had land in Donegal.'

'Aye, but there's land in Donegal and land in Donegal. You could have a thousand acres and every inch of it sucking bog.'

We parked the car in a gravelly forecourt, got out, knocked on the door.

After a minute's pause it was opened by a large, attractive red-haired woman about fifty-five. She was wearing a brown cardigan and a green corduroy skirt that went down to her ankles. She had a large bosom and her eyes were clear, hazel and intelligent.

'*Bail ó Dhia is Muire duit*,' she said.

'And to you,' I replied.

'What can I do for you?' she asked.

I took out my warrant card and showed it to her.

'Detective Inspector Sean Duffy, Special Branch,' she read frostily.

'That's right,' I said. 'I'm at Carrickfergus RUC at the moment and this is Detective Sergeant McCrabban, also of Carrick RUC.'

She grabbed the door and thought for a moment about

slamming it in our faces, but she wavered. 'This isn't about Lizzie, is it?' she asked dubiously.

'Uhhh . . . no. Who's Lizzie?'

'My daughter.'

'No. This is about Annie McCann.'

She nodded. Her face hardened.

'I see. I suppose you're looking for Dermot?' she said, with a groan of annoyance.

'Yes, and we were wondering if—' I began, but she cut me off immediately.

'Do I look like an informer to you?'

'What does an informer look like?' I asked gently.

She shook her head. 'You'll get nothing here. We don't know a thing about Dermot and if we did we certainly wouldn't be telling the RUC!'

And yet . . .

And yet she still stood there. And she didn't close the door.

Something was up.

I looked at the woman.

Something was going on here. Something I wasn't twigging.

She had gravity, this lady. Power. Her daughter had been married to Dermot McCann but it didn't come from that.

'We couldn't possibly get a cup of tea, could we? Then we'll get out of your hair and get on back to Carrick,' I tried.

She considered this for a moment, nodded, left the door open and walked into the house.

Crabbie and I exchanged a look.

'Could be a trap. After you, mate,' I said.

We walked into a large, comfortable living room that must have been the old dining room when this was a coaching inn. There was a massive stone fireplace, rugs over a stone floor, attractive watercolours on the wall, a bookcase filled with what looked like volumes of poetry and history.

I sat on an ancient red leather sofa and got up again when

the woman came back with the tea. She asked how we took it. I was milk and one sugar and Crabbie was milk with no sugar. She poured our tea into cups of fine nineteenth-century china. There was cake, too. Dundee cake, carrot cake, home made.

We both took a slice of the Dundee.

'I'm Mary Fitzpatrick. Annie's mother,' the woman said, sitting down on a high-backed armchair.

'Nice to meet you, Mrs Fitzpatrick,' I said formally.

'Likewise,' Crabbie said.

I took a sip of my tea. It was not laced with arsenic, which came as something of a relief. Mary Fitzpatrick might be the mother-in-law of a famous IRA operative but she wasn't pathological.

'Very nice Dundee cake,' Crabbie said into the silence.

'Thank you.'

'Do you happen to know where Annie is?' I asked.

'She's away with her da. I think they went rabbit shooting.'

'I see.'

'It won't do you any good, you know. Annie wouldn't tell you anything even if she did hear from Dermot, which she hasn't since he broke out of the Maze.'

'We were wondering if he'd contacted you or Annie or you knew where he might be?' I asked.

Mary smiled and shook her head. 'What incentive could I possibly have to help you, the agents of the occupier? Why on earth would I turn in my former son-in-law to the likes of you?'

'Dermot's planning a bombing campaign. He's going to kill a lot of innocent people,' I suggested.

Mary nodded. 'There will always be casualties in a war. It's regrettable, but there it is,' she said brusquely.

'And then there's the fact that the Brits have MI5 and the SAS looking for him and you know what those boys are like. They shoot to kill, don't they? But if Dermot were to turn himself in or we were to find him before then—'

She raised her hand. 'That's enough now, Inspector Duffy. Say no more. I am no fan of Dermot McCann. I have some issues with the way he treated my daughter. I won't go into the details but he did not exactly act the part of a gentleman. Be that as it may I will not under any circumstances talk to or cooperate with any person who works for the British government or its—'

'But Mrs Fitzpatrick—'

'Don't interrupt me, young man!'

The tone of her voice told me that she was teasing me a little, but only a little. There was a steely menace behind those attractive hazel eyes.

She set down her teacup and put her hands on her lap. It began to rain outside and I thought to myself that if it kept up it might force Annie and her father to give up their rabbit-hunting expedition and come home.

Mary was looking intently at me. 'What do you know about grief, Inspector Duffy, Sergeant McCrabban?' she asked.

'Grief?'

'Aye, grief. Are your parents still alive?'

'Mine are,' Crabbie said.

'Mine too,' I concurred.

'Have you ever lost a sibling or a child?'

'No.'

'No.'

'Well then. You don't know. Neither of you.'

'Is there something you want to tell us, Mrs Fitzpatrick?' I asked.

'Annie's had her share of troubles. But that's over and Dermot's not part of our life any more. He's out of all our lives. And life goes on, doesn't it? Where it can, life goes on.'

'Yes, I suppose so,' I said, utterly baffled by what she was talking about.

Mary got slowly to her feet. 'Well now, you've had your tea

and we've had a wee civilised chat and I think you should be leaving now, don't you?'

'If you want us to go.'

'I do want you to go, gentlemen. I've had enough of you for one day.'

She walked us to the front door.

On the threshold she took my arm and held it for a moment. She looked me keenly in the eyes.

'Yes?' I asked.

'You're not the first RUC detective that's been in this house,' she said.

'Oh?'

'No. But you're the first one who looks as if he knows his arse from his elbow.'

'Well, I'll be—'

'You'll be nothing, Duffy. You won't come back here again without an invitation. Do you understand?'

'I understand.'

We walked to the Beemer and when Crabbie had got inside she called me back to the porch.

'Yes?' I said.

'Orla McCann,' she said, and raised her eyebrows at me.

'What about her?' I asked innocently.

She smiled. 'Run along, Inspector Duffy. Run along now.'

I walked to the Beemer, got in, started her up.

'What did she say to you?' Crabbie asked.

'A final warning. "If I ever catch you round here" . . . they love that shit.'

Crabbie sighed. 'Another busted flush, eh?'

'You and the gambling metaphors, Sergeant McCrabban! What's the world coming to?'

He nodded ruefully. 'If the wife was to hear me say that. Oh boy! And on the same day I praised someone else's Dundee cake!'

I rubbed the stubble under my chin. 'You're right, though. Poker is Mrs Fitzpatrick's game and she's definitely got something up her sleeve. But what it is, I haven't the foggiest idea.'

12: ANOTHER LETTER

It was a week later when the letter arrived in my pigeonhole at Carrickfergus RUC. It had been an interesting few days for Northern Ireland. It had been quiet, so to prove they were still in business the Provos had carried out a small coordinated series of car-bomb attacks on market towns west of the Bann. Some of the car bombs had come with warnings, some hadn't, which represented the different operational procedures of the various IRA cells. Only one person had been killed in the dozen attacks but this was only luck and everyone knew that luck wouldn't hold for ever. The mood in Carrickfergus RUC was tense. This was not the 'big IRA push' we had all been promised but it would do just fine until the big push came along.

I had a busy few days driving to Derry, Limavady and Coleraine to interview the last remaining members of Dermot's clan; but if it hadn't been apparent before this it was obvious now: none of them would talk. Informers had a nasty habit of ending up face-down in a sheugh along the South Armagh border, with their right hand cut off and a hole in their head.

One morning Matty found me in my office tackling *The Times* crossword and listening to the *Hebrides Overture* on what the kids were calling a 'boom box'. He brought me a letter and a cup of coffee.

'A letter for you, Sean. Found it in your pigeonhole,' he said, plonking the white envelope down on my desk.

He had never brought me coffee or my post before and there was a hesitancy about him.

'Cheers, mate, what's the special occasion?'

He was reluctant to look me in the eye.

'Nothing,' he said.

'Have a seat, mate, and tell me what's on your mind,' I said.

'Ach, it's nothing, you've got a letter to read, I'll talk to you later, OK?'

'Are you sure?'

'Aye. I'll see you later.'

Strange, I thought, and opened the envelope, which had no return address on it and had been mailed to 'DI Sean Duffy, Carrickfergus RUC, Carrickfergus, Co. Antrim'.

It was a brief handwritten note on cream writing paper:

Dear Inspector Duffy,

I hope it would be convenient for you to meet me in the Rising Sun Café in Cornmarket Street, Belfast on Saturday June 26th at 10 a.m. to discuss an arrangement that may be mutually beneficial. I would appreciate it if you do not ring my home or RSVP by post as I am quite sure that my calls and post are being regularly intercepted by British Intelligence and I would like to keep this meeting discreet.

I would further appreciate it if you would be so good as to destroy this letter without photocopying or transcribing it first. I have looked into your background and I feel that I may rely on your discretion in this matter.
Aithníonn ciaróg ciaróg eile.

Yours faithfully

Mary Fitzpatrick

'Well, well, well,' I said to myself.

There was a knock at the door.

I put the letter quickly back in the envelope.

'Come in,' I said, and Matty stuck his head round the door.

'Sean, I was wondering . . .'

'Have a seat,' I told him.

He sat. 'A glass of Mr Walker's amber restorative?' I asked.

'Don't mind if I do,' he said, and I opened my desk drawer, took out two paper cups and poured us both a healthy measure of Johnnie Walker Black.

'What's on your mind, Matty?'

'Well, you see, the thing is, there's no future here, is there?' he began.

'You're moving to England and you want me to write you a job reference!' I announced.

'How do you do it, Sean?'

'They used to call me the Great Stupendo. I did children's parties and Butlins.'

He grinned. 'It's not England. It's Scotland. I'm applying to join the Strathclyde Police and I need two references and I was wondering if you could write one of them for me.'

'Of course! I'd be happy to. If you think it'll help.' 'You're a detective inspector, Sean, and you've got the Queen's Police Medal. I think it'll help.'

'Why Scotland?'

'There's nothing here, mate. It's fucked. We're all fucked. Some day I'll want to have kids. Can you imagine bringing up kids around here?'

I swallowed my Johnnie Walker.

'Nope, I can't.'

'I mean . . . don't think I'm bailing on youse, but there comes a time in a man's life when he has to look out for number one . . .'

'Jesus, mate, you're not bailing on anyone. You've done your bit and I'd be happy to write you a reference. You're a terrific police officer.'

Matty looked shyly at the floor, finished his whisky and stood up.

'Thanks, Sean, and if, uh, if you could keep this under your hat . . . I don't want any shit from upstairs until I have this thing in the bag.'

'Mum's the word, mate.'

'Ta.'

Matt had no reason to feel guilty. Getting out was the smart move.

I closed my office door, finished the Johnnie Walker and reread the letter. Then I held it over the metal wastepaper basket and set fire to it with my lighter.

The very last bit, *aithníonn ciaróg ciaróg eile*, meant something like 'a beetle recognises another beetle' or perhaps more pejoratively 'a cockroach recognises another cockroach', or if you wanted to turn it into criminal argot: 'a rat recognises another rat'.

The meeting with Mary was going to be interesting.

13: THE ENCOUNTER AT THE RISING SUN

Cornmarket was a pedestrianised shopping precinct off Royal Avenue. This was the original market street of Belfast when the city was little more than a row of houses along the Farset river.

As Dublin had stagnated Belfast had prospered through linen manufacture and heavy engineering. Grand Victorian banks and building societies had grown up around the City Hall and by the time of the First World War Belfast was building fifteen per cent of the ships of the British Empire. But after partition from the South in 1921 there had been little economic development or prosperity. In the Second World War the city had been heavily blitzed by the Luftwaffe and it suffered anaemic growth after VE Day. The *coup de grâce* had come in the period from 1969 until 1975, when this part of Belfast had almost been wiped off the map by endemic IRA bomb attacks. Hundreds of shops, offices and factories had been burned to the ground.

In 1976 the authorities blocked off vehicular traffic from the city centre and made all civilians entering Belfast go through a series of search huts, where they were patted down for explosives and had their bags examined for incendiary devices. The streets around Royal Avenue were then flooded with police and soldiers and although this was extremely inconvenient for all concerned, it had worked, and now Belfast city centre, paradoxically, was one of the safest places to shop in the world.

The Rising Sun Café dated back to the 1890s, when it had been an elegant tearoom. However, smoke damage from various nearby incendiary devices and an ugly 1982 refit had robbed it of much of its original chintzy charm. The elegant booths had been replaced with plastic tables and chairs: the wide black and white tiles had been ripped up and the bare concrete underneath covered with brown linoleum.

I arrived early for my meeting with Mary Fitzpatrick but she had arrived even earlier. As I entered the Rising Sun, a waitress asked me whether I was Mr Duffy.

I said that I was and I was escorted to a private dining room at the back of the café where, to my surprise, I found that many of the original Victorian features were still in place.

Mary was sitting at a table with a silver teapot in front of her.

The waitress led me to Mary's table and then excused herself.

'I didn't know this room existed,' I said.

'Few people do. I know Cameron, the owner. It's a nice quiet place to meet in the centre of town without any prying eyes. Neither of us will be running into any old friends.'

'I imagine not.'

'I hope you've not told anyone about our meeting.'

'I haven't.'

'Not even your sergeant?'

'Not even him,' I said, pouring myself tea from the pot.

'You knew Dermot personally, didn't you, Inspector Duffy?' Mary asked.

There was no point trying to dissemble. 'Yes, I knew him.'

'And you knew Orla too, didn't you? Orla, Fiona, all the McCanns.'

'I knew them.'

'And you even knew my Annie a bit, didn't you?'

'I knew Annie a little bit.'

'After you left I asked Annie about you,' she said, looking at me with her dark piercing eyes.

'Oh?'

'She remembers you right enough.'

'Does she?'

'She said that you and she and Dermot used to go to concerts in Belfast. Dublin once.'

'Is that so?'

'She says that you drove them down from Derry because you had a car.'

It was probably true – there had been a lot of rock concerts at the tail-end of the sixties and the beginning of the seventies. 'It rings a bell. Dermot didn't drive then so I could well have taken him to a couple of shows.'

'But of course you were a peeler by the time of the wedding, which is why *we* never met,' Mary said.

'I wasn't one of Dermot's closest friends anyway. And I certainly didn't blame him for not inviting me to his wedding. It wouldn't have been safe.'

She nodded and took off her coat. She was wearing a black jumper over faded blue jeans and boots.

She poured me some more tea and remembered to offer me the sugar bowl.

The waitress came back a moment later with a selection of cakes and pastries that she left on the table.

'Help yourself,' Mary said.

'I will, they look lovely.'

I grabbed a bun and a lemon slice.

She reached into her purse and pulled out a photocopied document and placed it on the table in front of her. I could see that it was some sort of report or file.

'What is that?' I asked.

'Eat your wee bun and I'll read it to you.'

'OK.'

She opened the file.

'So you joined the police out of Queen's University and

after two years in Enniskillen and South Tyrone you became a detective in Belfast. You did well there, were promoted to the rank of detective sergeant and were sent to Carrickfergus RUC. You solved a few cases and were promoted to detective inspector. But then you got yourself mixed up with the FBI DeLorean sting and it all started to go wrong for you, didn't it?'

'What exactly are you reading there? Is that my personnel file?'

'Never you mind. Last year you supposedly ran over some wean in a Land Rover you were driving, only you weren't driving, were you?'

'How do you know all this?'

'You resigned. And you were off the force.'

'Yes.'

'Which leads me to the conclusion that it was an *external* agency that brought you back in. An external agency that could only be MI5 or perhaps some intelligence unit within Scotland Yard. And why would they do that?'

I didn't say anything.

'I think they brought you back solely for the purpose of finding my errant ex-son-in-law,' she said.

'I can neither confirm nor deny any of that.'

'I didn't expect you to.'

I sipped the tea. It was too strong now and it tasted bitter even with the sugar.

'So now we know where we all stand, don't we?' she said.

'Well, you know about me but I don't understand why you're meeting me.'

'You're an interesting fellow, Duffy. You don't present yourself very well. You sell yourself short. I think you believe the reason MI5 recruited you to look for Dermot was because of this personal angle. Because you had a previous relationship with him. You knew Dermot and his clan and you think that's what makes you special.'

'Go on.'

She smiled again. 'But that's not the only reason they wanted you. MI5 recruited you because you're good. And *that's* what makes you special. You're good at what you do, Duffy, that's why they want you. That's why I want you too.'

'It's flattering to hear you say that but MI5 – if indeed it was MI5 – has more than enough bright people already, trust—'

She put up her hand to cut me off. 'Let's begin. In your dealings with Annie she never had you to our house in Ballykeel, did she?'

'No. I don't believe so.'

'And you weren't at the wedding, so you never got to meet Lizzie or Vanessa?'

'No.'

'Vanessa's my eldest. She's a doctor in Canada. In Montreal. Married to another doctor. They've a wee boy, my only grandchild. They've called him Pierre. I call him Peter.'

'Very nice. Do you get out there often?'

'I've been there once. It was enough. Jim doesn't like to fly.'

She closed the file she had on me, carefully ripped it up and put the remains in the nearest swing bin.

'Montreal's supposed to be lovely,' I said, to keep the conversation going, when she sat down at the table again.

She ignored this. 'You're not supposed to have favourites among your children, are you?'

'I wouldn't know. I'm an only child and I have no kids.'

She reached into her bag again and gave me a passport photograph of a tall, pensive, attractive girl with ginger hair. She was wearing a field hockey uniform and standing in front of a goal.

'You can keep that,' she said.

'Why?'

Next she passed over a brown folder sealed with two thick rubber bands.

'What's this?' I asked.

'This is a copy of the RUC report into my daughter Lizzie's murder. Lizzie was my youngest. The apple of my eye, you could say. Shouldn't say that, I suppose, but there it is. She was so funny and so sweet. There wasn't a vile bone in her body. She deserved more than this.'

'Your daughter was murdered?'

'It's all in there. It's not the complete file but I'm sure you can get that easily enough. I didn't want to look at all the grisly photographs and the autopsy report, but this should be more than sufficient to give the gist of what happened.'

I took off the rubber bands and opened the binder.

'It's what they call a cold case now,' Mary continued. 'They never found out who did it and the detective on the investigation has long since been assigned to other duties. Two years ago I hired a private detective but he didn't come up with anything either and he advised me to drop it.'

'What's this about, Mrs Fitzpatrick?'

'Lizzie's dead, Inspector Duffy. She's lying in the Arghall graveyard in Toome. My youngest daughter killed, her neck broken, by person or persons unknown.'

'When was this?'

'Four years ago this December.'

'And the RUC had no leads?'

'Leads? Well, there were three men in the bar, three suspects if you will, but there was no proof. No proof at all. I think one of them killed her and the other two are covering up for him. I need to know which one of the three did it. And I need proof. I need to be satisfied. It won't bring her back. Nothing'll bring her back, but the law, the old law, the Brehon Law, gives me the choice of penalty. Allows me to settle this score for her.'

She grabbed my hand and squeezed it hard.

I stared at her. Her eyes were fierce and her scarlet hair was straining at the clips that were holding it in place. 'Do you get me, Inspector?'

'I don't know. Are you saying . . . Let me make sure that we're talking about the same thing, Mrs Fitzpatrick. If I find your daughter's killer and give you sufficient proof of this person's complicity, then you'll . . . you'll—'

'I'll give you Dermot McCann,' she said with a cold smile.

14: WHAT BEFELL LIZZIE FITZPATRICK

M ary reached into her bag and took out a packet of Benson and Hedges. She offered me one but I declined.

'The story's all there in the file but I'll tell you the gist if you want.'

'Please do.'

'My husband used to run a wee bar in Ballykeel. Just on the edge of the village there. The Henry Joy McCracken.'

'Named after the rebel?'

'Exactly. We still have it but Jim will never open it now. Not since what happened to Lizzie.'

She took a sip of her tea and lit her cigarette. 'Lizzie and all the girls used to serve there now and again to earn some pocket money. And then Lizzie went away to England to study law. She wanted to be a lawyer like she'd seen on TV. Defending the weak, all that, you know?'

'Yes.'

'She was at the University of Warwick. Doing very well for herself. She'd come home in the holidays and sometimes work in the bar, but she was also interning at a solicitor's office in Antrim: Mulvenna and Wright, a top-notch firm, so we didn't see her much when she was back. Anyway, she was home at Christmas in 1980 and she wasn't supposed to be working in the pub at all . . .'

She sniffed and shook her head before continuing.

'Anyway, it was 27 December.'

'27 December 1980?'

'Yes.'

I wrote that in my book while Mary went on: 'Jim was in the Royal Victoria Hospital, Belfast, for surgery on his left knee. Arthritis, you know?'

'Sure.'

'He had the surgery that afternoon and he'd wanted to close the pub but Lizzie said she could handle it. I said OK because I could see she wanted a wee bit of responsibility. I'd been down to Belfast to see Jim and he was good and I came back to Ballykeel around ten thirty. I gave her a wee call in the pub and told her that her dad was doing fine. She was so glad to hear that. I asked her if she needed any help down the pub and she said that it was no bother because there were only three customers in the place. Well, closing time was in half an hour so I didn't think anything of it.'

'Were the police able to trace the customers?'

'Oh yes, the police found them. Very "respectable men", all of them. They weren't locals. They were all from Belfast. Come here for the fishing.'

'So then what happened?'

'Well, Lizzie didn't come home. It only takes ten minutes to lock up and walk to our house from the pub, so I was getting a bit anxious from eleven fifteen onwards.'

'What did you do?'

'I didn't do anything. I just waited. I thought maybe she was having trouble with the locks or something.'

'Then what happened?'

'Then at eleven thirty I got a call from Harper McCullough. He asked about Jim's operation and then he asked to speak to Lizzie. So I told him that I hadn't seen her yet. And he was quite concerned because she'd told him that she would be back home by eleven thirty at the latest.'

'Who's Harper McCullough?'

'Harper was her boyfriend at the time. Very nice lad. A Protestant, mind you, but we liked him all the same. Very close friend of the family.'

'Where was *he* when Lizzie was killed?'

'Oh, he was in Belfast at his rugby club's annual dinner. He was accepting some prize on behalf of his father. He was there from nine until he called me at half past eleven.'

'So what happened next?'

'Well, I told Harper I had no idea where she was and he said that I should call the police and that he was going to drive there immediately.'

'And did you call the police?'

She shook her head sadly. 'I got on my coat and I went down to the pub to see what was going on. Well, sure enough, it was locked up and the lights were turned off but there was no sign of Lizzie. So I knew something was wrong. At the time I thought that Lizzie had locked up the pub and something had happened to her on the way home.'

'How far is it from the pub to your house?'

'About three hundred yards.'

'Through the village?'

'You could go through the village, or you could take a short cut along the Love Lane, but she didn't take either of those.'

'What *did* she do?'

Mary stubbed out her cigarette and took a handkerchief from her purse. She dabbed her eyes and fought to keep the tears away. She resisted the urge to cry. This was Ulster, where even good Catholics like Mary had been infected by the Protestant sickness for repression of emotion.

'I got home and I called Annie. She was still living in Derry then and she told me to call the police straight away. I was a bit reluctant to do that because we've had our wee run-ins with the police, as you may know.'

I did know. I had done my research and I had found out that the Fitzpatricks of Ballykeel were a prominent Antrim-area Republican family. Maybe not active IRA, but certainly moving in high Republican circles. Mary Fitzpatrick had stood as an Independent Republican MP in the 1970 election and knew a lot of players back in the day.

'Harper arrived back from the rugby club do about a quarter to twelve out of his mind with worry and the police came shortly after that from Antrim and we all went looking for Lizzie. After midnight one of the policemen shone his torch into the pub and he thought he saw a body lying in there. We couldn't get in, of course, because Lizzie had the key, so they had to break the front door down with a sledgehammer. And that's where we found her. Lying on the floor, dead. All curled up there with her hair across her face. My God, I'll never forget that! I wanted to go to her and hug her and make her come alive again, but they wouldn't let me touch her!'

Mary lit another cigarette and I put my hand on her arm. She genuflected and I made the sign of the cross with her and together we said 'God and Mary and Patrick'.

She took a sip of her cold tea and continued her account. 'At first we all thought it was natural causes because a crime didn't make any sense. The pub was locked from the inside. The windows had iron bars on them, the bolt was across on the front door and the back door. Both doors were locked and the key was in her pocket.'

'But it wasn't natural causes?'

'No. There was a light bulb out above the bar and there was a new light bulb broken in her hand. For all the world it looked liked she had stood on the bar to change the dead bulb, slipped, fallen and broken her neck. Well, that's what the eejit police on the scene thought. But the next day the pathologist at Antrim hospital, a Dr Kent, told the police that he thought it looked very suspicious. He conducted the autopsy and he wasn't happy with the broken vertebrae in her neck or the wound on her head. And later at the coroner's inquest Dr Kent said that her broken neck was not consistent with having fallen off a bar.'

'What was it consistent with?'

'He thought that she had been struck on the head and her neck snapped by an unknown person. The police would have none of that but he was so adamant that the coroner had no recourse but to return an open verdict.'

'Did the police open a murder investigation?'

'It was half-hearted at best. I could tell that they didn't believe she was murdered. The place was locked, the broken light bulb was in her hand. Case closed.'

'They interviewed the men in the bar, of course?'

'Oh yes. It's all in the report. They all have the same story. They say that Lizzie kicked them out at eleven o'clock sharp. One of them, a man called McPhail, had his car parked in the village. They walked to the car and drove up to Belfast.'

'What did the police make of their story?'

'The police believed them.'

I rubbed my chin and considered it all. 'There was no one else in the bar?'

'No.'

'Is there any other way in?'

'No. A front door and a back door and they were both locked and bolted.'

'And the windows?'

'The windows are covered with cast-iron bars.'

'Can you take them off?'

'No. The police checked anyway. They were all intact.'

'Slip through them?'

'The gap's too narrow even for a child.'

I leaned back in the chair and skimmed through the police report. It was detailed and a nice job of work. The investigating officer, an Inspector Beggs, laid out the evidence in his conclusion. He was not convinced in any way that a crime had been committed. 'It's a tough one,' I said.

She nodded in agreement and blew out a thin line of blue smoke.

'You're certain she was killed?' I asked.

'I know it in my bones.'

'I'll look into it but I can't promise anything.'

She nodded and got to her feet. 'When you come to my house don't mention Dermot at all. Tell Annie and Jim that you're looking into Lizzie's death. I've told them that you came to see me already. That's how I was able to bring your name up with Annie. Listen to me now, Inspector Duffy, if you ask about Dermot they will tell you nothing and you will queer the pitch. Do you mind me?'

'I do.'

'Do not ask about Dermot!'

'I won't.'

'And when the time comes, if you fulfil your part of the bargain, I'll fulfil mine.'

'How will you be able to find out where he is?'

'Oh, don't you worry about that. I have my ways. My contacts.'

'You'd really give up your daughter's husband?'

'Ex-husband. I am as good as my word, Duffy. If you do this for me, I'll give you Dermot McCann.'

'I should tell you . . . I'm not an assassin. I want to arrest him but Dermot may not come quietly . . .'

'I'll tell you where he is. What happens next is between you and him.'

'I can promise you that if I have anything to do with it, I will give him a chance to surrender.'

'Very good.' She offered me her hand and I shook it.

'And if I need to get in touch with you I can come by the house?' I asked.

'And if I need to get in touch with you I'll write to you.'

'That's probably the safest policy if they're tapping your phones.'

'Good day, Inspector.'

She walked out of the back room into the café proper; I put the files in my briefcase, waited a decent interval and followed in her wake.

15: THE LOCKED-ROOM PROBLEM

The first thing I did on Monday morning was drive down to Antrim RUC to talk to the investigating officer. He was now Chief Inspector Beggs and he had moved from CID to admin. He was a ruddy, saturnine character with black hair and a moustache. He was about thirty-nine or forty, and if his heart or the booze didn't get him he would probably end up an assistant chief constable. He greeted me without suspicion, listened to my pitch, took the entire case file and asked a reserve constable to copy it while we adjourned to a nearby pub.

'Just a pint of Bass for me,' he said, and I got the same.

'So why are Special Branch interested in a four-year-old accidental death case?' he asked, taking a sip of his pint.

'I'm not at liberty to discuss that, sir.'

'Oh, it's one of those, is it?' he said good-naturedly.

'Yes, it's one of those, I'm afraid, sir. What can you tell me about the incident?'

'The poor wee lassie had locked up for the night, she was changing a light bulb, she got up on to the bar, she slipped, she fell, she broke her neck. End of story.'

'Dr Kent thought differently, though, didn't he?'

'Oh aye, him. He convinced the coroner to return an open verdict. The man's a menace. We've had trouble with him before. He sees conspiracies behind every corner. He got that poor wee lassie's mother worked up and no mistake. Three girls in that family. One falls off a bar and breaks her neck, another hightails it for America, the other's married to some IRA lifer in the Maze. It's like *Fiddler on the Roof*. It's bad luck is what it is.'

'You didn't think there was any kind of IRA connection in the girl's death?'

'No chance. It was an accident. The place was locked up tight. The key was in her pocket. The front door was bolted. The back door was bolted. The windows were barred. I tried to explain to Dr Kent and Mrs Fitzpatrick that it was a logical impossibility that anyone else was involved.'

I nodded and took a big swig of the Bass.

'Have you ever read—' I began, but he cut me off.

'*The Murders in the Rue Morgue, The Moonstone, The Hollow Man, The Rim of the Pit* . . . among many others.'

'Well, yes,' I said, a bit shamefaced. Clearly he was no eejit-brained country copper.

'You see, Inspector Duffy, the essence of the "locked-room mystery" is to assure the reader that the room is hermetically sealed when in fact there may be another way in. For example, in a lot of those stories there's a second key. Well, here the key was in Lizzie's pocket, and even if there had been a second key it wouldn't matter because both doors, front and back, were bolted from the inside.'

'What sort of bolts?'

'Heavy bolts on heavy rings that were used during a traditional "lock-in" for after-hours drinking. The bolts can only be slid across from the inside, there was no hole in the door for a wire to go through or any other way that they could be manipulated externally. I checked for that. In fact that was one of the first things I checked once the constable told me that the place was empty and the doors had been locked and barred from the inside.'

'In the *Rue Morgue* they got in through the window,' I

suggested.

'Yes. You know that story's very dodgy. I don't mean the trained killer ape, I mean the fact that an elderly French woman would ever go to sleep with the window open. The wife's mother's from Rouen. Believe me. No killer monkeys or vampires are getting into her flat. I don't think she's had the windows open since the Occupation . . . but that's, uhm, neither here nor there. In poor Lizzie's case the windows were covered with thick iron bars which were welded to the frames. This was to prevent burglaries and sectarian attacks. Needless to say, none of the bars had been tampered with . . .'

'In one of those stories the act of breaking the door down conceals the fact that the door wasn't actually locked from the inside after all.'

'I'm glad you asked about that, Duffy. I checked that too. The bolt was so strong on the front door that when they smashed it open it was the hinges that gave first.'

I took another drink of Burton-upon-Trent's finest.

'And the back door was definitely bolted?'

'I checked it myself.'

'A cellar door?'

'The Henry Joy McCracken has a cellar all right but the only way down to it is through the bar itself. I was thinking along those lines too. I went down there and had a look. It's completely bricked up along the walls and there's a solid concrete floor. I checked the walls: no loose pointing, no secret passages.'

'And the attic?'

'There is no attic. It's a hammer-beam ceiling.'

I finished the Bass and shook my head. 'Well then, I don't have an explanation.'

'It's not for me to question the wisdom of you lads in Special Branch, but what exactly has got it into your heads that this was a murder? Is there any new information that I don't know about?'

'No. No new information. We've just been asked to look at it all again.'

'Well, if my opinion's worth anything (and it probably isn't) I'd say that the simplest explanation is still the best. She locked up for the night. Closed the till, was about to head home when she noticed that a light bulb was out. She knew her ailing father couldn't fix it so she decided to do it herself. Accidents will happen . . .'

'And the lights were turned off why?'

'So she didn't electrocute herself when she put the new bulb in.'

'So she clambers up on the bar and tries to change the light bulb in the dark?'

'There was a little ambient light from the street lamp outside. She probably thought she could do it. Alas, she could not.'

'Tell me about the three men in the bar just before closing time.'

'I interviewed all three of them independently. They all had the same story. Lizzie kicked them out after last orders and they drove home to Belfast. They're all friends, so I suppose it's possible that they concocted the tale and they're covering for one another, but I didn't think so at the time and I don't think so now.'

I flipped open my notebook where I'd written down their names.

'Arnold Yeats?'

'He teaches history at Queen's.'

'Lee McPhail?'

'An election agent in Belfast. A bit of a political fixer. Works both sides of the street.'

'What do you mean?'

'For the Prods and the Catholics. As long as you've got cash.'

'He sounds promising. Bit of a dodgy character, eh?'

'He was the driver that night. The only one sober enough. He's connected up the Wazoo river and he's got a few convictions for various things.'

'Still, that's something, though, isn't it?'

He shrugged. 'If you want to make something of it, sure. It's three years since I interviewed him but I didn't detect anything suspicious at the time.'

'This last guy . . . Barry Connor?'

'Chef. He owns Le Canard in Belfast,' he said, looking at me as if I would have heard of it.

'What's special about that?' I asked.

'I see you are not an epicure, Duffy.'

'No. Not really.'

'It's Belfast's only Michelin-starred restaurant.'

'Didn't even know there was one.'

'I'm surprised the *Michelin Guide* people braved the Troubles to sample our less than spectacular local delicacies, but there it is.'

'An academic, a political fixer and a well-known chef. It's like an episode of fucking *Columbo*.'

'With an important difference . . . there was no actual crime committed here.'

We'll see what Dr Kent says about that, I thought.

'Tell me about the boyfriend. The one at the rugby club dinner.'

'McCullough?'

'Aye.'

'He's a good kid. His father was a builder who made a mint when they decided to develop Antrim as a new town. House up on the lough shore. He was a university boy studying architecture or archaeology or something.'

'You've always got to look at the boyfriend, don't you? What's his alibi like?'

'The rugby club dinner went on until one in the morning but he didn't stay that late. He called Mary Fitzpatrick from the dinner about eleven thirty asking to speak to Lizzie. Of course, she hadn't seen her. So he sped back home as fast as he could.'

'Was he definitely at the dinner?'

'Oh yeah. His father was getting an award and he had to give a speech on his father's behalf and then he had to hang around for all the other speeches. Look to the boyfriend, as you rightly say, but even without the impossibility of him being in two places at once I still don't like him for it.'

'Why?'

'He was knocked for six by Lizzie's death. His da had had a stroke earlier that year and he's an only child. Harper was looking after his dad at home and after Lizzie's death he went to pieces. Harper and Mary Fitzpatrick were the ones pushing me to open a murder investigation. He completely refused to believe that Lizzie would have died in so stupid a manner. He didn't buy it.'

'But you did?'

He took a big swig of his pint and grinned like a man content. 'That's how people die all the time, mate! You know how many non-terrorist-related murders Northern Ireland has in a bog-standard year?'

'I don't know, fifty, sixty?'

'In an average year: twenty. All domestics. Drunken husband kills drunken wife. You know how many accidental deaths there are every year?'

'No,' I said wearily.

'About four hundred. In other words you are twenty times more likely to die by accident than in a non-terrorist-related homicide.'

'I see.'

'Do you see, Duffy? Because Harper McCullough and Mary Fitzpatrick didn't see. And that batty doctor didn't see.'

'Did Lizzie have any enemies at all?'

'Nope. None that came out of the woodwork. We interviewed her friends. We talked to her professors across the water. She was well liked. She was even . . . she was even a bit dull. She was into the law, Harper, horses.'

'What about the Fitzpatricks? They were a Republican family, weren't they? Annie was married to Dermot McCann and he was doing time in the Maze. Could it have been some kind of revenge attack or something?'

'Without a claim of responsibility? And in this elaborate manner? And of a woman? Have you heard of such a thing before?'

'It's not really the MO, is it?'

'No.'

I ordered another couple of pints and two bags of salt and vinegar crisps. While they were getting poured I stuck twenty pence in the jukebox and went for three Elvis numbers: 'Suspicious Minds', 'In The Ghetto' and 'Suspicious Minds' again.

I sat back down with food, beer and music.

'Ta,' Chief Inspector Beggs said.

'Could the murderer have been hiding in the bar the whole time and then maybe snuck out the next day when no one would have noticed?'

'No.'

'How can you be sure?'

'Because the constables who broke into the bar that night treated it as a crime scene. The broken-down front door was kept under constant surveillance. I arrived on the premises some ten minutes later and I conducted a thorough search of the place. This included the cellar and every available crawl space or empty barrel, and the full barrels too! I can assure you, Inspector Duffy, that there was no one hiding in the Henry Joy McCracken waiting for a chance to escape.'

'OK,' I said, and wrote this in my notebook, too, with a note to myself to thoroughly search the pub for any concealed hiding places.

He smiled and began filling a pipe. 'Like I say, it's not my place to tell Special Branch their business, Inspector, but if you'll excuse the pun, you're barking up the wrong tree. Geddit?'

'I get it,' I said and finished my pint of Bass.

'All right, me old chum, I'll walk you back to the station and get you the photocopy of that file,' he said.

We went back to the barracks, I got the file, thanked the Chief Inspector for his time and made my way to Antrim Hospital. In the car park I read his full report on Lizzie's death. It was thirty pages long with complete witness statements, photographs of the body, of the pub, a comprehensive timeline, Dr Kent's autopsy report and the coroner's verdict. The file had been stamped 'No Further Action' and it was clear that Antrim RUC considered this to be a closed case. Chief Inspector Beggs was not the usual time-serving incompetent that you found in these out-of-the way stations. He was an astute, thoughtful officer who was well read and good at his job.

At this stage everything was looking like an accidental death, which was not what Mrs Fitzpatrick wanted to hear, but if that was the truth then somehow I'd have to break it to her.

I locked the car, buttoned my jacket and went inside the hospital.

Dr Kent, it turned out, was only a part-timer and he wasn't in the wards that day but the nursing station was kind enough to give me his home address.

He had no listed phone number so I drove out to a small sheep farm in a boggy townland south of Lough Neagh. Radio 3 were playing *The Legend of the Invisible City of Kitezh* by Rimsky-Korsakov – good head-clearing music if you're ever looking for some.

Dr Kent lived alone on a dozen desolate-looking acres. The wall of his barn had been painted with the words 'Jesus died so that ye might live! Repent now and accept Christ as your personal saviour!'

I parked the car and walked over the yard among chickens

and a friendly nanny goat. Dr Kent appeared with a border collie and I was a little dismayed to discover that he seemed to be well into his seventies. He had a full white beard and a rather wild hedge of white hair.

'Dr Kent?'

'Aye.'

'Inspector Sean Duffy of the RUC Special Branch.'

I shook his hand and observed him close up. His skin had a healthy country tan and he was lean but not frail. His watery brown eyes looked sharp.

'What do Special Branch want with me?' he asked, a little worried, looking furtively at his barn. He almost certainly had an illegal still over there, which was more the concern of Customs and Excise.

To put him at ease I quickly told him that Special Branch were taking another look at the death of Lizzie Fitzpatrick. He didn't initially recall the case, but when I told him the details it came back.

He invited me into his kitchen, where he made tea and offered me Veda bread and butter, which I accepted.

'Aye, that was an odd murder and no mistake,' he said, sitting opposite me at the sturdy, beautiful bog-oak kitchen table. He had a very slight Scottish accent which I knew would prejudice me in his favour. Everyone liked their doctors to be Scottish and their psychiatrists to be German. The Bible quote on the barn, the putative still and his age prejudiced me against him, so it would all balance out.

'Are you sure it was a murder, Dr Kent?'

'Aye, I am. She was struck on the head with a rounded wooden object, possibly a rolling pin, or a wooden pole, or a rounders bat, something of the sort. The initial blow knocked her unconscious and then the murderer snapped her neck with a quick and powerful lateral movement.'

'You were on the scene?'

'No, but I conducted the autopsy first thing the next morning.'

'It was impossible at that stage to be more precise about the time of death?'

'What did I write in the report?'

'Between 10 p.m. and midnight.'

'Yes, that sounds about right.'

'I've read your findings. There was no sexual dimension to the crime, no other signs of violence. Nothing under her nails. No struggle. Does that not seem strange to you?'

'Not strange at all. Her assailant struck her from behind. She fell to the ground unconscious, and the assailant manhandled her into a position where he could break her neck. There would be no defensive wounds in such a case.'

'Well, yes, Doctor, I see that, but it poses the question why, doesn't it? If there was no sexual motive and nothing was taken from the till . . .'

'There are other reasons to kill someone.'

'Of course, but Lizzie was well liked, she had no enemies that we know about, and there was no paramilitary dimension. And then there's the compelling fact that the pub was locked and bolted from the inside. Does it not seem more likely that she was the victim of an accident? The light bulb was in her hand, the bulb in the socket was dead . . .'

He shook his head, stood up and opened the window, letting in a salty breeze from the lough.

'I can't account for any of that. All I know is that the wound on her head was consistent with a rounded, blunt piece of wood, not a flat hardwood floor, and the snapping of her neck vertebrae was more consistent with a sudden violent lateral motion – exactly the sort of damage that would be inflicted if someone (admittedly a very strong or a very angry man) grabbed her head in his hands and snapped it to the back and right.'

'Who would know how to do something like that?'

'If you were raised in the country you might have done that to a rabbit or even a lamb more than once.'

'Is it *impossible* that she fell off the bar?'

He looked at me with annoyance. 'No, sonny! It's not impossible! I never said it was impossible. I wouldn't say that. I merely said that I think that this is the most likely explanation for her injuries. And as for that light bulb of yours. The light bulb was in her right hand, was it not?'

'I thought of that. It says in the file that she *was* right handed.'

'When you're taking out a dead light bulb don't you keep the new light bulb in your left hand and unscrew the dead one with your right?'

'Maybe you do, or maybe you wait until you're balanced and then switch the bulbs.'

'Ach, well . . . The killer put it in there, that's what I think. To fool us.'

'But with all the other circumstantial evidence, would it not seem, Dr Kent, that the probabilities are more in favour of an accident?'

'And who would change a light bulb in the dark? All the lights were turned off.'

'As Chief Inspector Beggs pointed out to me, you have to turn the lights off if you're going to change the light bulb, otherwise you could get electrocuted. Especially in an old pub with dodgy wiring. And there was light from the street lamp outside.'

He thought about this for a moment and fluffed the white flecks of beard under his chin. He sat down again and shook his head. 'I'm not a policeman, Inspector Duffy, I'm just a country physician. Fifty years I've been doctoring to this parish. Since 1933. You see a lot and you hear a lot in that time. And you learn to trust your instincts.'

'I'm sure you do, Dr Kent. I'm sure you've seen a lot more of life than I have.'

'Oh aye. Surely. It's been hard out here, alone.'

'You were never married?'

'Emily went to the Lord in 1944. Not the war. Tuberculosis. It took us both but I pulled through. I must have given it to her through contact with a patient. She was never a strong lass.'

'I'm sorry.'

'Long time ago. I've been out here by myself since then, although I cannae say that I have never felt her spirit about me from time to time.'

I munched on the thick, delicious, obviously home-made Veda bread.

'This is good,' I told him.

'Let me ask you a question, if I may, young man,' Dr Kent said.

'Go ahead.'

'Why do you think Lizzie Fitzpatrick locked the doors of the pub and put both bolts across if she was on her way home? She'd just sent the last of the customers packing, isn't that right?'

'Yes.'

'Well, all she had to do was clean up a few glasses and turn the lights off. She wouldn't bother to bolt the front door, would she? She'd maybe just turn the key in the lock so a passing customer wouldn't come in. But that big heavy bolt, why would she lock the door and bolt it if she was going to be heading out in a couple of minutes?'

'Why do you think?'

'I have no idea, but I thought it was a trifle odd myself.'

'Perhaps she was nervous. Maybe she was going through the till receipts and she wanted the place locked up nice and safe.'

'Aye . . . could be, could be . . .'

'Did you happen to know her before the, uh, incident?'

'No. Not really. I know the family to see, and I believe that I drank in the pub once or twice. It was a Catholic establishment and, well . . . it wasn't my sort of place. You're a Catholic, aren't you? I can tell.'

'Yes.'

'Do you not find that your religion causes problems in a largely Protestant, some would say sectarian, force like the RUC?'

'It's all right.'

'Hmmm,' he said dubiously. 'And it's very peculiar that the RUC Special Branch would take an interest in a four-year-old case of accidental death.'

I smiled. 'Aye, it is, but "ours is not to reason why . . ."'

He put down his teacup. 'Everyone misquotes that poem. It actually goes like this: "Theirs not to make reply/Theirs not to reason why/Theirs but to do and die/Into the valley of Death/Rode the six hundred." There's a difference of perspective between "our" and "their". Tennyson would never presume to speak for the soldiers, would he? Him, a rector's son?'

'I'm sure you're right, Dr Kent.'

I finished my tea.

'Shall I walk you out?' he asked me.

We went into the farmyard again. The chickens pecked at my feet and the nanny goat took an interest in the sleeve of my leather jacket.

'Someone has to speak up for that wee girl. Only I saw the truth. I'm the only one that believes she was murdered,' Dr Kent announced.

'Not quite. You and Mrs Fitzpatrick and the boyfriend.'

'Aye, I convinced them. A terrible thing to do, some might say. I've seen Mary Fitzpatrick from time to time and it's given her nothing but torment the last few years. It's a doctor's job to ease the minds of those who are suffering. But he also serves truth, doesn't he? Truth!'

'Dr Kent, would you be offended if I got a second opinion on your physical examination of Lizzie's body?'

'No, not at all. That's a fine idea! I'll look out my files and send them to you.'

I gave him my address.

'I'll be interested to hear what your doctor has to say. I only wish we'd taken an X-ray photograph. I did some drawings for the autopsy. That's what I was taught. That's the old way.'

He leaned in and said in a half-whisper, 'But of course, you could always exhume the body and take the photographs now if you need to. The flesh will most likely be gone but the bones will not have decayed.'

'Jesus, I can only hope it doesn't come to that.'

16: ANNIE McCANN

I drove to a phone box and put in a call to Kate at the number she'd given me. It was an odd area code and I wasn't sure whether I was calling her at the MI5 HQ in Bessbrook or the command headquarters in North Down. A secretary answered and when I told her who I was, she said she was putting me through to Kate Prentice. A surname at last.

'Long time, no hear,' she said with a playful but slightly annoyed tinge to her voice.

'I've been following leads.'

'Any promising ones?'

'Actually there might be one.'

'Really?'

'Yes. But it's not a matter I want to discuss over a telephone. I'll call you in a couple of days when I see how things shake out. It might be nothing, but then again it might be something. OK?'

'I knew you'd do it. I told them,' she said excitedly.

'I haven't done anything yet. I'm just saying that I might have a lead. OK?'

'All right, Sean, keep on it.'

'If I need to, say, exhume a corpse, I'd be able to get the powers to do that, would I? Even with my unusual status?'

'Exhume a corpse? What is this lead?'

'I just want to know that I've got the full authority of a regular cop.'

'Of course you do, and the full backing of our department.'

'Good . . . All right, that's all for now. I'll talk to you about this in a couple of days.'

'Yes. And well done, Sean!'

'Save your praise. The ball hasn't even got rolling yet.'

I hung up and drove back to Mary Fitzpatrick's house in Ballykeel village on the east shore of Lough Neagh.

I parked the Beemer outside the coaching house. The rain had stopped and the sun was coming out now. I opened the glove compartment and took out my old Dictaphone.

'Interviews Lizzie Fitzpatrick case, day 1 . . .' I began, and made a few notes to myself. I played back the notes and tried to make sense of it all but I didn't have it yet. I put the Dictaphone back in the glove compartment.

I walked down the drive, pushed the bell and after a pause Annie answered it.

She'd lost none of her looks. She had her mother's red hair, but hers corkscrewed in all directions in a way that some would find gypsy-like and charming and others a bit overboard for a woman who was inching towards the wrong side of thirty. She was pale, of course, and her striking blue eyes had lost none of their power and lustre. Her nose had the sharp angled prominence of the aristocrat's (an O'Neill bloodline perhaps) and her lips were full. She had always smiled easily and even now, after the death of her sister and her divorce from Dermot, her expression was warm.

She was wearing jeans and an enormous home-made woollen jumper with reindeer on it.

'Hello?' she said, not recognising me.

'It's Sean Duffy,' I said.

'Sean Duffy!' she exclaimed, and pulled me in for a hug. She kissed me on the cheek and then stood back to look at me.

'Sean Duffy as I live and breathe. Is it really you?'

'It's me.'

'You look thin. Police work doesn't agree with you,' she said.

'It can be stressful,' I agreed.

She looked at me with a trace of suspicion now. 'Me ma told me you'd been over.'

'Yes. I have. I work for Special Branch, I examine the cold cases. And I, uh, I came across your sister's file. I thought I would look into it.'

'Did you now? Lizzie. Poor Lizzie. Jesus. Not a day goes by when I don't think about her. Did you ever meet her?'

'No, I didn't. To tell the truth, Annie, I didn't even know you had a wee sister, or if I did I'd forgotten.'

'And you just happened upon her file?' she asked, and again there was a trace of doubt in her voice.

'It was passed on to me. They thought that I might be interested because I sort of knew the family.'

She accepted that, looked at me again and smiled. 'Dear oh dear! Sean Duffy as I live and breathe.'

'The very same.'

'What on earth possessed you to join the police?'

'It's a long story, Annie . . . You're not sorry I've come, are you?'

'No. Well, I don't know. You heard about Dermot? Out of the Maze, I mean?'

'Of course.'

'Look at you! A policeman! And you popping up to look into Lizzie's death after all these years. It didn't occur to you to let sleeping dogs lie?' she said in a lilting voice that had changed little in the years since I had seen her last.

'I have to do what I'm told, Annie, and for some reason they thought that this case was still something that we should look at.'

'Me ma thinks Lizzie was murdered,' she said in an undertone.

'But not you?'

'It's tragic. I mean, really tragic. But I mean, Sean, the facts speak for themselves . . . she fell off the bar, God love her.'

'It certainly looks that way.'

'Good luck convincing Ma. I think Harper finally believes it, but not her.' She reached out and patted my arm. 'Sure, why don't you come in?'

We were sucked into the large but claustrophobic and gloomy living room.

I greeted Mrs Fitzpatrick and we made an edgy eye contact.

'I'm sorry you're not going to meet Jim on this visit either, Inspector Duffy. My husband is fishing,' she said.

'Or what he says is fishing,' Annie said. 'Since we closed up the pub, he goes out every day. He sits by the lough with his pole. He never really catches anything although sometimes a trout will jump on to the line.'

Mary looked at Annie with a mixture of shock and dismay. How could she speak so glibly about her father in front of an outsider? In front of a policeman?

'Would you like a cup of tea, Inspector Duffy?' Mrs Fitzpatrick asked.

'No, thank you. I was wondering actually if I could take a look at the pub today, if that would be convenient? I've been reading the case notes and I've talked to the investigating officer and I'd really like to see inside the pub, to visualise exactly what happened that night.'

Mary nodded with satisfaction. It sounded like I was determined to do a thorough job. 'I'll get the key. Annie'll walk you over. It's not ten minutes from here.'

'I'm sure I can find it. I, uh, I don't want to compromise either of you by having you seen in public with a police officer . . . in the circumstances, you know?' I said.

'What, with Dermot on the run?' Annie offered.

'Yeah.'

'As far as I know no one elected Dermot McCann High King of Ireland! And no one will tell me who I can be seen in public with and who I can't!' Mrs Fitzpatrick exclaimed. 'I'll take you over there if Annie doesn't want to!'

'Jesus, if you'd let me get a word in, Mother . . . I don't mind taking Sean over.'

'No, really, it's OK, I can get there by myself, I—'

'If anyone asks me, we'll tell them the truth. You're a policeman looking into Lizzie's death. No one in Ballykeel or Antrim will object to that!' Annie insisted.

'And if they do they can answer to me!' Mary said, and gave me a brief look that I understood as a further injunction against bringing up Dermot's name.

Annie grabbed a coat and a pair of boots and I followed her through the house and out the back gate.

We walked along the boggy lough shore and along a tree-lined lane. There was a bluebell wood to our left and the village up ahead to the right. The trees were filled with wood pigeons and down by the water there were gulls, curlews, oyster catchers. Two wee muckers were in the wood swinging at one another with wooden swords, yelling obscenities and committing a messy angiocide on the wild flowers.

'It's a lovely place this,' I said to Annie.

'Aye, it is. This is an ancient forest, not a plantation, and just up there was where they massed for the Battle of Antrim. You know that story?'

'I do. Henry Joy McCracken led the attack on the British garrison. Protestant and Catholic fighting together against the English.' And before she could say it, I added, 'And here's me working for those self-same English.'

She turned to look at me. The smile was gone but that there was still an ironic glint in her eyes. 'I always liked you, Sean. And Dermot liked you. That's why he could not believe it when he heard that you'd joined the police. He was furious. You were like a wee brother to him.'

'That's bullshit, Annie. Dermot had no time for me at school and very little time for me afterwards. Dermot was in the cool crowd and I wasn't. Dermot was political and I couldn't give a shit. Dermot only kept in touch with me after St Malachy's because I had a car and he occasionally wanted me to drive him places.'

'Don't be silly, Sean.'

'I've thought a lot about this, Annie. Dermot never saw me as an equal. He condescended to hang out with me from time to time but that was all.'

'And yet you came to him after Bloody Sunday. You begged him to let you join the IRA, didn't you?'

'He told you about that?'

'It's true, isn't it?'

I nodded. 'Aye.'

'But he didn't let you join, did he? He didn't think you had the nerve for it. He thought you would lose your bottle at a crucial moment.'

I bristled at that. 'Jesus! Is that what he told you?'

'That's what he said.'

'I did ask Dermot if I could join the IRA and he did turn me down but he said it was because he wanted me to finish my PhD at Queen's. He said that "the movement need men with brains as well as brawn".'

Annie shook her head and gave a little laugh. 'That was a lie, Sean. That was a lie to spare your feelings. He didn't think you had the bottle. He didn't think you were reliable. He thought you'd fuck it up and get yourself killed.'

I felt chilled to the bone. 'Did he really say that to you?'

'You've gone all white. Don't get offended.'

'Don't get offended? That's a terrible thing to say about anybody. Bloody hell! If he told you that it doesn't sound like a man who liked me very much, does it?'

'I'm sorry, Sean, I'm a big blabber, so I am.'

Yeah, but you're not denying it.

We had reached the village now and I could see the Henry Joy McCracken pub next to a tiny newsagent and post office.

'I'm sorry I brought it up. It's water under the bridge, Sean.'

'I'm sorry you brought it up too. Jesus!'

She put her hand on my arm and gave it a little squeeze. 'He said a lot of things. Don't take everything so personally.'

'I'm not taking it personally. I'm not interested in Dermot. I'm only here to see if there's anything untoward in Lizzie's death,' I said.

She smiled and didn't reply and we walked across the quiet street to the Henry Joy McCracken.

'I forgot to bring a torch. Will the lights come on?' I asked.

'I have no idea,' she said, taking the key out of her pocket. 'I haven't been in here for years.'

'We don't need to go in just yet. Let me have a wee gander at these windows first.'

I walked around the pub, which was a small, single-storeyed building with no adjoining buildings or structures. It was a late nineteenth-century construction in an attractive red brick. The windows had been covered with cast-iron bars to prevent burglaries and as I examined them I saw that the bars were thick and six inches apart. No one was crawling through those. The bars were attached to heavy frames that were solidly bolted into the brick with a dozen thick 10mm hex bolts. I tugged on every single bar to see whether they were all securely fastened to the frame, but there was no give at all in any of them.

'Do you know when these window bars were put in? They weren't original features of the building, were they?'

'No. Me da had them put in at the start of the Troubles. 1971 maybe, somewhere around then.'

'Every one of them is rock solid,' I said. 'Did you notice the paint on them?'

'What about it?'

'It's consistent on the bars and the bolts.'

'Which means?'

'Well, to get through this you'd have to take the hex bolts out, all twelve of them, and even with a power tool that's not going to be easy. And then after the murder you have to stand here at the window and reattach the frame. Ten-minute job at least. Someone would have seen you. But let's say you did it and no one saw you . . . you're still screwed because you would have left traces of the power wrench in the bolt-head paint and the brick mortar would have been disturbed. But as you can see, the paint on the bars and the bolts on all the windows is undisturbed. Unless the killer also stood here on the night of the murder and painted every bolt head and every bar in all the windows.'

'Someone would have noticed the smell.'

'Indeed.'

'So no one came in through the windows.'

'No one came in through the windows. That's for certain. Let's go round the back and see this rear door.'

At the back of the pub there was a low breeze-block wall and a wooden gate that led into a yard with some pallets and a few empty beer kegs. The wall was easily climbable but the back door itself was a thick oak job with stainless-steel hinges.

I got down on my honkers to examine the lock.

The lock was a Portadown Lock Company tumbler lock from the 1950s. Model No. 13 by the look of it.

'I don't have the back-door key,' Annie said.

'I don't think we'll need it.'

I took my trusty lock-pick kit from my jacket pocket.

'Let me just see now,' I said, examining the mechanism.

'What are you doing?' she asked as I inserted the feeler pick into the lock.

'Gimme a minute,' I said confidently. But in fact it only took forty-five seconds with the tension wrench, an angle pick and a tiny amount of torque.

The lock clicked. I pushed the handle and as I knew I would I came right up against the deadbolt bar. The door didn't move a centimetre. If the bolt had been across the night Lizzie was killed the killer certainly didn't get in this way.

If there was a killer.

'Let's go to the entrance,' I said.

'All right.'

We made our way to the front of the pub again.

'No cellar doors, for delivering kegs and barrels?' I asked Annie.

'Nah. Da rolled the barrels right in the back door.'

'Do you know about any other way in?'

'I don't. And I played in here as a kid. Kids are always the first to find lost wallets and secret tunnels and things, aren't they?'

'Yeah, they are,' I agreed. 'How long has the pub been closed?'

'More or less since Lizzie died.'

'So what do you do for money?'

'That's a bit of a rude question,' Annie said.

'I'm a cop, Annie, I get to ask impertinent questions.'

'How is it relevant?'

'Everything's relevant. How are you getting by? I'm sure Dermot never paid you a penny in alimony. Your mother doesn't seem to work. The pub's closed. What do you live on?'

'Da inherited a lot of land from his dad in County Donegal. We've been selling it off in dribs and drabs for the last few years. Eventually we'll have to sell this place, too. It's a good location near the water. I'm sure somebody can make a go of it.'

We had reached the front door now and I could see where it had been ripped off the hinges by the police battering ram. They had reset the same door with different hinges on another part of the brick wall.

'So they knocked this door down?' I asked.

'Yes.'

'Were you there that night?'

'No, I was in Derry.'

'Who was there?'

'Mum, a couple of policemen and I think Harper had made it back from Belfast. Are you going to do your trick with the lock on this one?' she asked.

'Nah, you can get us in.'

The lock was an identical Portadown tumbler lock. A competent locksmith or burglar could easily have picked it, but that didn't matter much. The two deadbolts were what made this affair a locked-room mystery.

Annie put the key in the lock and opened the door. She fumbled for the light switch and after a moment the lights came on.

We walked inside. It was a single room with a long wooden bar at the back. About a dozen tables with wooden chairs stacked on top of them. Hammer-beam ceiling sure enough.

I had a hunch that Chief Inspector Beggs might have been exaggerating his own fastidiousness, so the first thing I did was examine the cellar.

I thought that this might be a key to the whole mystery but when we went down there I discovered no secret trapdoor or tunnel. The brickwork was solid, the floor thick. It was basically just a glorified storage room that you could barely stand up straight in. It would have taken two seconds to ascertain whether someone was in here or not.

'Do you think someone was hiding down here?' Annie asked.

'Beggs and his men searched down here, but I was more interested in the brickwork to see if there was evidence of recent pointing or a false wall or anything like that.'

'And?'

'Nothing like that.'

We went back upstairs and I examined the hammer-beam roof, which was a lovely job: a really nice pastiche of a medieval ceiling in stained pine planking.

The roof was planked and covered with slate tiles and was

about twenty feet above the bar. If you'd brought a tall ladder and a hammer, you could have smashed your way out through the roof, but how you would have concealed all the mess was beyond me, and surely the cops would have seen a great big honking hole.

Nah, you couldn't get out that way.

A dozen or so light bulbs were hanging directly from the ceiling, with one of them right above the bar.

'Is this the one she was supposedly trying to change?' I asked.

Annie was too upset to look at it, but she nodded her head.

I climbed on top of the bar. I could reach it without much difficulty but then I was five foot eleven.

'How tall was your sister?'

'About five two, five three, something like that?'

'This might have been a bit tricky for her,' I said.

'It obviously was.'

I climbed down and went to check the deadbolts on the front and back doors of the premises. They were heavy, sturdy iron bars that ran along the back of the door and hooked into a thick loop in the brickwork. The bar and the loop were held in place with two-inch Phillips-head stainless-steel screws. Even after the cops had used the battering ram on the front door these screws and the bolt had remained in place.

I ran the deadbolt back and forth a few times and locked it into place. It was heavy and just as solid as it looked. The door fitted tightly against the wall and there was only a negligible gap underneath it. The deadbolt was so heavy that attaching a wire to it and trying to somehow close it from the outside was the least likely of all the possibilities here.

'Well?' Annie said.

I shook my head.

'I'm perplexed. If these bolts were across then there was no way anyone could have got in here to murder her like Dr Kent suggests.'

'The bolts were across, weren't they?'

'Then unless you believe in the supernatural it must have been an accident. A tragic accident.'

We took two of the upturned chairs off one of the tables and sat down.

'Tell me about the boyfriend, Harper,' I asked.

'She was a great girl and of course Harper was mad for her,' she said.

'Harper loved her?'

'Oh yes.'

'And she him?'

'Yeah.'

'Talk of marriage?'

'I think so. Yes. Definitely. They would have made a lovely couple.'

There was something a little stilted about her remarks and I wondered whether Annie had been as close to Lizzie as she might have liked. But there was no percentage to be had in bringing something like that up . . .

I looked at the smooth bar covered with a thick coating of dust, dead moths and my footprints.

'It would be so easy to slip from here and break your neck,' I said.

Annie pulled out a packet of Rothmans Special Mild and offered me one. I took it and she grabbed a packet of matches from an ashtray on one of the tables. We lit our cigarettes and sat there for a while.

'You ever hear from your sister in Canada?' I asked, completely blanking on the name.

'Nah. Hardly ever. She wants to forget Ireland ever existed.'

'I don't blame her.'

'I don't blame her either. It's probably the right move. This country is fucked,' she said.

'Yeah.'

'Maybe if your English friends would piss off and leave us alone we could work it out,' she said.

She wasn't going to suck me in. 'Politics? Really, Annie? I mean, who cares?' I said.

'You used to.'

'Me? I never gave a shite about politics. I still don't. Certainly not bloody Irish politics. No, your sis has the right idea. Did you ever meet any of Dermot's brothers? I'll bet you didn't. They're all in Australia or America or somewhere. That's the play. Go to America. Sing a few songs about the Old Country from time to time, donate a few pennies to the cause now and again, but don't ever go back.'

'Why do you stay?' Annie asked.

'Why indeed?'

The vile Rothmans Special Mild was burning down to the filter unsmoked. Annie took it from me and stamped it on the floor. She wiped the ash from the back of my hand and gave my fingertips a little squeeze.

'Will you stay for tea, Sean?' she asked.

'Is that an invitation?'

'Yes.'

'I'd like that.'

17: VERTEBRAE

We locked up the Henry Joy McCracken and walked back through the village to the Fitzpatricks' house. We didn't talk, but I noticed that she sometimes stole glances at me when she thought I wasn't looking.

Still sizing me up, was Annie.

And me her, come to that. Feeling a little guilty now, too. How could I not be?

I stayed with the Fitzpatricks for tea.

Jim Fitzpatrick came home from his fishing at five o'clock, stinking of mud and whiskey. He was a big scary bastard, six foot two, bald, seventeen stone. An old-school Republican, but the sort who grumbles about the 'men of violence' and moves to a small town and opens a pub, not the sort who nurses grievances across the decades. And he came from money, which distinguished him from most of the guys who ended up in the H Blocks with nothing to lose.

He had in fact caught a fish. A massive brown trout that he had already gutted and beheaded.

Mary made us champ to go with the skillet-fried trout and onions and we talked about the weather and this and that.

I never mentioned the case and Lizzie's name did not come up. Lizzie's pictures had been removed from the walls and it was clear that the wound was still raw with the man. In fact it was a wound that was going to kill him. He was putting away at least a bottle a day and probably more.

I took my leave at six and drove back to Carrickfergus.

I debated whether I should keep this confidential or not, but I knew it was just delaying the inevitable so I called up Kate and told her the whole story.

She wasn't sure about it and told me that she felt that I shouldn't spend all my time investigating Lizzie Fitzpatrick's death because there was no guarantee that Mary Fitzpatrick could deliver Dermot.

I told her that she was right about that and that I would pursue all our other leads.

I laughed when I hung up. There were no other leads. There were not going to be any other leads. When Dermot finally activated his cell and started blowing people up, perhaps he'd make a mistake and leave a forensic trace, but no one in Ireland was ever going to give him up. Not without a very good reason.

The following Tuesday I drove to Aldergrove airport and caught the 10 a.m. flight to Aberdeen. I hadn't been to Aberdeen before but I felt I knew it because Telly Savalas was always telling us what a great city it was in a cheesy film that ran before every movie I'd seen for the last five years. Sometimes you'd only get to see TV's Kojak talking about Aberdeen for five minutes before there would be a bomb scare and the cinema would be evacuated.

I flew into the gleaming new airport and caught a taxi.

Aberdeen was a strange place to be in the summer of 1984. It was about the only place in Britain that wasn't in the crapper. After her brave boys had retaken the Falkland Islands, Mrs Thatcher had handily won the 1983 election. In early '84 a buoyant Mrs T had decided to end government subsidies to the coal industry. As she knew they would, the National Union of Mineworkers had come out on strike. The NUM had brought down the previous Tory administration and Mrs Thatcher was determined to get revenge for that and to end the union's power for ever. She had stockpiled years' worth of coal at power stations and had guaranteed to keep the pits open for any workers who wanted to defy the picket lines. Every day the English newspapers were full of pictures of battles between cops and picketers outside collieries in Wales and the north of England. But Aberdeen was above all this. It relied on a quite different fossil fuel. It was an oil-boom town. House prices were skyrocketing, wages were soaring – a house cleaner in the Bridge of Don made more than a detective inspector in the RUC.

My ex-girlfriend Laura had come here because she'd been offered a professorship in pathology at cash-rich Aberdeen University.

It was a chance to build a new life and she'd taken it.

I didn't blame her. Maybe I was even a little envious. She'd been able to cut through the guilt and the loyalties and the emotions and go.

Of course I missed her, but I don't think it went deeper than that. At least I hoped not.

We'd arranged to meet at the Student Union Bar, which she thought would be a nice neutral space. Of course, at lunchtime it was chaotic and it took me a while to spot her. She'd cut her hair short and it didn't suit her. She was wearing a subdued red dress, low-heeled black shoes and a diamond engagement ring.

She kissed me on the cheek and told me I looked great.

I said the same about her.

We were both lying already and that made me a little sad.

'Let's get out of here! It's more packed than normal,' she said.

We moved to a café adjoining a golf course overlooking the North Sea.

'Life's treating you OK?' I asked.

'It's treating me well,' she said.

'You're back as a detective, then, I see,' she said.

'Yes.'

'That meant a lot to you, didn't it? What was it you told me . . .

the classic peeler schism is between detective and beat cop.'

It pleased me that she'd remembered that. 'That's right,' I said.

A waiter came. I asked what was good and Laura said that it had to be the grilled haddock. We ordered two and a bottle of wine that she picked out.

'You're getting married,' I said.

'Did you run into my mother?'

'Is he nice?'

'You'd like him. He is a diver. A professional diver. A real guy's guy. He'd be right up your alley.'

I told her that he sounded great to pre-empt further discussion but she thought I really wanted to know and gave me the full treatment: his family history, his childhood, how they'd met. I listened politely and took none of it in.

Our food arrived and when we'd eaten I asked her about the case.

'Did you get a chance to look at those documents I sent you?'

'Yes, yes I did.'

'And?'

'Your Dr Kent seems to be a little . . .'

'What? Eccentric? Mad?'

'Old-fashioned in his terminology and technique.'

'He's in his seventies. Late seventies, I think.'

'That would explain it.'

'So is he off base?'

She opened her bag and removed the file I'd sent her by express mail.

'Do you want the details, or just a summary?' she asked.

'Oh, I'll take the details. You know me. Details Duffy.'

'There are seven cervical vertebrae. In his autopsy Dr Kent found that all seven had suffered trauma and the upper three vertebrae had suffered severe trauma. Dr Kent insists that the stress fractures on these vertebrae are primarily latitudinal, not longitudinal, and this convinced him that the trauma your victim suffered was a violent twisting motion, not an impact from a fall or blow.'

'What do you say?'

'I'd say that the evidence tends to bear out Dr Kent's thesis, although it's a shame he didn't think to take an X-ray photograph of the victim's neck. He includes drawings of his pathological study . . .'

'I asked him about that. I suppose in his day it was all drawings. But he said we could exhume the body if we needed to.'

'Yes, he's quite right. The bones won't have decayed. You could still take a good photograph.'

'Can you rule out a fall as a cause of Lizzie's injuries?'

She shook her head. 'Rule it out? No. In effect the human body is a massive spring, and when you drop a spring from a height . . . well, pretty much anything can happen.'

'I know it's not what you do, Laura, but if you were going to assign probabilities to the two scenarios: Lizzie fell off the bar while putting in a light bulb or Lizzie was hit on the head, someone snapped her neck and made it look like an accident . . .'

She thought about it for a while.

'Sixty/forty – murder/accident.'

'Jesus, that's not very convincing. I thought you were going to say eighty/twenty.'

'No. Like I say, it could have been a fall. I think your Dr Kent's hunch is the right one, but I wouldn't want to take it to court.'

I nodded and made a quick scribble in my notebook.

When I was done I found that she had crossed her hands on the table and she was smiling at me.

'How are you doing, Sean?' she asked.

'I'm fine.'

'Are you eating OK?'

'Yes.'

'And you're not drinking too much?'

'No more than everybody else.'

'Everybody else drinks too much.'

'Do you blame them?'

'No.'

She was so beautiful when she smiled like that. So beautiful I couldn't look at her.

'What about you, how are you doing?'

'I've never been happier,' she said, and meant it. 'When we're married and settled, I'm going to try and bring my parents out.'

Behind her the North Sea was a cold indigo with whitecaps scudding across the surface. There were tankers and other massive ships leaving the harbour and heading north-east towards the rigs. That's where the future lay, not west in Ireland, not down the ageing mines . . .

'Looks freezing out there. I suppose you never go swimming?' I asked.

'No. Never.'

'What shade of blue would you call that water? Indigo?'

She grinned a little. It was a feeble conversational gambit. 'Have you considered moving to Britain, Sean? I'm sure the Metropolitan Police would love someone of your abilities.'

'What abilities? I'm your classic big fish, little pond. Let me ask you something. If you're changing a light bulb and you're right handed, don't you need to have the new light bulb in your left hand? You need your good hand to unscrew the bulb, don't you?'

Laura considered this for a moment and imagined her own actions. She shook her head. 'I don't know about that. If it were me I would hold the new light bulb in my right hand until I was balanced and ready to unscrew the dead bulb and then I'd transfer the new one to my left and unscrew the dead light bulb with my right.'

'That's what I said. So you don't think we can draw an inference from the fact that the new light bulb was in her right hand. The hand she would need to unscrew the old one?'

'No.'

I shook my head. 'That seemed pretty thin to me, too.'

I stared at the sea again and Laura began stealing glances at her watch.

'This one's got you baffled, hasn't it?' she said.

'It has. If it wasn't for what you and Dr Kent were telling me I would say that this is a clear-cut case of accidental death. The pub was hermetically sealed from the inside. There was no other way in or out. There were heavy deadbolts on the front and back doors.'

'Could a murderer not have somehow manoeuvred the deadbolts into place from the outside?'

'I examined that possibility and eliminated it. They're just too heavy.'

'And if Dr Kent and myself are both mistaken, then everything becomes much easier, doesn't it?'

'It does indeed!'

'Isn't there a story about a locked room and a murderer who somehow gets in?'

I laughed. 'Are you kidding me? There's an entire literature! An entire genre. I've read a dozen of them in the last two weeks alone. *The Big Bow Mystery*, *The Murders in the Rue Morgue*, *The Mystery of the Yellow Room* . . . a couple of different Willkie Collins, Agatha Christie . . .'

'And how does the killer do it in those?'

'Various methods. The secret passage is one technique, a hidden trapdoor, killing the victim from a distance, then there are the magicians' tricks, the use of animals to do the killing, the supernatural . . . The two I seriously considered were the secret passageway or the possibility that the killer was hiding in the bar when the police arrived and then snuck out through the smashed-in front door some time in the next day or two.'

'And did he?'

'Sneak out, you mean?'

'Yeah.'

'No, he didn't. The cops who arrived at the bar were pretty sharp. They treated it as a crime scene, wouldn't let anyone touch the body or let anyone in or out. Detective Inspector Beggs arrived shortly thereafter and he conducted a thorough search of the premises. He assures me that there was no one hiding in the bar and I believe him.'

'A secret passageway?'

'A lot of those old pubs have a secret way in or out, or a creaky old cellar door where you deliver the barrels. But I checked that place from top to bottom and there was no other entrance except for those locked and barred doors.'

'So that leaves what? Ghosts? A lot of those old pubs have them.'

'There are other explanations. In one of the very first locked-room stories, *The Big Bow Mystery*, we find out that the victim wasn't actually dead until they broke down the door. The killer used misdirection and administered the *coup de grâce* while no one was looking.'

'That didn't happen in your pub, surely?'

'No, it didn't. But if you and Kent are right, something funny happened that night and it wasn't a ghost.'

She smiled and took my hand. The diamond caught the sunlight and sparkled in my eyes. 'It's an ugly circumstance, but it's nice to see that you're wrapped up in something, Sean. I got the feeling that you were fading away for a while there . . .'

I cleared my throat.

'Yeah, I was. I like this job. Finding things out. Restoring order. Putting the world to rights.'

'I'm glad,' she said, and gave my hand a squeeze.

'This case, though. It's a peach. It goes one, two, three, five. I've missed something. I'm not seeing it clearly.'

'You will. You always do, don't you?'

'No. Not always.'

'I'm sure it will be fine,' she said, and smiled patiently. The anodyne of her words just perfect.

'Do you go to mass much?' she asked.

'Mass? No. Never . . . Your fiancé? Is he a Catholic?'

'He's not. It's not a big deal over here. None of that matters.' She smiled.

'Do you think it could have worked? You and me?' I asked.

She shook her head.

'Why?'

'Different worlds. Different wants, you know,' she said diffidently.

'That's not much of an answer.'

She disengaged her hand.

She was in no mood to be pushed or interrogated.

'Do you think there's something wrong with me?' I asked.

She shook her head. 'Of course not!'

'The truth. I'd tell you,' I persisted.

'You want me to tell you if I think there's something wrong with you?'

'Yes.'

'There's nothing wrong with you, you know, just the . . . you know.'

'What, for heaven's sake?'

'You want a medical opinion?' she asked.

'Fire away!'

'Both barrels?'

'There's two barrels full? OK, I can take it.'

'All right. You've got manic-depressive tendencies. You have alcohol-dependency issues. You don't eat properly or exercise. You smoke too much. And working for the police has institutionalised you and, uhm, robbed you of some of your spark and personality.'

'That's a little harsh.'

'I'm sorry. I shouldn't have said that—'

'No. Don't be sorry, if that's what you think.'

She shook her head. 'It's not what I think. It just came tumbling out. You shouldn't have put me on the spot like that.'

'I shouldn't have. Sorry.'

'No, I'm sorry.'

We sat there embarrassed, with neither of us able to think of anything to say.

Laura looked at her watch again.

I stood up. 'Well, I have a plane to catch. I'm grateful for your time.'

I offered her my hand. She pulled me in for a kiss on the cheek instead.

'I'm happy to help, Sean. You be careful now, OK?'

'I will be.'

'Check under your car for bombs.'

'I always do.'

'There's a taxi rank just outside, let me walk you over.'

'OK.'

She walked me to the taxi rank and kissed me again and the cabby drove me through white granite Aberdeen, which was glistening and brilliant and lovely in the summer sun. Kojak would have been happy.

18: THREE MEN AND AN ALIBI

I showered, shaved, put on a shirt, tie, black jeans and leather jacket. I checked under the BMW for bombs and drove to Carrickfergus police station. I found Detective Sergeant McCrabban pretending to work in the CID incident room overlooking the railway embankment.

'Nothing pressing?' I asked.

He shook his head. 'It's been quiet. As they say in the pictures, too quiet.'

I nodded. The big IRA bombing campaign still hadn't started but they had the resources, the training, the targets and the men. It wasn't a matter of if but when it was going to happen. It was July in Northern Ireland, so of course there'd been boring old riots, but public disorder was a job for regular peelers, not detectives.

'You want to take a look at my case?' I asked him.

He stroked the moustache he'd been growing – with very limited success – for the last few months.

'Aye, OK.'

I gave him the file and my typed notes and made two cups of tea while he read it.

When he'd drunk the tea and eaten a couple of biscuits, he handed the binder back to me.

'Are you sure about this whole locked-room scenario?'

'Yes.'

'No secret tunnels, anything like that?'

'No secret tunnels. I checked the floor. Solid concrete, and it wasn't built in the era of priest's holes and the like.'

'*You* don't think it was an accident?'

'No.'

He shook his head and rubbed the back of his neck. 'I don't know, then, Sean.'

'I was going to take a run up to Belfast and interview the patrons who were in the Henry Joy McCracken that night. Supposedly they were the last people to see her alive and—'

Crabbie got to his feet. 'Of course I'll come. I'll leave a note for Matt and tell him to mind the shop.'

We booked out a police Land Rover and drove up the M5 into town. It was raining and sea spray was blowing over the lagoons on to the road. A man had crashed his Hillman Hunter and we had to pull in to help the eejit. His engine was on fire and he was standing next to the vehicle, sobbing. When the traffic cops showed up we bolted. Not so much as a thank-you.

'I did some research on "locked-room problems",' Crabbie said from the passenger's seat.

'Aye?'

'Quite the literature.'

'Indeed.'

'You've read the one about the killer monkey?'

'*Rue Morgue*. Yes.'

'The one about the ice bullet?'

'Yup, and there's a Charlie Chan film with a frozen blood bullet which is even better.'

'None of them seems to quite apply to our set of circumstances.'

'No.'

'Who's on our list of suspects today?' Crabbie asked.

'Arnold Yeats. He's the one at Queen's.'

'Won't he be away?'

'Nah, he has to run a summer school, the poor bastard.'

'Unlucky for him and lucky for us,' Crabbie concurred.

Belfast in the summer was one big tinderbox, and anyone who could get out of town usually did – one of the perks of being a school teacher or a university professor.

And this year the marching season had been worse than normal; my theory was that this was because the miners' strike in England was getting all the media attention: Belfast was the plain girl at the dance who was having to make a scene just to get noticed.

We saw the aftermath of rioting (overturned bins, smashed bus stops, burnt-out cars) as we arrived at Queen's University's Gothic façade. We parked in a tow-away zone and found Professor Yeats in a massive lecture theatre giving a talk on what he had titled 'Weird History'.

Crabbie and I slipped in at the back and sat down.

The lecture theatre was packed with a mostly older crowd and a few young East Asians.

Yeats was a small man with a black beard and bushy black hair. He looked about thirty, but, in fact, was closer to forty. He was wearing jeans and Converse high-tops and a black T-shirt. He was giving his lecture sitting cross-legged on top of his desk.

'One of the most unusual courts established in this period was the Court of Love. Has anyone heard of that?' Professor Yeats asked in a Home Counties accent.

No one in the lecture theatre had heard of the Court of Love.

'On Valentine's Day 1400 Charles VI of France established a Court of Love, a *Cour Amoureuse*, to regulate the rules of love and to hear disputes between lovers,' Professor Yeats went on. 'The Court's judges were selected by a panel of women on the basis of oral recitation or written samples of poetry. One of the first cases was of a man who had made wedding vows, but when he came into property after his father's death had renounced his vow and pledged himself to a woman of a higher station. The judges of the *Cour Amoureuse* decided that he could not be compelled to marry his former sweetheart since no law could force love upon a man who does not wish it. However, for his breach of the rules of courtesy he was made to compensate his former mistress to the tune of fifty pounds of gold, a sum tidy enough to help heal any wounded heart.'

Professor Yeats went on to talk about the penalties for pages who had stolen their mistress' billets-doux, for boastful lovers gossiping about their conquests and then, as a climax to all this, he segued into the story of Abelard and Heloise, giving plenty of eye-watering details on Abelard's fate.

When the lecture was over we walked to the front of the lecture hall and I introduced us.

'Detective Inspector Duffy of Special Branch, Detective Sergeant McCrabban of Carrickfergus RUC.'

'Is it about my car?' Yeats said excitedly.

'Someone stole your car?'

'I was hijacked last week by joyriders. Have you found it? It's a TR7, it's a bit of a classic.'

The chances of recovering a vehicle that had been taken by joyriders were close to zero. I hadn't heard of a case yet where the joyriders didn't run the car until the gearbox or transmission gave out, whereupon they would invariably set it on fire.

'No, we're here on a different matter. We're from the, uh, the Cold Case Unit, we're looking into the death of Lizzie Fitzpatrick.'

'Oh, I see,' he said, and looked grave.

Crabbie nodded at me and I nodded back. There had been no 'who's Lizzie Fitzpatrick?' bullshit from him.

'Shall we go to my office?' he said.

His book-lined, attractive office was on the fifth floor of a tower block on Stranmillis Road, overlooking the botanic gardens and the River Lagan. Now that last night's fires were out, from up here Belfast seemed like any other dull red-brick Victorian British city.

154 / Adrian McKinty

Professor Yeats caught me admiring the view.

'You wouldn't know there was a war on, would you?' he said.

'Just thinking that. You wouldn't,' I agreed.

He got behind his desk and Crabbie and I sat down in two comfortable leather chairs.

'That was an interesting talk today. Is that your speciality?' I asked.

He laughed. 'Heavens, no. I do British industrial history. But the purpose of the summer school is to pack in as many paying punters as we can, so it's all plagues, wars, chaos and castrations.'

'Sounds like Sandy Row on a Friday night,' Crabbie said. Yeats laughed at the jest.

'You're from England, Professor Yeats?' I asked.

'And everyone told me I'd lost my accent.'

'Nope. It's still going strong.'

'I'm from Hendon . . . near London.'

'And how long have you been at Queen's?'

'I came here in 1965, so it's nearly twenty years.'

'Ah, so they sucked you in before the Troubles kicked off, then, did they?'

He smiled. 'Yes, they did.'

'Married man?'

'Married, divorced.'

'Kids?'

'No.'

'Do you happen to remember what were you doing all the way over in Antrim the night Lizzie Fitzpatrick had her accident?' I asked.

'Yes, I remember it vividly. The three of us were fishing on Lough Neagh. Barry, Lee and myself.'

'That's you and Lee McPhail and Barry Connor?'

'Yes.'

'Fishing for what?' Crabbie asked.

'Dollaghan trout. Lee had been raving about the trout fishing on Lough Neagh for years and we finally decided to go and give it a shot.'

'Was it not a bit cold in December?'

'That was the perfect time to go. The trout had been feeding all summer so they would be heavy and by December flies would be few and far between so they'd go for an attractive lure. After dark we brought out the lights, the fishing was so sweet.'

'Anyone catch anything?' I asked.

'Oh yes. It was a great day. That's why we went for a drink before the run back to Belfast. I caught a nine-pounder, Barry caught two eight-pounders and Lee threw back everything he caught until he brought in a beautiful twelve-pounder.'

'So you had a good day's fishing and you went to the pub for a few pints . . .'

'No, we went to an Indian restaurant in Antrim first, which wasn't that great, and then Lee told us about this little pub he knew, the Henry Joy McCracken, and we went in for a few drinks.'

'The pub was empty?' Crabbie asked.

'No, initially there were a few farmers and old-timers, locals, I imagine, but by closing time everyone had gone but us.'

'The three of you and Lizzie Fitzpatrick?'

'Yes, although we didn't know her name then, of course.'

'So what happened then?' I asked.

'Nothing happened. It came to eleven o'clock and Lizzie rang the bell and told us that it was last orders, but none of us wanted any last orders because we'd all had a round each and Lee had to drive us home.'

'So what did you do?' Crabbie asked.

'We left. We walked through the village to where the car was parked.'

'Where was that?' I asked.

'Not too far away, just around the corner on the road down to the lough.'

'Did you see anyone about?'

'No.'

'Nobody at all?'

'It's a small village, I'm pretty sure there was no one.'

'No people or cars?'

'No.'

'Then what did you do?'

'We got in the car and drove to Belfast.'

'No incidents?'

'No. Lee dropped me first on the Stranmillis Road and then Barry and I assume he went home after that.'

'What time did you get in at?'

'I don't know. Eleven twenty or thereabouts? It's a pretty quick run in from Antrim.'

'What did you do next?'

'I washed up, put the trout in the fridge, got a book and went to bed.'

'What book?' Crabbie asked.

'I have no idea! It was nearly four years ago.'

'When you were leaving the pub, did you happen to see if Lizzie came behind you to close the door?' I asked.

He thought about it. 'I didn't notice, sorry. To be honest I was keeping an eye on Lee. I was a little worried about letting him drive us home with three pints of Guinness in him.'

'Did Lizzie seem agitated or upset that evening?'

'I didn't notice anything like that, although apparently her father was in the hospital recovering from knee surgery, so perhaps she was a bit subdued? I don't really know.'

'When were you contacted by the police about Lizzie's death?'

'I contacted them. I saw a news item about Lizzie's death and a police spokesman was asking for any witnesses who had been in the bar that night,' he said, a little unsure of himself. He looked at me and then at the floor and then out the window.

Crabbie had seen it too.

'That's not quite what happened, is it, Professor Yeats?' I asked.

'What do you mean?'

'You saw the news item on the TV and you called up Mr McPhail and Mr Connor and one or both of them told you to forget it. They told you it was best if you didn't get involved, didn't they?'

'Shit,' he muttered.

'But then, after some soul-searching, you decided to tell the truth, didn't you?'

Professor Yeats seemed stunned by this piece of deduction, although it was the most obvious thing in the world.

'Well, which one of them was it?' Crabbie asked.

'It was Lee. He said that he could get in trouble for drunk driving and it was best if we just didn't mention anything to the police.'

'But he didn't convince you, did he?' Crabbie said.

'At that time we didn't know her death had been an accident. The police were calling for witnesses to come forward to help them with an unexplained death. It could have been a murder or anything and I felt that we should come forward and tell them what we knew. So I called up Antrim RUC and the detective in charge came to interview me that afternoon. After that he talked to the others. But none of us knew very much. We had a drink, we barely talked to the poor girl. I think Lee chatted to her the most. Her father was in hospital for a knee operation and he was telling her that his dad had had the same operation.'

'How long were they chatting?' I asked.

'Not long. Two minutes.'

'Are you still friends with Mr McPhail?'

Yeats looked chagrined. 'Not really, not any more. He thought what I did was something of a betrayal and he more or less froze me out of his life after that.'

'How did you meet him in the first place?'

'He went to a talk I was giving on the great Belfast Police Strike of 1909. He asked a few questions and we met up afterwards. It turned out we had a mutual interest in labour activism and fishing.'

'And Barry Connor?'

'I got to know him through Lee.'

'Does he still speak to you?'

'Oh yes. Barry doesn't hold grudges.'

I looked at Crabbie to see whether he had anything else. He did. 'That night could anyone have slipped into the pub and been hiding, say, in the toilets?' Crabbie asked.

'It's possible, but I don't think so. I went to the toilet just before we left and I didn't notice anyone.'

'Did you look in the stalls?' I asked.

'No, I just used the urinal.'

'I suppose you didn't go in the women's toilet, by any chance?'

'Definitely not.'

'Do you have anything else to add, Sergeant McCrabban?' I asked Crabbie.

He shrugged. 'Do you have any more information that you think might be pertinent, Professor Yeats?'

'Uhh, I don't think so.'

I got him to reiterate the timeline but he was consistent so I got up and offered him my card. 'Well, thank you so much for your time, Professor Yeats. Here's my card – if you think of anything else please don't hesitate to give me a call.'

He walked us to his office door. 'May I ask you a question, Inspector?' he said.

'Of course.'

'Why now? I mean, it's been four years. And this seemed like a simple story. The poor girl fell off a table or something, right?'

I nodded. 'It seems that way, but the coroner returned an open verdict so the case never really closes. If you think of anything give me a call, OK?'

'OK.'

'Oh, one more thing, did you happen to notice a problem with any of the lights in the pub that night?'

He sighed. 'I don't remember. Sorry.'

'Ah well, thank you very much.'

Crabbie and I walked downstairs.

'Fancy some lunch while I pick your brain?' I asked him when we'd reached street level.

'I'd take a wee bite to eat,' he agreed.

'Good, because I've heard about a wee place round the corner that I've been meaning to try. Follow me.'

19: LE CANARD

We walked over to Botanic Avenue and found Le Canard just finishing its lunchtime service. It was a French bistro in the style of the Deux Magots with outside tables, expensive coffees and snippy waiters. Anywhere else this would have been a cliché but in war-torn Belfast in the summer of 1984 it was a breath of fresh air.

Getting a table would normally probably be quite difficult, packed as it was with folks from the BBC and the surrounding offices but our warrant cards did the trick with the maître d'hôtel and he found us a table in the back near the toilets.

I ordered a glass of red for me and an espresso for Crabbie.

'Cheers,' I said, taking a sip of the house plonk.

'Chin chin,' McCrabban said, sipping his coffee.

The wine was excellent and I ordered another almost immediately.

'Ever read Roald Dahl?' Crabbie asked.

'*Charlie and the Chocolate Factory*?'

'He's got one. It's not exactly a locked-room mystery but it's a good one. Do you wanna hear?'

'Sure.'

'The police are called to a house where a man has been found by his wife apparently bludgeoned to death. The policeman very gently and sympathetically chats to the bereaved woman, and notices the delicious smell of a leg of lamb, roasting in the kitchen. The distraught widow begs the detective to partake of a little of the meat, as it was her husband's favourite meal etc. And thus the murder weapon (the frozen leg of lamb) is consumed.'

'Nice. Sort of a variation on the frozen bullet theme . . . But our girl had her neck snapped. It was either an accident or a human being snapped it after he'd knocked her down. I don't think there's any trickery about murder weapons in our locked room.'

'No,' Crabbie said sadly.

'You wanna talk about the timeline?' I asked cheerfully.

'I'm all ears.'

'Lizzie gets a call from her mother Mary at ten thirty. All is well. She kicks out the three fishing comrades at eleven. All is well. Eleven twenty our new mate Professor Yeats arrives home. At eleven thirty boyfriend Harper calls Mary Fitzpatrick's house asking to speak to Lizzie. Lizzie isn't back yet. Mary goes to the pub looking for her, finds that it's locked up and the lights are off. She comes back to the house, rouses the neighbours, calls the cops. Eleven forty-five or shortly thereafter Harper arrives back from Belfast, worried sick. Antrim peelers show up shortly after that and a second search begins. Midnight, a cop shines his torch through the window of the pub and thinks he sees something lying on the floor. They break the door down and find Lizzie lying there with a busted light bulb in her hand.'

Crabbie nodded. 'That sounds about right. Lizzie dies between eleven and eleven thirty.'

I took another sip of wine.

'You think Yeats is telling the truth?'

'I think so. Why, what are you getting at?'

'Do you think Yeats or one of his mates came on to Lizzie and there was a scuffle and they accidentally killed her and concocted the accident scheme and hightailed it out of there?'

Crabbie nodded. 'It would take some nerve, wouldn't it? To get away with it and then offer yourselves up to the police.'

'That would be the last thing the police would suspect.'

'And then there's the barred front and back doors.'

'One of them hides in the toilet and waits until Lizzie's body is found and slips out when all the commotion has died down.'

'He didn't react when you suggested that.'

'Could be a good actor. And he's had three and a half years to prep for this line of questioning.'

Crabbie shook his head. 'It's way too risky. Nobody would have the bottle to do something like that. Why not just leave? And anyway, your Inspector Beggs did a thorough search of the premises, didn't he?'

'So he says.'

'Do you have a reason not to believe him?'

'You and I know, Crabbie, that all peelers cover their arses . . . But actually no, he seems like a pretty thorough copper.'

'So it had to be an accident.'

'It would appear that way for now.'

Crabbie sighed. 'No offence, Sean, but this case seems like a bit of a waste of time.'

'That's the speciality of the RUC.'

A waiter came to take our order. I found that I wasn't really hungry after the murderous leg of lamb story, but Crabbie was and he got the *pot au feu* after I explained what it was.

I ordered another glass of the house red and when it came I found myself ruminating on what Laura had said to me. After the waiter had gone I leaned over to Crabbie. 'Listen, mate, do you think I'm manic depressive? I'm depressive, sure, we're all depressed, but I've seen no evidence of a manic phase, have you? Bad judgement. Some rashness. But not foaming mania, right?'

The conversation was far outside McCrabban's comfort zone but he listened to me politely. When he saw a response was called for he put down his coffee.

'I think I'd take issue with your premise, Sean. I wouldn't say everybody's depressed. I'm not.'

'Aye, but that's because you think you're going to be raptured up to heaven any minute, isn't it?'

'You could join me if you would accept Jesus as your personal saviour.'

'I'm sorry I asked now. Anyway, here's your grub.'

Crabbie's food came and when he was done I asked to speak to the chef.

'The chef is very busy,' the waiter replied with an unctuous smile.

I showed him my warrant card. 'He'll want to talk to us.'

As was the wont of many chefs, Barry Connor was a thin, bird-like man who looked as if he survived on water biscuits. He was balding and he had shaved the rest of his brown hair into a buzz cut. He was medium height, with piercing grey eyes.

He was dressed in some kind of chef's jacket over a white T-shirt and brown corduroy trousers. He looked extremely nervous.

'What can I do for you two gentlemen?'

I gave him our names and told him we were working on the cold case of Lizzie Fitzpatrick.

'Who's Lizzie Fitzpatrick?'

'27 December 1980. She was a barmaid in the Henry Joy McCracken in Antrim. You were her final customers. She kicked you out at last orders and after that she had a rather mysterious accident that resulted in her death.'

A little smile of relief showed on his face. We hadn't come to ask him about the protection money he was shelling out to the Loyalist and Republican paramilitaries. Nor had we come to ask about the dodginess of his books. We'd actually come calling about Lizzie Fitzpatrick . . . Whatever had happened with the three of them and Lizzie it was nothing our mate Barry Connor was too stressed about.

Unless of course he knew that I'd be thinking that and he was one step ahead.

That would be diabolical.

'Let's talk,' I said.

'Do you mind if I finish lunch service first? We're nearly done. Just a couple of tickets left.'

'Nah, let's talk now, Barry.'

He sat down at the side of the table.

'This is fantastic, by the way,' McCrabban said. 'Really hits the spot.'

'Thank you,' Barry said.

'How do you know Alan Yeats and Lee McPhail?' I asked him.

'I met Alan through Lee. Lee and I went to Queen's together.'

'Studying?'

'We were both reading English and Politics. We both wanted to be journalists. He did become a journalist at first, but I . . . I never followed through on it.'

'How did you get into this cooking racket?' I asked.

'My mother's French. These are all her recipes. My mother's and my grandmother's.'

'Your mother's French, did you say?'

'Yes.'

'Whereabouts in France?'

'Brittany.'

'Does she ever sleep with the window open?'

'What?'

'Does she ever sleep with the window open at night?'

'Now you come to mention it . . . I don't think she does. Why do you ask that?'

'No reason. All right. So tell me about the night of 27 December 1980 as best as you can remember it.'

'We'd all gone fishing and done really well and we'd had a bite to eat and Lee told us about this pub he knew. We had a few beers and then we drove back to Belfast. That's about it.'

'Did you interact with Lizzie at all?'

'We all got a round, so we all went up to the bar and gave our order. But that was about it. She didn't invite conversation.'

'She wasn't particularly friendly?'

'No, she wasn't hostile, she just seemed as if she had other stuff on her mind. I read later that her father had been in the hospital for an operation . . .'

'She chatted to Lee, though, didn't she?'

'Oh yes. Lee's very gregarious. He could get a Carthusian nun to have a chinwag with him.'

'Was he trying to pull her?'

'Lee's always trying to pull somebody.'

'I'll take that as a yes.'

'Did it go farther than she wanted? Was there any kind of argy-bargy?' Crabbie asked.

'No. Nothing like that. Lee tried a few lines on her. She wasn't interested. End of story.'

'So you finished your drinks and headed home?'

'Exactly.'

'What time was this?'

'Last orders. Eleven. Possibly slightly before.'

'And what time did you get back to Belfast?'

'Lee dropped Alan off at about eleven twenty and me about two minutes after that.'

'And what time did he get home?'

'I have no idea. He's only about five minutes away down the Malone Road so I assume not much longer after he dropped me.'

'When did you first hear about Lizzie's death?' Crabbie asked.

'Two days later. Alan called me. He said we had to go to the police about what we knew.'

'And what did you say to that?'

'I thought it was a good idea.'

'And Lee, what did *he* think?'

'Uhm, I don't know.'

'Sure you do,' I insisted.

'Uhm, well, I think it was his opinion that we shouldn't get involved.'

'Why?'

'I think just on general principles. He didn't think cooperating with the police was a good idea.'

'But Alan thought otherwise.'

'Alan was quite insistent . . . anyway, he called the cops and they interviewed us. But the whole thing turned out to be an accident.'

I rubbed my chin and looked at Crabbie.

He had nowt.

'While you were all sitting there having a drink in the Henry Joy McCracken, did you notice if there was a problem with any of the light bulbs in the place?'

'No. But I don't think that's the sort of thing I would have noticed.'

'Why?'

'I don't know. Had a good day's fishing. Three pints of beer. You're not thinking about light bulbs, are you?'

I gave Barry my card.

'If you think of anything else, I'd appreciate a call,' I said.

He nodded.

'Is that it?' he asked.

'Yes.'

He stood up and smiled.

'That was pretty painless, wasn't it?' I said.

'Yes, it was.'

'Thank you for your time, Mr Connor.'

I finished my wine and when we went to pay we discovered that it was on the house. I didn't insist.

We went outside and I lit a cigarette.

'You know what I think?' Crabbie said.

'What do you think?'

'I think Lizzie Fitzpatrick fell off the bar and broke her neck.

I think the girl's father can't accept the fact that a random act of God killed his little girl. I think he's pressuring Special Branch to reopen the case and Special Branch are doing it because he's a big wheel in the Republican movement and nobody wants to piss him off.'

I tapped McCrabban on the bonce. 'You're not as thick as you look, are you?'

'Am I right?'

'And where does Dermot McCann come into your little scheme?'

'You think if you find out what happened to Lizzie Fitzpatrick somebody in the Fitzpatrick clan will give you a tip on Dermot, which, frankly, is a stretch even for you . . .'

'You know what I like about you, Crabbie?'

'What?'

'You keep me grounded, mate.'

'I'll take that as a compliment. Where to now?'

'Let's go see the last of these three fearless fishermen.'

We checked the Yellow Pages and found Lee McPhail listed under Managers and Agents. His office was on Botanic Avenue near Shaftsbury Square.

We walked over and found that he was up on the third floor of an office block overlooking the Ulster Bank. It was an old building but the office had recently been renovated. There were two secretaries. An older and a younger. One to get the job done, the other to provide eye candy for the punters. The younger one was a fetching blonde who was nonplussed by our questions about her boss's whereabouts. The older one informed us that Lee was unavailable as he was showing VIPs from America around the city.

'And who might these VIPs be?' I asked.

'Joe Kennedy from Massachusetts for one,' she said, with a look of triumph.

'Will Mr McPhail be in the office at all this week?'

She reached in a drawer and looked at Lee's schedule. 'Nope. It's jam packed,' she announced.

'Mind if I have a look?' I said and took the schedule out of her hand, but it was no good. He was indeed thick as thieves with the Kennedy clan all week.

'Have you got a photocopier?' I asked her.

She reluctantly admitted that she had.

I photocopied McPhail's busy life and gave her the book back.

We took our leave and I examined the schedule as we walked down the stairs. Kennedy was meeting priests and politicians, visiting prisons and factories in his visit to Northern Ireland. One trip that caught my eye was to the old DeLorean plant in Dunmurry – a factory that I had visited myself when they were still turning out clunky, underpowered gull-winged sports cars. Now it was a *business park* – whatever that meant.

'Do you fancy coming with me tomorrow to meet McPhail at the old DeLorean factory?' I asked Crabbie.

'I'd love to, mate, but I can't. I'm in court all day.'

'What have you done? Something to do with sheep?'

'I haven't done anything. I'm testifying.'

'A likely story.'

We walked back to the Land Rover, checked underneath it for bombs, and I took Crabbie back to Carrick. I signed the Land Rover in again, got in my Beemer and drove to see Mary Fitzpatrick in Ballykeel.

Annie answered the doorbell. 'You again,' she said.

'Me again,' I agreed.

'You want to come in? Me ma and da aren't in. They're away to Belfast.'

I hesitated on the doorstep. 'Uhm, it was your mother I wanted to see. I just wanted to fill her in on our progress in our investigation.'

'After four years there's been progress?'

'Well, not as such, but I wanted to tell her what I've been up to.'

'You can tell me. Come in. Have a cup of tea.'

I went into the living room and sat down on the sofa. *Countdown* was on TV.

'Let me know when it's the numbers game!' Annie yelled from the kitchen.

It was a word game. Both contestants only got five-letter words but the guy in Dictionary Corner got a nine-letter one.

'It's the numbers!' I yelled, and Annie came in with two mugs of tea and a plate of chocolate biscuits. While she watched the screen I watched her. She was very beautiful. It was the eyes, I think. Those extraordinary eyes. It wasn't surprising that it had been Annie who had finally got a charismatic fellow like Dermot to settle down. She had eyes like his sister's and his mother's. Intelligent and haughty and dangerously dark. 'Ten plus five equals fifteen. Fifteen times fifty equals seven fifty. Seven fifty plus nine equals seven hundred and fifty-nine!' Annie squealed with delight, and was pleased even more when neither of the two contestants got the solution.

She turned off the TV.

'Sorry about that. I have to do the numbers. It's the only thing that keeps me sane around here.'

'Don't you have a job or a part-time job or . . .'

'No.'

'Weren't you training to be a teacher at Magee?'

'I was. I gave that up. Dermot, that old romantic, said that no woman of his was going to have to work!'

'Wee bit Stone Age, no?'

'That's Dermot. He's old-fashioned. But I didn't really need to work, did I? Dad always spoiled me rotten and Dermot was getting a good, uhm, allowance.'

'What did you do when Dermot was inside all those years?'

'I still got the allowance from you know who and Dermot pulled a few strings and I wrote a few articles for *An Phoblacht*. I quite enjoyed that. I thought maybe I could parley that into something more permanent, but then, well . . . you know what happened next.'

'What happened next?'

'Well, Lizzie died and we closed the pub and Vanessa went to Canada. It was a bad few years and then the maddest thing of the lot!'

'What was that?'

'*He* divorced me!'

'I heard about that.'

'The eejit divorced me from inside the Maze! Just like that! I couldn't believe it. I really couldn't believe it. He wouldn't even see me.'

'Did he give you a reason?'

'No reason. Just a terse remark through his lawyers.'

'What was the remark? If you don't mind me asking.'

'I have it bloody memorised. He said, "I trust that Annie will not contest this divorce. I have no desire to drag her name through the mud or hurt the cause we both believe in so deeply."'

'What did he mean by that?'

'You know what he meant. And it was a load of shite. Somebody must have been spreading gossip or something . . .'

Annie shook her head and turned away from me, looking through the window at the back garden.

There was a distant gunshot and hundreds of ducks lifted off from the lough en masse.

Annie crossed and uncrossed her legs. The clock on the mantel ticked. 'Well, I suppose I better be running along, Annie. If you could tell your mother we're still on it, I would appreciate that.'

Annie sniffed and turned to face me again. 'Are you going back to Carrickfergus?'

'No, not yet. Since I was in the area I thought about paying a wee visit to that kid who was seeing your sister.'

'Harper McCullough?'

'Aye, that's the one.'

'Do you know where he lives?'

'I've got his address in my notebook.'

'Ach, I'll walk you over. It's about a quarter of a mile up the lough path ... That is if you don't mind me tagging along. I wouldn't want to spoil your investigation.'

'No, I don't mind. In fact it would be my distinct pleasure.'

20: HARPER McCULLOUGH

We dandered along the Lough Neagh path. The sun was setting over the west shore and the light had taken on a colour that you see sometimes in dreams. Wading birds of a dozen varieties were settling down for the night and the wind was stirring gently among the reeds. The blue lough itself was still and motionless but for a yacht cruising the north coast on an easy tack.

'It's remarkable here,' I said.

'Yes,' she mumbled.

We walked farther along the track. A family of ducks got out of our way. Annie put her hand on my arm to stop me.

'What?' I asked her.

'You don't judge me, do you, Sean? You never seemed the sort.'

'What are you talking about?'

'I mean, what did Dermot expect? He was in prison for five years. Five years. And before that he said that he knew they'd catch him sooner or later. He knew it. He gets to be the hero and where does it leave me? Alone. Living with my parents?'

'Annie, you don't have to explain yourself—'

'You know what some of them say? They say that the first thing they'll do when they get an independent thirty-two-county Ireland is to ban abortion and take away votes for women. Put women back in their place. The men in the fields, the women in the kitchen. That's the kind of mind-set we're dealing with here. You know?'

'I can't believe Dermot ever said anything like that.'

'No . . . not really . . .' Her voice faded away.

The last arc of the sun had dipped behind the Sperrin Mountains and all the birds on the lough seemed to give a great collective sigh.

'Come on,' she said, and we walked a little farther on until we reached a huge Georgian house on the water's edge with a pier and a boat dock to which a twenty-foot cabin cruiser had been moored.

'This is it,' Annie said.

'They have money, do they?'

'Aye. Harper's father, Tommy McCullough, was a big . . . what's the word?'

'Fish? Enchilada?'

'Magnate in these parts. His construction company built half of Antrim town. He was a Protestant but he was liked well enough by everybody. A real . . . uhm . . . character. Used to have these big Halloween and Christmas parties for all the local kids. That's how Lizzie, Vanessa and me got to know Harper. We've known him since he was a wee nipper. His dad was big into fishing and the rugby club.'

'He had a stroke, didn't he?'

'Yeah. He was in a bad way for a while and died not too long after Lizzie's accident. Harper was completely lost.'

'What about his mother?'

'Don't mention his mother. She ran off to England with some actor when Harper was only five. She's been pestering Harper for money since Tommy's death. Of course, he gives it to her because it's his mother, but she's a frightful woman by all accounts.'

We opened the back gate and began walking up the garden path to the house, which I could see now was a lovely red sandstone manor from the 1780s or '90s.

Annie took us to the back door, which led into a large scullery off the kitchen.

'Wait a minute, will he mind us coming in the back door like this?'

'I've come in this way a thousand times!' she scoffed.

I followed Annie through the scullery and the kitchen into an enormous, slightly old-fashioned living room which overlooked the lough.

'Hello!' she yelled. 'Hello! You've got company!'

'Is that Annie McCann?' a man's voice asked from an adjoining room.

'Annie Fitzpatrick, if you don't mind!' she said.

A side door opened and Harper McCullough came in. He turned on the light and gave Annie a hug and a kiss on the cheek. He was tall, six four, handsome, about twenty-six or twenty-seven. He had an open, clean-shaven face with a sharp, square jaw, thick black hair and dark brown eyes. His frame, however, was slight and he was skinny, and when he walked it was with a stoop. In another age you would have had him down as a consumptive artist. He was wearing a mustard-coloured sweater, blue jeans and no shoes. If he put on a few stone he'd look like one of those wankers who are born with money and good looks and who swan through life; but this character wasn't swanning anywhere. His mother had abandoned him, his father had passed away recently and his girlfriend had died in some kind of bizarre accident . . .

'Is this your new beau?' he said to Annie, offering me his hand.

'God, no!' Annie laughed. 'This is . . . well, I suppose you could say that this is an old friend of the family . . . Detective Inspector Sean Duffy of the famed Special Branch.'

I shook Harper's hand and his grip was firm.

'A policeman? How can you bunch of rebels have a policeman as a family friend?' Harper asked with a laugh.

'You have slandered us, sir! We're actually a diverse and

pluralistic lot,' Annie said, poking Harper in the chest.

Harper shook his head and winked at me. 'You know her ex-husband is a famous IRA commander! You're in trouble, pal. This is a classic honey trap if ever I saw one.'

Annie punched him on the shoulder. 'Stop it! I'm not seeing Sean! I'm not seeing anyone. He's here on official business.'

'Oh?' Harper said.

'Yes, I am, Mr McCullough. I'm in the Cold Case Unit of the RUC Special Branch. We're looking into the death of Lizzie Fitzpatrick.'

Harper's eyes widened. 'Finally!' he exclaimed. 'Lizzie never got justice! I don't care what they say. That whole thing was very suspicious, to say the least.'

'How so?' I asked.

'They say she fell off the bar and broke her neck? Impossible! She was very coordinated. She had terrific balance. She could do a handstand with one hand!'

Annie groaned. 'The handstand thing again? We can all do that! Look!'

She got down on the kitchen floor, did a handstand and lifted her left hand off the ground. She fell and did it another two times until she managed to hold it there for a ten count. Harper looked at me, embarrassed, and I was embarrassed for Annie too.

She finished her handstand and sprung back to her feet.

'There! What do you think of that?' she said.

Harper smiled. 'That was brilliant, Annie. All three of you girls were always incredibly talented.'

Annie smiled from ear to ear and unconsciously gave me a little nudge on the back.

'What is going on in here?' a female voice said behind me.

I turned to look.

She was blonde, winsome, pale, very pretty and nine months pregnant.

'There she is! Ready to pop!' Annie said, and kissed the pregnant woman on the cheek.

There was the customary cooing over the baby bump before Harper introduced me.

'This is my wife, Jane. Jane, this is Sean Duffy. He's a police detective. He's looking into Lizzie's death.'

Jane frowned and shook her head. 'Poor Lizzie. Don't believe them when they tell you she could just have fallen off a table. She could do these one-handed handstands that were—' Jane began.

'I was just showing them! I was just after showing them. Right this minute!' Annie interrupted.

'So did you all go to school together?' I asked.

'Aye. Antrim Grammar. I was a couple of years ahead of Harper. And Jane was in Lizzie's year,' Annie said.

That would put Harper at about twenty-eight and Jane at about twenty-five, I thought, and made a mental note of it.

'I lived about a mile that way,' Jane said, pointing down the lough.

'Jane was one of Lizzie's best friends,' Annie added.

'*The* best friend!' Jane insisted. 'Now just because I'm ready to explode I am not going to forget my duties. Who wants a cup of tea?'

Jane and Annie went to make the tea, which gave me a chance to talk to Harper alone.

'If you don't mind, Mr McCullough, I'm reinterviewing everyone. Can I ask you a few questions?'

'Of course.'

'I'd like to bring you back to the night Lizzie Fitzpatrick died, 27—'

'27 December 1980, I'll never forget it.'

'That night you were at some rugby club dinner in Belfast?'

'Yes. It was the Antrim Rugby Club Awards Dinner at the Montjoy Hotel. They were giving an award to my father.

Lifetime achievement thing. I was his representative.'

'He'd had a stroke.'

'Aye. A month before. I didn't want to go to the dinner, not with my old man sick and Lizzie's dad in the hospital for his knee surgery. Did they tell you Jim was in the hospital for his knee?'

'Yes. That's why Lizzie was running the pub.'

'She didn't have to. It could have closed for one bloody night. She was going to be a lawyer. It still makes me furious. I think Mary guilted her into it.'

'So you were reluctantly at this rugby club dinner.'

'Reluctantly is right. It hardly seemed a time to be getting blitzed with the bloody rugby club. A game I've never liked, incidentally. And if I hadn't gone none of this would have happened.'

'Why do you say that?'

'Well, I would have been with Lizzie the whole time, wouldn't I?'

'What do you think happened to Lizzie, Mr McCullough?'

'Somebody killed her. Had to be. She would never have fallen off that bar. I've seen her jump from twice that height as happy as Larry.'

'How did they do it, with all the doors locked and bolted from the inside?'

'I don't know. You're the detective! She wouldn't die like that. So random like that.'

'What do you do for a living, Mr McCullough?' I asked him.

'I'm a builder.'

'You physically build things?'

He laughed. 'Me? No. Look at me. I run a construction company. My dad's company.'

'Were you working for your father when you were going out with Lizzie?'

He shook his head. 'God, no. I was at Queen's.'

'Studying?'

'Archaeology.'

'A fascinating subject.'

'Oh yeah,' he said, his eyes lighting up for the first time in our interview. 'I've always loved that stuff. I wanted to do underwater archaeology. You know what that is?'

'No. Not really.'

'I got a book on it when I was ten. I've been entranced ever since. You dive on drowned cities. Alexandria, Piraeus, places like that. It's a brilliant field and they've barely, er, scratched the surface.'

'Why don't you still do that?'

He shook his head and sighed. 'Somebody has to run the bloody firm, don't they? After my dad had his stroke, I sort of got sucked into it. And then after Lizzie's . . . after she died, well, I sort of buried myself in the work . . . And it's too late now, isn't it? I've a kid on the way,' he said, looking a little panic-stricken.

'I see.'

'Do you have any kids, Inspector?'

'Me, no.'

'I mean, how do you raise kids?'

'I think it's all quite straightforward, sir. Uhm, you get the book and everything's in the book.'

'What book? There's a book?' he said, hopefully.

'My next-door neighbour, Mrs McDowell, has ten or, possibly, eleven kids. I'll ask her.'

'Thank you. Where *are* the girls with the tea?' Harper said, distracted.

I didn't want to lose this moment. 'OK, so bringing you back to the night of Lizzie's death. What time did you leave the rugby club dinner?'

'The whole thing was supposed to go on until one in the morning with the disco and the bloody karaoke, but the speeches and the awards and the pats on the back were all done by about half eleven.'

'That's when you called Lizzie's house?'

'Yeah. I thought she'd easily be finished by then. Glasses cleaned, pub locked up and home. The pub is only five minutes from their house. So when I called up and she wasn't there I was worried. I told Mary that I thought something might be wrong and of course that daft old bird told me not to concern myself! I said she should call the police and she said she wasn't having a policeman in her house! She said she'd go down to the pub and check on her. And then she hung up.'

'What did you do next?'

'I was worried. I ran out to the car and I burned rubber getting back to Antrim. I got there roughly the same time as the peelers.'

'So she did call the police?'

'Yeah, Mary had walked to the pub and seen that it was closed and come back and called the cops.'

'And then what happened?'

'We all went looking for her in the village.'

'And?'

'One of the policemen shone his torch into the pub and he thought he might have seen someone lying on the floor. So we all ran over and started trying to break the door down.'

'And did you break the door down?'

'Yes. It took some work because the bar was across but the cops had a battering ram in their Land Rover and we all gave it a good charge each. And, well, we got in . . .'

'And?'

'She was lying there on the floor, all crumpled up and that stupid light bulb in her hand.'

'How did you see her if the lights were turned off?'

'One of the policemen turned them on.'

'And that's when you saw the dead bulb in the socket?'

'I didn't notice that, but one of the peelers did.'

'Is it possible that there was someone hiding in the bar?

Waiting there until the door was open so they could slip away?'

He shook his head dubiously. 'No. There was nobody in there.'

'How can you be so sure?'

'Where would they hide?'

'The toilets.'

He shook his head. 'I doubt it. We were all milling around. One of us would have bumped into somebody hiding, wouldn't we?'

'What do you mean, milling around?'

'We were all just milling around. A policeman had already determined that she was dead. Beyond saving, you know? And Mary was sobbing and I was just *devastated.* And we weren't allowed near the body and nobody was allowed to leave until the detectives came.'

'Was there a search of the premises?'

'Not then, but it didn't matter because when that inspector showed up from Antrim RUC he had the pub searched from top to bottom.'

'How long after you broke the door down did the inspector show up?'

'Ten minutes? I don't know.'

'That seems like a good enough time to make a getaway.'

He shook his head again. 'No. You're not understanding the layout of the pub. She was in the middle of the main room about fifteen feet from the door. There were four policemen, Mary and me all waiting for the detectives to show up. No one could have slipped past us in that time. And there was one guy on the front door the whole time.'

'And the back door, Mr McCullough?'

'I checked that myself. Locked and bolted.'

'But you didn't check the toilets?'

'No. Why would I?'

'And what exactly happened when the inspector came?'

'He looked at the body, determined the situation, and then conducted a thorough search of the premises.'

'And apparently found nothing untoward?'

'That's what he said.'

I made a note of all of this.

I'd read Inspector Beggs' report and all four police officers at the scene had said the same thing. No one had left the pub in the time before the search had been carried out.

Annie and Jane came with the tea on a silver tray. The good china, Ceylon tea, fresh milk. They set it on the coffee table and sat there on the edge of the sofa while I continued my questions.

'Did Lizzie have any enemies, Mr McCullough?'

'I doubt it. She was very good-natured. She wouldn't hurt a fly.'

'Do you have any enemies? Someone that might have wanted to hurt you by getting her?'

He considered it for a moment. 'Not back then. I was just a student. Maybe now I'd have a few. People complaining about how slowly we're building their house or something.'

This was getting me nowhere. 'Mr McCullough, you appreciate that both the pub doors, front and back, were barred and locked from the inside?'

'Yes, I know that.'

'And all the windows were barred.'

'Yes.'

'Which pretty much means that it *had* to be an accident,' I said.

'So they say.'

'But you're not convinced?'

'She was so physically capable. Agile. She rode horses and stuff and never fell off those. As if she's going to fall off a bar?'

'In the dark, trying to change a light bulb . . .'

'I don't believe it.'

'You don't want to believe it.'

He ran his hands through his hair. 'Ach, I don't know,' he said, with a bitter sigh.

Jane put her arms around her husband's shoulders. 'Did you tell Inspector Duffy about the break-in?' she asked her husband.

'The break-in?' he said, puzzled.

'At Mulvenna and Wright's. Just before Christmas,' Jane said.

'Oh yes. The break-in. Inspector Beggs didn't think too much about that, did he?'

'Tell me,' I said.

'Well, Lizzie had worked for James Mulvenna in Antrim. She'd clerked there. She was very good. He let her draw up trusts and contracts and everything. She really had a head for detail and—'

'Oh my God, Harper, you have to get to the point. I'll tell it,' Annie interrupted. 'There was a break-in at the law offices where Lizzie used to work. They took some money and smashed the place up a bit. Druggies. It wasn't a big deal.'

Harper shook his head. 'No, it *was* a bit of a big deal, actually. I remember Lizzie being upset. It added to all the stress of that week with her dad going in for his operation and everything.'

'When exactly was this?' I asked.

'The twenty-third I think,' Harper said. 'Or maybe the twenty-fourth – no, that would have been Christmas Eve. The twenty-third. Definitely.'

'Don't you think there could be a link between that break-in and Lizzie's death?' Jane asked me.

'I don't know. This is the first I've heard about it,' I said.

Annie rolled her eyes. 'Some druggie broke into the offices and stole the cash box. End of story.'

'Was she actually working there that Christmas?' I asked.

'No. Old Mr Mulvenna had passed away and his partner Harry Wright said he couldn't afford to pay her for holiday work,' Harper said. 'Another reason she was working in the pub, maybe.'

Annie shook her head. 'That's not even the real story,' she said. 'James Mulvenna finally passed away that October when Lizzie was back at Warwick.'

'How did he die?'

'He had multiple sclerosis. Anyway, James was a Catholic and his partner Harry Wright was a Protestant. It was a brilliant idea really because James got all the Catholic farmers and Harry all the Protestant ones hereabouts. James was as mellow as you please but Harry was a different sort. DUP councillor. Real Proddy Prod. And he wouldn't take Lizzie on over Christmas. I reckon he just made up that nonsense about the money and it was really about me and Dermot. He didn't want a famous IRA man's sister-in-law under his roof.'

'I liked Mr Mulvenna. My father used him even though he was the Catholic solicitor. They played rugby together. Do you play rugby, Inspector?' Harper asked.

'No.'

Jane piped up with a recollection of Harry Wright's meanness when they had gone carol-singing one time and Annie said that she remembered that incident very well. She also remembered that Wright's wife used to throw a bucket of water on anyone who came to their door on Halloween.

It was all very interesting but it was beginning to sound like a sidetrack. Irish villages were full of gossipy sidetracks like this. But I made a note to ask Chief Inspector Beggs about the burglary, to see whether there was anything in it.

'Was Lizzie worried about stalkers? Weird phone calls, anything like that, in the days or weeks leading up to her death?'

Harper shook his head. 'I don't think so.'

'Nothing she told me,' Jane said.

'Or me,' Annie chipped in.

'If you don't mind me asking, what exactly is the deal with your mother? She's not around?' I asked Harper.

'The deal? She's in England with her boyfriend. That's all it is.

She's not . . . as some people would paint her. She's made a lot of progress in the last few years.'

Both Jane and Annie rolled their eyes at that. Jane bit her tongue but Annie couldn't help but blurt out: 'Harper gives her a huge cheque every month. We've told him not to but he doesn't want a legal fight on his hands. God knows what she spends it on—'

'Annie, that's enough!' Harper said.

Annie saw that she'd goofed and to change the subject she asked the sex of the baby and Harper said that they didn't know because they wanted it to be a surprise, but he would love a little girl.

'When was the last time you spoke to Lizzie the night she died?' I asked Harper.

'I called her from Belfast about nine. She was in the pub.'

'How was she?'

'Stressed about her da. She'd spoken to Mary and her dad was out of surgery but still in intensive care. I told her not to worry and that I'd speak to her after the rugby club dinner, you know? I never did. I never spoke to her again.'

Harper's eyes began to water. Jane took his hand and squeezed it. It was awkward for her. Harper getting emotional about his dead ex-girlfriend, one of her best friends. And I couldn't think of anything else to ask right now anyway.

'Maybe we should call it a night there, folks,' I said, closing up my book.

'Finish your tea, Inspector, please,' Harper said.

While Jane rubbed Harper's back I stole a glance at Annie. She was trying to conceal whatever emotion she was feeling by munching loudly on a cream cracker.

'It was an awful time for Harper. Lizzie died in December. His dad passed away in the New Year, his mother was demanding a share of the estate, and then there was the recession. He had nobody. He had to manage all by himself,' Jane said reflectively, squeezing his hand and looking at him with pride.

'That's not quite right, Jane. His friends and neighbours all rallied around. We were all there for him. And he was there for us,' Annie said, with a brittle edge to her voice.

'Aye, it wasn't as dramatic as all that. We all helped each other if I remember rightly. My poor old man passed away and your da came out of the hospital and we had that memorial for Lizzie down by the water. It was . . . cathartic. Do you remember?' Harper asked Annie.

'I do indeed. That filthy beggar of a priest refused to do it on the lough shore because he said it was the site of pagan worship. Bloody fool. I think Ma actually had to bribe him. Ireland's never going to get anywhere until we kick out all the priests and all the ministers,' Annie said.

Jane yawned behind her hand and I took that as my cue.

I got up. 'Well, yes, I really should go. My car's parked back at Annie's house and I've a bit of a drive to get to Carrick.'

Harper got to his feet and shook my hand again. 'I hope you can sort this out. It's been hanging over all of us for nearly four years. First we hear one thing, then another, then it's an open verdict, which basically means nobody has a clue, doesn't it?'

'I can't promise you closure but I'll do my best,' I said.

Harper walked us to the back gate and we waved goodbye and walked down to the water.

'He's nice, isn't he?' Annie said.

I was slightly annoyed with her. 'You never told me his wife was pregnant,' I said. 'In fact I don't think you ever told me he had a wife.'

'Why would I?'

'Aren't you supposed to bring a present for the baby?'

'That just sounds like some middle-class bullshit thing,' she said irritably.

'I think it's basic civility, Annie.'

'You know what your problem is? You've got a servile

mentality. That's why it's so easy for you to work for the British. You fit right in. You'd have done great in the fucking Raj or something.'

'You think so?'

'Aye, I fucking do.'

I didn't reply and we walked in silence along the water's edge.

It was full dark now and the sky was full of summer constellations. We were far from city lights here and I could see Pegasus and the nebulae in Orion's belt reflected in the lough. Clegs and dragonflies buzzed above the water and the occasional plop was one of those famous trout coming up for a bite to eat.

'And listen, don't be thinking I'm one of those mean bitches that hates kids,' Annie said, as if we'd been talking the whole time. 'I asked Dermot about kids and he said that we couldn't even think about having weans until Ireland was on the path to freedom. Those were his exact words. Jesus! Can you believe that crap?'

'Annie, I—'

'And now what am I going to do? Divorced. Ex-husband is a scary fucking terrorist on the fucking run. No job. No qualifications. No prospects. I'm thirty! I mean, Christ. I might as well have leprosy.'

'Come on. Look at you. Your whole life is ahead of you. There's plenty of time for you to meet somebody and have kids and a—'

'That's not even the point! Christ, Duffy, you are so dense. How *did* they make you a detective?'

'What *is* the point?'

'Can you not see?'

'No.'

She didn't reply for a beat or two and then muttered, 'Forget it, just bloody forget it.'

We had reached her house now.

'There's no use in you coming in, Duffy. Me ma and da are seeing Joe Kennedy speak in Belfast and they won't be back till late. I'll tell me ma you've still got your thumb up your arse or, as you call it, are working on the case.'

'My car?'

'You can get to your car round the side of the house there.'

I wasn't offended by her. I knew her hostility was being displaced from Jane or Harper or both of them. 'All right, goodnight, then,' I said.

I walked round the side of the house.

It was a Republican area so of course I kneeled down and checked under the BMW for bombs but I didn't find any.

When I got back to my feet she was standing there. Crying? Crying.

I put my arms round her. She cried for a minute and then sniffed. I tilted her face up and kissed her on the forehead.

'It's OK,' I said.

'It was him, OK? You wanted to know? It's none of your business. It was him! All right?'

'I know.'

'Aye, of course you know! With your fucking peeler brain! Or was I just that bloody obvious?'

'No—'

'I suppose I made a real arse of myself in front of her *again*,' she sobbed.

'You were fine, Annie.'

'Oh God!' she moaned. 'I'm such a fool.'

'It's OK,' I said, and held her against me. I could feel her heart beating and her breasts against my chest.

'It wasn't anything to do with Lizzie. Please don't think that, Duffy. It was after Lizzie. A year and a half later. I was the rebound girl. The rebound girl between Lizzie and Jane.'

'You should have let her be the rebound girl.'

'I know.'

'Did you love him?'

'Ach . . . aye . . . I did. I loved him before Lizzie did. Before Jane did. Even before Dermot came along. His da. Jesus. His father was such a tyrant. Don't believe that lovable eccentric stuff even when I tell it. Harper was such a lonely little boy. He used to have dinner at our house more often than not. He was like a member of the family. His bloody da. All he cared about was his birds and the bloody rugby club.'

'Birds?'

She sniffed again and disengaged from my arms. 'Oh aye. He was president of the Antrim chapter of the Royal Society for the Protection of Birds. I went out with him a few times. He used to sit there and drink gin from a flask and watch the birds. He never took Harper with him. He liked me. And not in a creepy way, the old bastard. I used to draw the birds. I used to have all these interests. All this stuff I was into and it's all gone now. What have I got to look forward to now? *Countdown* on the TV? Dinner with Ma and Da?'

'Were Lizzie and Harper childhood sweethearts?'

'Christ! Do you always have to be on the job? Have you been listening to me at all? Have you heard anything I've been saying? You weren't like this before, Duffy. You've changed. They've turned you into a cog in the machine.'

I'm the same, Annie, and you're the same. Although perhaps we both exist in a slightly different key. Your song's got shriller and less restrained and mine's got a little more melancholy . . .

'I haven't changed.'

'You have! You used to be OK. You used to be cool.'

'Never as cool as Dermot.'

'Who could be?'

I laughed at that and she smiled at me. I tucked a strand of hair behind her ear. She'd always been a looker, Annie. In that dark, Basque, black-Irish way.

She took my hand and held it against her cheek for a moment.

Then she caught herself, disengaged my hand and took a step back.

'Well, Sean, I think you should . . .' she said.

'Yes, I should be going, actually . . .' I said.

I put the key in the lock. Her hand was on my arm. I could see her tear-stained cheeks in the moonlight.

She wanted to say something.

She hesitated.

The seconds went past, falling backwards into the abyss with the hours and the years.

'If I asked you to kiss me, Sean Duffy, would you do it?'

'I would.'

'Kiss me, then.'

I kissed her.

My God, I'd waited a long time for this.

I kissed away her tears and my tongue found hers and I pulled her close. She loosened her shirt and grabbed my hand and put it on her breast.

'Quickly! Now! Before I change my mind!' she said, breathlessly.

She unzipped my fly.

'Do you want to go inside or—'

'Make love to me. Fuck me. Fuck me here! Now. Fast!'

I took her up against the car. There was nothing beautiful about it. When she climaxed she screamed loud enough to wake half the colonies of wildfowl on the lough shore. She laughed and I laughed and she kissed me and took a breath and pushed me away. 'Go,' she said. 'Go on now, you big eejit.'

'Can I see you or—'

'Never! Not with a peeler! Not with you!'

'Then what can we—'

'We can't! Just go. Just. Fucking. Go.'

I watched her march up to the house and slam the door behind her.

I drove back to Carrickfergus with no music. Just the window down and me fags and the night blowing in. I parked the Beemer on Coronation Road, waded through the bills and junk mail and went upstairs.

I had a good gander at myself in the bathroom mirror.

Ten years I'd been waiting for that. Was it about Annie? Or was it to get one over on Dermot? Whatever it was it left me feeling foolish, numb. Happy.

'Eejit,' I said to the reflection. I ran the bath and as the room filled with steam my reflection blurred and faded and finally disappeared completely, which was the way I wanted it to be.

21: KENNEDY HAIR TORT

In the morning I drove to Antrim and called on Inspector Beggs to ask him about the break-in at the firm of Mulvenna and Wright where Lizzie had interned.

'Aye, I checked that out,' he said, putting the pipe cleaner into the bowl of his briar.

'And?'

'It was small potatoes. You want the details? Course you do, you boys always want the details. Hold on a minute and I'll check with the robbery squad,' he said.

He went down the hall and came back with a file. He flipped it open and began to read. 'Let me see, from Mulvenna and Wright they stole the cash box, two hi-fi speakers and an ornamental ashtray. It was the fourth in a series of robberies on commercial properties that Christmas in and around Antrim.'

'So it was a pattern.'

'Aye. And we caught them in the end.'

'You caught the burglars?'

'Oh aye. They weren't master criminals, believe me. They were tinkers. We caught three of them red-handed breaking into a butcher's shop at two in the morning. And unsurprisingly they knew nothing about Lizzie Fitzpatrick's death.'

'Can I talk to them? Are they inside?'

'That's a laugh. As soon as you let them out on bail they flee over the border or to England. Talk to them, he says.'

'All right. But if I understand what you're saying, you don't see a link between the break-in at the law firm and Lizzie's death a few days later?'

'How could there be?'

'I don't know. I suppose you got the names of these burglars?'

He handed me the arrest sheet. 'I don't think that'll help you much either,' he said with a grin.

The names were Michael Mouse, Dick Turpin and Robin Hood.

'So these burglars had done a whole series of robberies in Antrim?'

'That's right. Mulvenna and Wright were just one more place on their list.'

'Linked how? Fingerprints?'

'Modus operandi. Geography. Chronology. Four break-ins within a couple of streets.'

'Hmmmm,' I said, and rubbed my chin. 'So it's a dead end?'

'We thought so . . . How's your investigation going?' Beggs asked me when I had sufficiently digested all this.

I shrugged. 'I'm nearly finished, I suppose. I've interviewed everyone that I can think of except this Lee McPhail character.'

Beggs grinned. 'You'll love him. He's quite the customer.'

'Is he?'

'Oh yes. Big tall baldy cunt.'

'You said he had a few convictions?'

'That he has. Unemployment benefit fraud. Odometer fraud. Statutory rape.'

'Tell me about the rape.'

'Fancied himself as a bit of a ladies' man in his day. The girl was sixteen. He was thirty-seven. Her da found out. No question of force but that's why they call it statutory rape, isn't it?'

'That wasn't in the file.'

'The case was expunged because of her age.'

'How did you find out about it?'

'Maybe I'm not the lazy country copper you take me for, Duffy.'

'That's not fair. I don't take you for anything. It seems that you've done a good job here.'

'Oh, thanks very much.'

'Do you like McPhail for Lizzie's death?'

'I wouldn't put anything past him but I don't like him for her death because her death was an accident.'

I sighed and shook my head. 'I may be coming round to your way of thinking.'

'Oh, don't let me influence you, Inspector Duffy! You're *Special* Branch,' he said.

I didn't take the bait. Instead I thanked him for his time and drove to Belfast.

It was a tough run in, it was raining and there were army checkpoints everywhere and soldiers have never liked the cut of my jib. I parked the Beemer at Queen Street police station and took a black taxi out to the former DeLorean plant.

When I got to Dunmurry, prospective Congressman Joe Kennedy was already inside. The old factory was being converted into what a banner proclaimed were 'Exciting new public–private sector partnerships'.

There was a pro-Kennedy crowd and an anti-Kennedy crowd waiting for the politician outside the plant. I showed my Special Branch warrant card and easily got to the front of the control barriers. It was raining and the two crowds amounted to maybe a hundred people. The Reverend Ian Paisley, MP, MEP, was trying to whip the antis into a frenzy with talk about the Antichrist and the End of Days but it was a bit of a hard sell in the rain.

I waited by the gates.

A dreary, typically Belfast scene: low clouds, power-station chimneys pumping out grey death, greasy pavements, police Land Rovers, army helicopters, a rent-a-mob of religious nuts, TV camera crews hunting for visual sight bites for the evening news.

We waited and waited. Finally a limousine pulled up in front of the gates but no one got in or out and the cameramen turned their lights off again.

A wind blew from off the lough and there was a smattering of hailstones.

'Send the Antichrist back to America!' Paisley bellowed before launching into an obscure hymn that no one else, including his synthesiser player, seemed to know.

'Where are you from, mate?' an inspector from the riot squad asked me.

'Special Branch,' I told him.

'Jeez, I thought you boys had better things to do with their time than shite like this.'

Before I could answer the gates began trundling open and the crowd surged against the crash barriers. Police radios began to crackle and the Belfast coppers linked arms.

'Have your men ready, McDougal,' a riot-squad officer said to a square little red-faced man in a crash helmet.

'OK, lads, if we're needed, we go in softly. The whole world is watching as they say,' the red-faced man told his officers.

The limo door opened, the driver got out, walked to the rear door and opened it. A limo – God save us, even Thatcher and the Queen didn't use a limo.

There were jeers and cheers and catcalls and then I could see Kennedy and his minders and the government men walking out of the former car plant. Paisley began singing 'Jesus Loves Me This I Know' in his apocalyptic Ballymena staccato.

Kennedy seemed unfazed by the rain or the hail or his reception. His father was the martyred senator from New York, his uncle the martyred president, his other uncle, Teddy, was the current senator from Massachusetts. And he was the Dauphin.

He grinned and waved at the unsmiling faces. I had to admit that he was impressive. You noticed the hair first. Kennedy hair was far in advance of anything Ireland had to offer. It was space-age hair. It was hair for the new millennium. Irish hair was stuck somewhere in 1927. Kennedy hair had put man on the fucking moon.

Joe Kennedy had much of his uncles' charm and their recklessness around women: in the early 1970s he had crashed a jeep that had left one female passenger paralysed but from which he had walked unscathed. Not that that mattered in Ireland: what mattered here now was the blue suit, the well-calibrated poise oozing from every tanned pore and the Alexandrian curl of his blond locks.

An attractive female reporter – obviously American – rushed forward with a microphone.

'What do you think of your reception here today, Joe?' she asked.

'I am always delighted to meet Irish men and women, Sandy, even when they don't agree with me,' Kennedy replied smoothly, his teeth gleaming like an anti-missile laser.

'Go home, you bum!' someone yelled from the crowd.

'I am home!' Kennedy replied good-naturedly.

'Do you have any plans to run for congress?' the reporter asked.

Kennedy smiled and shook his head. 'Sandy, I'm not here today to talk about the congress. I'm here to talk about justice for the Irish people. I'm here to talk about ending the British policy of dividing Ireland!'

More catcalls from the crowd.

'And what is the purpose of your visit to this particular factory?'

'Our fact-finding team's primary concern here is to make sure that any project getting US taxpayer dollars is employing equal numbers of Catholics and Protestants. For, as you know, Sandy, for centuries, for millennia, for far too long, Catholics in Ireland have suffered at the hands of British imperialism!'

The reporter and the entourage nodded. This was going to

play very well tonight in South Boston. The protesters knew their part and booed again en masse. For them Joe Kennedy and the Kennedy clan stood for everything they despised about the Irish-American diaspora: rich, interfering, good-hearted but essentially kind of stupid . . .

I had stopped listening to the reporter and was focusing on the entourage. Two men were standing next to Kennedy. One of them was the local MP, the Sinn Fein president, Gerry Adams, and the second was the fixer for this trip, Lee McPhail. I'd taken Lee's photo from the file and studied it but that was unnecessary as he was absolutely unmistakable. Six eight, bald, with huge hands and a lupine face almost concealed by a straggly salt-and-pepper beard.

'Say no to the terrorists and their sympathisers! Say no to Rome rule! Say no to the Beast and to the Antichrist!' the Reverend Ian Paisley, MP, MEP, yelled, without the need of a megaphone.

The crowd surged against the frail-looking temporary crash barriers.

And then, quite suddenly, it all went to shit.

The barriers went down, the small squad of police were engulfed by the protesters and the prospective congressman no doubt wondered whether he was about to be the latest victim of the Kennedy curse.

'Get him out of here!' someone screamed.

An egg hit Kennedy on the head and he was lucky it wasn't half a brick. The inspector from the riot squad and myself pushed aside the TV reporter and began shoving him towards the car.

'What are you doing?' Lee McPhail screamed.

Kennedy thought that we were attacking him and lashed out at me with a neat left hook which caught me square on the face.

'For fucksake, I'm a policeman, you've got to get out of here!' I yelled, and shoved him towards the open door of the limo.

The crowd surged behind us. I heard the boom of a plastic

bullet gun, Paisley started screaming about the Whore of Babylon switching between the hieratic and the demotic. McPhail, Adams, Kennedy and myself all tumbled into the limousine together.

'Drive on!' I yelled to the chauffeur.

'There's people in the way!' he said.

'Drive slowly, then, but keep fucking moving!'

McPhail closed the limo door and we began edging our way through the crowd. Protesters were thumping on the roof and the windows and there was a tense five minutes or so before we made it on to the main road.

'The police did that on purpose!' Gerry Adams declared.

Joe Kennedy was too shook up to say anything. I handed him a handkerchief to get the egg out of his hair.

I looked at Adams. He had no recollection at all that we had met once before in the Maze prison. Probably a good thing, as I'd been a bit pissy with him on that occasion.

'You are?' Adams said, catching me in a stare.

'Inspector Sean Duffy of RUC Special Branch,' I said.

'I shall report this. This whole thing was obviously orchestrated by British Intelligence to humiliate the Kennedy family,' Adams said.

'Obviously you haven't had many dealings with British Intelligence if you think they could pull off something like this,' I said.

'I think Inspector Duffy saved our bacon,' Lee McPhail said.

'That's what we are expected to think. The whole thing was a set-up,' Adams insisted.

'Where's Helen? My hair's ruined,' Kennedy whined.

The limo had reached the centre of Belfast now and was making its way towards the Falls Road.

'Time for you to get out of our car!' Adams said to me.

'Do you mind if we have a chat?' I said to McPhail.

'You want to talk to me?' he asked.

'You're a hard man to track down.'

'Chat about what?' McPhail asked breezily.

'About Lizzie Fitzpatrick's death. I'm from the Cold Case Unit and we're taking another look at her death. Do you know what I'm talking about?'

He nodded. 'I do indeed. Aye, I'll get out with you. Stop here, driver!'

'Who's Lizzie Fitzpatrick?' Kennedy asked.

'Yes, who is Lizzie Fitzpatrick?' Adams wondered.

'Dermot McCann's sister-in-law,' McPhail said. Adams didn't have to be told who Dermot McCann was.

The limo pulled to a halt on Great Victoria Street. Lee opened the limo door.

'Thanks for the handkerchief,' Joe Kennedy said.

'You're welcome. Enjoy the rest of your stay in Belfast. We're not all mental. It just seems that way.'

Lee and I got out and the limo pulled off into the traffic.

'The Crown Bar?' Lee suggested.

'Perfect.'

We dodged the buses, police Land Rovers and black taxis and went into the Crown.

The Crown was my favourite Belfast pub, not just because it was a beautiful gas-lit Victorian drinking saloon or because my favourite film had been shot there (Carol Reed's *Odd Man Out*) or because they did an excellent pint of the black . . . no, I liked it because it was divided up into dozens of individual snugs, private booths, where you could close the door and have a confidential conversation.

'What's your poison?' I asked him.

'Whatever you're having,' he said, which was a nice way of getting my measure.

'Two Black Bushes and two Guinnesses please,' I said to the barman.

We took them to an intimate snug near the windows at the front.

'So, Lizzie Fitzpatrick,' Lee said.

'I've spoken to your fishing buddies,' I said.

'I suppose that fucker Arnie Yeats told you I didn't want us to go to the police.'

'He did tell me that. Is it not true?'

'It's true all right. I'm from the Ardoyne, son. Born and bred. And if there's one thing I've learned in this fallen world, it's that you don't go to the police with information.'

'Why not?'

'Two reasons. You don't rat. And second, they'll try and pin it, whatever *it* is, on you.'

'You want to tell me about the night of Lizzie's death?'

'All right.'

He took me through the same timeline that Yeats and Barry Connor had given me. Either that part of it was true or they had all agreed to tell the same story.

'So by eleven thirty you'd dropped both your friends off in Belfast. What did you do next?'

'I went home.'

'Where do you live?'

'As if you don't know . . . Botanic Avenue.'

'Two minutes away from Barry's house.'

'Aye.'

'So by eleven thirty-five you were safe in your bed?'

'Aye.'

'You were flirting with Lizzie Fitzpatrick on the night of her death, weren't you?'

Lee took a big drink of his Guinness and grinned at me. He had a quick smile and an alert eye.

'Am I to understand your line of reasoning here, Inspector Duffy? You think I left off my mates in Belfast at eleven thirty and then I gunned it back to Antrim to murder some girl who had rejected my advances and then I set up this elaborate fucking scheme to make it seem as if the pub was locked from the inside and she'd fallen off the bar? And I did all this just in the nick of time before the police showed up and broke the door down?'

'Well, did you?'

He laughed.

'Who's put you up to this? Annie McCann?' he asked with a sly look from under his thick black eyebrows.

'No one put me up to it. I'm in the Cold Case Unit. That's what we do,' I said. I didn't need him pursuing this any further.

'What you do is investigate unsolved murders. The coroner's inquest said that Lizzie Fitzpatrick's death was an accident.'

'No, the coroner returned an open verdict.'

'Ach, it's the same thing.'

'Not quite.'

Lee finished his pint and put the glass down on the table.

'Another?' he said.

'Aye, OK.'

He came back with two pints of Guinness and two bowls of Irish stew.

We ate and drank and when we were done Lee offered me one of his Camel cigarettes.

'So,' he said. 'How did a high-flyer like you end up in the RUC's Cold Case Unit?'

'High-flyer?'

'You took down those Loyalist queer killers from Rathcoole, you got yourself a medal. I did some digging on you, Duffy.'

'Digging?'

'Had to, after Barry calls me and says you're asking questions about me.'

'That sounds reasonable.'

'You were headed for the top, but the record goes all quiet for a while and now you're in some bullshit Cold Case Unit? What happened to you, boy?'

'I pissed off the wrong people.'

'What wrong people?'

'It's none of your business, McPhail.'

He nodded. 'It was the Chief Constable, wasn't it? A little bird told me that you fucked up their DeLorean case. Didn't you?'

'Jesus! Where do you get this from?'

'The same little bird.'

'Your avian informant was mistaken. I didn't fuck anything up. Don't you read the papers? DeLorean's under indictment by the FBI. He's going down,' I said.

'That's not what I hear. I hear he's going to walk.'

In truth I'd been avoiding all mention of the DeLorean case in the papers but Lee's assessment didn't surprise me. The FBI DeLorean team that I had run into did not appear to be the most competent bunch of policemen on the planet.

'Let's talk about you, Lee. Quite the step up from journo to petty crook to rapist to a character who hangs out with the likes of the Kennedys.'

'Steady on with the rape remarks, Duffy. She was a week from her seventeenth birthday. Across the water that wouldn't even be a crime.'

'Still . . . the Kennedys.'

'The future congressman's grandfather was a petty crook, bootlegger and small-time hood. The whole fucking family is corrupt from top to bottom. Bobby was the only decent one of them.'

'Jesus, that's a nice to thing to say.'

'You're a Catholic, aren't you?'

'Yeah,' I said.

'Well, I'll leave it there, then. I'm sure your mother and father have a framed picture of JFK up in their parlour.'

'They do, actually.'

'He was no Saint Jack and Joe's no saint either. Everybody thinks he could be president one day, but between you and me and the gatepost . . . no chance.'

'I met Adams once before in the Maze. He doesn't remember me,' I said.

'Count yourself lucky, Duffy. You don't want to be remembered. The only way to survive is to keep your head down. Keep your head down for fifty years.'

'Fifty years? Is that when the Golden Age is due to begin?'

'No. That's when the rest of Europe will be as blighted as Ireland. That's when the oil will have run out and the Americans will have gone home and the Chinks will be running the world.'

'Let's get this train back on the fucking track.'

'Go on.'

'That night in the Henry Joy McCracken . . . is it possible someone was hiding in the bog?'

'The bog?'

'Aye. The Ladies maybe?'

'Maybe the Ladies. Not the Gents. We were all in there at one time or another and there was no one there.'

'Are you sure?'

'Of course. And how did they get out? The doors were locked and barred from the inside, weren't they?'

'Locked doesn't mean shit. You could pick those old locks with a bit of skill. What I can't get past are the deadbolts on the front and back doors. Big heavy sliding bolts that you can only pull across from the inside. But if the killer was hiding, say, in the women's toilets and then somehow got out after the door was broken down . . .'

'That sounds like a possibility,' Lee said.

'Yeah, but it's not. That's not what happened at all. When they broke the door down a constable guarded the entrance until CID showed up. And when CID showed up they searched the entire premises and they found no one.'

'It's a real mystery, then, isn't it?' Lee said.

'It's only a mystery if it wasn't an accident.'

'Well then, you're in the clear, Duffy. It was an accident.'

'I've got two pathologists who think differently.'

He laughed. 'I'm glad this is your headache and not mine.'

'Did you happen to notice if there was a problem with any of the light bulbs in the place?'

'I didn't notice any problems with the light bulbs. I'm not saying there wasn't but I never noticed any.'

'And then there's that bloody burglary.'

'What burglary?'

I told him about the burglary at Lizzie's law offices and how Chief Inspector Beggs, the original detective on Lizzie's case, thought it was just a series of robberies done by a bunch of tinkers.

'Tinkers, eh? Don't listen to him. Lazy peelers are always blaming every unsolved crime on either the IRA or the tinkers. Is your Inspector Beggs any good?' Lee asked.

'That's another problem. He is actually.'

'And what does he think about Lizzie Fitzpatrick?'

'Oh, he's very clear on the matter. It was an accident.'

'It's nice to have certainty.'

'Isn't it? Here, how did you get that statutory rape charge expunged?'

'I married her.'

'That helps, does it?'

'It does.'

'Are you still married to her?'

'It didn't work out. Another round?'

'Aye, why not.'

He got another round and I got another round and it went on like that for the rest of the day.

My eye started to throb where Kennedy had punched me and Lee went off for five minutes and came back with a frozen steak.

'Put that on it and you'll be right as rain. And if you're not, sue the bastard. He can afford it.'

I liked Lee McPhail. I didn't want to, but I couldn't help

myself. He was gleefully amoral and had contempt for all sides in Northern Ireland's pointless religious wars. For him nationalism was a perverse hangover from the nineteenth century, and the sooner everyone started thinking of themselves before their country the better.

We drank until last orders and I walked to Queen Street police station, where I'd parked my Beemer. The cops there wouldn't let me take it because they said that I was intoxicated, which may have been true after nine or ten pints of stout, but I still kicked up a stink about it.

'Forget it, Duffy, we'll get you a taxi,' Lee said.

We found a taxi rank and parted like old friends . . .

There was rain all the way back to Carrick and the driver charged me an extra fiver because I was out of area. I paid him and when he'd gone I noticed a strange car parked outside my house. A black Jaguar. I knew it could be an assassination squad come to kill me from pretty much any side, but I was too blitzed and tired and fed up to get agitated about it.

I got halfway down the path when I noticed that there was music coming from the living room. With some difficulty I drew my service revolver and put the key in the lock.

'Who's there?' I demanded, pushing the door open.

'What time do you call this?' Kate demanded from the living room. 'The dinner's ruined. I knew this was a bad idea.'

I put the gun away.

She came into the hall and looked at me with concern.

'What happened to your eye?'

'President Kennedy's nephew punched me in the face.'

'What?'

'Don't go all diplomatic incident on me. He didn't do it on purpose. At least, I think he didn't.'

'Do you have a steak? You should put a steak on that,' she said.

'I've done the whole steak thing. I could do with a drink,

though. Anything non-alcoholic. I think there's lime juice in the fridge.'

I went into the living room. She'd been listening to my Motown collection and had made her way through to Gladys Knight and the Pips.

She brought me the lime juice and a bag of ice.

'Maybe I should run you a bath or something,' she said.

'Did you really make dinner?'

'Yes. Pasta.'

'That would be nice.'

'It'll be all sticky now.'

'I'm sure it will be fine.'

We ate at the kitchen table.

'And I'll be with him on that midnight train to Georgia. I'd rather live in his world than live without him in mine . . .' Gladys sang from the living room.

The pasta was a little dried out but still good. When we were done with it, it was well after midnight.

'Aren't you going to ask me how I got in here?' Kate said.

'I assume MI5 have their methods.'

'The neighbours let me in. Mrs Campbell. We had a nice chat about you.'

'Uh-huh?'

'Yes. She told me that she was worried about you for a while there,' Kate said, with a twinkle in her eye.

'Not any more?'

'Not any more. She thinks you're doing much better now.'

'That's good.'

'Are you doing better now, Sean?'

'Despite appearances . . . yeah. I've got something to get my teeth into. We all need a job of work. Otherwise you think too much and you know what that leads to . . .'

I put a finger gun to my head and mimed pulling the trigger.

'We've received some new intelligence. We think Dermot

might be in Germany.'

'Germany. Why would he be in Germany?'

'Preparing an attack on one of the British army bases there?'

I shook my head. 'I doubt it. When Dermot announces himself it's going to be something huge. A spectacular. It's not going to be an attack on an out-of-the-way British army base in bloody Germany.'

I suddenly got a stabbing pain in my eye. 'Jesus! That fucker really clocked me.'

'Let me draw you a bath, Sean,' she said, rather sweetly.

'That's surprisingly intimate.'

'Don't get any ideas. It's just a bath.'

When she went upstairs I made a hasty vodka gimlet and followed her up.

She had lit the paraffin heater on the landing and was looking at my bookcase. It wasn't as badass as my record collection. Mostly novels but quite a few of them were Penguin classics. The usual suspects: nineteenth-century biggies, the Americans, a Frog or two and the Beats. I left her to it and got in the bath. A minor miracle that there was hot water at this time of night. I started to drink the vodka gimlet in the tub and it went straight to my head.

'Mind if I read this?' she asked from my bedroom.

'What is it?'

'*The Counterfeiters*.'

'It's not about what you think it's going to be about . . . Oh, wait, you probably know that. Grab me a book too, will you?'

'What book?'

'Any book . . . No, on the bottom shelf, on the far left, get me that biography of JFK.'

She opened the door and primly slid the book across the tiled floor.

'Ta.'

I picked up the big hardback, which had been a Christmas

present from my parents that I had never had the motivation to read. I flipped it open, read a couple of paragraphs and put it aside. I couldn't care less about the bloody Kennedys. I finished the vodka gimlet and put the glass on the floor next to the tub and sank deeply into the water. I gazed fixedly at my map-of-the-world shower curtain. Australia was all bunched up in the corner. Greenland was way too big.

'I suppose you wanna know about the investigation?' I said.

'I wouldn't mind hearing what you've got.'

'I haven't found Lizzie's killer. In fact I don't even know if she was murdered. And if she wasn't murdered I don't know if Mary Fitzpatrick will give me Dermot's whereabouts.'

'If she even knows them.'

'Fair point. But she does move in old Republican circles. She's got some old contacts. Hey, I should have asked Gerry Adams where Dermot was. I was talking to him today.'

My head was spinning now. The vodka was a mistake.

Kate said something. 'What?'

She said it again.

I ignored her and sank beneath the water. I surfaced and my eye still hurt.

'Hey, you couldn't make me another gimlet, could you, I'll never get to sleep with this eye,' I said.

She said something that might have been 'I think you've had enough'.

'I'm dying of thirst.'

'Are you decent?'

'The bath's quite foamy.'

'I'll bring you some water.'

She came in with a pint glass of iced water. I drank it and gave it back to her.

She sat down on the laundry bin.

'I found out your name. Shoddy security at your end. Kate Prentice!'

'I would have told you. It's not a secret.'

'That's what you say now, after I found out. Do me a favour and pass me that book.' She gave me the JFK biography and I went back to the paragraph I'd just been reading. 'Listen to this . . . It all comes down to the Kennedy hair. Listen. It says here that on the morning of 22 November 1963 Jack Kennedy was given a Stetson at the Fort Worth Hotel by the Fort Worth Chamber of Commerce. His aides begged him to wear the Stetson on the motorcade route through Dallas because they knew it would be a real crowd-pleaser. But Jack Kennedy had great hair and he had a policy of never being photographed in a hat. He *refused* to wear the Stetson and we all know what happened next.'

'What?'

'Oswald's third shot was aimed at the dead centre of JFK's unmistakable helmet cut. If he'd been wearing the Stetson the whole history of the world would have been different.'

'Did you tell this to the president's nephew? Is that why he punched you?'

'He punched me by accident. It was a misunderstanding!'

'I think you should take a couple of aspirin and go to bed.'

'OK.'

'I'll leave while you get out.'

I put on my dressing gown, took two aspirin and lay down on the bed. My head was spinning again and my eye throbbing.

Kate sat beside me and helped me under the covers.

'Kiss it better, will you?' I said. 'And say "there, there".'

'There, there,' she said.

No kiss but that was OK. I smiled under the cool sheets and within half a dozen heartbeats I was asleep.

22: DEATH IN THE AFTERNOON

I pulled back the curtains. Another dishwater sky and rain falling so slowly that you wondered how it was coming down at all. As if it had to be dragged from the clouds to water yet another dreary Ulster morning.

I stood there looking at the hills. I thought about the three fishermen and their alibis. I thought about Lizzie. I thought about the impossibility of the crime.

I thought about Annie. Poor, lost, beautiful Annie.

When I went downstairs I was surprised to find Kate still there. She'd grabbed a sleeping bag from her car and had dossed down on the sofa. She was awake, drinking a mug of tea. The Open University was on the telly.

'Watcha watching?'

'It's about volcanoes.'

'What about volcanoes?' I asked.

'Volcanism. Magma. Iceland. Hawaii. You know the story.'

'Pompeii in there somewhere?'

'Do you want some tea?'

'Aye, OK.'

'You want some Weetabix?' she shouted from the kitchen.

'Nah.'

She made me the tea and sat next to me on the sofa. 'Where were you last night?' she asked.

'The Crown.'

'Nice?'

'Never been?'

'No.'

'They filmed *Odd Man Out* in there.'

'They didn't actually. Carol Reed had the whole place remade in Alexander Korda's London Films Studios. Same place that they made all those wonderful Michael Powell films.'

'Do you know everything?'

'Yes. I do. Look, I have to head on, Sean.'

'OK.'

'How do you feel?'

'Like I've just read one of those Philip Larkin poems you come across in the *Observer*.'

'We're having a meeting about you at the end of next week,' she said, biting her lip.

'Is that so?'

'It is.'

'What are you going to tell them?'

'I'm going to tell them that you're working very hard.'

'I *am* working very hard.'

'Good. And, er, is everything all right?'

'Everything's fine! Apart from a splitting headache.'

She looked at me affectionately. 'Do you think maybe the time has come to shut down this lead and pursue other lines of enquiry?'

I shook my head. 'I don't think we're there yet. It's beginning to look like Lizzie's death was an accident but I can't say it definitively and I don't want to go to Mary Fitzpatrick until I know for sure. There's this *coincidental* burglary I don't like the look of, for a start.'

'OK, well, you know best.'

She got up and went into the hall. She put on her coat, came back in, rolled up her sleeping bag and tucked it under her arm. 'Please don't lose sight of the fact that the reason we brought you back was to help us find Dermot McCann. That's your job. Nothing else. All right?'

'All right! Don't get all eggy,' I said wearily.

'I'm not "eggy" or even cross but do remember we'd really like to find him before the IRA's big push. It's the last thing we need with the miners' strike starting to cause tremors. If the government falls, God knows what will happen.'

'The government's not going to fall. Who calls a miners' strike in the summer when nobody uses coal and when the power stations have been stockpiling it all year? Thatcher's manipulated this whole situation. She's pulling all of our strings.'

'Quite,' she said, and went outside to her car.

On the TV a beardy guy with glasses was blathering on about earthquakes and tidal waves. Mrs McDowell came over to borrow sugar. I asked her the name of the famous baby-rearing book and she told me that no book was necessary – the slightest wee dash of Irish whiskey in the bottle was all you needed for a good night's sleep.

I showered, had a quick breakfast and drove to Carrick police station. I chatted to Matty and McCrabban about their cases and I left my office door open so that they could come in whenever they wanted to talk to me about mine.

I did this every day. I reread Chief Inspector Beggs' case report and I examined the photographs of the locks on the two doors of the Henry Joy McCracken.

In the Oxfam shop I grabbed a copy of Edward Thomas' *Icknield Way* and a brand-new copy of *Baby and Child Care* by Benjamin Spock. When I paid, the Spock fluttered open, revealing a news story cut out from the *Daily Mail* that I picked off the floor.

'What's that?' Peggy asked.

It was a lurid December 1983 account of the suicide of Dr Spock's grandson, who had jumped to his death from the roof of Boston's Children's Museum. I handed Peggy the clipping.

'He's not foolproof, then, is he?' Peggy said, tapping Spock's face.

'Few people are, Peggy.'

'Except for you, Inspector Duffy. There are no flies on you.'

On the Wednesday, Crabbie asked me to interrogate an elder who had been accused of stealing money from a Presbyterian kirk because he felt that he would lose his rag with the man. It was a walk in the park. After only forty minutes in Interview Room 1 the poor guy broke down and confessed. Gambling was at the root of it, he said, in tears. It was an ugly business, and to show his gratitude Crabbie offered to drive to Antrim to look over the Henry Joy McCracken and give me his professional opinion.

I took him up on the offer the following Friday.

We drove to Antrim in the Beemer and because of a police action we were diverted into the housing estates and got completely lost. Ballycraigy Estate, in particular, afforded us an intense, Hogarthian snapshot of human misery before we found the road to Ballykeel.

We called in on the Fitzpatricks: Annie and Mary had gone to Omagh to visit Mary's mother but Jim Fitzpatrick was home watching a fishing programme on Channel 4. It was ten in the morning and the poor sod was half wasted. I asked him for the keys to the pub and he brought them to us without saying a word.

'Was that the dad?' Crabbie asked as we walked into the village.

'Yeah.'

'He's sixty, is he? He looks ninety.'

'Lizzie's death has hit him hard.'

'He was half tore. Did you notice that?'

'I noticed.'

'It's a shame. A crying shame. Strong drink is the curse and ruination of Ireland.'

'That it is.'

We drove to the village and parked the car. We were just getting out of the BMW when we bumped into Harper McCullough and his wife, Jane. I introduced them to McCrabban and a stressed-out Jane informed us that the baby was now officially overdue.

'If she doesn't start going into labour by the weekend they're going to have to induce her,' Harper said, with a wild-eyed look of terror in his eyes.

'They did that to my missus. It's nothing to be afraid of,' Crabbie assured him.

'I want to give birth naturally, that's why we're walking round and round the village,' Jane said. 'My mother says it might help.'

'Her mother said she should go for a ride on a horse! She said that that would fix her!' Harper said with amazement.

'Me ma was joking,' Jane protested.

Harper rolled his eyes. 'The previous generations have some mad notions. I'm surprised any of us are here at all,' he said.

'Here, Harper, me old chum, I got this for you,' I said, and opened the BMW's boot and gave him the copy of Dr Spock's *Baby and Child Care*.

'Oh, this looks great!' he said, clutching it like a lifebelt.

'And I meant to tell you, I saw this Open University programme the other morning about earthquakes and tidal waves. This guy with a fantastic beard was talking all about Alexandria and how much of it was underwater. You would have liked it. With the new baby you'll be up all hours of the night. You should look into the Open University, you could take up archaeology again,' I said.

Jane gave me a grateful smile. 'You really could, you know,' she said to him.

'We'll see. Let's get this baby born first. Where are you two gentlemen off to today?' Harper asked.

'I'm going to get Sergeant McCrabban's professional opinion on the layout of the pub,' I said.

'The locked-room problem,' Crabbie muttered darkly.

'The locked-room problem, indeed,' I said.

'Of course, if the killer couldn't possibly have got out of there then there's no problem,' Crabbie added.

'Because?'

'Because there was no killer.'

'And my two doctors?' I asked.

Crabbie shrugged. 'You know why you always have to get a second opinion? Because doctors are often completely wrong.'

'Lizzie had exceptional balance, you know,' Harper said to McCrabban.

'So I've been told, but changing a light bulb is a tricky business,' Crabbie said. 'Me da fell off his tractor one time in Ballymena. He'd got on and off that tractor every day for forty years. One day he slipped and broke his pelvis.'

'Was he all right?' Jane asked.

'He was in pain for a day or two but then he went to the Lord,' Crabbie said.

'Jesus,' I muttered under my breath.

'We could walk over to the pub with you. We could help you out,' Harper said keenly.

Jane looked less than enthused at this prospect. A dusty pub, the place her husband's old girlfriend died . . .

'Uh, no thanks, Mr McCullough, it's official police business and we can't really involve civilians.'

Harper looked disappointed. 'Well, if there's anything we can do to help, give us a ring.'

'And tell Annie I was asking for her, if you see her,' Jane said.

We said goodbye to them, wished Jane luck and continued on to the Henry Joy McCracken.

I opened the door and turned the lights on. I walked Crabbie through the pub, showed him the bar, the toilets, the light bulb fixtures. I didn't offer any further information. I let him take it in for himself.

He examined the basement, looked at the roof and finally the front and back doors.

'Obviously they had to repair the broken-down front door but the back door is the way it was?'

'Aye.'

He went outside and tested the strength of the bars on all the windows.

'No way anyone's getting through those,' he said.

'I agree.'

'The paint is consistent, too.'

'Yes.'

He inspected the basement, shone a torch at the hammer-beam ceiling, walked inside and outside for ten minutes and then pulled up a chair.

I sat opposite him.

'Well?'

'If both doors were bolted from the inside the killer must have been inside when the police came. But Beggs searched the pub from top to bottom and no one was hiding here, right?'

'Right.'

'Ergo no killer.'

'That's your opinion?'

'That's my opinion . . . However . . .'

'However what?' I asked him, with a tremor of excitement.

'Her dad's in the hospital, her mother's on the way back from the hospital with a status report on her dad's health, she's so keen to get home she kicks the punters out at exactly eleven o'clock . . .'

'Or maybe even a little before.'

'Right. She gives McPhail, Yeats and Connor the bum's rush 'cos she wants to get back home. So why on earth does she decide that she has to change the light bulb that's been annoying her all evening? I mean, think about it. She has to look for a replacement bulb, she has to turn all the lights off so she doesn't get electrocuted, she has to bolt and lock the front door. She has to get up on the bar and start fiddling with a dusty old light bulb in the dark that she can barely reach 'cos she's only five foot two. She does all that instead of just leaving, locking the front door and rushing home to see how her da's doing.'

'What are you saying, Crabbie?' I asked him.

'I'm saying that now that I'm sitting here thinking about it I'm not buying it.'

'I'm not selling it.'

'I know you're not. But the killer is, isn't he?'

'He certainly is. He wants us to think that an accident happened. That a murder is impossible,' I said.

'This isn't a sex crime. Nothing's been stolen. Which poses the question . . . why did he do it? It was something about Lizzie. Had to be.'

'What about her, Crabbie?'

'I don't know. Something she'd done? Something she knew?'

'I like the way you're cooking here. Look around you. Was there anywhere he could have been hiding that we might have overlooked?' I asked.

Crabbie considered it and shook his head. 'No, Sean, he wasn't hiding in the pub. He was long gone. If he was careful enough to kill her and make it look like an accident he wouldn't have taken the risk of hiding in the pub,' Crabbie said.

'My way of thinking, too.'

Crabbie took out his pipe and I took out me fags. I borrowed his lighter and sucked down a Marlboro Light.

'Do you know why magicians don't reveal how they do their tricks?' I asked him.

'Why's that, Sean?'

'Because the way they do it – twins, misdirection, looking at your card while you're not looking – is usually so stupid they know you'll have nothing but contempt for them when you find out. I bet we're missing something here that's really stupid and obvious.'

'It's not obvious to me.'

'Or me . . . yet.'

We sat and smoked for twenty minutes, but even though we were at the scene of the crime, we had two good cop brains and we were lubricated by our tobacco of choice, still illumination did not dawn.

We locked up the pub and walked back through the village to the Fitzpatricks'.

Mary and Annie were home now and we gave them the key and said a quick hello. I introduced McCrabban and I explained what we'd been doing.

Mary asked whether we'd made any progress.

'Unfortunately not,' I said. 'But we're still working on it.'

'I'm glad to see that you're still working on it,' Mary said, looking at me significantly.

'I'll keep on it until I'm easy in my mind one way or the other,' I said.

'That's good,' Mary said.

'Well, we should be off. Jane was asking for you,' I told Annie.

Instead of pleasure a look of jagged annoyance sliced across Annie's face.

'Asking about me, was she?' she said, a little testily.

'In a very nice way,' I insisted.

'She's overdue, isn't she? I knew she'd pull something like that. She's quite the drama queen when all is said and done.'

'Annie! Don't be ridiculous. She can't force the baby out!' Mary insisted.

Annie looked at me for support, but I wasn't getting involved in this.

'We should go.'

'Aye, we better get back,' McCrabban agreed, and we hurried out to the Beemer.

'Can you tolerate Radio 3?' I asked him.

'It's your car, mate. Your rules,' he said.

It was Brahms' Symphony Number 3, which wasn't that objectionable.

We drove back to Carrickfergus in rare August sunshine. I took us in along the Tongue Loanen, through the sheep fields and cow pasture.

We drove to the station along Taylor's Avenue and the bridge over the railway lines. There was a grubby man standing there next to a Toyota Hilux. He was wearing a green and white Glasgow Celtic bobble hat. There was a lankness about his features. A measured insolence. Something about him that made Crabbie and me both take notice. There was a driver in the Hilux with a ginger beard and in the back of the pick-up something that resembled building materials under a tarp.

A few hours later Crabbie and I were able to give them a description of the two men and the vehicle.

But they never caught them.

They never do.

I went through the checkpoint and parked the Beemer at the rear of the police station in the space near the wall reserved for CID personnel.

The sun was shining. The birds were singing. There hadn't been a riot for days but Northern Ireland's stuttering journey to normality abruptly came to an end that afternoon with a series of bomb attacks on police stations.

Carrickfergus was an out-of-the-way police barracks. And it was this which had probably saved it from the worst of the Troubles. Everywhere, however, has their time. The reason the USAAF targeted Hiroshima was because it had, up until that point, got off lightly . . .

Crabbie was out of tobacco so we walked down to Sandy Walker's newsagents. He went inside and I waited for him. There was a nice view of the lough and the castle, and it could have been lovely but for the fact that the tide was out and Downshire beach was littered with its usual modern-art ensemble of plastic bags, shopping trolleys, tyres, sewage and the odd dead sea creature.

Crabbie paid, we walked back to the barracks and went upstairs.

Matty was at the coffee machine talking to a pretty, pale, dark-haired reserve constable I didn't know. I felt a minor spasm of guilt that I hadn't got to his letter of recommendation yet, but he hadn't hassled me about it so maybe he'd had a change of plan.

Matty asked McCrabban and me whether either of us wanted a cup of tea.

'I think we're all right, mate. And it looks like you're busy enough,' I said, and winked at Crabbie. 'I'll get on with that letter you wanted, mate.'

'Ta very much,' Matty said.

I went into my office and booted up the Apple, but instead of writing the letter of recommendation I played Beyond Castle Wolfenstein, determined this time to get to the level where I could kill Hitler.

Time ticked.

Death made his way along the lough . . .

I closed my eyes for a moment.

There was an enormous bang and a crash and then two more bangs.

The last mortar landed very close, the percussion wave smashing the windows in my office and throwing me out of my chair into the wall.

Dust was everywhere. Blood in my mouth.

Bomb, I thought. *No . . . gas explosion. No . . . bomb.*

I rubbed my eyes and looked at the wrecked room. My chair was on top of the filing cabinet. My desk had been overturned, the window had imploded.

Being in a bombing inside a building is like no experience one has ever had before. The only thing to compare it to is an earthquake. All your certainties have gone. The solid world has collapsed and what is left is fear and awe and the momentary exhilaration of being alive.

Time slows.

Adrenalin spikes.

Hysteria and shock, even among us hardened professionals.

I heard screaming. The ringing of a fire alarm. I got to my feet, steadied myself and opened my office door. I was surprised at how little damage there had been. Later we learned that only two of the mortars had hit their target and the rest had missed and arced harmlessly into the sea.

The roof had caved in and there was smoke and debris, but there was no fire and the walls of the station were intact.

'Are you OK?' a man asked me.

'I'm fine,' I said.

'Over here,' he said.

Two uniformed officers were trying to lift a concrete slab off a woman's smashed legs. I felt absurdly strong and I tried to help, but twenty men wouldn't have been enough. And it was too late anyway. A girder from the roof had impaled her through the abdomen and she was losing blood by the mugful.

She was crying and someone took her hand.

I sat down for a moment.

Breathed in dust, coughed.

'You're bleeding,' someone said.

I touched my scalp. It was only a scratch.

'We have to evacuate. Here, let me help you up, sir.'

Outside into the August sun.

Ambulance men came. Firemen came. There was even a helicopter.

A blanket went around my shoulders, sweet tea was pressed into my hands. A girl with blonde hair wiped my face. 'Drink your tea,' she said. 'It'll make you feel better.'

I drank it and it did make me feel a little better.

I was triaged into a low-priority group and it wasn't until an hour later that I was taken to the Moyle Hospital in Larne where I got half a dozen stitches in my scalp and a splint on a sprained wrist.

It was in the recovery room of the Moyle surgical ward that I learned that six police stations and four army bases had been targeted that afternoon in a simultaneous assault. The mortars they'd launched at Carrick police station had only ten-pound shells, whereas in a similar attack Newry police station had been hit by half a dozen fifty-pounders, just one of which had killed nine policemen and injured thirty-seven.

Carrick police station had suffered only two fatalities. Reserve Constable Heather McClusky and the person she had been talking to at the coffee machine: Detective Constable Matty McBride.

23: SEPTEMBER

After two days the doctors still didn't like the swelling on my head and refused to give me permission to attend Matty's funeral, which meant that I had to sign myself out between nurses' shifts and get Crabbie to meet me in the hospital car park and drive me to the small churchyard in Magheramorne.

Matty's father, a Dunkirk veteran and an old-time peeler, gave the eulogy. He talked about Matty's love of the police and how his son had wanted to bring a better future to everyone in Northern Ireland.

Every cop there knew that all Matty really cared about was fly fishing and girls, and that, perhaps foolishly, he had treated the cops as a civil-service job that gave him a lot of time off to drive to the Fermanagh lakes.

My head was on fire at the wake but I managed a couple of jokes and told his father that I was proud of him and that I'd think of Matty every day for the rest of my life.

His old man thanked me and I could see that he was moved.

Crabbie wanted to drive me back to the hospital after the wake but I got him to take me home instead.

Heather McClusky's funeral was the next day in Ballycarry but my head was throbbing and I was running a fever and I just couldn't make it. It didn't matter. Apparently the Chief Constable and the Secretary of State came down for that one.

The IRA attacked more police stations, army bases and

shops in the coming weeks. They used a variety of techniques: mortars, drogue bombs, truck bombs, grenades and rockets. This, apparently, was the beginning of the Libyan team's big push. I read in the paper that my old friend the luxuriantly coiffed Joe Kennedy had exculpated the actual terrorists and blamed all the attacks on the British army's continuing presence in Northern Ireland.

Kate called to see whether I was doing OK and I said that I'd need a few weeks to get back in the saddle, which I knew would buy me some time without any pressure.

In other news the miners' strike across the water was generating increasing chaos for Thatcher's government, Mrs Gandhi attacked the Golden Temple in Amritsar, killing two thousand people, and John DeLorean was acquitted of all charges stemming from his cocaine bust.

I spent some time at home doing nothing and MI5, to their credit, left me alone. I didn't really know why they were giving me all this string. Perhaps they were desperate or perhaps I was one of a dozen crazy lines in the stream and they only needed one of them to bite.

I appreciated that they had gone off the reservation to bring me in. And I felt some sense of obligation. But what I didn't have I didn't have. I wasn't going to bang my head against a wall. Magnum PI did that on TV and other cops in books. But few people in the RUC ever banged their head against a wall about a case. We conserved our psychic energy for the day-to-day. We were all too busy trying to stay alive. At Stalingrad no one cheered when the tractor factory finally fell. I knew how they felt. Emotion was a luxury none of us could afford.

In the middle of September I drove to Antrim to talk to Mary Fitzpatrick.

I told her what I had and what I didn't have.

She listened politely and it wasn't what she wanted. She wanted definitive answers. I said that I would keep working on it.

Annie was there and she walked me out to my car.

'I heard about what happened at your police station,' she said. 'Are you OK?'

'I'm fine.'

'The newspapers say it was the boys from Libya.'

'Maybe. Who knows?'

'If it was Dermot's cell, then I'm sorry, Sean.'

I nodded and she took my hand.

'I'm glad you're OK, Sean,' she said.

'Yeah, I'm all right.'

'I've got something to tell you. I've been thinking about things and I've made some decisions.'

'Like what?'

'I'm going to go to Canada. Montreal. Vanessa says they need teachers out there. I'm not too old to start something new.'

'Of course not.'

'New country, a whole new life.'

'I think it's a great idea.'

'I'm worried about my mum and dad, though, you know?'

'Your mother's a strong, capable woman and she'll cope just fine without you.'

'You think so?'

'I know so.'

She smiled sadly, kissed me on the cheek and went back inside the house.

So the IRA didn't get a permanent propaganda coup, they quickly repaired Carrickfergus police station and rebuilt it with a reinforced roof and a huge fence around the outer perimeter wall. I went back to my office but it was so morbid in there I immediately abandoned the idea and started working in Carrick library instead, booking one of the study rooms and reading the case notes over and over . . .

That's where McCrabban found me one afternoon with a look of mild satisfaction on his face. 'I've got something for you,' he said.

'What have you found out?'

'Our friend who owns that nice French restaurant we had lunch at. Turns out he has a teenage burglary conviction.'

'Barry Connor?'

'Mr Barry Connor to you,' Crabbie said, giving me the arrest sheet.

It was a teen rap sheet on a newsagent and post office, in Bangor, County Down. We'd all shoplifted at some point in our teenage lives and everyone dreams about robbing a bank when they're a kid, but the interesting part of Barry's epic tale was the fact that he had picked the newsagent's lock before tripping the silent alarm.

McCrabban grinned when I got to that bit. 'Barry knows how to get into locked rooms,' he said.

'This is good work, mate! You fancy some free French lunch?'

'I might.'

We drove the Beemer into Belfast and parked it at Queen Street cop shop.

We walked to Le Canard, took a discreet seat near the back and ordered off the à la carte. 'And we'll talk to the boss. Tell him it's Detective Inspector Sean Duffy,' I told the waiter.

When Barry appeared he was sweating, purple-faced and harassed-looking.

'You can't keep doing this. Not in the middle of lunch service, it's not right!' he said.

'Why don't you write to your MP?' I suggested.

'I will!'

I pulled a chair from a neighbouring table and set it next to me.

'Let's talk about your burglary conviction, shall we, Barry?'

He sat down with a groan. 'That was twenty years ago,' he hissed.

'How did you learn how to pick locks?' I asked him.

'From a book.'

'What book?'

'A book of magic. *Houdini's Secrets Revealed*,' Barry said.

'Weren't you saying something about magic tricks, Inspector Duffy?' Crabbie said to me.

'I was indeed, Sergeant McCrabban. I was saying that only a magician could have killed Lizzie Fitzpatrick and got away with it,' I replied.

'I didn't kill Lizzie Fitzpatrick! I was home in my bed!' Barry said, sweating even more profusely now. The dishes from the à la carte arrived but I was off my grub.

'Tell me about this book,' I said.

'It taught you how to pick every lock. Handcuffs, that kind of stuff. The one time I tried it on a shop, I got caught. I was seventeen, for heaven's sake!'

'Do you happen to remember what the locks were like on the Henry Joy McCracken?'

'I have no idea! I grew out of all that!'

'How would you escape from a locked room if you had to, Mr Connor?'

'I wouldn't have the faintest idea,' he protested.

'How would Houdini do it? Come on, son, rack your brains.'

He wiped the sweat from his forehead with the back of his sleeve. 'Houdini? I don't know. A trapdoor. A hidden wall. A false bottom. That kind of thing,' he said desperately.

I looked at McCrabban and he gave me the minutest little shake of the head. I agreed with him. This guy wasn't our man. I popped a piece of bread into my mouth.

'Do you have any questions, Sergeant McCrabban?'

'No, I don't.'

'All right, Mr Connor, you can go back to your lunch service.'

'That's it? I'm free?'

'That's it. You're free. But if you think of anything pertinent to this case next time you better call me before I come calling on you, OK?'

'OK, yes, officers, yes!' he said with palpable relief.

Crabbie ate his lunch and we asked for the bill but naturally it was on the house again. Not only that but we were given half a dozen vouchers for a free lunch. Since we were in the neighbourhood I tried to see Lee McPhail but he was escorting another American politician around Belfast. This time it was some guy called Peter King, who was the Comptroller of Nassau County and Grand Marshal of the New York St Patrick's Day parade. While he was in Ulster, King got a lot of publicity by calling Gerry Adams 'the George Washington of Ireland' and by championing IRA bomb attacks and assassinations as part of the legitimate struggle against British imperialism. On the TV news that night Lee looked like the cat who got the cream. King was even better than Kennedy at generating headlines.

Ennui. Anomie.

I took riot duty, even though I didn't have to. Belfast in silent tableaux: skeleton cars, men in balaclavas, men in riot gear, bonfires, the tea-coloured lough, bombsites growing with fern and alyssum, Venus above the Pleiades, petrol smell as sweet as new-mown hay, felled telegraph poles, feral kids, smoke curled over the city streets like some great dragon . . . Days like this. Nights.

A vodka gimlet. *Dr Who*. A knock at the door. Mrs Hamilton from over the way in floods of tears. The problem was Jessie Watson, who had stolen one of her kids' go-karts to use in the 'ark' he was building in his back garden. I knew all about Jessie Watson: a lay preacher in one of those apocalyptic American sects that had been blossoming in Carrickfergus recently. God had told him that the polar ice caps were melting and he was the one to build a boat. Jessie, who'd had no previous experience with carpentry, naval architecture or the interpretation of divine visions, did have a history of violence and psychiatric problems, so I went over with my revolver and opened his front door with extreme caution. I found him sobbing on the kitchen floor, naked and covered in what I hoped was brown paint. The go-kart was in the back garden, undamaged. I didn't see any evidence of any 'ark', which wasn't surprising, considering that it was bonfire season. I returned the go-kart to Mrs Hamilton.

'Thank you,' she said. 'A man like that should be locked up. That's part of your job, Mr Duffy, to protect the public.'

'Aye, but we'll be laughing on the other side of our faces when the flood does come and we're scrambling for a berth, eh?'

A few days later Mrs Hamilton brought over a ticket for the Monsters of Rock concert at Castle Donington. It was a wee thank-you, and her brother-in-law was looking for a driver—. We drove over in the Beemer, pitched our tent, drank a lot, saw AC/DC and Van Halen and copped off with a couple of strumpets during the Mötley Crüe gig, which Mötley Crüe would have approved of.

The night we got back a sergeant in charge of incinerating seized drugs, guns and pornography came out to my house with a bag of Moroccan blond cannabis resin the size and shape of a dog turd. 'Are you interested?' he asked.

Why did he think I'd want to buy it from him? I suppose I just had that kind of face. The street value was about 5,000 quid. I offered him 200 pounds. He took it, no questions asked. I suppose I could have suspected an Internal Affairs sting operation, but I knew the RUC wouldn't dream of fucking me while I was protected by MI5.

And speaking of MI5. A helicopter to Bessbrook. Grim faces. Questions. I stalled them as best as I could. *Following leads, testing stories, new developments* . . . but they could see that I was never going to solve the Lizzie Fitzpatrick case. Like the *Mary Celeste*, the Bermuda Triangle and the popularity of Spandau Ballet, some things you were never destined to know the answer to.

Kate liked me, didn't she? Maybe she would let me string them along for a few more months before quietly letting me rejoin the RUC full-time in the new year.

A helicopter ride back to Carrick.

Days. Nights. Bombs. Riots.

Simmering civil war.

Circling.

Circling . . .

There are cops who push through the blocks in a case through the sheer force of their intellect. I am not one of those cops.

I'm a cop who needs a break.

In October I finally got one.

24: A FIXER CALLS

'White Rabbit' was on the stereo, I had rolled myself a fat joint of Atlas Mountains kif and the sweetest North Carolina pipe tobacco, and I was about to get in the bath when I heard the phone ringing downstairs in the living room.

It was fifty-fifty whether I would ignore it or not.

If I had ignored the call Lee said that he wouldn't have called back because it was his instinct never to offer the police information in any circumstances.

I *did* go downstairs. I did pick the phone off the table. 'Yeah?'

'It's Lee McPhail.'

'Lee. Good morning. I saw you on the telly. Your boy Peter King made quite a splash.'

'I expect big things from him. He's not presidential material but maybe V-P. And he's not cheating on his wife like our other friend.'

'What can I do for you, Lee?'

'It's what I can do for you.'

'Go on . . .'

'About those tinkers.'

'What tinkers?'

'The tinkers your Inspector Beggs thought broke into the Mulvenna and Wright law offices in Antrim in December 1980.'

'You've got my full attention.'

'The RUC couldn't trace those tinkers but I have contacts

that the RUC doesn't have.'

'I was told they were in England.'

'Well, they aren't.'

'Can I speak to them?'

'I'm not going to tell you who they are, Duffy. I don't shop friends of friends to the peelers. What's important for you is the fact that they did not break into the Mulvenna and Wright law offices. I talked to those boys myself and they are not eejits. They knew there wouldn't be much ready money in a place like that.'

'Of course not!' I said, and slapped my head. 'Your information's completely reliable?'

'My word on it, mate.'

'OK.'

'Do you understand what I'm telling you, Duffy?'

'I do. Thanks, Lee. I appreciate this. I owe you one.'

'You don't owe me anything. Just get the person who killed Lizzie Fitzpatrick.'

'I'll do my best.'

'Oh, and naturally, we never had this conversation.'

'I understand.'

He hung up. I unplugged the bath and threw the joint down the toilet. I shaved and dressed in a white shirt, black tie, black cords and a black sports jacket.

I put on my shoulder holster and checked that there were six rounds in my .38.

I went outside. No rain yet but there was some in the forecast.

I said good morning to Mrs Campbell and Mrs Clawson. I checked under the BMW for mercury tilt bombs, didn't find any and drove down Coronation Road until I hit the Barn Road. I took the Barn Road to the North Road and then the open country of the Raw Brae Road, where I gunned the Beemer up to a ton and change.

Sheep, cows, hills, high blackberry hedges, woods.

I kept to the B roads where traffic was light and I could speed.

I was in Antrim in fifteen minutes, coming in on the single-track lane through Lenagh.

I parked the Beemer in the police station for safe-keeping and got directions to the Mulvenna and Wright law office, which was now known as JJ Wright and Son, Solicitors-at-Law.

It was a glass-fronted building next to a dentist's on the high street.

An attractive young woman with very red lips and a black bob asked me whether I had an appointment.

I showed her my warrant card and asked her whether Mr Wright was busy.

She said that she thought not but she would see.

I was shown into his offices a couple of minutes later and the receptionist asked whether I would take a cup of tea. I told her that that would be lovely, milk, one sugar.

'So what can I do for you, Inspector Duffy?' Mr Wright asked.

He had curly ginger hair, which was miraculously ungreyed despite his age, which was around fifty-five. He was a big man with the build of a prop forward, and knowing how many rugby players became solicitors, that's probably exactly what he was. He had a ruddy, maroon-coloured face, massive hands and a dangerous mien.

I told him who I was and that I was looking into the case of Lizzie Fitzpatrick.

He nodded, said nothing.

'Your former partner, James Mulvenna, when did he pass on?' I asked.

'November 1980, although he was confined to his home from that summer onwards.'

'He had multiple sclerosis, I believe.'

'He did.'

'How old was he when he died?'

'James was fifty-one. The doctors said that he'd be lucky to make thirty. He told me that when we became partners, but by God he showed them.'

'After he died you took on most of his clients?'

'Some, not all. Others preferred to take their business elsewhere.'

'Because you were a Protestant and Mr Mulvenna was a Catholic?'

'You'll have to ask them that, I have no idea.'

'When Lizzie Fitzpatrick wrote to you asking to intern at your office over the Christmas holiday of 1980, why did you turn her down?'

'Why *would* I take her on?'

'Because she had interned for the previous two Christmases and the previous two summers.'

'She had interned for James Mulvenna, not for me. He knew her family.'

'Didn't Lizzie do a good job?'

'She did an excellent job by all accounts.'

'But still you didn't take her on?'

'I didn't have the time or the money to take on an intern that Christmas. In fact I haven't taken on an intern since. James cared a lot more about mentoring than I did,' he said.

'It wasn't because Lizzie was from a prominent Republican family and her sister was married to the IRA bomb-maker Dermot McCann?'

'That wouldn't endear me to her or her family. But that wasn't the reason I didn't bring her in. You have to pay interns in Northern Ireland, Inspector Duffy. The Law Society says you have to pay them a wage commensurate with a junior solicitor. I simply didn't have the money. To be honest, I wasn't sure if the firm was going to survive James's death. James brought in half of our clients and he did all of our court work.'

'Even with MS he did the court stuff?'

Wright nodded slowly and looked at me as if I were a simpleton.

'Oh, I get it. And I'll bet he hardly ever lost.'

'Hardly ever,' Wright agreed.

'All right, if I can switch gears for a minute . . . The burglary that took place here on 23 December 1980. Do you have any idea what was taken?'

'I know exactly what was taken. Brenda and I made a full inventory and called the police immediately.'

I flipped open my notebook. 'The Antrim robbery squad said it was an ashtray, speakers and a cash box. How much was in the cash box?'

'About 15 pounds.'

'And the ashtray was worth how much?'

'I don't know. A quid?'

'And the speakers?'

'A fiver?'

'How did they break in?'

He hesitated.

'Go on, tell me!'

'Through the window in the bathroom at the back. There were so many layers of paint on it we were . . . we were never able to properly close it.'

'So they didn't even have to smash the window?'

'No. They didn't, they just had to push it up and climb through.'

'Don't you have a duty of care to protect your clients' documents?'

'James didn't— It had been like that for years . . . a decade . . .'

I read through my notes. 'As well as the thefts, apparently there was some vandalism in the office?'

'Well, we thought it was vandalism.'

'What else would you call it?'

'You could also call it the *actus reus* of a deliberate criminal act.'

'What do you mean by that?'

'Because they did it on purpose.'

'Am I to understand that something else was taken from your office that night? Something that you didn't tell the police about?'

'We didn't think anything else had been taken at the time,' he said shiftily.

'*At the time*?'

He nodded.

And I knew that this was it.

This was bloody it.

This was the case.

I stopped doodling the picture of him in my notebook and put my pencil down.

I looked at Mr Wright and smiled.

He didn't smile back. His eyes were black, beady, suspicious.

Behind him on Antrim High Street a green Saracen armoured personnel carrier crawled past the window like a creature from the Jurassic.

'But you subsequently found out . . .' I began for him.

'The filing cabinet had been smashed and toppled over but in it we discovered that one of the, er, files was missing.'

'Which file?'

'A folder that contained wills.'

'Which wills, Mr Wright?'

'The folder containing the "M" wills had been taken.'

'Wills beginning with the surname "M"?'

'Yes.'

'When did you find this out?'

'After the Christmas holidays in January.'

'And you never thought to tell the police?'

'We considered it a confidential matter between our clients

and us. We didn't want it generally known. And by that time the police had caught the burglars and taken them into custody. I, uh, I made a few discreet enquiries but the missing wills had not shown up in the tinkers' caravan. Maybe they'd hoped there would be money in there or . . . I don't know. Tinkers are illiterate so they probably just burned them or something. That, at any rate, was our thought.'

'You told the clients that their wills had gone missing?'

'Of course! We called them all immediately when we discovered what had happened.'

'Were there copies of these wills?'

Wright looked shamefaced. 'Yes, but the notarised copies were in the same file.'

'You stored the copies in the same place as the originals?' I asked with a tone of amazement.

'I'm afraid so. We have rectified that policy since then.'

'How many wills are we talking about here?'

'Twenty-one wills and four codicils.'

'If the wills were gone and the copies were gone how did you know what was missing?'

'From our accounts. We cross-checked with our account books. Fortunately every will had to be paid for. And the account book had the fee that was paid to the solicitor and the fee to the official witness.'

'What's an official witness?'

'Under Northern Irish common law neither the person who draws up the will nor the witness can be a beneficiary to that will. You need a solicitor and a witness to make every will legally binding.'

'And the witness and the solicitor are both paid a fee?'

'Yes.'

'Who is this witness?'

'When I'm drawing up a will here in the office I generally use Brenda. She's a notary public.'

'So when you found out that someone had stolen the twenty-one wills and the four codicils, what did you do?' I asked.

'We called up each of the clients, told them the situation and offered to make them a new will for free. It was the least we could do to make restitution,' he said with some complacency returning to his voice now.

'Did anyone not take you up on your offer to make a new will?'

'Yes,' he said.

'Do you want a minute to look up your files?'

'No. I remember who it was. Only one client didn't take us up on our offer.'

'Who was that?'

'I'm not sure that I'm at liberty to—'

'I'm conducting a murder investigation here, Mr Wright.'

'I appreciate that, but there is also the issue of attorney–client priv—'

'Is there? If he didn't employ you to make this will for him you didn't have a privileged relationship. You can't protect a negative, can you? A judge will probably see it my way, and of course on learning about this sorry affair he'll have to refer your lack of candour in the reporting of this missing file to the Law Society. Won't he? What do you think?'

'No, I—'

'Who didn't want you to make them another will, Mr Wright?'

He sighed. 'Harper McCullough.'

The tips of my fingers felt cold. 'Why did he turn you down?' I asked.

'His father had made the will but his father had had a stroke and was not expected to survive. He couldn't put him through the process of making another will. I understood completely and I refunded him the money that his father had paid for the will and testament.'

'Do you happen to know what was in that will, Mr Wright?'

'No, I do not, and even if I did, I certainly would not be obliged to tell you that.'

'But you don't know?'

'No.'

'Because you didn't make the will?'

'That's correct.'

Could he feel it?

The electricity?

Could he see my hands shaking? The fire in my eyes?

'Can I hazard a guess here, Mr Wright, that the will was made by your partner James Mulvenna and the official witness to the will was the late Lizzie Fitzpatrick,' I said slowly and deliberately.

'I believe that's right.'

'Would you mind checking for me in your account book?'

He left the office and came back with a wide black leather double-entry ledger.

'There is it is. The third row down. August 1979. A fee of 130 pounds for Mr Mulvenna and 20 pounds for Miss Fitzpatrick.'

I looked where he was pointing. The will had been made on 4 August 1979, drawn up at the home of Tommy McCullough, 2 Loughshore Road, Ballykeel Village, County Antrim, by James Mulvenna, solicitor-at-law, and witnessed by Lizzie Fitzpatrick, clerk and notary.

'I'd like to get a photocopy of that, if I may,' I said, trying to keep my voice from breaking.

It was difficult getting the wide account book on to the Xerox machine but we managed it.

I took the photocopy and thanked Mr Wright for his time.

'Is that it?' he said.

'That's it for now,' I told him.

I ran, sprinted, to Antrim Town Hall and found the Births and Deaths office.

I looked up the death certificates for James Mulvenna and Tommy McCullough.

Mulvenna had died on 1 November 1980 from 'natural causes, due to complications related to multiple sclerosis'. The notes on the certificate referred to a hospital stay of sixteen days prior to his death. To my line of thinking James Mulvenna's death was almost certainly not murder.

The death certificate for Tommy McCullough was equally innocuous. He had died at home on 8 January 1981. Only thirteen days after Lizzie's 'accident'. Tommy McCullough's death had officially been recorded as occurring from 'post-stroke bronchopneumonia'.

I photocopied both death certificates and drove to Antrim Hospital. I flashed my warrant card and asked whether Dr Kent was in.

He was.

'502,' the nurse said.

I legged it up five flights.

Caught my breath.

I found him in a dingy fifth-floor office with a compensatory view over Antrim, Lough Neagh and most of western Ulster.

'Inspector Duffy, what can I do for—' he began, and stopped when he saw my face.

I handed him the death certificates. 'I need you to pull some records for me. I need to know if either of these deaths was in any way suspicious.'

Dr Kent read the death certificates and shook his head. 'They were both signed by Dr Moran. He's a competent physician.'

'I want you to pull the files, Dr Kent.'

'The files won't help that much. Without an autopsy it will be impossible—'

'I'm sure you'll do your best, Doctor. I'll wait here for you.'

He came back an hour later.

He had put on a white coat and had brushed his wild hair, presumably to impress the people in charge of the records.

I vacated his chair and let him sit back down.

'Well?' I said.

He shook his head. 'I have nothing conclusive.'

'What have you got?'

'I think it's fair to say that James Mulvenna died from advanced multiple sclerosis and not from any outside agency. This was his sixth hospital visit in three years. He was a very sick man.'

'And Tommy McCullough?'

'That death is a little more puzzling. Certainly many stroke patients do die from bronchopneumonia . . .'

'But . . .'

He began reading from the file. 'Mr McCullough had his first stroke all the way back in 1974 and had almost completely recovered. His second stroke occurred on 1 October 1980. He was admitted to the casualty ward of Antrim Hospital at 11 a.m. on 1 October and transferred four days later to a general ward. He was eventually released into his son's care on 30 November. He had lost most of his vocalisation and many of his motor skills, which is common in stroke patients, but when he was released he was able to sit up without difficulty, he was not on a ventilator and he could eat solid food.'

'In other words he was out of danger?'

'It seemed that way . . . Shall I continue?'

'Please do.'

'He had regular physical therapy and outpatient visits, including one on 7 January 1981, just a day before his death,' Dr Kent said, and looked at me for emphasis.

'Is that significant?'

'Oh yes. Oh yes indeed. Very significant. The nurse was Aileen Laverty. I know Aileen a wee bit. A very competent sort. According to the file on Mr McCullough, Nurse Laverty took a sample of Mr McCullough's blood on 7 January during that visit. The blood was tested and the blood work showed no signs of pneumonia.'

'Would it be possible that he could have developed a fatal

strain of pneumonia in the next twenty-four hours after the blood work?'

'Entirely possible.'

'But unlikely?'

'I'd rather say not very probable.'

'You think we could talk to Nurse Laverty?' I said.

'I'll see if she's on call. This might not be one of her days.'

He paged Nurse Laverty and when she came up to the fifth floor I found that she was a staff nurse in her forties, thin, dark-haired, serious.

I told her who I was and showed her the file and, yes, she remembered Mr Tommy McCullough.

'Really? You must have had hundreds of patients since then,' I said, with devil's advocate scepticism.

'Even so, I remember him,' she said, with an attractive West Cork accent. 'I had visited him several times in an outpatient capacity. He was making good progress. His death surprised me.'

'Did you think it was suspicious?' I asked.

'No. Not suspicious, but surprising. He had seemed in very good spirits and when we left he said "goodbye", which was the first word I'd heard him say.'

'And in the blood sample you didn't find pneumonia?'

'To be honest I wasn't even going to test his blood. When a patient is under watch for pneumonia normally you would take a sputum sample. But Mr McCullough wasn't coughing or having difficulty breathing. I only took a test as an extra precaution. Sometimes you do that with elderly patients. Patients who are between sixty and ninety.'

'What if they're over ninety?'

Nurse Laverty looked at Dr Kent. He cleared his throat and didn't say anything. But I could see what they were getting at. If they were over ninety they let the pneumonia take them.

'So you sent his blood test off and it came back negative and then he died?' I asked.

'No, it takes a week to get the tests back from Belfast. He was dead and buried by then.'

'And when you did get the test back? Did you tell anyone of your suspicions?' I asked.

'I didn't have any suspicions. His white count was low. He showed no evidence of pneumonia but the test is not foolproof. And he was an elderly man who'd had a stroke. Pneumonia can come on a patient very suddenly, and in this case it must have done so.'

I asked her a few questions about Harper McCullough, his demeanour, his behaviour, but she had seen nothing but good things.

I excused her and let her go back to her shift.

'How many elderly patients die of bronchopneumonia in this hospital, Dr Kent?'

'I don't know, quite a few I suppose.'

'Would you say that the majority of elderly patients die of pneumonia?'

'Yes.'

'So if Dr Moran found a stroke patient dead at home in his bed, he probably would have written bronchopneumonia as a useful catch-all on the death certificate, especially if the distraught son of that stroke patient didn't authorise an autopsy?'

'He could have written bronchopneumonia or cardiac arrest or just death from natural causes, something like that,' Dr Kent concurred.

'If Mr McCullough had been suffocated, would it have been obvious?'

'Deliberately murdered?' he said, taken aback.

'Yes. With a pillow or a blanket or a plastic bag over the head. Something like that.'

'A plastic bag would have left ligature marks perhaps but a pillow . . . aye, you could easily mistake suffocation for death by bronchopneumonia. Of course, an autopsy would have told you the truth.'

It was getting late now and the sun had carved up the sky between Lough Neagh and the Bluestack Mountains in Donegal. 'You think there's been a murder, Duffy? What's this all about?' Dr Kent asked me.

'I'll tell you what it's about. It's about three deaths in three months and two of them more than a little suspect.'

'Which three deaths?'

'James Mulvenna, Lizzie Fitzpatrick and Tommy McCullough.'

'But what's the connection?'

'That's what I'm going to find out, Doctor,' I said.

'I knew I was right! I can help you,' he said.

'No. This is a police matter. There's no proof of wrongdoing here. And you won't be saying or doing anything. If I need your help I'll bring you in.'

He nodded.

'I have to go,' I said. 'Thank you, Doctor, you've been of great assistance.'

I went down to reception, called directory assistance and got the home address for Dr Moran. Another enquiry and I got the phone number for Antrim Rugby Club. Two more calls got me the rugby club chairman, Andrew Platt, who happened to be at the club right now.

I asked him whether he could wait there for me for an hour or so. He said it was no problem.

I went outside, checked under the Beemer for bombs and drove to Dr Moran's house, reaching 80 mph in a 30 zone. Mock-Tudor four-bedroom on a cul de sac. Moran a married man, three kids, all of whom were under five. Grey hair, thin, cheerful. A damn sight less cheerful when I hit him with the possibility that Tommy McCullough had been murdered. No, he didn't recall the details of the case. I showed him the file. Was there evidence of pneumonia? Not as such. As such? Well, how else could you explain the poor man's sudden demise? How else? Read the *News of the World* any given Sunday.

I drove to the rugby club.

I met Andrew Platt in the rugby club's oak bar, which was a long, elegant affair decorated with club ties, trophies and rugby shirts from touring parties. Platt was quite the Colonel Blimp character. Handlebar moustache, puffy face, chrome dome, black blazer, trousers too high and too tight. He was about sixty years old, which would have put him slap bang in WW2.

He shook my hand and offered me a drink.

'Whatever you're having,' I said, and the barkeep made us two double gin and tonics.

I thanked the barman for the drink and told him to scram while I asked Platt some questions.

When he was gone I went straight to the rugby club dinner of Christmas 1980: what time had Harper McCullough got there, what time had he left?

Platt hadn't the foggiest but he thought he had an old agenda in his office.

'Let's go, then, we'll bring our drinks,' I said.

Platt's office was neat and well maintained. A couple of plants. An empty desk. He was clearly a military man.

'The Christmas dinner of 1980, you say?'

'That's the one.'

He opened a metal filing cabinet and began rummaging inside.

I noticed that even his shoes were shined to a brilliance.

'By any chance were you in the war, Mr Platt?' I asked, to satisfy my own curiosity.

'Indeed I was, my boy. RAF. Dumfries.'

'Spitfires?'

'Hurricanes.'

'Any kills?'

'A Ju-88 and I shared a kill on a 111.'

'That's not too shabby.'

'No, it isn't,' he said, grinning from ear to ear.

He handed me a file that contained press clippings, photographs and a schedule for the rugby club Christmas dinner of 1980. There were lots of awards and presentations. I couldn't make head nor tail of it.

'Harper McCullough got an award and gave a speech that night, didn't he?'

'Oh yes. A speech on behalf of his father. It was the President's Award.'

'And what time would that have been given at?'

'That would have been the next-to-last presentation, at about ten o'clock.'

'And how long was Harper's speech, if you remember?'

'Two minutes, not more, we like to keep the speeches short,' Platt said, sitting on the edge of his desk and gulping the last of his gin and tonic.

'You don't happen to remember seeing Harper after his speech was over, do you?' I said, with the chill marching up my spine again.

I could almost predict the answer, word for word.

'Harper? He gave a very gracious speech. Very gracious. After it was over he excused himself to go to the Gents. Did I see him after that? Hmm, I don't know. There was no reason for him to stay there until the bitter end . . .'

In other words, from about 10.15 onwards Harper's movements were unaccounted for. He'd said that he'd stayed until 11.30 but would there be any witnesses who could back up that story?

'Did you ever speak to the police before about this dinner?'

'No.'

'Did you ever talk to an Inspector Beggs?'

'No, I don't think so.'

Beggs had missed it. Beggs had bloody missed it! He had taken Harper at his word and assumed that there would have been dozens of witnesses at the dinner who would have backed up his alibi.

'How well did you know his father? Tommy McCullough?'

'As well as anyone else. Tommy loved the rugby club.'

'He was a builder, wasn't he?'

'A contractor. Very successful. They say his company built half of Antrim town.'

'I heard that. How would you say that relations were between father and son?'

'They were good.'

'Are you quite sure?'

Platt opened his mouth and closed it again.

'Go on, please, Mr Platt,' I prompted him.

'I don't like to speak ill of the dead . . .'

'He didn't like Harper?'

'It's not that he didn't like him . . . Well, it's more that he never . . .'

'Please, sir, I'm a homicide detective conducting what could be a murder inquiry.'

'Well, one time . . . it's probably nothing . . . one time I heard him call Harper "Carol's wee bastard".'

'He didn't think that Harper was his child?'

'They weren't alike in temperament and they certainly didn't look anything alike.'

'Did he say this sort of thing often?'

'God, no! One time. Just that one time. He'd been drinking!'

'Nice of Harper to pick up that award for his father. Had he done anything like that before?'

'No . . . but his father had just had a stroke.'

'Is there a picture of Tommy here in the club? Harper didn't have one in the house when I went to visit.'

'Of course!'

He walked me out into the corridor and showed me several pictures of Tommy at various club functions and a couple of him playing for Antrim 1st XV. He was a big, strapping second row with blond hair, huge thighs and shoulders. Harper was tall like his father, but dark-haired and thin.

'Harper never played the game?' I asked.

'Never. And his dad didn't force him, which was right. You can force someone to play football or cricket but with rugby you have to be committed or you're going to get yourself hurt.'

I studied the photograph for a while.

'Mr Platt, did Tommy ever talk about leaving any money to the rugby club in his will?'

'Gentlemen don't discuss things like that. I would never have asked him!' Mr Platt said, affronted.

'Of course not.'

We studied the photograph for another moment or two.

'Although . . .' Mr Platt said, *sotto voce*.

'Yes?'

'Well, he did say to me once that the house was going to the RSPB after his death. He wanted it to be some kind of birdwatching centre or something. He loved the birds.'

'I heard that. Did the club get *any* money after Tommy's death?'

'No. Not a penny. It all went to his boy and, like I say, rugby wasn't his game. Not at all.'

'It's a shame that he died intestate, then, isn't it?'

'Aye. But a man never knows when his number's up. Even in the war you never really thought about that. They could have said to you, OK, chaps, this is a dicey mission and only one out of ten of you is going to make it back. You would have thought to yourself, oh, those poor bastards, I shan't be seeing them again.'

I thanked Mr Platt for his time and asked him where I could make a phone call.

He said there was a payphone next to the squash court.

I got some change out of my pocket and called McCrabban at home in Ballymena.

I bounced my idea off him. He liked it. He thought it was entirely possible.

'There's an expression in Irish, Crabbie. *Ólann an cat cluin bainne leis.*'

'Which means?'

'The quiet cat also drinks the cream.'

'I know what you're getting at.'

I left it at that. I didn't say that I was going to make a collar. We both knew that all the evidence was circumstantial.

This wasn't his case. It wasn't even my case. This one belonged to Mary Fitzpatrick.

I told McCrabban that I'd see him next week and told him to give my best to his missus. I hung up and walked outside to the waiting BMW. It was a dark sky. A sleekit line of storm clouds had drifted up from the Mourne Mountains and the sun had finally set into the Atlantic. I felt the first spit of rain and looked underneath the Beemer for an explosive device and when I found none I got inside.

I wondered whether it had all been Lizzie's idea.

After Mulvenna's death from MS she must have known that she was the sole witness to Tommy McCullough's spiteful will. All they had to do was get rid of the will and that would be that. She would marry Harper and they would inherit the estate and live happily ever after.

But then why would he kill her?

And how did he kill her?

A dozen raindrops fell on the roof and then a score and then the heavens opened.

'Shit,' I said. There was no point putting it off any more.

I drove to Ballykeel village, parked outside the Henry Joy McCracken and took my lockpick kit from the glove compartment.

I walked to the front door.

I knew the lock now and I was inside the pub two minutes later.

I turned the lights on, took an upturned chair from off the

table and sat down.

I flipped through my notebook for the hundredth time.

Always with this case one, two, three . . . five, six.

I looked at the bar and the front door and the back door.

How did he do it?

How?

How did he—

One beat.

Two.

Three.

And just like that.

I knew.

I knew everything.

25: HARPER'S FAIRY

I drove out to Harper's house through the rain and dark. Perhaps I should have called McCrabban in for this one, but I didn't want to bother him this late at night and Harper surely wouldn't be much trouble.

I parked the car next to an open horsebox in the muddy yard.

I opened the glove compartment and put brand-new AAA batteries in the Dictaphone.

I set it running in my inside pocket. It was a corny technique and it wouldn't hold up in court, but I didn't need it to hold up in *court* . . .

It was raining hard so I turned up my collar and put on my baseball cap.

I opened the car door and ran, but I still got soaked in the ten seconds between the car and the porch and I was lucky not to go arse over tit on the wet grass.

I took off my cap, rang the bell and ran my hand through my hair to get rid of some of the water.

Jane McCullough came to the door holding the baby. She had that tired but happy look of new mothers.

'Oh, hello, Detective Duffy,' she said.

'Congratulations,' I said.

'Thank you. Madam finally decided to join us.'

'A little girl, then?'

'Yes.'

'Well done. What was the weight?'

'Seven pounds on the dot.'

'That's great. Congratulations. I'll get you something. Is pink still in these days?'

'Oh, that's not necessary. We have a room full of stuff.'

'Listen, Jane, I've come to see Harper, is he about?' I asked tentatively.

She smiled sadly at me. 'You're still working on what happened to Lizzie?'

'I'm still on the case, yes,' I agreed.

'You're a regular plodder,' she said, and yawned.

The baby looked at me. She was a beautiful little girl with her mother's blonde hair and green eyes.

If I told Mary what I suspected about Harper she would grow up never knowing her father.

'Have you picked a name yet?'

'Grania.'

'Pretty. From *The Fenian Cycle*?'

'Yes! Cormac mac Airt's daughter. Harper knows all about that stuff. History . . . all that.'

'It's a nice name.'

'Like I say, Harper came up with it, but I love it.'

'And where is the man of the house?'

'I think he's in the library. Do you know where that is? Next to the living room on the ground floor,' Jane said. 'Go on ahead. Will you be staying for a bit of dinner?'

'I don't think so.'

'I'll be putting the wee sprog down in a minute, it won't be chaos.'

'It's not that, it's just that I've another appointment tonight.'

'All right, then, but if you change your mind let me know.'

'I will, Jane, thank you.'

The library was a rectangular chamber clearly modelled after Trinity College's reading room. It had quite the collection of books, possibly three or four thousand of them, going back several hundred years. Harper was in a comfortable leather chair facing the boat dock and the choppy waters of the lough.

He wasn't pleased to see me but he got up quickly enough and forced a smile on to his face. And he wouldn't have smiled at all if he'd known that I was the fucking herald for the Angel of Death.

The book he was reading was called *Archaeology under Water: An Atlas of the World's Submerged Sites*. It fell to the floor with a heavy bang as he stood up.

'Hello, Inspector Duffy, it's great to see you.'

'Hello, Harper.'

'Are you staying for dinner?' he asked.

I closed the library door and sat down opposite him.

'I'll talk and you'll listen and when I've done talking you'll have a chance to respond, OK?'

'What's this all about? Have you found something out—'

I put my finger to my lips.

'Lizzie Fitzpatrick *was* murdered,' I said.

'I told you. One of those characters who was in the bar that night. I—'

'It was a smart play, Harper. Always pushing the murder angle because you couldn't believe that an accident could have befallen your beloved Lizzie. It made you sympathetic. The man who was so consumed by grief he couldn't see reality.'

'What are you talking about?'

'She wasn't killed by any of the men in the bar that night.'

'How can you know that?'

'It was you, Harper. I know it was you. You were there, outside in the shadows. You waited until last orders. You waited until McPhail, Yeats and Connor had gone.'

'I was at the rugby club dinner!'

'No. You were done by ten fifteen. You were in Ballykeel. Waiting.'

'I was in Belfast!'

'You waited until the three fishermen had gone. And then you knocked on the door and told her it was you. She opened it. She was excited to see you. You locked the door behind you. Did you say anything to her?'

'I wasn't there!'

'No, you wouldn't have said anything. Maybe "go get your bag", and when her back was turned you smacked her on the head with a tent pole or an axe handle. And when she was unconscious you snapped her neck. You made sure that she was dead and then you climbed up on the bar and put a dud light bulb in the socket and you put a good light bulb in her right hand. And you cracked the good light bulb to make it look as if she had fallen.'

Harper shook his head. 'This is crazy! Why would I do such a thing? She was my girlfriend. I loved her! We were getting on great!'

'It was because you were getting on so well that she decided to let you in on a secret.'

'Secret? What are you—'

'She clerked for James Mulvenna. She spent the two summers before you killed her clerking for him. Appearing in court, filling in forms, filing briefs, witnessing wills . . .'

'So?'

'She witnessed your father's will, Harper,' I said.

I waited for a reaction but he played an impressively straight bat.

'And as your relationship blossomed the secret was eating away at her. After Mulvenna's death from MS it occurred to her that she was the only living witness to the will. That will in James Mulvenna's filing cabinet and Lizzie's word – the only two things between you and a fortune.'

'This is the most ridiculous thing I've ever heard.'

'I don't think it is.'

'Where is this mysterious will that you're speaking about? Show it to me,' he said, his voice moving into a slightly higher register.

'Oh, the will's gone. Lost in the burglary of 23 December. But there's a record of it in Mulvenna's account book that I've made a photocopy of. James Mulvenna kept meticulous accounts.'

I passed him the photocopy of the account book.

'What does that prove?' he said dismissively.

I took back the photocopy.

'Your father paid Mulvenna 130 pounds for work on his will,' I said. 'As the official witness Lizzie got 20 pounds.'

He laughed. 'That's pretty thin, Inspector Duffy. This is what you're going to take to a jury?'

'Mr Wright might testify that he had a conversation with you about replacing your father's will and you declined because your father was in poor health.'

'I wasn't going to drag him through making a new will.'

'But he was getting better, wasn't he? He was getting better every day. And that's what you were afraid of. The old will and the possibility that he might make a new one.'

'The will, if it ever existed, is long gone, Inspector Duffy. And I'm afraid you're going to need this mythical will of yours if you're going to convince anybody about these wild speculations,' he said, with some complacency.

'This is what I think happened. Lizzie had no intention of telling you what was in your father's will. It would be a breach of professional ethics and by all accounts she was quite serious about her legal career.'

'She was.'

'But after James Mulvenna's death and as your relationship grew she knew that the only thing making the difference between you inheriting this estate and the construction firm was a silly piece of paper that your father had almost certainly drawn up in a fit of pique.'

'That sounds like him.'

'What did she tell you, Harper? Who was he leaving all the money to? A school? A charity? The rugby club? The Royal Society for the Protection of Birds? You weren't getting a bloody penny, were you? That's what shocked her. That's what made her tell you.'

Harper linked his fingers behind his head. 'You're trying to get me to blurt out some confession? This isn't fucking *Miss Marple*, mate. I'm not confessing to anything. I'm not confessing because I didn't bloody do anything.'

'How do you explain this?' I said, holding up the photocopy of the account book.

'You're going to try and hang me on that? You'd be laughed out of court.'

I pulled my chair a little closer to his.

'She must have told you the week she came back from university at Christmas break. She knew that time was of the essence. If you were going to act you had to act soon.'

'Maybe I killed Mr Mulvenna too, did I?'

'No, you didn't. But his death was the catalyst. She knew there was an opening here. A tiny window of opportunity where you could act, where you could break into Mulvenna's office, find the will and destroy it.'

'You should write a novel, Duffy.'

'So she told you about the will. But here's the thing, Harper. She couldn't have known what kind of a man you were. Your father knew what sort of a person you were but she couldn't have known how ruthless you could be.'

'I'm enjoying this. It's pure fantasy,' he said, attempting to light a cigarette with a box of matches. I pulled out my Zippo and offered it to him. He lit his cigarette and threw the Zippo back at me.

'Poor Lizzie. All she thought that you had to do was break into the office and get the will and destroy it and everything would be fine.'

'Go on.'

'But that wasn't your plan, was it, Harper? She hadn't thought things through. Your father was on the mend. Every day he was getting a little bit better. The outpatient visits were working. The physiotherapy was working. He was a tough old bird. He had recovered from one stroke and now he was going to recover from a second one. He still despised you. When the law office eventually found out about the missing will he'd just make a new one, wouldn't he? You'd be right back to square one. No, no, no. Lizzie hadn't thought things through, but you had. You knew you'd have to kill him, didn't you? You had to destroy the will and make sure your father could never make another. But she was the hitch, wasn't she? She trusted you but you didn't know if you could trust her. A burglary seemed harmless enough but would she countenance murder?'

'I can smell smoke! I've told you about smoking in there! Please go outside, gentlemen!' Jane yelled from the kitchen.

'Sorry, Jane!' I yelled back.

The rain had stopped now so I opened the French doors and let in the cold, damp night air.

'After you,' I said, pointing the way out on to the balcony.

He went first and I followed.

The air was cool. Lough Neagh was the silent, dark vacuum to the west.

'She trusted me but I couldn't trust her? Is that your bullshit theory?' Harper said.

'You had to do three things. Mulvenna was dead but the will was still there, sitting in his office like a time bomb. The will, Lizzie and your father in that order. First the burglary. You needed Lizzie's help for that. She had to tell you exactly where the will was and how to get in through the dodgy bathroom window. She was the brains. She was the fairy godmother behind this part of the plan.'

'Nonsense!'

'You did that on the 23rd.'

'As if I would know how to do a burglary.'

'Then poor Lizzie had to go. What happened there, Harper? Did you tell her that you were going to have to kill your own father and she objected to that? Or were you afraid to tell her because you knew that for her burglary was one thing but murder was the line she wouldn't cross? Maybe you could have killed him and just not told her anything. But she might have been suspicious, and then you would have had that hanging over you for your entire married life. No, the best way was to get rid of her and then wait a month or so to finish the old man.'

'Rubbish!'

'When you found out that she was going to be working in the pub alone, that must have got you excited, eh? You knew that you could use that. And you were at the rugby club dinner that night. You had an alibi. Did you ask her to give you the key? Did you make a copy? Or did you already have a copy? Maybe you lifted the key from Lizzie's purse and got a copy made in Antrim.'

'This is bollocks, Duffy. Pure speculation.'

'The key isn't important anyway. It was an old lock. Easily picked. Easily locked from the outside. I'll bet you any key from the period would have worked in that lock. Nah, forget the key. The real challenge was the bolts on the door, wasn't it?'

'Exactly, Duffy. The doors were locked and bolted from the inside. No one could have got in or out.'

'It was perfect, Harper. Lizzie was alone in the pub in a locked room. She tried to change the light bulb and she fell and broke her neck. You and her mother were the only people who couldn't believe it because you were warped by grief.'

'This is—'

'Let me tell you how you did it. You gave your speech at the rugby club dinner and you excused yourself to go to the bog and then you drove back to Antrim. Everyone would assume you were still at the dinner but you were already back in Ballykeel. You knocked on the door. Lizzie's all "Oh, Harper, what a surprise, I'm so happy to see you" and then bam! Broken neck. Light bulbs. Then you make sure the front door is locked and bolted. Then you use your key to go out the back door. You lock the back door from the outside but of course you can't possibly pull the deadlock over, can you? You don't need to. You wait until eleven thirty and you call Mary Fitzpatrick from a phone box in Antrim, not from the rugby club dinner. You show up at Mary's house and you join the search party. The police officer shines his torch into the pub and all of you break down the front door.'

'Where we found the pub locked and bolted from the inside!' Harper exclaimed, with more than a touch of desperation in his voice.

'You find the body and while Mary screams and the beat cops call it in . . .'

I flipped open my notebook and read aloud from it: '"We were all just milling around waiting for the CID to come." That's right, isn't it? Everyone was just milling around waiting for the CID. Ten minutes of that waiting around, Mr McCullough.'

'So?'

I flipped over the page in my notebook. 'Do you remember I asked you this question: "And the back door, Mr McCullough?" This was your answer: "I checked that myself. Locked and bolted." That's when you did it, Harper. While the cops were guarding the front door and comforting Mary and telling her not to touch the body and you were staggering around in despair . . . You took ten seconds to go to the back door and slide the deadbolt across. As simple as that.'

'I just locked the door when no one was looking?'

'Yeah. That's all you did. You know why magicians never reveal their tricks?'

'Why?'

''Cos the tricks are all so fucking stupid.'

Harper shook his head. 'That's not what happened, Duffy. The place was locked.'

'Tell me the truth, Harper,' I said, with a malevolent insistence.

'I'm not telling you anything, Duffy! I've had enough of this! I think you should be leaving now. From now on any further communication between us should be conducted through, and in the presence of, my solicitors.'

I stood there looking out at the black water.

I wondered whether my word and my theory would be good enough for Mary?

Almost certainly not.

She'd probably had suspicions about Harper herself. But suspicions weren't bloody good enough, were they?

I tossed the fag, unbuttoned my sports jacket, reached into my shoulder holster and pulled out the .38.

'What the f—' he began before I cocked the revolver and pointed it at his face.

'No sudden moves, Harper. This thing has a hair trigger. Do you understand?'

'Yes,' he said. His eyes were wide, terrified. He didn't know me. Maybe I was one of those bent peelers you were always reading about in the papers. One of those coppers who was capable of anything.

'All I have is guesswork, Harper. You've got a decent alibi and there's no will, which means there's no motive. So not only will I never be able to prove any of this in court in front of a jury but I'll never even be able to convince the Director of Public Prosecutions to take up the case. You will not be sent up for this, I guarantee you that.'

'What?'

'As you so rightly point out, Harper, I have nothing but speculation and circumstantial evidence. Not a shred of proof. I give you my word that you will not be arrested for this crime, much less sent to trial.'

'So . . . so . . . so what do you want from me?' he said.

'I want you to tell me your side of it, Harper. How the whole thing was an accident that night. How you just came to talk to her. You didn't mean to kill her. You got in a fight. One thing led to another . . . I want to know your version of events.'

'If . . . if . . . I say I killed her it won't be the end of it. You'll kill me. Here and now!'

'If you tell me the truth, Harper, I'll leave you alone. You'll never hear from me again.'

'As simple as that?'

'As simple as that. I know I can never prove this, not in a million years, but I want to know! I want the intellectual satisfaction of knowing that I was right.'

'And if I don't speak?'

I grabbed Harper by the throat and shoved the gun against his cheek.

'I'll shoot you in the fucking head and I'll tell Jane and everybody else that after I confronted you about Lizzie's death you went for me and we fought and you grabbed my gun and turned it on yourself.'

'You w-w-wouldn't,' he stammered.

'You want to take that chance?'

He thought about it for a few seconds.

Sweat was pouring down his face.

'Speak!' I ordered.

'I . . . I . . . I . . .'

'Tell me, you motherfucker! Tell me or I'll fucking blow your brains out!'

'You were right! It was her idea! It was all her idea!' he sobbed.

'Elaborate.'

'She'd heard about Jim Mulvenna's death when she was still at Warwick and when I picked her up at the airport she was bursting to tell me. She knew my dad had had his stroke and was in no condition to make a new will. She knew we could do it.'

'Do what? Tell me, Harper!'

'Like you said. To get the will and destroy it.'

'What was in the will?'

'Dad must have been out of his fucking mind. I mean, I knew he didn't like me but what she told me was evil. She said that I was getting next to nothing. The house was going to the National Trust. His firm was going to be sold and the assets were going to be divided between the RSPB, Oxfam and the rugby club. James Mulvenna had known that I might sue so he made the will fucking ironclad. I'd get a pittance. Me and Lizzie would get a pittance!'

'How much money would you stand to lose?'

'The house and the firm? Jesus! Three million.'

'So what was Lizzie's plan?'

'That we'd break into James Mulvenna's office and steal the will and destroy it and then when my father died intestate I'd get everything. The house, the firm, the bank accounts.'

'But your dad was the wild card, wasn't he? He was getting better.'

'Euthanising the old man was never part of her plan. She wanted me to wait until he died from natural causes. How long would that be? Five years? And you were right. He was on the mend. I knew he'd be speaking soon. Within six months the old bastard would have been fully recovered . . .'

The words were spilling out now. Everybody, I supposed, needed a confessor. I released my hand from his throat and took a step away from him. The night was perfect for it. I could smell peat burning in fires up and down the lough shore and there was a sea mist moving in from the water.

'So you wanted to kill your own father but you knew you couldn't trust her not to turn you in? That's it, isn't it?'

'She was a good girl, was Lizzie. How could I trust her with something like that? But it didn't matter. That was only part of it. There was something else . . .'

'What else?'

'She was away at university. I mean, I'd loved her once, but . . . They say absence makes the heart grow fonder, but it's not true, is it?'

'You didn't want to marry her?'

'I already knew Jane. We'd gone out for a drink a couple of times. You can't blame me, what with Lizzie across the water half the year.'

'Lizzie didn't know about Jane?'

'Of course not!'

'But if she found out the whole deal would be off.'

'Exactly.'

He fumbled for his smokes and I lit him a second fag.

'Ta,' he said, almost as if we were mates now.

If the tape hadn't been rolling I'd have told him what I knew about Annie, too. But Mary didn't need to hear about that.

The conversation had momentum now. I kept the gun on him but I took another step back to give him some breathing room. He was relieved at that.

'Could you have offered her money? Would she have taken a million, say?' I asked.

'I didn't even consider it. She was besotted with me. She wanted it all. The house, the money, the lifestyle. She wasn't like her sisters. She wasn't interested in the fucking cause. She just wanted a bit of comfort. And she thought she could have that with me. And she thought that her knowledge of the will would be something she could keep in her back pocket so I'd never leave her or have an affair. It was a kind of blackmail.'

Poor girl. She had no idea who she was dealing with.

'So when you heard that she was working alone in the pub the same night you'd be in Belfast you concocted a plan . . .'

'Concocted is the wrong word, Duffy. It all just came to me the day before.'

'Tell me about the key.'

'Are you joking? That was the easiest part. I asked her if I could borrow some change from her purse. I told her I had to run to the supermarket. I drove into Antrim, got the key cut and was back in fifteen minutes.'

'You needed to lock the back door after you left, just in case someone came by.'

'Yes.'

'And if you didn't get a chance to pull the deadbolt over after you and the cops had broken the front door down, you knew that, at the very least, the back door would be locked.'

'Exactly.'

'That's why you needed the pub key. As insurance. But it didn't really matter in the end. No one saw you slip off to push the deadbolt over.'

'No.'

'And hey presto: the back door and the front door were locked and bolted.'

He nodded. I closed my eyes and let out a long sigh. 'Where did you get the idea for a locked-room mystery?'

He pointed behind him at the books. 'Da has hundreds of the bloody things.'

I nodded. I wondered whether Mary needed the details about the actual killing itself. Do parents want to know exactly how their children died? Did Harper talk to her? Was there a struggle? Were there last words?

I didn't want to hear the details. You got enough stuff like that in my line of work. 'Did she know you were going to kill her?' I asked.

'She never knew a thing about it. I hit her from behind and then I did it quick. I read that SAS book about how to break someone's neck. I hate to say it but it was easy.'

'The weapon?'

'A rolling pin.'

'Dr Kent was right. Where is it now?'

'Long gone.'

'No qualms about any of this?'

'Do you think I'm a monster? Of course there were qualms. Of course! But what choice did I have? What would you have done?'

I wasn't going to get on my high horse. 'All right, Harper,' I said, and walked off the balcony back into the library. I uncocked the revolver and returned it to my shoulder holster. He followed me inside. 'That's it? You're done?' he asked.

'I'm done.'

'No charges? No nothing?'

I shook my head. 'No proof, so no charges, no nothing.'

He grinned and breathed a sigh of relief. 'You're a Catholic, aren't you?'

'Yeah.'

'Is that what it's like going to the priest?'

'Usually the priest doesn't need to resort to firearms.'

I walked back into the hall. Harper followed me. 'And this is really it? You're going and you won't be coming back?' he said, unable to believe his luck.

'I gave you my word, Harper. You're never going to see me again.'

'Inspector Duffy, where are you off to? Are you not staying?' Jane yelled from the parlour.

'No, I'm not, I better go,' I said.

'The rain is supposed to get worse before it gets better. Stay! A wee bite to warm you up,' she insisted.

'Aye, stay for dinner,' Harper said.

He thought we were friends now. His grinning face was inviting a right hook.

'No. I better go. I'm late for another appointment,' I said, and left the house for the last time.

26: MARY FITZPATRICK'S WORD

As Jane had predicted the drizzle had become a hard rain. I walked down the Fitzpatricks' drive and stopped outside the living-room window. I could see the family illuminated by the blue light of the TV screen.

I stepped on to the porch, hesitated and rang the doorbell.

Annie answered it. She was wearing a green sweater and a long corduroy skirt. She was barefoot. Her hair was tied back Mary Tyler Moore-style. She looked pretty.

'Hello,' she said, pleased to see me.

'I've got something for you,' I said. I undid the elastic band from my notebook and took the free luncheon vouchers Barry Connor had given me for his restaurant.

'Take these,' I said. 'You've got to get used to that French food if you're moving to Montreal.'

'Wow! I've heard about this place. Thank you!' she said, and kissed me on the cheek.

'You're welcome.'

'What are you doing here, Sean?'

'I'm here to talk to your mother.'

'Oh, is it about Lizzie?'

'Yes.'

'Any news?'

'No. No news. In fact I think we're going to have to shut down the case.'

266 / Adrian McKinty

'A waste of precious resources, eh?'

'Something like that.'

'So I won't be seeing you again, Sean?'

'I don't think so.'

'OK,' she said. She frowned and wanted to say something, but didn't have the words.

'You'll do great in Canada, I'm sure,' I said.

'It's better than here anyway.'

She sniffed and touched me on the cheek and then she turned and ran into the back kitchen.

I'll tell Dermot that you're doing well, Annie, I said to myself.

'Ma! Somebody at the door for you!' Annie yelled.

Mary appeared in the hallway.

'Who is it?' Jim asked from inside.

'I'll talk to the policeman, Jim,' Mary said.

'Maybe we should talk outside,' I said.

I stepped backwards on to the porch and Mary closed the front door. We stood there with the rain bouncing three feet back off the granite steps.

'Well?' she said, folding those blue meat-axe arms across her ample chest.

'I've got a name for you,' I said.

Her eyes narrowed.

'Go on.'

'Before I give it to you I want you to think about something,' I said.

'What?'

'Revenge is a mug's game, Mary. The person getting revenge injures himself far worse by the act of vengeance than he was ever suffering before. He ends up living miserably. I've seen this first hand. A few years ago I revenged myself on a man who did terrible wrongs and it has brought me no satisfaction and considerable regret.'

She scowled at me and grabbed me by the shoulders.

'Tell me the name, Duffy!'

'Tell me you'll think about what I said.'

'I'll think about it, Duffy.'

I nodded.

I counted to ten in my head.

If I told her it would be his death warrant.

'Harper McCullough,' I said.

'Are you sure?'

'Yes.'

'Why?'

'She was the witness to his father's will. His father was going to leave him nothing.'

I reached into the pocket of my leather jacket and took out the Dictaphone tape recorder and gave it to her.

'Play this. It's all on here.'

Her fist closed on the machine.

'He admits it, but it was a confession obtained under duress. It won't stand up in court.'

Of course, that wouldn't matter at all.

The Fitzpatrick family hadn't bothered lawyers and judges with their problems for twenty generations and were unlikely to start now.

'You should destroy the tape after you've played it.'

'I will.'

'What about your side of the bargain . . .' I said.

'My side of the bargain?'

'Dermot. Your son-in-law.'

'When do you need this information by?'

'As soon as possible.'

'Will twenty-four hours do?'

'It'll do.'

'Where do you like to stay when you're in London?' she asked.

'What?'

'When you're in London, what hotel do you stay at?'

'I don't have a hotel that I normally—'

'Someone will call you at the Mount Royal on Regent Street tomorrow night. Be prepared to move. If you fuck this up it won't be my fault.'

'The Mount Royal Hotel tomorrow night? Should I register under my own name?'

'How else will I be able to find you?' she said.

'All right, I'll be there.'

There were tears and an insane wildness in her eyes.

'Thank you, Duffy,' she said, and pushed me gently off the porch into the rain.

She opened the front door and went back inside.

I could see Annie looking at me through the living-room window. When she caught me peeping she turned away.

I walked back to the BMW and drove to the nearest phone box, which was outside the post office in Antrim town.

I called Kate.

'I think he's in England. My informant wants me to go to London,' I said.

'London?'

'Yes.'

'When are you going?'

'Tomorrow.'

'Are you sure he's in England? Our intelligence still says he's going to attack a British army base in Germany.'

'That's where my informant is sending me, so I imagine that that's where our boy is.'

'I'll go with you.'

'OK.'

'If it's true he's in England that scares me,' she said.

'Why?'

'Conference season has begun. The Tory Party conference

begins in Brighton next week. The prime minister will be outside her usual security protocols.'

'I'd get those protocols stepped up, if I were you.'

'Yes, that might be a good idea.'

27: TWENTY MILES TO BRIGHTON

Kate, Tom, myself and 'Alex', a young MI5 driver, waited by the phone in Room 301 of the Mount Royal Hotel. The SAS and the Met's Special Branch were on stand-by, ready to roll at a moment's notice.

Nothing happened.

We got hungry and ordered room service and played poker and watched *Porridge* and the snooker on BBC2.

The phone didn't ring until a quarter to midnight.

She was calling from a phone box.

She asked for me by name and the front desk put her through to my room. We had the phone on speaker.

'Duffy?'

'I'm here.'

'11 Market Road, Tongham, Sussex. If he's not there now he will be soon.'

'Will he be alone or—'

The line went dead.

Tongham was a large village twenty miles to the north of Brighton. 11 Market Road was right on the outskirts of town. A cottage with woods behind it and fields in front. An out-of-the-way spot where no one would bother you.

Kate made calls on the way down and the research team found out that it was a rental property. The owner was in Spain.

We arrived in six Range Rovers. One for us, two for Special Branch and three for the SAS Rapid Response Unit.

We parked a quarter of a mile along the road and waited while the blades did their work. They were wearing black camouflage gear, bulletproof vests and balaclavas. They were carrying MP5 assault rifles and some were armed with heavy machine guns.

They scouted the place for an hour and twenty minutes. They used heat-seeking cameras and they drilled a hole in an exterior wall and inserted a pinhole video camera.

We contributed nothing. We just sat there watching, waiting and smoking in the car.

Nobody talked.

Suddenly the SAS team went in. They broke down the front door and piled into the house SWAT-team-fashion.

Ten minutes later they came out.

One of them signalled for us to come up.

We drove to the house to see what they'd found.

We could tell the place was deserted by the utter lack of excitement in the team.

Kate questioned the SAS commander, a Geordie sergeant who was already smoking a fag on the downslope of his adrenalin crash.

'Is there anyone in there?' she asked.

'No, and I'm no expert but I'd say there hasn't been for a while,' he said with an air of disgust.

'Our intelligence was good,' Kate said defensively.

'Yeah. Fantastic. We better go, our job's done and it's a hell of a long drive back to Hereford,' the sergeant said.

'It's good practice for your lads,' I offered weakly.

'If you say so,' the sergeant mumbled.

When the SAS were gone Kate sent in the Special Branch forensic team, who were dressed in white hooded boilersuits and wearing latex gloves.

This wasn't *1984* any more. Now we were in *Clockwork Orange*.

Kate produced a thermos of tea and we drank it while the droogs did their work.

'Are you sure about your information, Sean?' Kate asked me. It was the first time she had expressed any doubt.

'You know who the source is. And you know why she told me the information.'

Kate frowned. 'Would Mary Fitzpatrick really give up her son-in-law?'

'Apparently there's no love lost between them. And like I say, she gave me her word.'

Kate nodded.

The plod hooked up a noisy diesel generator to power their lights and other equipment. The peeler guy in charge, a Chief Inspector called Dawson, gave us his initial report half an hour later.

'It looks like this intelligence is somewhat out of date. It's hard to say exactly when, but from the mouse droppings and the layers of dust I'd say that no one's been resident in this dwelling for several months.'

'Are you sure?' Kate asked.

'Well, I can't be certain about the dates, but those are good rough estimates. No one has been here recently, that's for sure.'

Kate looked at me. It was hard to read her expression. Not quite irritation, not quite disappointment, but something along those lines.

'Did you get any fingerprints?' I asked.

'We dusted for prints, but we didn't find any,' Dawson said.

Tom shook his head and groaned. 'What a bust.'

'Don't you find that rather unusual, Chief Inspector?' I pressed him.

'Unusual how?'

'You didn't find any prints at all in the whole house? Have you ever been at a crime scene where you've found *no* prints?'

Dawson was a tall guy with a moustache and salt-and-pepper hair. He didn't project an air of stupidity but with coppers you could never really tell.

'No prints. Not a one. That's very strange, no?' I insisted.

Dawson nodded. 'Yes, that is a little uncommon.'

'What *are* you getting at, Duffy?' Tom asked.

'Sean is suggesting that at some point this *was* an IRA safe house,' Kate said.

'But the intelligence is months out of date,' Tom said, and glared at me in the moonlight.

Dawson looked at me with evident distaste. My Irish accent and lack of a police uniform presumably indicated that I was some kind of scumbag informer.

'I think we're missing something,' I said.

'They played you, Duffy. Your informant played you. They gave you a real lead but they made sure it was a dead one. It's a classic move. We see it all the time,' Tom said.

'Can I have a look around?' I asked Kate.

Kate raised her eyebrows at Dawson.

'We're done, help yourselves,' Dawson said.

The three of us went in.

A rather shabby cottage with an odour of mildew. The coppers had rigged up arc lamps but when I flipped the light switch the lights came on, which told me two things: the police sometimes neglected the obvious and someone was still paying the electricity bill.

The furniture was nondescript. A couple of sofas, plastic chairs in the kitchen, a black and white Grundig TV, circa 1970.

Two bedrooms with two single beds each.

'Four beds in total. That's what you'd need for your typical IRA cell,' I suggested to Kate.

She nodded and made a note of it.

Cutlery in the drawers, crockery in the cupboard. An old box of cornflakes, powdered milk, sugar in a glass jar, tea sealed in plastic bags.

Next to the toilet there was a copy of the *Sun* from March 1983. I read through the paper to look for messages or filled-in crossword clues but there was nothing. The page-three girl was a big-breasted blonde called Suzanne, who hoped one day to be a singer on a cruise ship.

274 / ADRIAN MCKINTY

I ran the taps in the sink and checked that the gas worked.

'No phone, but there's electricity and gas and running water,' I said to Kate.

'What does that tell you, Sean?'

'They've used it before and they're coming back,' I said.

It was getting on for four in the morning now.

Kate sat next to me at the pine kitchen table. 'Don't beat yourself up about this, Sean. I'm sure you've done your best,' she said soothingly.

'We should stake this place out. They're coming back. Soon. We have to repair that front door and put everything back the way it was.'

'Sean, look, you—'

'Mary wouldn't have given me bum info. They're coming.'

'How would she even know, Sean? We're monitoring her phones, we're lifting her mail.'

'She knows!'

Kate put her hand on mine.

'You have to learn not to take these things personally.'

'I don't take it personally. I know I'm right. I want this house watched. If they're not using it now they're going to be using it. I want a team on this place twenty-four hours a day. I'll be part of it.'

She thought about it. 'I know what they'll say back on Gower Street, they'll say that we've got to use our resources in the most sensible way possible. That this is a wild-goose chase.'

'Then you've got to convince them, don't you? A team of watchers, round the fucking clock.'

Kate sighed. 'For how long, Sean?'

'As long as it takes.'

'Gower Street will want to know. They'll want to know the exact commitment.'

'That's your job, Kate. Finesse them. Convince them. Dermot's coming here. I know it. I can smell the bastard. He's planning a spectacular and he and his team are coming here.

This is where they do the final prep or this is their bolthole when it's done. Halfway between the ferry ports and London. Twenty minutes to Gatwick. It's perfect.'

She smiled indulgently. 'If you say so, Sean.'

'You'll do it? You'll watch the house?'

'As you say, we'll need to fix the front door and put everything back the way it was.'

'And the fucking dust and the mouse droppings. He's cautious, clever.'

'All right.'

'I want to be part of it. I want to be here when he comes. I don't want you to shoot him when he's got his hands up.'

'Don't you trust us?' Kate said.

'No, I fucking don't. And I don't trust the SAS either. I'm not in the assassination business. I'm a policeman. We try and bring in our suspects alive if we can.'

She raised her eyebrows slightly. *That's not what she had heard.* She brushed the dust off her slacks.

We walked outside.

'I have a field office to run. I'll have to go back to Northern Ireland,' Kate said.

'OK.'

'Which means you'll be under Tom. You'll have to do what he says.'

'I can live with that.'

'And there won't be any heroics either, Sean. I'm going to be leaving strict instructions with the watch team. If you spot Dermot or indeed anyone coming here you're to call it in and we'll let the SAS take care of them. Your job will be to observe, nothing more. Is that understood?'

'Understood loud and clear,' I said.

'Well then, I'll call our wise and venerable masters and I'll see what we can do.'

28: DEATH'S AMBASSADOR

The van was parked on a layby half a mile from the house under an ancient copper beech tree. It was a beautiful location for an observation post because although it wasn't that far away we were on a completely different B road from the house itself. We were parked opposite a scrapyard which got intermittent use, and we were on a slight hill, which meant that you could look down on the house across the rapeseed fields. You could see any vehicles approaching on the London Road and you could see whether anyone was entering the house either from the front or the back. There was even a phone box at the scrapyard, which we could use if the battery on our wireless ever died.

Dermot was a circumspect character, but if he did scout his safe house first to check for watchers it was unlikely he'd notice the dirty old Ford Transit half a dozen fields away next to the town dump.

We had repaired the farmhouse's front door, got rid of our footprints and even put down that additional layer of dust I'd asked for so it would look as if no one had been inside in months.

MI5 watchers came in teams of three. Shifts were twelve hours on and twelve hours off, which meant that you needed, at minimum, six personnel. Since this whole thing was my gaff I insisted on taking the place of at least one team member on the hated night shift.

Our base was MI5's own rather seedy safe house in nearby Brighton, and to save money and time we all stayed there rather than London.

I shared my room with a young Scottish intelligence officer who called himself Ricky. He said he was from Glasgow, he played in a ska band and he had a beard. I liked him and I always let him beat me at Scrabble because I could see how important it was to him. He said that he'd been recruited at St Andrews because of his proficiency in foreign languages. He'd been studying Russian literature but could also read Czech, Polish and Serbo-Croat – no doubt these skills were why they had put him on the Northern Ireland desk.

Ricky was Tom's deputy and the two of them ran the show.

After the first three days Ricky and Tom stayed but all the other personnel changed because, as Tom explained, observation-post duty was a notorious way to burn out intelligence officers.

There were a few other developments: we tracked down the owner of the property, an octogenarian English accountant called Donoghue who had moved to Spain five years previously. He had a dozen properties along the south coast and he'd rented this cottage out to various people over the years, none of whom, it materialised, were in any way connected to the IRA. Because of the damp no one had apparently rented the place for nearly a year and if it was a safe house it was one that was almost never used. After the op was over he'd have to be brought in and questioned, but at this stage it seemed that if the IRA was in fact staying in one of his houses he didn't know anything about it.

They were patient lads on the whole, and it wasn't until Day 5 that I began to hear the mutterings about a 'false lead' and 'bad intel'. I sympathised with the agents who thought it was shite. If it hadn't been for Mary's word and if I'd been outside this investigation looking in I'd have me pegged as the sap, too. And as time wore on I began to suspect, not that Mary had deliberately lied, but more that *she* had been given bad information. Perhaps she *had* played me, but, more likely, she'd just been given junk.

Day 6 and Day 7 crawled by. Dreary hours in the van watching an unoccupied house, or dreary hours in Brighton playing poker with a rotating team of intelligence officers who lost money with depressing ease.

At the end of the first week, Tom, Ricky and myself drove up to London and met with Kate in Gower Street. Tom and Ricky were convinced that the operation was a waste of time, but I insisted that my source was unimpeachable.

Kate had the final say and after a slight hesitation agreed to sanction another full week's surveillance. As she explained to us, and subsequently her superiors, the Tory Party conference was upon us and the IRA 'safe house' was suspiciously close to Brighton . . .

The crew changed but the routine seldom varied.

I would usually spend the night shift with two other intelligence officers in the Ford Transit watching the house in Tongham through night-vision binoculars or on the infrared scanners. It was smelly and a bit uncomfortable, but one of us could usually get some kip while the other two kept their eyes on the house.

At eight in the morning Tom or Ricky would meet us with the day shift and then we'd drive the short run back to Brighton.

I'd usually go immediately to bed and sleep until two in the afternoon. The safe house was on Hove Street near a kebab shop and a video rental place.

Sometimes I'd walk down to the beach, but most of the time I'd lounge around with the others, playing cards and watching movies on the VCR.

By the beginning of Day 9 even I was now convinced that Mary had somehow fucked up or betrayed me, getting from me what she wanted and giving me nothing in return.

And now the environs of Brighton seemed a very unlikely

place indeed for any kind of IRA activity. The Conservative Party conference had begun and the place was chock-full of law enforcement. Because of the IRA's bombing campaign and several death threats from disgruntled mineworkers, Special Branch and the Sussex constabulary had flooded the town with beat cops, special constables, riot police and plainclothes detectives. You couldn't swing a stick without hitting a bunch of peelers looking for something to do or someone to stop and search.

As a man with an Irish accent and a week's facial hair I was stopped three times in two days and asked to provide proof of ID. My warrant card usually did the trick, but not always. But that wasn't the point. An attack in Brighton this week seemed well outside even Dermot's capabilities. Mrs Thatcher's hotel and the conference centre had been thoroughly searched and MI5, Special Branch and even the SAS were providing the security for all cabinet officers going in and out of the various conference venues.

On the third day of the Tory conference, after another fruitless night in the watchers' van, I went out for a lunchtime drink with Tom and told him that I felt we should probably pack it in at the weekend.

'So you're giving up on your informant?' he said.

I took a sip of lager. 'It looks like the tip she got was old information.'

'Who was this mysterious Mata Hari, if you don't mind me asking?'

'I'd rather not say. But she's not someone who is operationally involved with the current Provisional IRA command. She's someone from the previous generation.'

Tom nodded and took a gulp from his bottle of Budweiser. We were sitting in a beer garden that overlooked the beach and the English Channel. It was pleasant. The wind off the water was mild and there was plenty of autumn sunshine.

'Or it could be that she just straight conned you,' Tom said.

'Aye.'

'It's a shame, though. We have absolutely no other leads on Dermot's whereabouts, apart from that Germany tip, and I haven't seen any follow-up on that in the green sheets.'

I finished my pint. 'I did what I could.'

'I know,' Tom said. He ran his fingers through his hair and sighed. 'I'll be transferred out of Northern Ireland.'

'You'll be glad about that. It's got to be a shite posting.'

'Not really. They'll probably put me on the fucking miners' strike.'

'MI5 are bugging the miners?'

'Of course we are. Fucking Trots.'

For an intelligence officer Tom was very lippy, but I liked him.

'Do you want another one? We're getting a nice tan here,' Tom suggested.

I nodded and thanked him when he brought back two Stellas.

'Cheers, mate.'

'Cheers yourself.'

'Why don't we give it until Sunday morning? What do you think about that?' I suggested.

'I'll tell Kate. She'll be pleased. The forms she's had to fill in over this. Believe me, you don't want to know.'

Kate called me later that afternoon.

'You're packing it in?' she said, with neither approval nor disappointment in her voice.

'It's been nearly two weeks. He's not coming here. Brighton's too hot now anyway.'

'So what do you want me to do?'

'We'll give it until Sunday morning and then I'll fly back to Northern Ireland. I'll talk to Mary again. Maybe she's got more up-to-date information.'

She said nothing.

There was nothing to be said.

It was over.

We had tried but Dermot was an escape artist.

An escape artist with lots of money and passports and identities.

He was a mover. A gypsy. A ghost.

'Have you tried looking in the Libyan embassy?' I asked.

She laughed and then added in an undertone: 'Yes. We have.'

'I'll see you on Sunday,' I said.

'I'll see you on Sunday,' she agreed.

Tom, Ricky and I walked to the Grand Hotel to gawk at the BBC camera crews and the Tory Party faithful. The only place that wasn't packed was the Kentucky Fried Chicken where we got dinner.

After that we walked back to the house and Ricky, myself and an officer called Kevin (a Brummie who had only arrived that afternoon) drove up to Tongham to relieve the day crew.

We got there shortly after seven. It was dark now and of course the house across the fields was its usual black and empty self.

'Anything new, lads?' I asked.

They rolled their eyes and said nothing.

'He asked if there was anything new,' Tom repeated angrily.

'You can read the log. There's nothing new.'

Kevin, Ricky and myself climbed into the Ford Transit.

Tom drove the others back to Brighton.

Kevin took the first shift sitting in a camp chair and looking through the rear window of the Transit with the night-vision glasses. Ricky sat up front and read the newspaper and I lay on the camp bed on the van's floor listening to my Walkman. Every fifteen minutes Kevin had to log what he had seen on a clipboard.

Every fifteen minutes he muttered 'sweet Fanny Adams' to himself in an amusing Wolverhampton accent.

A couple of hours had gone by and we were well settled in when there was a polite knocking on the rear door of the van.

I was listening to Leonard Cohen on the Walkman and I didn't hear it but Kevin must have because he put down his clipboard and opened one of the back doors in a very relaxed manner.

Maybe he thought it was a local bobby wondering why we were parked outside the scrapyard or maybe it was somebody who had got lost. We were so lulled by tedium that none of us could really contemplate anything but an innocent explanation.

Even so I don't think I would have opened that door as blithely as he did.

There was a flash of light and Kevin tumbled backwards into the van with a hole in his head. At the same moment there was a flash of light up front in the cab. Another flash of light and an animal shriek and I knew that Ricky was dead.

Kevin had a gun in a shoulder holster but before I could even think about making a try for it a man in a balaclava tore open both doors of the Ford Transit and pointed a suppressed 9mm Glock at me.

Leonard Cohen was still playing loudly in my head.

At least it was a decent soundtrack to die to.

I couldn't think what else to do so I put my hands up.

'What are you listening to?' the man with the gun asked in a Derry accent.

I swallowed.

'What are you listening to?' he repeated.

'Leonard Cohen.'

'Leonard Cohen, did you say?'

'Yes.'

'Which album?'

'*New Skin For The Old Ceremony*.'

'Which track?'

'"Chelsea Hotel #2",' I said.

The man in the balaclava was joined now by another man in a balaclava.

'I topped him,' the second man said.

'Aye, I saw.'

'What's going on here?' the second man asked.

'He's listening to Leonard Cohen, so he is,' the first man explained.

'What?'

'He says he's listening to Leonard Cohen. *New Skin For The Old Ceremony*.'

'Never heard of it,' the second man said.

'You wouldn't. Ignoramus.'

The first man took off his balaclava.

Of course it was Dermot. His hair was a long blond mane. He was tanned and fit. His eyes were clear blue pools in the desert. His face was lined and his jaw like a fucking anvil. He looked young and strong and merciless. A stone-cold killer. An usher for *Mag Mell*.

'Do me a favour there, pal. Pass *me* the Walkman. Do it slowly now, though,' Dermot said.

I sat up and gave Dermot the Walkman. He put it on and listened to the track. He watched me while the song played. He watched me without so much as blinking. When it wasn't quite over he gave it to his mate.

His mate wasn't impressed. 'What was that all about?' he asked, when the song was done.

Dermot took the Walkman back and pressed the stop button.

'It was about Janis Joplin,' Dermot said.

'Janis Joplin?' the second man said, dubiously.

'Isn't that right, Sean?' Dermot asked me.

'Aye, that's right, Dermot,' I said.

Dermot looked at me for a moment and grinned.

So this is it, then, I thought bitterly. *Bested by Dermot yet again. Just like every day in fucking St Malachy's. This is how it fucking ends . . .* And it was in St Malachy's, too, that Father Pugh had told us that the dead would sleep for a million years and be resurrected on the Day of Judgement when they would join the Mother of God in Heaven, whereas the bad, the bad would burn for ever in a lake of fire.

Where would I go?

Could you work for Mrs Thatcher's government and still be a good man?

Could you shoot a man in cold blood and expect to avoid the fires of hell?

And Dermot, what about him? Could you blow up innocent people and still make it to Paradise? What would Father Pugh think of the pair of us now?

'Well?' the second man asked Dermot.

Dermot nodded. 'Aye, you best get out of the van, Sean, anyone could be along in a minute. We can't stand here gabbing all night.'

'Get out?'

'Aye, get out, and I don't need to tell you that you better not try any sudden moves, 'cos, you know . . .'

'You'd fucking shoot me,' I said.

'I really would,' Dermot said, with a little chuckle.

'I don't doubt it.'

I got out of the van while the second man dragged Ricky's body from the front cab and tumbled it into the back. Poor Ricky. He was a good bloke. I knew almost nothing about him but I'd liked what I did know.

Dermot patted me down and the second terrorist closed the two rear doors of the Ford Transit. He went back to the front cabin and got inside.

'Destroy the radio, take the log books, throw the keys away!' Dermot said.

Dermot walked back over to me.

'I watched you change shifts at eight o'clock. Now is it six hours on and six hours off or twelve hours on and twelve hours off? Or maybe four?' Dermot asked.

'Twelve.'

'So your friends won't be by for you until eight tomorrow morning?'

'That's right.'

'If you're lying . . .'

I had always found it difficult to lie to Dermot. 'It's the truth. Twelve-hour shifts.'

'Radio check, anything like that?'

'Nothing like that, Dermot. The new shift comes in and reads the log. That's it.'

Dermot nodded. 'Well, that gives us a few hours, then, doesn't it?'

'I suppose so.'

'Have a wee seat there, Sean. Just there on the ground. That's right.'

I sat down on the moss.

'It's a lovely night, isn't it? A gorgeous night. Crisp, cold. Morrigan the crow is flying tonight, isn't she? Looking down with her black eye. Looking down on you and me,' he said.

'Yes, Dermot.'

'Do you ever read Hobbes, Sean?'

'No, Dermot.'

'You should. It's all there.'

He squatted in front of me, pointing the 9mm casually in my direction. 'The state of nature is a state of war.'

'I expect you're right, Dermot.'

'I am right! Look at us! We exterminated the great grazing herds of mammoth, elk and buffalo. We grew in numbers, painted images on cave walls and we drove our poor cousin *Homo sapiens neanderthalis* to the fringe of the western sea. That wasn't very nice, was it?'

'No, Dermot.'

'And when the ice retreated and a time of plenty began we turned our bellicose passions inward! Inward, Sean. We just can't help ourselves,' he said, and for emphasis poked the barrel of the Glock into my chest.

'No, Dermot,' I said, trying not to sound afraid.

He gave me that easy, handsome grin of his and patted me on the head.

'You get it. I know you do. You were always a smart lad. "War is the locomotive of history." You know who said that, don't you?'

'I can't remember.'

'Trotsky! Come on! You knew that, didn't you?'

'Yes, I think so.'

'Trotsky. I visited his house. They've buried him in the front garden. Imagine that. Huge place. Lovely part of the city. Very close to the house of Fri—'

'Dermot, I think we should bloody go!' his mate said.

Dermot turned on him furiously. 'Don't you fucking interrupt me, you fucking ingrate!' he screamed.

'All right, take it easy,' his friend said.

'And don't fucking tell me to take it easy!'

'OK.'

Dermot turned back to me. 'Now where were we?'

'Frida Kahlo.'

'Oh aye. Forget that. It's not important. The point, Sean, is that violence is the only way to bring down the Empire.'

'Gandhi?'

'Fucking Ben Kingsley is the exception that proves the rule! Right?' he said.

'Right.'

'On your feet. Walk to the car.'

'OK, Dermot.'

'Yes, Dermot, no, Dermot, OK, Dermot, is that all you fucking say? Jesus!'

He gave me a shove and looked at me with utter hatred for

a moment, but then he put his hand under my shoulder and pulled me upright.

'Come on! Let's go over to the house. We'll be more comfortable there. We'll take him with us, Marty. I'm sure Sean's got a lot more information he's willing to spill.'

'Not the house. It might be bugged, they might be listening in,' the second man said.

'We just killed the listeners, Marty,' Dermot said, and then he turned to me.

'Is it bugged, Sean? You can tell me, just between us, like.'

'No. There are no bugs. We didn't want to have anything in the house to give the game away. It was all just observation.'

'And then what? What were you supposed to do when you saw us? Don't lie to me, Sean boy!'

'As soon as we saw you guys appear we were supposed to call the SAS Rapid Response Unit. They would have been down here sharpish.'

'A death squad.'

'No. We wanted to take you alive. You were a potentially valuable source of intelligence, what with the whole Gaddafi angle and everything.'

Dermot nodded. 'Aye. That makes sense. Of course, I would never have told youse anything.'

I nodded.

'Come on! This way, Sean boy.'

We walked around the bend in the road, where a black sports car had been parked. Dermot put a gloved hand on the back of my neck and squeezed.

'And speaking of valuable sources of intelligence. You don't mind coming for a wee ride with us, do you, Sean my lad?'

'No,' I said.

'You'll like the wheels. Toyota Celica Supra. Bit of a squeeze in the back, but you won't mind that either, will you?'

'Not at all, Dermot.'

'It's just a short run for you, anyway. We'll go to the house. I mean, why not, eh, Martin?'

'You're the boss,' Martin said.

Dermot grinned at me and looked at his watch. 'Not too long now anyway, Sean,' he said.

'Too long for what, Dermot?'

'We'll talk over a cup of tea,' Dermot said. 'Here, mate, put those on for me, will you?'

It was a pair of handcuffs. I put them on with a bit of give in both wrists but Dermot quickly saw through that little scheme and squeezed the ratchets so that they were good and tight. He pushed me into the back of the Toyota. Martin kept the 9mm pointing at me while Dermot drove.

'Not too long for what, Dermot?' I asked again.

'Until Guy Fawkes Night!' Dermot said, laughing.

29: TICK, TICK . . . BOOM

Somehow, in the hilly half-mile between the scrapyard and the safe house he managed to get the Celica Supra up to 70 miles per hour. We pulled up to the cottage with a squeal of brakes and the smell of burning rubber.

'This isn't exactly low-key for an IRA car, is it?' I said.

Dermot laughed. 'That's what everybody tells me!' he said delightedly. 'Last time I saw you I couldn't even drive!'

'Out!' Martin ordered.

I got out. Dermot produced a key and let himself inside.

'So MI5's been all over this place?' he asked.

'Yes.'

'I hope you didn't touch my tea. It was vacuum-sealed. If you've gone and spoiled it there will be hell to pay.'

'I don't know about that,' I said.

'Why don't you have a seat in the living room there, Sean, while I get the kettle on? Martin, do me a favour and keep an eye on him. A beady eye. He's a character is Sean, could get up to anything.'

'How long are we going to stay here?' Martin asked. 'The original plan's fucking broke, isn't it?'

'Aye, it's broke. We'll debrief Sean here and then we'll head up to London,' Dermot said.

This remark sent me into something of a tailspin.

He was letting me know where he was going to go next and

he wouldn't do that if he was going to let me live at the end of it.

I sat on the dusty living-room sofa while Martin anxiously looked at his watch and tried to get the radio station he wanted on my Walkman. When he took off his balaclava I could see that he was a bit of an ugly spud – red hair, a shock of teeth pointing in all directions, a prominent broken nose, hollow cheeks, blue-white chip-butty skin. I didn't recognise him from any of the mugshots of the Maze escapers so he must have been someone new, someone not on the books. You didn't need to be Henry Higgins to figure out that his West Belfast hardman accent meant that he was trouble.

'Are you sure we shouldn't just go, like now?' Martin said, looking at his watch again.

Clearly, whatever was going to happen was going to happen soon. Tonight, possibly. Something big. A real show to impress the folks back home and Irish America . . .

Dermot came back into the living room two minutes later with three cups of tea.

'Only powdered milk, I'm afraid, Sean,' he said, handing me a Mickey Mouse mug. 'Milk, one sugar, that's right, isn't it?'

Unless someone had been in touch with him about my tea habits his memory had gone all the way back to the sixth-form study when as Head Boy and Deputy Head Boy we'd made tea and biscuits for the other prefects every lunchtime. Fifteen years ago, in that heady school year of 1968/69, when the whole world seemed to be on the verge of some great spiritual change.

Spiritual shitstorm more like.

'Ta,' I said, and sipped the tea.

He sat facing me on the opposite sofa. 'So the MI5 were in here looking for us, eh?'

'Yeah, and the SAS.'

'The SAS too.' Dermot whistled.

'And Special Branch.'

'How did youse find out about this place?'

'An anonymous tip to the confidential telephone.'

He nodded. 'And how long have you been out in that van, if I may enquire?'

'About ten days.'

He sipped his tea and narrowed his eyes.

'That's a lot of faith in an anonymous tip.'

'Well, we were clutching at straws, really. We had no idea where you were,' I said.

'I wonder who Mister Anonymous was?' Dermot asked semi-rhetorically.

'I have no idea.'

'You're still an RUC detective, aren't you, Sean?'

'Uh, it's a little bit complicated.'

'That sounds intriguing.'

'I was drummed out of the police by Internal Affairs. They said I ran some guy over in a Land Rover.'

'That doesn't sound like you.'

'It wasn't me. I was fitted up for it. And there were other things. Insubordination. Disobedience of a direct order.'

'You were always such a good boy in school.'

'Be that as it may. I pissed off the Chief Constable and I was a convenient fall guy.'

'So what are you now if you're not RUC?'

'I was taken back on a temporary basis. MI5 got the RUC to take me back and put me in Special Branch.'

'Why?'

'To help look for you.'

He nodded sagely and folded his gloved hands under his chin. 'I see, so it was all about me, then, was it?'

'What was?'

'You noseying around my family and friends, asking questions about Lizzie Fitzpatrick's death.'

'Oh, that? Initially that was about you, but then I got

292 / A D R I A N   M C K I N T Y

sidetracked. I didn't like the fact that everyone was willing to let Lizzie's death become a cold case.'

'And did you find out who killed her in the end?'

'No. Not yet.'

He sipped more of his tea. 'I'm not sure I believe you, Sean.'

'Well, it's the truth. If I'd had more time, more resources, maybe I would have been able to come up with something.'

'Resources. Ha! Look at me and Marty here, we have nothing and yet we're about to change the world!'

'That's right!' Marty said.

'Well, we have my knowledge of chemistry, of course! Never much use for it in school, but now you should see what I can do! For instance, did you know that in a decomposition reaction the result is usually exothermic? You're probably wondering what a decomposition reaction is, aren't you, Sean?' he said, and gave me a friendly tap under the chin.

'Yes, Dermot.'

'Well, decomposition reactions occur in materials such as trinitrotoluene (TNT) and nitroglycerine. The molecules of these materials contain oxygen. When the molecule decomposes, the products are combustion gases, which are produced at extremely high temperatures, generating resulting high pressures at the reaction zone. Fascinating, no?'

'Extremely. Is it OK if I ask you a question, Dermot?'

'Perhaps.'

'How did you get the bomb into Brighton, through all that police security, I mean?'

His eyes widened and Marty stopped messing around with my Walkman. Both men looked at me in horror.

'Say that again,' Dermot commanded.

'I was just curious how you got the bomb into Brighton. I mean, the place is swarming with peelers. How could you risk getting it through a roadblock?'

'What bomb do you mean, Sean? Specifically.'

'The truck bomb that you're going to blow up outside the Conservative Party conference.'

He breathed a sigh of relief.

Martin laughed.

'You're a good guesser, Sean, I'll give you that much, but you haven't quite got it right, have you?' he said.

'It's too much of a coincidence. Why else would you be down here near Brighton when there are, no doubt, safe houses all over the country?'

Dermot grinned and nodded. 'But let's talk about you, Sean. I never figured you for a traitor.'

'Traitor how?'

'Working for the Castle.'

'The police, you mean?'

'Aye, the fucking SS RUC. How'd that come about? Was it the money? I've heard you get paid quite a bit.'

He was bristling now, ready for a fight, but I wasn't going to take the bait.

'The money? Is that what they tell you? I'm living in a council house in Carrickfergus and my car certainly isn't a Toyota Celica Supra!'

Of course, I didn't tell him that I owned the house and my car was a BMW – that would have diluted the message.

'So why did you join the black bastards, Sean?'

'I wanted to put a stop to this madness. To hunt down nutters from both sides and put them away where they can't do any more harm.'

He sipped more of his tea and grew thoughtful.

'I remember a rather different Sean Duffy who came to see me in Derry in 1972 begging me to take him into the Provisionals. A Sean Duffy that I turned away with tears in his eyes because he was doing his doctorate at Queen's University. I told the soppy wee shit that the movement needs thinkers! Do you recall that, Sean Duffy?'

'I do. It was right after Bloody Sunday. I'm sure you had every man in Derry knocking down your door that weekend.'

'That I did, Sean. That I did. But I remembered you. With your long hair and your beard and your sheepskin jacket and your university scarf. And I remember that look on your face when I said no . . . Is that what this is all about? Is that why you joined the fucking peelers? To get back at me?'

It was a fair point. Dermot, who'd been Head Boy, Dermot, who'd captained the hurling team, Dermot, who'd always been on top of the latest music, the latest trends, Dermot, who always got the girls, always impressed the boys . . .

'You think too much of yourself, mate. Until I was recruited to get on your trail your name never crossed my consciousness. When I made detective you were already in jail, weren't you? And who are you, anyway? You're nobody in the big scheme of things. What have you done since you escaped from the Maze? Written a few poems in the Benghazi Hilton? Cooked up a few wee plots and schemes? But what have you actually done?'

Martin could contain himself no longer. 'You'll see what he's done very fucking soon, mate! You'll see! Lee Harvey fucking Oswald will be a fucking footnote.'

So it *was* Thatcher.

I was right.

And if not a truck bomb? What?

A Carlos the Jackal-style machine-gun attack? No. Too many cops and soldiers.

What, then?

A lone gunman in the conference hall?

How could they possibly get a rifle through the metal detectors?

I raced through schemes and came up empty.

'What's going on in that noggin of yours, Sean?' Dermot asked.

I grinned and shook my head. 'I can't figure it out, Dermot.

I'm baffled. How are you going to get near enough to get her?'

Dermot lit himself a cigarette and offered me one. I nodded and he lit it and handed it over.

'It's your turn, Sean,' he said. 'What have you got on me?'

'Me personally?'

'You, the MI5, the RUC.'

I drew in the tobacco smoke. There was no angle to be had in giving Dermot any bullshit. He'd see right through that in an instant.

'They've got a whole team on you, Dermot,' I said, flattering him. 'They seem to think that you're the leader of all the cells that trained in Libya. That you're some kind of kingpin. I told them that all the cells would be operating independently once they hit the UK but I don't know if they really listened to that.'

'What intel have they got on me?'

'Well, we know Gaddafi had you arrested and kept you in a cell for three months. MI5 or maybe MI6 got a hold of the journal you were writing there. We read that, looking for clues, but you were too clever to leave any clues there . . .'

Dermot smiled. He liked having his ego stroked just as much as the next man.

'What else have you got?'

'That's it. Of course, they've been wire-tapping the phones. Your ma, your sisters, your mates. Annie's ma and da. Your aunts and uncles. All your bloody friends and neighbours. But you never called any of them, did you?'

'Of course not!'

'There was a rumour that you were in Germany. Most of them still believe that one.'

'Germany? What the hell would I be doing in Germany?'

'They seem to think you're going to attack a British base there.'

He shrugged. 'Aye. That's not a bad idea. But that's more the Red Army Faction's turf, you know?'

'Well, that's all we have. A waste of thousands of man-hours.'

Martin laughed. 'We've got you running in circles!'

'We had nothing at all until we got the anonymous call about this safe house. And even that was beginning to look like a hoax until, well . . .'

'You have no idea who called this place in?' Dermot asked.

'Search me. It was the confidential telephone and you know they don't tape those calls. Policy.'

'Yeah, I know.'

Before he could ask me whether I was, maybe, *lying* about the anonymous nature of the information I quickly asked: 'Have you got any enemies within the movement? Someone jealous of your position?'

Dermot rubbed his chin. 'Maybe. We'll have to have a wee think about that, won't we? Was it a man or a woman who left the tip?'

'A man.'

'Hmmm, I wonder.'

Martin examined his watch again. 'We should fucking top this guy and head on, don't you think, Dermot? If this place is blown it's going to be crawling with bloody peelers in a couple of hours, isn't it?'

Dermot nodded. 'Yeah, Marty, me old mucker, I suppose you're right. It wouldn't do for me to ignore my own rules, would it?'

'No, it bloody wouldn't.'

Dermot passed Martin his teacup. 'Wash these out thoroughly and put them back on the shelf.'

'What for?' Martin said.

'If you would broaden your reading from *Penthouse* to *New Scientist* magazine, Marty, me old china plate, you'd know that there's this thing called DNA evidence. If you so much as spit in the wrong place these days the police can track you down and nail you.'

'It's not quite as accurate as all that,' I suggested.

'Better safe than sorry, eh, Sean?'

I nodded weakly.

Martin took my teacup and went into the kitchen.

Dermot eyed me in a bored, abstracted way. Rather the way an old cat does a much-toyed-with mouse.

'So you don't really know anything, do you, Sean?' he surmised.

'I know you're going to try and attack Thatcher.'

'But you don't know when and you don't know how and that's the key thing, isn't it?'

'I suppose so.'

'I could leave you here and you'd have no idea where we were going to go next, would you?'

'You already told him London!' Marty shouted from the kitchen.

'Aye, but where in London?' I said. 'And maybe it's a double bluff.'

I began to have a glimmer of hope. Was it possible that he was going to let me live? Tie me and gag me until it was too late for me to do anything about it? It might be just his thing. Cloak an act of sadism in an act of mercy – by allowing me to live while others died, my failure would be manifest. I'd have to go the rest of my long days knowing that he'd bested me. The great Dermot McCann outfoxes the not-so-great Sean Duffy once again.

'I really have no clue where you're going next, Dermot,' I said.

He looked at his watch. 'Well, this has been very interesting. And fun. And there's so much more I'd like to ask you, but as my rambunctious young colleague keeps reminding me, we must be away. Tick, tock, tick, tock.'

Realisation flooded over me. 'I think I get it,' I said.

He smiled. 'What do you get?'

'A time bomb. That's it, isn't it? Planted weeks ago. No, months ago. In the hotel? Right?'

Dermot laughed again. 'You're too clever for your own good, Sean. Martin! Get in here!' Martin came back into the living room and stood next to me, ready to do the necessary when his boss gave the order.

'I told you he was a tricky customer, didn't I?'

'That you did, boss.'

'When is the bomb going off, Dermot? Is it tonight?'

No reaction.

'It *is* tonight, isn't it? When? How long have they got?'

Dermot raised the Glock and pointed it at me.

'How long?'

'They've got a bit longer than you, mate, that's for sure.'

I was suddenly terrified. I didn't want to die. Not here, not like this.

'No. Dermot, don't! Please, I'm sorry,' I said, pathetically. *I'm sorry for joining the wrong side. I'm sorry for fucking your ex-wife. I'm sorry about everything . . .*

'Sorry?'

'Maybe you made the right choice and maybe I made the wrong one. We were both doing what we *thought* was right, weren't we? Are you going to kill me because of that?'

Dermot sighed and looked at Martin. 'Did you know that in India there's a priest who spends his entire life counting the integers. 1, 2, 3, 4, 5, 6 and so on. You know why he does that?'

'No idea, Dermot,' Martin said.

'Do you know why, Sean?'

'No.'

'He's doing it to make sure they're all there. Do you understand, Sean?'

Yeah, I understand. You're fucking nuts, pal.

'Not really, Dermot,' I said.

'You have to be meticulous. You have to count the integers. There are half a dozen reasons why I have to kill you, Sean. Being a traitor is certainly high on the list, but denying British

Intelligence even a single clue as to who planted the device in Brighton has got to be a more pressing consideration. *Is binn béal ina thost.* You're a canny lad, Sean boy, surely you can see that I can't possibly let you live?'

'We were friends, Dermot.'

'And if our positions were reversed would you let me go or would you do your duty and—'

I sprang to my feet, hooked my right leg around Martin's calf and toppled him backwards with my right elbow. As he went down I fell on him and as his face smashed into the hardwood floor, I made sure my elbow crashed down on his temple. A bullet whistled past me and another round thudded into the floor inches from me. I flipped the unconscious Martin over and grabbed his 9mm. Another bullet whizzing past centimetres away.

I scrambled into the kitchen, adjusted the semi-automatic in my handcuffed wrists, shot out the living-room light and sent another round into the bulb directly above me in the kitchen as I dived under a table and Dermot shot twice into the space where I had been.

I put the gun down to flip the kitchen table over.

It landed on the linoleum floor with an almighty crash.

'Everything OK in there, Sean?' Dermot yelled from the living room.

I crouched behind the table and picked up the gun again.

'It's an impasse, Sean. You're in there and I'm in here. How are we going to resolve this little stalemate?'

Always the talker, always the big mouth. I grabbed a teacup from the sink and threw it towards the sound of his voice. It crashed somewhere near him and, furious, he shot into the kitchen twice.

I shot back three times at the muzzle flash of his 9mm.

Silence.

Five seconds.

Ten.

'Dermot?'

'Ugh.'

'Dermot, are you hit?'

'Ugh.'

I walked into the living room, turned on a side lamp and saw him sprawled face-down on the living-room floor. He was still holding the 9mm.

I stood on his wrist and kicked the gun away from him.

I rolled him over. It was a stomach wound, a bad one, gut shot.

I knelt beside him and took his hand. 'When is the bomb going to go off, Dermot?'

'Is that you, Sean?' he said in the darkness.

'Aye, it's me, Dermot.'

'How did it come to this?' he groaned.

'I don't know, Dermot.'

'Am I hurt bad?'

'I don't think so. I can get you help. But the bomb, Dermot. Innocent lives . . .'

He thought for a moment. 'Sean boy, listen to me.'

'I'm listening . . .'

'You want to be the hero?'

'Tell me.'

'You've got until four in the morning.'

'It's going off at four?'

'The sixth floor, Sean, get yourself to the sixth floor by four—'

A sudden gunshot in the darkness that smacked Dermot in the face.

Fuck!

I hit the deck.

Martin had a second piece or had grabbed the gun I had scooted away from Dermot.

I shielded myself behind Dermot's body and tried to figure out where the bastard was.

A shadow flitted past the window, heading for the front door.

I shot at it.

The shadow shot back twice.

I emptied my clip.

The shadow fell.

30: BRIGHTON ROCKED

Martin and Dermot were both still. Blood was weaving serpentine trails on to the cork floor from the place where Dermot's face had been ripped open by a bullet.

And me?

I was unhurt. I wasn't hit at all. Not even a scratch. Shook up. But untouched.

I knelt next to Dermot McCann.

Morrigan of the crows, daughter of Emmas, goddess of war, receive thy faithful son.

I looked in the pocket of his trousers, found a key chain with the car key and the handcuff key. I uncuffed myself, went to the sink, turned on the tap and poured water into a mug.

I opened the window, drank and took a deep breath.

The room dissolved momentarily. I could smell the water under Brighton Pier, hear the voices on the promenade and perhaps, just perhaps, I could feel the waves of pain leaking into the present from the future . . .

I looked back into the living room. I saw Dermot breathe.

Blood bubbles formed on his tongue.

His chest moved a centimetre.

Perhaps he could be saved to lie brain dead in some grim hospital ward for the next fifty years.

He didn't deserve that.

His mother wouldn't like that either and her strict Catholicism would never permit them to pull the plug.

Better he die a martyr.

Better for both of them.

I went over to Martin and took the 9mm out of his hand.

I walked back to Dermot and placed the gun against his heart.

'*Codladh samh*,' I said, and pulled the trigger.

I dropped the gun and ran outside to the Toyota.

I drove to the phone box at the scrapyard. I looked in my pocket for change and found two fifty-pence pieces.

I put in one of them on hearing the pips and dialled Kate's temporary number. The phone rang and rang but there was no answer. I hung up before her answerphone kicked in and ate my money.

I called Tom in Brighton. 'Yes?' he said drowsily.

'I found Dermot. They've planted a bomb in the Grand Hotel. They're going to assassinate Thatcher.'

That got his fucking attention.

'What!'

'Thatcher's the target. The Grand Hotel. There's a bomb in a room on the sixth floor. The sixth floor. Have you got that?'

'Are you sure about this, Duffy? I'll have to wake up the prime minister!'

'Wake her up! Wake up the whole town! It's a bomb on a time delay. It's going to go off at four in the morning.'

There was a pause while Tom processed the information through his cautious MI5 filters.

'This can't be right, Duffy,' he said after a moment.

'It is right. It's what Dermot told me.'

'It must be another target. Scotland Yard thoroughly searched the entire hotel before they let the cabinet stay there. They went through every frigging room with sniffer dogs. Top to bottom. And when they were done the prime minister's own security team went through her suite and the entire floor.'

'I'm telling you, Tom, it's the Grand Hotel, Brighton. You've got to start getting people out!'

'Where's Dermot now? Do you have him secured? I want to talk to him.'

'He's dead, you fucking arsehole! Prick up your ears! He ambushed us. Everybody's dead. Get everybody out of that fucking hotel! I'll be there in twenty minutes!'

I slammed the phone down, put in my last fifty-pence piece and tried Kate again. Again no answer, but when her message kicked in I said: 'Dermot's trying to assassinate the entire cabinet. The bomb is in the Grand Hotel, Brighton. It's timed to go off at 4 a.m!'

I hung up and looked at my watch.

Two twenty-two a.m. We had an hour and forty minutes, give or take a minute or two.

But we had an entire building to evacuate. Should have called in a bomb threat to the front desk myself! Damn it!

I ran to the Toyota Celica Supra, opened the door and got inside. I stuck the key in the ignition, gunned her and put on the lights.

I'd never driven one of these bad boys before, but I liked the fact that the speedometer went up to 130 mph.

I stuck my foot on the gas and burned through the gears.

Zero to sixty in six seconds.

Only 160 horses, only 160 pounds of torque, but the thing moved like a Formula 1 car. Radio Luxembourg came on and I turned it up.

Hendrix and then the Velvets kicking it just for me.

I raced through the gears and I was already at hundred miles an hour through the village of Clayton.

On the straights I forced it up towards a ton and a quarter, the chassis vibrating, the understeer brutal, but the engine loving it.

I wound down a window and lit a cigarette.

Night. Speed. Virginia tobacco. England.

I didn't need to look in the mirror to know that I was grinning.

If the disease of modern times was angst and boredom, we in Northern Ireland had found the cure. The constant presence of death collapsed ambition, worry, irony, tedium into a single word on the page. *Live!*

To live was miracle enough.

Yes.

I scorched down the A23 through empty towns and hamlets until the sprawl began and I knew that I was reaching the outskirts of Brighton.

The A23 went up over a rise and there ahead of me I could see the whole sleeping town: the houses, the hospitals, the railway station, the hotel strip, the pier, the pavilion and the coal-black sea beyond.

Everyone asleep.

Everyone oblivious to the fact that they were going to remember this particular October morning for the rest of their born days.

I looked at the dashboard clock.

Two forty.

There wouldn't be time to get a disposal crew in here. The bomb was going to go off no matter what we did. The only question was whether it would take anybody with it.

I ran a red at the A27 junction and almost killed a man at Preston Park. I kept on the road south and when I hit the seafront I skidded to a halt and looked for the hotel. There it was to my right, a couple of hundred yards away, lit up with fairy lights.

The dashboard clock said that it was 2.44.

There was no need to hit the panic button, but even so when I got to the front of the hotel I was alarmed to see that there had been no general evacuation. No people wrapped in blankets, no ambulance guys, no journalists, just two uniformed policemen outside talking to one another like everything was hunky-dory.

I skidded the Celica to a halt in a burn of tyre and brake pad.

'Oi, you can't park that here!' one of the coppers said as I got out.

I showed him my warrant card.

'You still can't park that here,' he muttered.

'There you are!' Tom said, running out to me from the lobby.

I cursed him and his mother and his ancestors all the way back to the time of the chimps swinging breezily in the primordial forests.

'What the fuck is going on, Tom? Didn't you hear what I was saying? There's a fucking bomb in here!' I said.

The two coppers looked at me in amazement.

Tom's pale face was glib and unrepentant. 'I called up Nigel Cavendish in Special Branch and he assured me that every room in this hotel has been searched by sniffer dogs. Mrs Thatcher's own security detail have—'

I pushed him aside and ran into the lobby.

I sprinted to the front desk and showed a sleepy-looking girl my warrant card.

'What room is the prime minister in?' I asked.

'What?'

'The prime minister. Which room?'

'I'm afraid that I'm not at liberty to—'

Tom put his hand on my shoulder and turned me round to face him. 'Sean, he's had you. Wherever Dermot put the bomb, it's not in here! This place has been thoroughly searched. This is clearly a diversion from the—'

'There's a fucking bomb in this hotel!' I insisted.

The desk clerk's eyes widened.

Tom shook his head. 'Not inside. The only possible way he could do it is with a car bomb parked outside. I've got a team discreetly going through all the vehicles on the—'

'You're a fucking idiot! It's on the sixth floor. I'm getting everybody out of there!'

The clock above reception said 2.50.

I looked at the clerk. She was a brunette. About twenty-five. Seemed like a smart girl. 'Call the prime minister's suite! Get them woken up!'

'They're already up, I think,' she said.

I ran to the lift. In front of the elevator there was a big copper in a Metropolitan Police uniform, sitting behind a desk and reading a Frederick Forsyth novel.

He put down the book. 'Can I see your pass, sir?' he asked like a bloody fool.

I pushed the Up button.

'He's with me!' Tom said.

We got into the lift together.

I pressed the button for the sixth floor. Tom looked ridiculous in a black sweater over purple pyjama trousers that were covered in cartoon mice.

'What are you going to do? Knock on every single door on the sixth floor and wake them all up?' he asked.

'That's the idea!'

'Don't you see, Sean? This is Dermot's last laugh on you! Disrupt the Tory Party conference with you as the fucking joker.'

'I don't think so. I think he was telling me the truth.'

'I can't let you do it, mate. The press will have a field day with this. Scaring the shit out of everyone the night before the prime minister's big speech.'

I grabbed him by the ears.

'Open those lugholes, fuckhead. There's a bomb in here! We're getting everybody out!'

The lift began to climb.

Second floor. Third floor.

I looked at my watch.

It was 2.53. We only had an hour and seven minutes now. How to proceed?

I took a breath. OK. First, start banging on the doors and get everyone off the sixth floor. Second, use one of the room phones to call in the bomb threat to the BBC and 999. That would get everyone's attention and they'd have to bloody evacuate whether they liked it or not. Third, find the prime minister's suite and make sure she knew exactly what was going to happen . . .

The elevator dinged and the doors opened

I walked out on to the sixth floor.

I noticed a red carpet and a large mirror in a gilt frame.

I saw my own face. I was haggard, thin, with an almost full beard. My eyes were sunk deep in my head. The beard, I noticed, had flecks of grey. Some time in the last year I had become an old man.

'Sean, come on, please—' Tom began, and tried to grab my arm.

I brushed him off and marched towards the hotel room that was nearest to the lift.

I banged on the door.

I looked at my watch.

It was 2.54.

This time I wasn't safe in a back office.

This time I was right there.

The sound of a percussion cap. The unleashing of Dermot's chemical bonds . . .

My head half turned. My mouth open . . .

An immediate rush of pain. Like a car crash. Like a massive electric shock.

This was high explosive, not some home-made fertiliser bomb.

Semtex.

The Czechs had manufactured it with no markers and it was undetectable by sniffer dogs. And of course the biggest importer of Semtex was Libya.

These thoughts jumped across my synapses as the walls imploded and part of the roof came down.

I rocked forward on my feet, tried to get my balance and then dropped with the rest of the floor on to the level below.

Tom grabbed at me but there was nothing I could do to save me, never mind him, and we fell together.

And as we tumbled into the nothing, we saw the floor above come down on top of us.

Burying us.

Tom's expression: *You were right.*

Mine: *You were right. He played me, he told me four o'clock so that I'd be in the middle of the blast during the evacuation.*

All explosions have two phases. The initial expansion and then, after the outward blast, the gas rushing back into the partial vacuum, creating a second wave.

I felt the air getting sucked from my lungs.

I couldn't breathe.

I couldn't yell. The air like glass: aqueous, hard, a poisonous black liquid . . .

I punched my chest, I grabbed at sky, I landed heavily and then a ton of debris folded everything into darkness.

. . .

. . .

. . .

Moments. Moments that might have been years. Darkness. The dark of mine shafts. The dark of event horizons. Down I went. Deep down where it was colder and blacker. Far from the world of men. Into the realm of things that were not quite human. Where the golems and shape-shifters lay unmoulded in the clay. The stuff of night—

I woke suddenly. I was pinned by debris in the smothered dark. Pain. But pain was good. It meant that you were alive and the nerve endings were firing. Dust in my mouth and throat. I coughed. I was folded in the foetal position. I flexed my fingers. I could move both hands and my left leg. My right was wedged under something heavy. My left hand was up against my face. And my watch was working.

The luminous hour and minute hands were both pointing at six.

I had lost consciousness only for a few hours. I could hear voices and the distant sound of a helicopter. I wanted to cry out but my throat was dry. I sucked on a finger to generate saliva.

'Over here!' I yelled.

Silence above.

'I'm under here!' I yelled again.

'We hear you, mate! We'll have you out in no time. Hang in there!' someone said.

'He's got an Irish accent. He's probably the cunt that blew the place up,' someone else muttered.

Digging.

Light.

They had me out in ten minutes.

They put me on a stretcher but it wasn't necessary. I could have walked out. Nothing was broken. I'd been blown up and buried in the Grand Hotel and all I had were cuts and bruises.

I learned later that five people hadn't been so fortunate.

Three of the dead were women, none of whom were in the cabinet or indeed were even Members of Parliament.

The bomb had been planted in Room 629, under the bath.

Mrs Thatcher had been awake at the time, working on her conference speech in the sitting room of her first-floor suite. Her bathroom was destroyed but she had escaped unscathed.

You'll die in a hotel, Maggie, but not this one.

She had been taken by her security detail to Brighton Police College to recover and rewrite her conference speech.

She got calls there from President Reagan and all the heads of government in the EEC.

She gave her conference speech on schedule to a rousing chorus of approval. She vowed that the IRA terrorists would never triumph over a democratically elected government.

The IRA released this statement: 'Mrs Thatcher will now

realise that Britain cannot occupy our country and torture our prisoners and shoot our people in their own streets and get away with it. Today we were unlucky, but remember we only have to be lucky once. You will have to be lucky always. Give Ireland peace and there will be no more war.'

I read the statement that night in the *Evening Standard*.

The IRA didn't realise that luck was a commodity that some of us had and some of us did not.

Thatcher had it. I had it. Dermot did not.

I spent two days in the Royal Sussex County Hospital.

On the evening of the second day I had a visitor. Half a dozen detectives entered before her. Then Kate. Then Douglas Hurd, the Secretary of State for Northern Ireland. Then Mrs Thatcher herself.

'Is he the one?' she asked Kate.

'Yes,' Kate said.

The prime minister leaned over my bed. 'Can you hear me?' she asked.

'I can hear you,' I told her.

'I am in your debt, Inspector Duffy. I owe you a great deal.'

'I didn't do anything,' I said.

'Your modesty does you much credit, Inspector Duffy. And I appreciate that the full extent of your heroism will never become public knowledge. But as long as I have any influence over Her Majesty's Government I will make sure that your name will be mentioned with respect – something that has not always been the case in the recent past.'

Even if I hadn't been pumped full of drugs I wasn't sure I would have been able to follow what she was talking about.

Was this that bloody apology I'd wanted?

'How's Tom? No one's told me about Tom,' I said.

Kate took that question. 'Tom's at the Royal Free Hospital in London. He broke both his legs, a couple of ribs and punctured a lung. He's been very badly burned but he's recovering and is expected to live.'

Mrs Thatcher put her hand on my shoulder and leaned over the bed. For one horrifying moment I thought she was going to kiss me on the forehead, but she merely said: 'Good luck, Inspector Duffy,' and with that she nodded to her security detail and exited the ward.

When she was gone it began to rain outside.

I thought of the people who hadn't made it, the people I couldn't save. I thought about Matty and Reserve Constable Heather McClusky and I thought about Dermot.

And I thought about poor incompetent Tom.

But he had survived.

And that was the great thing, wasn't it?

To live.

I drove the BMW north through the rain, hugging the coast of Ireland until the land suddenly came to a halt in the wild, broken country that had once been the sea bridge between Alba and Hibernia.

I had been home from England three weeks now. Hunkering in my house in Coronation Road. Waiting for a letter or a phone call.

But no one had contacted me. I didn't know where I stood. I didn't know anything.

I drove north through Ballypatrick and Ballycastle and Ballintoy.

I parked at the Giant's Causeway and when the rain cleared off I got out my Walkman, zipped my leather jacket over my hoodie and went out on to the rocks as far as they would go into the north Atlantic.

It was well after midnight. There were no people, birds, anything.

I could see a few lights from the villages on the Kintyre peninsula in Scotland. Nothing else. I sat on one of the hexagonal columns closest to the water and put Led Zeppelin's *Houses of the Holy* into the player. I fast-forwarded the cassette until I got to 'No Quarter'. I burned a little cannabis resin and rubbed it into a roll-up.

I lit it and pulled back my hood. The sky was mirrors. Bleary-eyed stars of whose true names and stories we were destined to know nothing. I drew in the black cannabis. I held it. I let it go. The moon knew. Much she had seen in her four-billion-year ellipse. It would be a long time before she forgave our sacrilege of coming unbidden into her presence in 1969.

I closed my eyes. It was warm. There was an odour of salt and spray. The sea breaking gently on the cape, on this hidden path between the kingdoms. *The path that still exists for those who can truly see.* I lay back on the flat rocks.

'What'll I do now?' I said aloud to the sea. 'What'll I do now that I have set the world to rights?'

The sea, as always, kept her own counsel. *I'll lie here and offer myself to Lyr, the god of broken water.* The cassette ended. The water lapped the stones and the great stave of night had only this one faint note in all that epic silence.

I slept. Dreamed.

Grey light.

Yellow light.

Dawn over Scotland.

I got up and shook the stiffness from my bones and walked to the car.

I drove to Ballycastle and caught the first ferry of the day to Rathlin Island.

I was the sole passenger and the crossing was calm over a strange, milky, phosphorescent sea. We docked on the little stone pier in Church Bay.

I asked directions to Cliffside House. Up along the road towards the West Lighthouse, I was told. I walked the hilly road and found the place. It was at the end of an isolated lane through oak and hazel trees.

I had expected this.

I could hear the ocean all around.

The house was a three-storey medieval fortified manor built of massive stones that had been repointed and whitewashed. The gate was a large iron swing bar over a cattle grid. A sign said

'Strictly No Trespassing'.

I opened the gate, stepped across the cattle grid and walked under two massive white oak trees.

The front door was painted red and was Canadian maple, four inches thick.

The windows were bulletproofed.

I knocked on a brass knocker shaped like a goat's head.

'It's open,' she yelled from inside.

I turned the handle and went in.

I found myself in an eighteenth-century manor house with thick stone walls that were decorated with shields, ancient bows and claymores.

There was even a harp.

The furniture was wooden, handmade, ancient.

'I'm right at the back of the house, Sean,' she said.

I walked through a small living room, an old-fashioned kitchen, and found myself in an airy, modern conservatory. She was sitting on a rattan sofa with her back to me, looking out to sea.

The conservatory window was made of one enormous sheet of curved plate glass. I saw now that we were almost at the edge of the cliff. To the west Malin Head in County Donegal, the northernmost point in all of Ireland, seemed close enough to touch. To the east the Mull of Kintyre in Scotland was even closer. I didn't know what we were looking at to the north across thirty miles of blue Atlantic Ocean. Islands in the Hebrides? I wasn't going to ask. I wasn't here to talk about the view.

She raised herself a little to look at me. Her eyes were green and her hair was cut into a Louise Brooks-style bob. She was wearing jeans, a black sweater, socks.

She could have been anything from twenty-five to fifty-five.

'Have a seat,' she said.

I sat on a leather armchair next to a telescope.

'Would you like some tea?' she asked.

I shook my head.

'What do you want?' she asked.

'I want, I want . . .'

But my voice was flat and weak and the words died.

'I'll make the tea,' she said.

She got up and went into the kitchen.

I watched a tiny sailing boat cutting west into the impossible expanse of blue sea. I wondered whether the landmass behind the Kintyre peninsula was the Isle of Arran in the Firth of Clyde, where St Brendan the Navigator had rested before his journey to the New World.

She came back with a teapot wrapped in a handmade cosy.

'Shall I be Mother?' she asked.

'All right.'

'Milk and sugar, isn't it?' she asked.

I nodded. She poured the milk and sugar into a bone-china teacup and passed it to me on a saucer.

'Thanks,' I said.

I sipped the tea and we sat there saying nothing for a few minutes.

When my tea was done she offered me another cup.

I shook my head.

'Why did you come here, Sean?' she asked.

'I have questions,' I said.

'And you think I'll have the answers?'

'Aye, I do,' I said.

She folded her hands across her lap.

'Go on, then,' she said.

'What happens next, Kate?'

'For you?'

'For me.'

'Whatever you want to happen, Sean. Do you want to continue your police career?'

I don't know.

'Why are you keeping Dermot's name out of the papers? It's been a month since his death was announced in the Republican press and I haven't heard his name mentioned once in relation to the Brighton bombing.'

'I imagine that it suits the purpose of Scotland Yard to assume that the bombers are still out there . . .'

'So they can fit someone else up for it?'

'You would know more about the ways of policemen than I.'

I leaned back in the chair and smiled at that.

'The ways of policemen . . .' I said to myself.

She put down her teacup and took my hand. 'It's been a terrible few months for you, hasn't it? You must be exhausted.'

I nodded. Exhaustion wasn't the word.

'What's your real name?' I asked.

'It's Kate,' she insisted.

'Is it really?'

'Shall I tell you about this house?'

'If you want to.'

'My grandmother's house. My father was Irish. Of a sort. Didn't I tell you that?'

'Yes. You did.'

'She had it built over an old fort. She liked the place because of its defensive properties. The walls are two foot thick. There's an escape tunnel that leads to the cliff path. Quite the character, was my grandmother.'

She smiled and looked through the window.

A tiny sailing ship tacked, freezing in mid-water, before sliding northwards across the sea.

'Is my future safe in the RUC? What are you going to tell the Chief Constable?'

She laughed. 'That's what you're worried about?'

She leaned across and gave my hand a squeeze. 'As long as Margaret Thatcher draws breath no one can touch you, Sean.'

'So I can resume my career in the CID?'

'Anytime you want with any rank you want at any station you want.'

'I was that good, huh?'

'You were that good. You kept history on track.'

I shook my head. 'I did nothing. I didn't stop the bombing. I didn't prevent those people from being killed . . .'

Kate let go of my hand and shook her head.

'I shouldn't be telling you this,' she said, in a half-whisper . . .

'What?'

'You saved her life.'

'Who?'

'The prime minister.'

'How?'

'As soon as you called Tom, he got through to me and although we didn't think there could possibly be a bomb we had to get her out. No fuss. No drama. We woke her and Denis and she and her staff were all across the street when the bomb went off.'

'Jesus!'

'Of course, this information can never be allowed to come out. Everyone has had to sign the Official Secrets Act. This is a deep one. This one has been sealed under the hundred-year rule.'

'But her room was untouched, it wouldn't have made any difference.'

'Again, that's the official story. In fact her room was completely destroyed by the bomb. Dermot knew what he was doing. He knew where she had stayed in the past and where she would likely stay again and he planted his bomb for maximum effect. He knew that her room would be thoroughly searched, but a few floors above . . . Well, they might be a little more lax about that. And as we all know now, sniffer dogs cannot detect Semtex.'

'Tom knew this when I met him at the hotel?'

'Of course. We thought it was bollocks, but you don't think we're complete idiots, do you?'

Bloody Thatcher. Jesus. Maybe Dermot had had the right idea.

She patted my arm. 'As I say, Sean, you kept history on track.'

'For good or ill.'

'For good or ill, indeed, but it'll go the way it's supposed to go.'

'And the PM knows it was me.'

'You've got the golden ticket, Sean, you can do anything you want; as one of my earthier colleagues said, you could fuck the Princess of Wales in the dining room at Balmoral and no one would say boo to you . . . You wouldn't be the first one either, but that's another story.'

I sat there for a long time. My tea grew cold.

'Why do you do this? What's in it for you?' I asked.

'For me personally?'

'For you, for the service, for the Brits? Why?'

She withdrew her hand from mine and folded it back on her lap. She was sitting there with her legs curled underneath her. Feline. Intelligent. Sinister.

'We play the long game,' she said.

'The long game?'

'Yes.'

'What is this long game?'

'Do you study history, Sean?'

'Some.'

'I'll tell you a little story. After victory in the Franco-Prussian war, an adjutant went to General von Moltke and told him that his name would ring through the ages with the greatest generals in history, with Napoleon, with Caesar, with Alexander. But Moltke shook his head sadly and explained that he could never be considered a great general because he had "never conducted a retreat".'

'And that's what you've been doing here, is it? Conducting a retreat?'

'That's what we've been doing since the first disasters on the Western Front in the First World War. Conducting as orderly a retreat as possible from the apogee of empire. In most cases we've done quite well, in some cases – India, for example – we buggered it.'

'And Ireland has the potential to be the biggest disaster of all, doesn't it?'

'Oh yes. If Britain pulled out tomorrow we could be looking at thousands of casualties, right on our doorstep. It would be quite intolerable.'

'It wouldn't be thousands, it would be tens of thousands.'

'Indeed. Would you like to hear some fortune-telling, Sean?'

'Yes.'

'Mrs Thatcher has survived the assassination. She will win the next election. Easily. And the one after that. At some time point in the 1990s, perhaps ten years from now, she will resign or lose to a Labour Party that has been shifted to the right. Never again will a Labour Party advocate a unilateral withdrawal from Ireland.'

'If you say so.'

'The Falklands War and the Brighton bomb have made it an inevitability.'

'And then what?'

'The IRA are becoming increasingly marginalised. They already know that their campaign has failed. They have failed to capitalise on the momentum of the hunger strikes. We know just how demoralised they have become.'

'You've got one of your own on the Army Council, haven't you?'

'I couldn't possibly comment on that, Sean, even if I knew that to be the case, which I don't . . . But I will say that they have already begun putting out feelers to end this conflict through disinterested third parties.'

'So that's it, is it? That's the next twenty years sewn up, is it?'

She laughed a little. 'Twenty years? I can go farther than that if you want.'

'Go on, then.'

'Some time in the 1990s there will be a ceasefire.'

'No.'

'Oh yes.'

'Ten years from now?'

'Or perhaps longer. Fifteen, maybe. But it'll come. We'll make a deal with the IRA. They lay down their arms and we'll release all their prisoners, withdraw the British army and establish a power-sharing parliament in Belfast.'

'Paisley will never agree to that.'

'Ian Paisley will be the one leading it. The extremists will be the ones who make this deal happen, not the moderates in the middle. The moderates, I'm afraid, will be squeezed out of existence. It always happens.'

'And then what? What happens next in this great scheme of yours?'

'Well, then there will be a period of calm for a long time. There will certainly be IRA splinter groups who will commit atrocities, but they will be marginalised and largely unimportant. Maybe this period will last another twenty years.'

'We'll be long-retired, or more likely, long-dead.'

'Speak for yourself.'

'All right, I'll bite. What happens then?'

'We cannot escape demography. By that time there should be a comfortable Catholic majority in Northern Ireland and hopefully, after sixty years of European integration, borders won't even matter any more . . .'

The penny dropped.

'So that's when you withdraw. That's when a united Ireland will take place.'

'European money will have been pouring in for half a century. Incomes will have risen. The middle class will have expanded.

The small Protestant minority will hopefully not rise up and begin a civil war.'

'You'll withdraw without a bloodbath. You'll have managed the retreat.'

'We will have managed the retreat.'

I looked at her for a long time.

Those eyes had seen much. That brain had thought much. I'd been wrong about her age. She was old. She was ancient. And she had lied to me about her position in the Service. She was much higher up the chain than she had let on.

'Who are you?' I asked.

She opened her mouth and then closed it suddenly, like a toad.

She waved her hand dismissively. 'I am not important.'

I stared at her. I was cold. I got to my feet.

'I suppose I should go.'

She nodded. 'Yes,' she said.

'I don't expect I'll be up this way again,' I said evasively.

'I don't expect you will,' she said. 'Let me see you to the front door.'

She walked me through the house.

She opened the door.

I stepped out into the autumn sunlight.

The door shut heavily behind me.

32: *ARMA VIRUMQUE CANO*

Rathlin. This is where the first people entered Ireland. This is where the human story of this island began.

'Like I give a shite,' I said to myself, and walked under the oak boughs away from Cliffside House.

I digested what she had told me and I tried to feel something: hope, despair, anything. But I was empty. This was a shadow play. A puppet theatre.

She pulled the strings and at the other end of them I jumped. And to mix my metaphors: she'd known exactly how much line to give me. She was the master fisher, not I. I walked down her lane and I took a short cut over the stone wall and through the heather down to Church Bay and the harbour.

I bought a packet of cigarettes and the *Belfast Newsletter*, which had just been delivered to the shop.

I climbed aboard the ferry. The *Isolde,* a sixty-foot converted Second World War cargo boat. Getting on with me were a dozen schoolkids in uniform and an old man with a horse on a piece of rope. I lit a cigarette and thought about Kate.

I felt used. Manipulated. But what had I been expecting? The job of the Prince was to rule, not to explain the game to the merest of the pieces.

I finished my fag, lit another and read the paper while I waited for us to get going.

'MRS GANDHI ASSASSINATED,' the headline screamed.

Murdered by her Sikh bodyguards in retaliation for her assault on the Golden Temple. I read the report, which went on for four pages.

It was horrific stuff. There had been retaliatory massacres of Sikhs in Delhi, gun battles in the streets.

The Brits certainly had buggered up India.

On page five another story caught my eye:

CONSTRUCTION COMPANY HEIR
SHOT DEAD

Harper McCullough, CEO of McCullough Construction of Ballykeel, County Antrim, was shot dead last night by two masked men, as he drove out of the company car park shortly after 7 p.m. No terrorist group has claimed responsibility for this attack. A police spokesman has not ruled out robbery or an attempted kidnapping as a—

I carefully folded up the paper and threw it in the rubbish bin. The last of the passengers got on: a couple of wee sprogs also in school uniform.

'All aboard that's going aboard!' the pilot said.

We sailed out of the harbour and into the chop.

We rode under the black sky.

We navigated the green waters . . .

The Antrim coast advanced. Rathlin Island and the Kingdom of Scotland receded.

I should never have come. I had always been curious to a fault. It was better not to know. Life was easier lived in the dark.

Ballycastle loomed out of the sea mist. The row houses, the school, the proving-ground for the horse fair.

'Fenders away!' the pilot said as we glided into the harbour.

He nudged the ferry up to the pier and they threw securing ropes to men in oilskins who fastened the boat to concrete bollards.

'Sheets tight!' the pilot said when the *Isolde* was securely tied to dry land.

He cut the engines.

A deckhand lowered a wooden gangway. The schoolkids ran through the rain to the waiting school bus. The horse and man went more gingerly down the ramp.

I cupped my hands around the Zippo lighter and kindled life into a cigarette.

I went down the springy wooden gangway and walked to a sheltered overhang at the pilot house.

Dry land.

Ireland.

Land of my fathers and of my birth. I had no love for it. All it was fit for was the ash from my cigarette and the slurry from the heel of my shoe.

A klaxon sounded on the far pier where the hundred-and-twenty-foot-long daily car ferry, *The Lady of the Isles*, was about to depart for Campbeltown in Scotland.

I was seized by a wild impulse.

Run for it.

Flee.

Get on the boat and escape to Britain and leave all this . . . all this madness behind.

Yes! Get out. They've got their plan but you don't have to be part of it.

Go to Scotland, England.

Go.

To do what?

Something else. Anything!

'All aboard that's going aboard!' the skipper of *The Lady of the Isles* yelled through a megaphone.

Was there anything keeping me here?

I was beyond their words.

I was free of honour and obligation. What use was a cop? A

cop was a pawn. A cop was never in the endgame.

'Last call for Campbeltown!' the harbourmaster shouted. 'Last call for the port of Campbeltown!'

He looked at me. He sensed my interest. He was a trim man with a black beard, a black coat and a cap that was reassuringly nautical.

I caught his eye.

The futures split.

The paths diverged . . .

For an instant.

For the merest instant.

And then they merged back into one.

I shook my head, took a final draw on the cigarette and threw it into the sea.

I turned up the collar on my coat and walked towards the car, readying myself for what was evidently going to be a long, long war . . .